The Donovan Dynasty

BIND

SIERRA CARTWRIGHT

Bind
ISBN # 978-1-78651-854-5

Interior text design by Claire Siemaszkiewicz
Totally Bound Publishing

Published in 2016 by Totally Bound Publishing, Newland House, The Point, Weaver Road, Lincoln, LN6 3QN, United Kingdom.

Totally Bound Publishing is a subsidiary of Totally Entwined Group Limited.

BIND

Dedication

For Sierra's Super Stars. You are simply the best!

"Let me help you with that."

At the sexy, intimate sound of a man's voice, Lara stopped shrugging into her coat and turned to glance over her shoulder. Her pulse slammed to a stop. *Connor Donovan.*

When he'd entered the hotel's ballroom an hour earlier, she'd immediately noticed him. Even at an event attended by Houston's power elite, the man had commanded attention.

Her friend Erin had introduced her to Connor, her older brother, and president of Donovan Worldwide.

He'd been polite, though courteously distant, as if his attention was focused elsewhere. She'd found that his icy demeanor was the perfect complement to his cool, intimidating gray eyes.

In spite of herself, she'd continued to watch him.

After only fifteen minutes, he and a couple of other men had made their excuses and left the ballroom. Since all were moguls, their absence had been noted.

Connor had been the first to return, and she'd seen the delicious way that he'd adjusted one of his starched, white cuffs.

And now, he was standing only inches behind her.

"May I?" he prompted.

His voice was friendly, but his implacable tone sent a shudder through her. She realized it wasn't really a request.

"I'd appreciate that," she said.

When his fingers brushed hers, she felt his touch as if it were a sliver of lightning.

Their proximity felt intimate, making her aware of how devastatingly handsome he was. She made a conscious decision not to let him know how much he flustered her. She'd grown up around authoritative men, but he possessed a unique aura of command.

He continued to hold the jacket until she'd settled into it.

"Thank you," she said as she turned to face him. Though she was tall and wore cripplingly high stilettos, she had to tip her head back to meet his gaze.

He looked at her without blinking, and for a moment, she was the focus of his attention.

"It's my pleasure to help a beautiful woman."

She told herself not to take him seriously. The man hadn't been named president of Donovan Worldwide at such an early age without learning to consider the impact of his words. Still, his genteel Southern manners impressed her. No one could have faulted him for walking past the coat check area. But he hadn't.

He turned his hand palm up, indicating she should precede him through the revolving glass door.

Outside, a cold rain fell in wind-whipped torrents. Thank goodness the portico was covered but, of course, there were no vehicles waiting in the taxi lane.

A sedan pulled up, and Connor said, "I'll give you a ride."

"That won't be necessary."

Just then a valet hurried over. "Taxi, ma'am?"

She nodded as she brushed her hair back from her face.

The valet went to the curb and blew a whistle to summon the cab.

"Are you certain?" Connor asked.

The idea of being in the back of a vehicle with him even for a few minutes gave her shivers in a way that had nothing to do with the outside temperature. "I promise you, Mr. Donovan, I'll be okay."

The cab arrived.

Connor waved off the valet. Despite the weather, he opened the door to the taxi and handed her into the vehicle.

"I'll see you again soon," he said. The words were laced with promise.

His gaze lingered. His eyes no longer seemed as cold, yet

they appeared ten times more dangerous.

With a decisive move, he closed the door then walked away, each stride purposeful.

In the scant few minutes they'd spent together, she'd felt the vortex of his authority. She knew she could have refused his help, but there had been something mesmerizing—something seductive—about the way he'd instinctively taken control of the situation.

She gave the driver her destination and tried to shake off Connor's effect.

"You should ask my brother to marry you."

Shocked by the statement, Lara jerked her hand, causing wine to slosh over the rim of her glass. *"What?"* Even the thought of suggesting such a thing made her heart stop before rushing on in a fury. Absently, she reached for her napkin to blot at the red stain that was seeping across the white tablecloth.

"You should marry Connor. You remember him from the cocktail party, right?"

As if she'd ever forget.

"You two would make a fabulous couple." Erin Donovan reached for her glass of chardonnay and sat back, wearing a huge smile. "So there you are. It's the perfect solution."

"Perfect? I don't see how marriage changes anything."

"First of all, you'd have access to Connor's advice."

"I've already hired advisors."

"Who aren't running companies as successful as Donovan Worldwide."

"I can't argue that," Lara agreed.

"If he thinks it's worthwhile, he may help with the financial issues."

Which her father would never consider.

"Surely you could get him a seat on the board if he were your husband?" Erin persisted. "You'd have someone to back your position. And most of all, you'd have a lover to share the emotional burden with. Stop scowling. You'll give yourself frown lines."

Lara stared at Erin. They'd known each other since graduate school, and they'd continued to meet once a week to discuss business, as well as other issues in their lives. Years had made them more than friends, it had also made them confidantes.

Until this moment, Lara had considered Erin to be extremely intelligent and a gifted problem solver. But her suggestion that Lara marry someone she didn't love, especially the aloof and dynamic Connor? Even though her father's stubbornness meant BHI's situation was dire, marriage wasn't the way to solve the problems plaguing her family's business. "You've lost your mind."

After taking a sip of wine, Erin put the glass down and leaned forward. "You should think about it."

"Not in a million years." Even though her interaction with Connor had only been a few minutes long, its impact had stayed with her. The next day, she'd caught herself thinking about him, wondering what might have happened if she had let him drive her back to her bungalow.

Probably nothing, she'd told herself. Just because he'd offered a ride didn't mean he was sexually attracted to her.

Unfortunately, she'd been so turned on by him that it had taken several ridiculous days and lots of determination to free herself from the hold he had on her.

Now, more than three weeks later, the tendrils of the memory still unnerved her. "Rumor has it he's not in the market for a wife." Not only that, but according to reports, he rarely dated.

"Which means you looked him up!" Erin pronounced.

"I didn't say that," Lara protested.

"How else would you know?" Erin grinned cheekily. "I think you'd be ideal for him. You saw him. He's too damn serious about everything, always has been. Since Dad died, it's gotten worse. Not that I can blame him. But he's recently become even more of a hard-ass than he used to be, like he doesn't deserve to be happy. He needs a vacation. Or someone to shake up his careful little world. Aunt Kathryn agrees." She tipped her head to the side, as if considering Lara's suitability.

"Don't look at me," Lara said. "I'm not that woman. My life is complicated enough." When she went out, it was generally for happy hour with a group of friends. She could kick back, have fun, have an occasional hook-up, but keep her time free. "Besides, I like a different kind of man."

"That's absolutely true," Erin agreed. "You like men who are milquetoasts."

"I prefer the word uncomplicated."

"Uh-huh," Erin said. "Remember Randy? He was milquetoast."

"He was a nice guy."

"It took him four dates to kiss you."

"Three," Lara corrected.

"Which is three too many."

Lara fought back a small smile. Erin would tease her relentlessly if Lara admitted the truth. She'd had to initiate the intimacy. And when it had happened, the kiss hadn't curled her toes or made her swoon. In fact, she'd been strangely unaroused. When they'd slept together, it had been perfunctory, leaving her unsatisfied. When she'd hinted that she'd wanted more, he'd scowled, obviously half offended, half puzzled.

She'd told herself that great sex—hell, even good sex—was overrated. Randy had been a good man, always understanding, never protesting when she'd worked late or canceled dates to deal with one of her father's dramatic pronouncements. In the end though, lack of sexual chemistry had made them drift apart.

One night at dinner, when they hadn't seen each other in more than a week, she'd suggested an amicable parting. He'd smiled, in relief, she imagined.

And since she was swamped with work, she'd opted not to pursue dating for a while. Her vivid imagination and her vibrator collection were enough. She might not have a man as a partner in her life, but she told herself that was okay, for now.

"Consider it," Erin encouraged.

Instead of responding, Lara reached for her wine.

"You should at least schedule a meeting with him," Erin persisted.

"Do you ever stop?"

"I could give you his cell phone number."

The image of him made her shiver. All that power and intensity? "No. Absolutely not. Thanks."

"In that case, I'll give you the secret code to get past his personal assistant in case you decide to call the office. You can find the number online."

"A secret code?"

"Don't laugh," Erin said. "A lot of enterprising reporters and salespeople will use all sorts of tactics to get past the gatekeeper."

"She must be tough."

"He," Erin corrected.

"Your brother's personal assistant is a man?" The information shouldn't have shocked Lara, but it did.

"Oh, yes."

"Oh?"

With her index finger, Erin skimmed the rim of her glass. "He's...interesting."

"In what way?"

"Uh-uh. You're not getting any information out of me. Go see for yourself."

"Stop it!" Lara protested. "Tell me."

"Not a chance." Erin made a show of fanning her face with her hand. "Okay. I'll tell you this much...Thompson is a gem. Gorgeous. Ex-military. I don't know, he's... forbidding."

"Forbidding? That's an interesting word."

"Like he has all these secrets. He doesn't talk about himself much. The man scares the hell out of me in the most exciting way possible."

"Now I'm intrigued."

"That was my point, exactly."

Forbidding. If you added handsome, enigmatic and powerful, the same description could apply to Connor.

The waiter brought them coffee and the slice of the renowned key lime pie they'd ordered to share.

"This'll cost me an hour on the treadmill," Erin said as she stuck her spoon in one side.

"It's worth every single minute," Lara pointed out.

After they'd paid the bill, they went outside. Humidity and heat from the unseasonably warm spring evening swamped Lara, settling over her, making her suddenly restless.

"Seven, seven, three, four," Erin said.

Lara scowled.

"That's the code so that you can contact Connor."

"I won't need it."

"I want you to be my sister-in-law." Erin waved a cheery goodbye and headed for her car while Lara walked back toward the skyscraper that housed her family's business, Bertrand Holdings, Inc. Since it was technically after hours, she shrugged off her black blazer then tucked it through the handle of her oversized bag.

Earlier she'd debated whether or not to cancel her dinner plans with Erin, but since she'd been working so many hours, Lara had decided to keep the appointment but go back to work to wrap up the day's final details, straighten her desk then stop by the workout center before heading home. Lately, it seemed as if she spent more time behind her desk than anywhere else.

Problem was, she couldn't see an end anytime soon. They needed more help than they had, but cutbacks had left all departments woefully understaffed. Doing more with less had become a mantra. Unfortunately for her, that resulted in a lot of twelve-hour days, and Saturday had become a regular workday.

She entered the high-rise through the revolving glass door and exhaled in relief as the air-conditioning cooled her damp skin. At least the brisk walk should have worked off part of the key lime pie.

As she strode across the marble floor toward a bank of elevators, she waved to the security guard.

"No rest for the wicked?"

"I'll have to make a note to be a saint in my next life," Lara said.

"You and me both, sister," the woman replied.

Since most workers had gone home hours before, the building was quiet. It amazed her how different downtown became after hours. The lack of energy was palpable, weighty. An elevator was even waiting to whisk Lara directly to the eighteenth floor.

She was deep in thought when she exited the car and almost walked directly into someone.

He reached for her, grabbing her upper arms to steady her.

"I beg your pardon," she said.

"Are you all right?"

Lara looked up. Electricity hummed through her when she realized Connor Donovan was holding her. For a breathless moment, time seemed to stop.

"Well, well," he said. "Ms. Bertrand." He continued to hold her.

Self-preservation instincts told her to pull away, but she didn't...couldn't.

Their gazes held. He drew his dark eyebrows together, making him look even more intimidating. Rather than scaring her, his frown, his presence, compelled her attention.

She wasn't sure how much time had passed before she found a thread of equilibrium. "I'm...surprised to see you here." And why was he?

In his dove-gray suit, starched shirt, red tie and polished wingtip shoes, the man was impossibly handsome, made even more so by the slight shadow of stubble on his strong jaw. And his voice... It wasn't just his words, but his deep, well-modulated tone that made her think of summer nights and hot, hot sex.

His eyes, though, accentuated by the color of his clothing, were as chilly as she recalled.

Slowly, slowly, he released her. She took two small steps back. Where he'd touched her, she throbbed.

"I was sorry you didn't let me give you a lift home a few weeks ago."

"I'm sure you're a busy man."

"I always take time for the important things and people."

Was she ridiculous for thinking that he, too, felt the attraction between them? She shook her head. He was a powerful man, of course he had a strong sex drive. It didn't mean anything.

Under his scrutiny, she was hyperaware of her bare skin, the damp tendrils of hair curling against her nape, the way her silk shirt showed her silhouette. She wished she'd kept her blazer on.

Lara mentally took hold of herself before his power consumed her. "I was having dinner with your sister. If I'd known you had business with BHI, I would have rescheduled."

Something dark ghosted across his eyes. "I had understood I'd be meeting with the board of directors. Or at least with you *and* Pernell."

She adjusted her grip on her bag to cover the shock that her father hadn't said a word to her.

"At any rate, my proposal is no longer on the table."

"What proposal?"

"Regarding your communications division."

One that had been losing money, one she wanted to sell. Lara took in his pricey leather briefcase, no doubt containing a file folder with papers, or, more likely, a flash drive. "And you've changed your mind?"

"Pernell made it clear he wasn't open to discussion."

"I see." Her knees went weak. Was this another instance of her father's stubbornness? "I wish I had been there."

"I do, as well. Things might have worked out differently. Better."

She scrambled for time. Perhaps her father had been out of line. On the other hand, maybe Connor's offer had been a bad one. And she needed time to sort it out, learn what was going on, and mostly, think it through. "Are you open to continuing the negotiation?"

"Under my original terms? No."

Connor took another step closer to her, and she remained in place, waiting, wondering.

He was close enough that she could once again inhale his scent...that of relentless determination spiced with masculine power.

Her heart seemed to pause then raced when he reached for the elevator call button.

"If you're interested in hearing more, contact me." He paused long enough to pull out a business card. "My personal cell number is on there."

She accepted the card.

"Good evening," he said when the doors slid open.

Her voice suddenly constricted by the thundering of her pulse, she nodded and watched him enter the car.

Within seconds, he disappeared from view.

She exhaled, feeling simultaneously relieved and disappointed. What had she expected?

Lara straightened her shoulders and headed down the hallway to her father's office.

Lara knocked sharply then pushed the door open without waiting for an invitation.

Pernell raised his eyebrows as he glanced up. "Lara, darling." He cleared his throat. "I didn't expect you back today."

"Obviously." She took a seat across from him and dropped her bag onto the thick carpeting. The unyielding green leather, high-back chair squeaked as she sat. The rest of his office was just as uncomfortable. Dark mahogany bookshelves overflowed with civic awards, mementos and antique clocks. His gigantic desk had a huge phone, a blotter, a few fine pens and a cup of pencils. Begrudgingly, he'd allowed the IT team to install a computer, but it was behind him on a credenza. If he'd ever turned it on, she'd be astounded. His entire space reeked of old-world tradition or, in her opinion, an outdated way of doing business.

In contrast, her work area was minimalistic, equipped with modern electronics. It was designed for focus as well as flexibility. Its small, sparse confines were accented only by a shocking arrangement of red flowers displayed in an artistically shaped alloy metal vase, all designed to encourage creativity.

Their offices were only the beginning of the differences between Lara and her father.

"I just ran into Connor Donovan."

"Oh?" He glanced away, as if to avoid her gaze.

She gripped the chair arms. "He thought he had a meeting with both of us."

"Did he, now?"

"Dad, please. Don't patronize me." She held on to the tendril of frustration that threatened to unravel inside her. "Why didn't you mention we had an appointment with him?"

"I thought I'd see if he had anything interesting to say first."

How long had it been this way, the thrust and parry as she tried to dig necessary information from him? When she'd been young, he'd doted on her. Lara would hurry to him every chance she had. He'd encouraged it. Every time he'd had to work on a weekend, he'd brought her along. He'd allowed her to work summers while she was in high school, and he'd been her greatest mentor. Even while she'd been in college, she'd looked forward to the opportunity to spend time with him.

It wasn't until after grad school that she'd realized he was attached to outdated ways of doing business, and she'd started to challenge his decisions.

More and more, he'd begun to leave her out of conversations, and the wedge seemed as unbridgeable as it was wide. Now she understood the frustrations that had led her mother to divorce him five years ago. The man was stubborn.

Opting for the direct route, Lara stated, "Connor said the offer is off the table."

"It was never on it," her father replied, relaxing back in his seat, obviously once again feeling in control.

"Meaning?"

"He has some ideas on how we can work together on some projects. But essentially he's arrogant enough to think we should sell the communications division to him."

"Did you look at his proposition?"

"It was missing a comma and some zeroes. I never even looked at it." He clapped his hands together and left them steepled. "I tossed him out on his ass. Told him to take his insulting offer with him."

"You did *what?*" Energy ripped through her, bringing her to her feet.

"Sit down," Pernell instructed. "I don't like tipping my head back to see you." For the first time in weeks, he smiled. It erased years from his face, banished the shadows from beneath his eyes. His eyes, dark like her own, all but twinkled.

"You're enjoying this."

"Lara, you should have seen his face."

Since BHI was a private firm, they didn't answer to shareholders, just a seven-member board of directors. She and her father both held seats, along with her mother, Helene who had retained her position as part of her impressive divorce settlement. But because of her annoyances with Pernell, her mother hadn't been to a meeting in at least a year. Occasionally she threatened to show up, mostly to irritate him, Lara assumed.

The other four members had been appointed by Pernell over the years. They were colleagues and of a similar age and mindset.

Lara believed the company's financial problems could be solved with a steady, firm hand, a compelling five-year plan, some management shake-ups and, above all, getting rid of certain divisions.

At the last board meeting, she'd presented the dismal financial report, for the third quarter in a row. They could not afford for this spiral to continue.

Despite her passionate entreaty urging them to make changes, they'd voted to continue on the course they'd set.

One of the board members had stated that they had weathered decades of market fluctuations. Things would come back. They always had. Pernell's ever-steady philosophy had served the company in good stead.

Now, her father's stubbornness was damaging BHI's valuation, and he refused to see the truth.

For the past eighteen months, she'd been steadfast in her conviction that they needed to make changes immediately. The resulting tension coiled between them, gnawing away at their relationship. "Dad—"

"Go home," he interrupted. "Get some rest. You've earned it. Have a glass of wine."

From experience, she knew she'd get no further with him. He could be right that the offer had been an intentional lowball, but she didn't know that.

"Go home, Lara Marie," he said softly.

"Only if you will," she countered.

"Donald will be coming for me in half an hour."

His driver, confidant, butler. She nodded. "We are not finished with this conversation."

"Believe me, Lara. I know." He sighed. Then, obviously realizing he'd revealed a weakness, he stood. "I'll see you tomorrow."

She was being thrown out. Like Connor had been.

Her father waited for her to pick up her bag before escorting her to the door.

Once she was out, he snapped it shut.

Frustration churned through her. Instead of cleaning up her desk, she exited the building and headed for the parking garage. She knew she should follow her original plan and hit the gym, but she wanted to go home, have some peace to think things through. It'd been a hell of an evening.

Her fast pace didn't alleviate any of her anxiety, and she was still simmering as she slid behind the wheel of her sedan.

Her car was cool, and she took a moment to unpin her

hair and roll her shoulders, trying to ease some of the knots there. Unfortunately they seemed to have become permanent.

This evening there was no baseball game or concert, so traffic was as light as it ever was in Houston, and it took her less than twenty minutes to reach her historic bungalow in the Heights.

All the way home, she turned over Erin's words and the unexpected meeting with Connor.

Before going inside, she stopped long enough to water the bougainvillea and the potted plants that looked as wilted as she felt.

She headed straight for the bedroom to stow her bag, kick off her shoes, remove her thigh-high stockings then pull her shirt over her head. As usual, she left everything in a discarded heap. At times she was grateful she lived alone and wasn't dating anyone. There were benefits.

After she'd changed into a pair of shorts, a tank top and flip-flops, she went into the kitchen for that glass of wine her father had suggested. Since the day had been so frustrating, she added sparkling water to the glass to cut the alcohol in half. She had a feeling she'd be wanting at least one refill.

Glass in hand, she grabbed her iPad from the counter and went into the backyard, her favorite retreat. The outdoor space was the feature that had convinced her to offer full price for the house. In addition to the covered deck, there was a small vegetable garden, numerous oleander trees, lush banana plants, several types of palms and a fishpond that she had to constantly replenish thanks to the hungry local bird population. It was a small oasis in a busy city.

In cooler months, she had a heater on the deck, but today, she needed the overhead fan to churn through the humidity-laced air.

Lara sat on the porch swing and took a long drink before putting down the glass. Then she powered up the tablet. While she waited for it to connect, she used her toes to push off and set the swing into motion.

She became aware of children playing in the yard behind

her. And soon after, the sounds of dogs running around. Mrs. Fuhrman, her next-door neighbor, must have let her five rescue animals outside.

Their excited yips and barks soothed her.

Without conscious thought, she did a search on Connor's name.

Not for the first time, she scrolled through a few articles about him. Most of it, she knew from Erin, so Lara only read the first couple of paragraphs before moving on.

After their father's death, Connor had been called home from his graduate school studies back east to take the helm of Donovan Worldwide. Though his grandfather, William, referred to as the Colonel, still served as CEO, Connor was president, and he was responsible for most of the decisions. According to unconfirmed reports, the Colonel had recently had a stroke, which meant that Connor had assumed even more obligations.

Lara saw a couple of references to Erin's role as a human resources guru, while Connor's younger brother handled research. According to Erin, they had a step-brother, Cade, who was the eldest child. Though she seemed to adore him, he wasn't around much, and there were only hints about the scandal of his birth. He ran a ranching operation—or, as it was referred to deeper in the story, the family's agribusiness interests—in west Texas.

As she'd mentioned to Erin, Lara had previously looked Connor up online, searching for any indication he had a girlfriend. She hadn't seen recent pictures of him with any women, though he'd been photographed at a Boston event with Julien Bonds, the renowned technology genius. But there was frustratingly little to give her a glimpse of who he really was or what mattered to him.

Without conscious thought, she pulled up the bookmarked images of him. All of them were mouth-watering. No matter what he was wearing, from khakis and a polo shirt with deck shoes, to a suit like he'd worn today, the man looked delicious. Tall and handsome, he had the lean frame of a runner or bicyclist. He was powerful and sexy. And he tripped all her physical responses.

She glanced up from the screen and stared into the distance, replaying their unexpected meeting near the elevator.

As a professional, she'd understood that Connor had been visiting on business, but the woman in her had pulsed with awareness.

Unbidden, Erin's words returned to tumble through Lara's mind.

Marry Connor?

The idea was absurd.

But for a moment, the idea of being with him tantalized. She wondered what it would be like to be with him, to surrender to his kiss. Would he be as bold in the bedroom as he was outside it? For a moment, she pictured him with his fingertips poised to open the top button on her favorite blouse. Would he skim her skin as he bared it, or would he move aggressively to the next button?

How restrained was he?

Would he tear the material in his haste to have her? That thought was followed by another, and she imagined him undressing, taking off his belt then looping it around his hand as he approached her.

She shook her head.

What was wrong with her? She wasn't sure where the unbidden fantasy had come from. And, as she'd found out, men thought she was too kinky as it was. She'd do better to banish the thoughts.

Adding Connor Donovan to her evening fantasies was a prescription for disaster.

Determinedly, she shoved her musings away.

She had real issues she needed to focus on, a family business that needed serious attention. And Connor had already indicated his willingness to help.

The idea of approaching him made rockets of ice shoot up her spine to settle at the back of her neck.

Lara reached for her glass and took a deep drink, contemplating. No doubt her father would see her action as disloyal. But her job as CFO was to advise and make recommendations, even if the owner didn't want to hear them.

Resolved, she went to shut down the tablet, but was once again riveted by a picture of Connor, this time adjusting one of his starched cuffs.

Damn, everything he did radiated appeal.

She headed inside and deposited her iPad and unfinished drink on the counter, telling herself she wasn't going to use her shower massager to masturbate while she thought of Connor.

But as she turned on the water in the bathroom, Lara admitted she was lying to herself. She was aroused—consumed by naughty thoughts of him—and she needed relief.

Lara Bertrand.

Christ.

Five minutes before his alarm clock was set to shatter the silence, Connor Donovan threw back the sheet and crawled from bed.

Last night, he'd taken a long swim after he'd gotten home, hoping to get rid of the memory of her. It hadn't worked. Instead, he'd been tormented by thoughts of her dark brown eyes, long hair that he wanted to pull and her beautiful sun-kissed skin that reflected her Cajun heritage. Her delectable fragrance—lemony and spicy—evoked magnolias and made him think of sultry, endless summer nights. He recalled the way she'd felt when he'd momentarily held her in his arms. Her softness, responsiveness, had scorched him, igniting physical hunger.

Connor rarely spent any time thinking about women. Work obsessed him, and he'd discarded the idea of dating because relationships mattered to him. They demanded and deserved an investment of time and energy. It would be selfish to ask a woman out while knowing it wouldn't progress beyond something casual.

His subconscious obviously hadn't been impressed by the decision of his rational mind, and thoughts of Lara had haunted him all night.

He'd dreamed of her, imagining the sight of her in his bed, naked with her arms over her head, wrists secured to the headboard, not with silky ties, but with rope. Hemp would leave tiny marks that he could enjoy for hours. Her eyes would be closed, her back arched, legs spread as she begged for his touch, his domination.

Now, he all but inhaled the scent of her on his pillow—spiced citrus and feminine seduction.

Connor shook his head. What in the hell-fuck was he doing thinking about an opponent's daughter? Picturing her in a submissive pose would lead to nothing other than a hard-on.

Shoving thoughts of her aside and determined to keep his focus, Connor followed his typical predawn ritual by heading for the bathroom to take a one-minute cold shower.

Wide-awake, invigorated, he dragged his fingers through his wet hair then dried off before pulling on a pair of compression workout skins.

Silence surrounded him as he went into one of the loft's spare bedrooms. He'd set up a television and a couple of pieces of cardio equipment for the times he didn't want to take advantage of the building's fitness facility.

He grabbed a bottle of water from the small refrigerator and downed all twenty ounces before cranking up 1980s rock music. Then he turned on the wall-mounted television and pushed the mute button.

Focused on the hour ahead, he settled onto the seat of the rowing machine and reached for the handle. As he pulled, he concentrated on his breathing until he reached the cadence he wanted.

Occasionally, he glanced at the television screen, noting what was happening with the world's financial indexes. He'd only been ten when his grandfather had started instructing him on the importance of understanding how each market was connected to another, explaining that a hiccup overseas could cause disaster in the Donovan portfolio.

Connor had paid attention. How could he not? The man was affectionately known as the Colonel. Even though he'd never risen higher than the rank of captain in the army, he'd married Libby Sykes and had become honorary patriarch of the family and its fortune. He'd worked damned hard to increase the family's wealth, and he constantly reminded his descendants of their obligations. Connor had dutifully taken it all in, even filling notebooks with the man's wisdom.

His father had been killed in a horrific car accident. Connor's half-brother, Cade, had survived—physically, at least. Guilt at being the driver continued to gnaw on him.

Connor had returned home to work alongside his grandfather at Donovan Worldwide. Four years ago, at the age of twenty-three, Connor had accepted the mantle of president, two decades earlier than expected. Like all trials he'd been presented with, he'd conquered it.

There was nothing that made his blood flow more than a challenge. The bigger the challenge, the greater the reward. He'd known acquiring BHI's communications division would be difficult. But they had a number of patents that he wanted, patents that would give Donovan Worldwide a greater international platform. When he'd asked his younger brother, Nathan, to gather as much information on the Bertrands as possible, Nathan had said Pernell would never agree to it.

That didn't stop him.

Like the generations before him, Connor realized that he had to take risks—calculated ones—to grow. Hell, even to remain relevant.

He spent many hours each day performing risk assessments. He carefully considered all ideas that made it past his Aunt Kathryn, his grandfather or his brothers. The ones really worth pursuing, he studied in depth, for weeks, even months. He didn't rush the process. By the time he acted, he did so with complete confidence.

Little caught him off guard.

Connor had a reputation for dealing with issues straight up. At times, his forthrightness took others by surprise. BHI Communications was prime for a takeover. Rumors had been out there for months. Pernell should have been looking to sell or at least merge.

When Connor had arrived at BHI, he'd expected to meet with the board of directors—Pernell and Lara at the least. Connor had been prepared with an offer, willing to talk, open for negotiation.

Instead, Pernell had been in his office, alone. He hadn't even stood to greet Connor. The older man was as stubborn as his Cajun roots were deep. Without even looking at the offer, he had told Connor to get out and not to come back unless he tripled the upfront cash.

No doubt Pernell considered himself to be cunningly brilliant. But for Connor, the strategy hadn't worked. With a tight smile, he'd responded that the offer was no longer available.

He'd watch as BHI's various communications holdings withered, just like some hotel investments had. Then Donovan Worldwide would pick at the remains. The problem was the damned patents. They were potentially worth more than the whole deal. And he wanted all of them, not just a few of them.

Which brought him back to Lara.

He missed a beat. With determination, he resumed his smooth rowing motion. He tried telling himself that his unusual reaction had been because he'd been shocked by Pernell's behavior.

Somewhere deep inside, he knew that wasn't true.

He had never experienced that kind of visceral reaction to a woman.

He'd been captivated by her the first night they'd met, when Erin had introduced them at the cocktail party. Holding Lara's coat for her in the lobby had been natural. He'd been strangely disappointed when she'd refused his offer of a ride home.

Last night, near the elevator, her surprise at running into him had been genuine.

Attraction had sent a ragged surge of energy through him. It had made him forget his own anger.

He'd wanted to spend more time with her.

The rower's timer sounded, and he eased off with a loud exhalation. As he slowed his workout, he reminded himself that he exercised to clear his mind. Obsessing over the brunette beauty wouldn't get him anywhere.

He headed into the kitchen for a mug of coffee. He

guzzled that while he sliced veggies for an omelet. As that bubbled in a satisfying amount of olive oil, he checked his email, looked at his calendar and scanned the agenda that Thompson had prepared for the monthly family business meeting.

As usual, the man had already secured RSVPs. Not surprisingly his half-brother, Cade, had declined. The distance from Corpus Christi was a challenge, even if he took a commuter flight. Erin, Nathan, Aunt Kathryn and his grandfather would all be there, though.

After eating and methodically cleaning the kitchen, he showered. This time, he didn't hurry. Instead, he allowed the hot water to work out the kinks and soothe his muscles.

By the time he had downed a second cup of coffee and was dressed in his customary suit, dawn was meandering across the horizon, changing the downtown Houston skyline from black to dark gray.

Since there was no rain in the forecast and the humidity was relatively low for this time of year, he decided against driving or calling for his car. Instead, he walked to work.

The numerous office buildings still stood dark, devoid of the energy and drive that would pulse through them in less than an hour. The city would wake, fortunes would be made, lost, traded. At the end of the day, he intended to be counted among the victors.

The sun was barely cresting the horizon when he entered his office suite.

Thompson, his assistant, was already there, near the coffeepot. Most other employees wouldn't show up for another thirty minutes, and Thompson would be at full speed by then.

"Coffee, Mr. Donovan? I'm willing to share."

"You're a good man, Thompson. Thank you." The man had a first name, but he'd asked Connor not to use it. He respected that. Some addressed him as Mr. Thompson. Others called the man Badass Thompson. That worked, as well. He was former military, and with his massive shoulders, bald head that showcased an impressive scar and intimidating posture, he'd earned the reputation.

Truth was, Thompson didn't share much about his time in the service, and Connor had never been inclined to push for details.

The man possessed amazing organizational skills. "You never want to look for your bullets or your weapon when you're under fire," Thompson had explained during his interview. He'd started at Donovan Worldwide a few years ago when the company had launched their military veterans outreach program. Thompson had been in the IT department and had repaired one of Connor's notebook computers, which was no easy task. The machine had been a gift from Julien Bonds. Notoriously, Bonds' equipment could only be fixed by people with genius technical ability, which Thompson possessed.

But the man hadn't stopped there. He'd integrated several programs, made sense of scheduling, set reminders and generally made Connor's work life much more streamlined. Though Thompson didn't have the usual skills Connor looked for in an executive assistant, when an opening had occurred, he'd asked Thompson to apply for the position. What he hadn't known, he'd figured out, even putting himself through school in the evenings to earn a business degree.

Connor considered the hire one of his best decisions.

With a nod, he accepted the mug. He took a slug of the strong brew then shook his head to clear it. "Damn. This could dissolve a spoon."

"As I always say—"

"I know. I know. Only pussies and ladies add cream or sugar."

"And you are neither, Mr. Donovan."

"So I'm told." He choked down a second swallow.

"Fortitude, sir. You'll be wide awake after finishing it."

"Or trembling badly enough that I'll measure on the Richter scale." Ignoring the man's big grin, Connor nodded his thanks then continued through to his office, hoping to find a packet of sugar stashed somewhere.

His schedule lay neatly in the middle of the polished desk, and several pieces of paper were stacked next to it. When advertising campaigns required his signature for approval, he preferred to look at a printout rather than a computer image. There was something tactile about handling paper that appealed to him.

He placed his briefcase on the credenza and set down the cup of coffee, absently hoping the brew didn't chew through the ceramic and into the wood beneath.

Thompson had already opened the blinds, and all that was left for Connor to do was to add a splash of fresh water to the bamboo plant that had been a gift from his Aunt Kathryn. She was on a kick about the impurity of the building's air, and office by office, she was adding greenery. He had to admit he liked the potted plant, and he spent an inordinate amount of time relocating it so it had the best indirect sunlight and proper water. Over the past three months, it had grown four inches.

He grabbed the coffee then slid behind his desk to power up his computer and its screens. While he was waiting, he opened a drawer and riffled through pens and paper clips to finally find buried treasure, in the form of a sugar packet.

He ripped it open, poured in every granule then tried another sip.

It didn't help.

Giving up, he wadded the packet into a tiny ball so that Thompson wouldn't find it in the trash. Some knowledge was sacred.

He scanned the pages on his desk. He scribbled notes on a few, signed off on others. By the time the computer monitors were displaying the company's logo, he was ready to tackle the onslaught of weekly reports.

At noon, he joined his attorney for lunch then arrived back at Donovan Worldwide in time for the family meeting.

He entered the smallest of the conference rooms to find Aunt Kathryn, Erin and Nathan already there. No one noticed him. Kathryn was gazing out of the window, no doubt ignoring her niece and nephew while daydreaming about her upcoming Panama Canal cruise. Erin and Nathan were seated at the table. If their body posture was anything to go by, they'd been there for a while. Erin was speaking animatedly, waving her hands, while Nathan was leaning forward, a frown on his face.

"A corset store is a fad," Nathan said when Erin took a breath. "It won't last."

"I disagree. Corsets and bustiers are enjoying a renaissance. There's huge demand for them. And there's not a better location than Kemah."

The town wasn't far from Houston, close enough to be considered part of the metropolitan area. Situated on Galveston Bay, Kemah's boardwalk area had an amusement park, restaurants, specialty shops and boutiques that attracted tens of thousands of visitors annually. The right stores did well, Connor had no doubt.

"I'm not arguing that point," Nathan replied. "But correspondingly, rents are high. How many corsets would she need to sell per month to pay the bills and keep the lights on, not to mention the inventory and advertising?"

"Women go crazy for them," she said. With a wicked glint in her eyes, she added, "And some men, too."

"It's too specialized. Even a boutique concept needs something more. Accessories. I don't know..."

"Toys? Vibrators and such?"

To his credit, Nathan didn't pick up that gauntlet. Instead he responded as a businessman. "Bring me a projected profit and loss, show me the cost of goods sold and make sure the numbers work. Or go ahead and invest your own money. Even if you do that, I recommend you take a hard look at the realities of the business. Don't let your enthusiasm get in the way of a sound decision."

"By that, you mean emotions."

Before Nathan could respond, Connor cleared his throat. "Hate to break up this argument..." Not that it was anything unusual. His family had a diverse range of interests, thoughts, opinions, pet projects. Including, seemingly, more plants. "What's that?" He pointed at the oversized pot in the corner.

"Hibiscus," Aunt Kathryn responded, turning around. "I thought the peach blossoms would brighten up the space. Needed something."

Besides the bold, red painting on the back wall? "Aren't they supposed to be outside?"

"Many people grow them indoors and they do well in pots as long as they're fertilized properly and kept out of direct sunlight. You can make a tea out of the blossoms. Calms the nerves."

"You can muddle them into a mojito, too," Erin supplied.

"I'm thinking of replacing this one with a peace lily." She moved to a counter that held refreshments and a single-cup beverage maker. She brewed a cup of green tea, which she slid in front of Erin.

His sister wrinkled her nose.

"Drink it," Kathryn said. "And I mean it."

Erin drew the cup closer.

"For you, Connor?" Kathryn asked. "Coffee?"

"Ah, no. As it is, I'll be awake until well into the next century."

"Thompson must have shared his coffee with you," Erin surmised.

He nodded.

"I think he makes it strong to prove something about masculinity," she said.

"I think it's more a statement about moral fortitude," Connor corrected, taking a seat.

"Tea for you?" Kathryn asked Nathan. "Something nice and soothing?"

"Not in this lifetime. I'll have water." He grabbed himself a bottle while Kathryn popped another tea pod in the brewer.

Connor joined Erin. One of his first acts as president had been to replace the more formal oblong conference table with a round one to encourage unity along with a less structured meeting hierarchy. Despite that, they all more or less sat in the same places, the Colonel to his right, Nathan to his left.

"Any word on Grandfather?" Erin asked.

Aunt Kathryn sat erect, shoulders pulled back as she allowed steam to waft across her face. Erin ignored her cup of tea. Nathan uncapped his bottle then reached for one of the agendas that had been piled in the middle of the table.

"He said he'd be here," Connor replied. And the Colonel would no doubt keep his word, no matter how difficult the challenge. Since his stroke five months ago, he spoke more deliberately, moved slower and he used a cane. He was too damn stubborn to use the walker the doctor had prescribed. He still went to see a physical therapist every day. No matter what the woman suggested, the Colonel did more. "Other than Erin's corset shop, is there any new business?"

"About that," Erin said. "This isn't the first time one of us have had an idea rejected."

"I didn't reject it," Nathan countered.

"Semantics."

Connor shuffled his agenda to the side.

"I think we need another type of investment category." When Nathan started to interrupt, she held up her hand. "We have a great procedure set up to award grants from the foundation."

Nathan nodded.

"And rigorous guidelines we follow when looking to make a major acquisition. But what about doing some smaller loans, for businesses like this one? As long as they're within our community."

Nathan shut his mouth. The youngest Donovan brother might be risk-averse, but their great-grandmother had set a requirement that the company keep the majority of its funds in the area where her family settled five generations earlier. Their Texas roots ran deep and proud.

"Come up with a set of guidelines," Aunt Kathryn suggested.

Connor wondered if she'd always been the peacemaker. He couldn't remember a time she hadn't been.

"Bring it back to us next month. I think we can consider it."

Erin looked to Connor. "Fine with me," he said.

The Colonel entered, slowly, but without a cane. Connor stood to offer assistance, but was waved off.

"Where's your cane—?" Kathryn started.

"Button it," he interrupted, "otherwise I'll give in to your mother. She's always wanted to see the Panama Canal."

"Panama Canal?"

"Your mother talked to a travel agent. Your cruise isn't sold out."

"Consider it buttoned."

"She doesn't want her mother and I knowing that she's going to be spending two weeks with Neil Lathrope."

"Grandfather!" Erin scolded.

"Man's thirty years younger than her. Everyone knows they're seeing each other."

"Thirty-one," Kathryn said easily.

"Lathropes only want women for one reason. And it isn't the money."

"Probably true," Kathryn agreed. "And that's not all bad. Should have started dating younger men years ago."

"I can't unhear that," Nathan protested.

Connor wondered if the stroke had removed some of the Colonel's polite-society filters. Either that, or it was the privilege that came with age. Five years ago, he would have never said such a thing.

Once the Colonel was seated, an act that took some time as well as concentrated effort, he asked, "Are we waiting on Cade?"

"He's not coming," Connor replied.

"He missed last month, too. He has obligations, and being part of the family is one of them. That damnable mother of his—"

"I'll call him," Kathryn said.

"We talk once a week," Connor added, grateful his aunt had derailed that rant. No matter how much family mattered to the Colonel, his relationship with Stormy,

Cade's mother, continued to irritate him.

"That's not good enough."

"Agreed." Connor nodded. Cade did need to interact more. Their conversations were short, and Connor generally initiated them. Connor understood his brother's reluctance—he was protective about his mother, and he carried the burden for their father's death. It didn't matter that no one blamed him.

"I want him at the next meeting."

"I'll see to it," Kathryn promised.

"Let's get through this." The Colonel reached for an agenda. "I have an appointment with my trainer."

"You mean physical therapist?" Kathryn asked.

"No. I hired a personal trainer. She has me lifting weights and building my endurance. Yes, yes, before you become the appointed nagger, the cardiologist, neurologist and a whole host of other names—all ending in ist—said it was okay. I'm going to participate in a five-k walk later this year."

"Go, Granddad," Erin said.

Connor looked down to hide his grin.

"I'll be raising funds for stroke victims," he added. "I expect you all to sponsor me. The foundation, as well."

It wasn't a question, and they all knew it.

Kathryn nodded. "Name the amount."

"The more people from Donovan Worldwide who participate, the better."

"On it," Erin replied. "I'll set up a team." She ran the HR department, and she had a particular interest in wellness programs and getting employees involved in special projects.

As always, the Colonel's determination impressed Connor.

"Now, where were we?" the man asked.

Erin updated him on the corset shop idea, ending with her proposal to invest in more small, regional loans.

He nodded. "Of course. Nathan will want to see how it can be profitable, but if Connor doesn't object, neither do I, unless you overextend yourself." He picked up an agenda and scanned it. "I don't see BHI on here."

"BHI?" Erin asked. "What about BHI?"

"Nothing much to report," Connor said. "I had a meeting with Pernell and he threw me out of his office. I didn't get to meet with the board or his daughter."

"Not surprised," the Colonel said.

"When was this?" Erin asked.

"Yesterday."

"I had dinner with Lara." Erin scowled. "She didn't mention it."

"Conniving bastard," the Colonel added. "Nothing good comes of associating with the Bertrands."

"That's a broad brush," Erin objected. "Lara's one of my best friends."

"Erin's right." Connor tapped the top of his pen against his agenda. "I don't get the sense she's much like her old man."

"How would you know?" Nathan asked.

"Erin introduced us a few weeks ago. And I ran into her last night. She was getting off the elevator after I met with Pernell."

"And?" Erin prompted.

"She obviously knew nothing about the meeting." Her wide-eyed reaction to seeing him had been real. No doubt about that.

"You could call her," Erin said.

"I gave her my card."

"Oh?"

"If she wants more details, she can contact me." He was surprised, and more than a little disappointed, that she hadn't. Loyalty ran deep, perhaps. Most times, that was an admirable trait. But when it was blindly given, it bordered on an emotional reaction rather than a strategic choice.

"What's our next step?" the Colonel asked.

"We wait."

"I like it." The Colonel nodded. "Vultures will swoop in eventually."

"There's a danger in that," Kathryn said.

"Oh?" Connor leveled a glance at her.

"If the rumors are true, BHI is making some bad decisions. There may be nothing worth saving if Pernell does something stupid."

"The patents make it attractive," Nathan said.

They were the game changer.

The five of them spent the next hour discussing other interests. Kathryn outlined her plan for Erin to fill in at the foundation while she was on her cruise.

"You are planning to come back?" the Colonel demanded.

Kathryn was slower in responding than Connor expected. "It's no surprise that I'd like to cut back on the time spent at the office."

"But?" Connor prompted.

She looked at him without blinking. "I'd like Erin to start looking for someone to take over more of the day-to-day responsibilities."

Until now, he hadn't thought much about his aunt's hopes and aspirations.

"I want to travel more. But don't misunderstand. I'm not resigning."

"It's the influence of that youngster," the Colonel insisted.

"Perhaps."

Was it? She'd never married, had never had children. Until now, Connor hadn't wondered why. She was certainly still young. Fit. Trim. Obsessed with eating well, taking vitamins. She often said she had no intention of aging gracefully. She was going to fight the temptress at every turn. So far, she was doing a hell of a job. "Erin, get with Kathryn offline."

Erin nodded.

The meeting wrapped up shortly afterward. Erin hung back for a private word.

"What did you think of Lara?"

"Meaning?"

"I've known her for a very long time."

"And?"

"She knows her father is not making the best decisions. Convincing the board is another thing. She needs a friend. An ally. Even better, a mentor."

"I don't plan on eating her for lunch, if that's what you're worried about."

"I was rather hoping you would. Call her, at least?"

He shook his head.

"Aunt Kathryn is right. Waiting for BHI Communications to implode is risky. Maybe we should be more strategic? Talk to board members. Some of them have to be sympathetic. There's no doubt they've heard the rumors. And so have our competitors. There's no guarantee we'll win the battle. You need to gather support, make a preemptive strike. I know for a fact that Lara's an excellent place to start." With that, she left.

He rapped his knuckles on the table before gathering the discarded agendas and feeding the pages into the shredder.

Erin made a good point. Perhaps part of his hesitation was from Pernell Bertrand's lunacy. Pushing aside the unwelcome thought, he went back to his office, returned a few phone calls, responded to a dozen emails then opened up a preliminary month-end financial statement.

When his mind kept returning to the topic of BHI and the best way to approach the problem, he opened a drawer and pulled out the file Nathan had provided on the company.

Connor found the section detailing the biographical information on each individual board member. He spent the next hour reading through the profiles, but he skipped the one on Lara.

Overall, there were few surprises.

The board was comprised mostly of Pernell's associates. With the exception of Lara, he was surrounded by people of a similar age and thought process. Nothing new. No innovation. No bold moves.

He'd read the information on Pernell before but he reached for it again, just the same, wondering if his run-in with the man would give him new insight.

It didn't. The Bertrand fortune was slowly being gnawed

away. Pernell had recently been forced to sell their hotel holdings. Yet he remained stubborn, believing his divisions were worth more than they were.

Connor had saved the profile on Lara for last. He picked it up and studied it.

Initially, there weren't a lot of unexpected revelations. She seemed well adjusted, the adored only child. She'd gone away to college, then had returned to Houston to earn her Master of Finance degree. After that, she'd taken a job at an insurance company. That was his first surprise.

As he read deeper, he learned that she'd completed a number of summer internships, one at an Internet startup in California, another at an oil company in Houston, followed by two at the same financial firm back east. It seemed that she'd tried to broaden her work experience as much as possible, and he applauded that effort.

He wondered then about the relationship between Lara and her father. Was it fractious or harmonious? Her lack of knowledge about his meeting with Pernell suggested the former. Or perhaps the man just ran his business that way.

Connor was the first to recognize that Donovan Worldwide operated differently from a lot of privately held family firms. The informal monthly meetings ensured everyone knew all of the big decisions being considered. Information was shared rather than hoarded. Differences of opinion were discussed and respected.

He scanned the rest of the report. There was a lack of information about her personal life. As he'd surmised, she wasn't married and there were no reported engagements or even serious relationships. That didn't necessarily mean anything. Perhaps, like him, she was too focused on business to consider dating.

If so, no doubt they both deserved a diversion.

It didn't matter that she hadn't telephoned him as he'd expected. The way she'd reacted to him last night had said things that words could not.

Her pulse had accelerated. Her mouth had opened slightly as she'd momentarily lost her composure.

Yeah, he wasn't above spending a little time with the delectable Lara Bertrand.

He flipped to the attached picture.

It was a corporate one, probably taken for the times a headshot was required, the company's website, press releases and such. Since there were no more photos, he dropped it on top of the report and closed the manila folder.

After waking up his computer, he searched her out on social media. Clever girl had her accounts locked down. So he searched his sister's recent albums. Still nothing. A general search showed only the professional photograph. It showed her as tough, unapproachable, formidable. It didn't show any of her vulnerability, appeal, or the depth of her rich brown eyes.

Another half hour of online searching didn't turn up any information that Nathan hadn't already supplied.

Connor sat back and closed his eyes, considering.

Erin's earlier suggestion had been spot on. Lara was probably the best person to approach about BHI's position. If she were amenable, she could then advise him on who else to talk to. The next step would be to garner the support of the board. He didn't need everyone, just the right people. Once others were on his side, Pernell would have no choice but to capitulate. At the moment, that seemed to be his family's preferred course.

Fine by him. The opportunity to spend time with Lara suited him.

The intercom on his desk phone beeped.

"You have an unscheduled visitor, Mr. Donovan."

The interruption surprised him. No one got into his office without an appointment. When Thompson refused admission, they went. "And?"

"Lara Bertrand."

Well. Well.

"She knew the code and said you were expecting her."

Her move took him off guard. He'd been prepared for her phone call, but not a visit. "Send her in." He opened his top drawer and slid the BHI file inside. Her picture, he put under his keyboard.

Connor moved to the middle of the room and waited.

Seconds later, Thompson opened the door.

Lara walked in, wearing sky-high stilettos and a pencil skirt with a matching blazer. The suit was red. Libido red. She'd likely selected her outfit carefully, believing she had chosen a power color. If his guess was right, no doubt she'd discarded black as too obvious and a pastel as too feminine. All would have been a better choice. Red made him think of sex.

Beneath the jacket, she had on a white lacy something. Perhaps a camisole. Definitely something he'd want to move aside as he bared her shoulders.

She radiated a cool, timeless elegance. The small patent leather clutch in her left hand added an ultrafeminine touch. Factor in the way her long, dark hair spilled across her shoulders, and testosterone short-circuited his brain.

She was part Audrey Hepburn, part pin-up girl. And he had to force himself to remember his manners and the fact Thompson still stood there, a puzzled frown buried between his eyebrows.

"Ms. Bertrand," Connor greeted, extending his hand. Better than giving in to temptation and curling it behind her neck to hold her still for his kiss.

Though her hand disappeared in his, her grip was strong. Despite their size differences, she was meeting him with courage, as an equal. But damn, he noticed that her nails had been manicured with those sexy French tips. And he wondered what they'd feel like on his back. "To what do I owe this unexpected pleasure?" he asked. The handshake ended much too soon. The morning's image—of her bound to his bed, unable to get away—raced through his mind.

Thompson cleared his throat and said, "I informed Ms. Bertrand that you have a very busy schedule and only have a few minutes available."

"Thank you. Would you like coffee, Ms. Bertrand? Perhaps a bottle of water?" The questions were part of the code he and Thompson had prearranged. If Connor didn't offer a beverage, Thompson would return shortly to escort the visitor out.

"Is the coffee strong?"

"Very," Thompson replied. "If that's the way you like it, you'll be pleased." He paused. "Cream or sugar?"

"Black is fine," she replied.

"Damn," Connor said, as Thompson closed the door behind him.

"Damn?"

"I was hoping you'd ask for sugar at least," he confessed.

"Oh?" She frowned, drawing her eyebrows together.

His packet stash was almost completely depleted. "Long story. Have a seat?"

Though he had a small area with a couch and several armchairs for informal discussions and meetings, he extended his hand toward the chair in front of his desk. Until he knew the nature of her business, keeping some distance between them was wise.

"Thank you," she said.

He waited until she sat, then he took his chair.

She placed her small bag on the carpet then crossed her legs.

Fuck if he didn't hear the sweet whisper of silk.

She inhaled then expelled the breath quickly before starting with, "I know you're a busy man and I have an unusual proposal—"

A sharp knock on the door forced her to cut off her words. She sighed at the interruption of what was obviously a carefully constructed and rehearsed speech.

Her beautifully pursed lips turned upward when she looked to see Thompson approaching with a mug of coffee.

"I don't know if I've ever been more grateful."

Both men watched her as she took a sip.

She closed her eyes momentarily. "It's excellent."

"It is?" Connor asked.

"You sure you don't need cream or sugar, ma'am?"

"It's exactly the way I like it."

"That's what I'm talking about," Thompson said, words

almost sing-songy.

"Any possibility of stealing you away from Mr. Donovan? Name your price."

"I'll keep that in mind." Thompson's grin was sloppy, ridiculous. A former Special Forces badass should know better than to be fraternizing with a potential enemy.

Not that he should judge. Connor suspected that he had looked much the same the moment she'd walked through his office door.

"Anything else, sir?"

"Out," Connor said.

The man was still grinning like an idiot when he left.

"You really like it?" Connor couldn't help but ask when they were alone again. "You aren't just being polite?"

"About coffee? Never. Getting a cup like this ranks up there with receiving manna. Filtered water, no doubt. Freshly ground. Your man Thompson has elevated it to an art form of types. No doubt takes great pleasure in the ceremony of it."

"All that from a cup of coffee?" And from his assistant? He'd hired a secret barista? Was there no end to the man's talents?

She inhaled the aroma. "It has a nice flavor." She licked her upper lip.

God help him.

"Caramelly, a hint of chocolate perhaps. A good acidity around the edges of my tongue. I understand some people lack appreciation of a strong brew. I take it you're one of them?"

He didn't answer.

"You could always switch to hot chocolate."

Now his manhood was at stake. Connor told himself that Thompson had made her coffee weaker than usual, just for her. After all, she was a lady. "Where were we?"

She put the still-steaming mug on a coaster. He noticed that her hand shook a little. Immediately she put it in her lap. Good move. In business, opponents looked for tells that gave away a person's thoughts or reactions. She'd betrayed her nerves and, realizing it, had taken steps to hide it.

This was no social call. "You had a proposal?" he prompted before leaning back.

"My father can be very..."

He pressed his palms together and waited for her to find the right words.

"Committed to his ways."

"That's polite."

"I apologize for the way he treated you. Even if he hadn't wanted to consider your offer, his actions were inexcusable." She took a breath. "You told me last night to call if I had questions. I do. A number of them. I'm curious about the offer you took to him last night."

"You asked him?"

"I understand he didn't consider it."

"Regardless. It's off the table."

"I understand that. I'm hoping we can find a way to work together."

"Go on."

"You obviously know of the challenges we—meaning BHI—are having."

"Some," he agreed. "Since you aren't required to file public reports, the extent is nothing more than rumor and conjecture."

"We have divisions that are doing well. Others are not."

"And that brings you to your proposal?" Connor noticed she was twisting her hands together. The mug of coffee sat there, untouched and cooling. He waited. The only sounds were those of the air-conditioning's whisper and her rapid breaths. Whatever the woman had to say, it was costing her in terms of emotional energy.

"I know this is unexpected, ridiculous, outrageous..." She closed her eyes, then opened them again and locked her unblinking her gaze on him. "We're not even on a first-name basis."

"But?"

Her words had been jammed together, rushed, unpolished. While she'd been speaking with Thompson and with him, about the coffee, her tone had been light, not forced. Now, tension wove through her voice. Connor had no idea where she was going, but he sure as hell expected it would be interesting, suspected he'd be willing to do anything she suggested, as long as she kept looking at him like that, as if he were hope, promise, threat and redemption all in one. Fucking heady stuff.

After a short breath, she rushed on, "Will you marry me?"

Of all the things he'd been expecting her to say, that wasn't it. Connor wasn't sure he'd ever been more stunned. He took great pride in being prepared for all eventualities. He thought in terms of flow charts. Each thought led to a different result. Since he enjoyed considering various possibilities, he was rarely caught off guard, and she'd managed it twice.

Silence hung in a whisper, an expectation.

Possible responses crowded his mind. But only one mattered. "You have no idea what you're asking."

"I'm sure you're right. It was forward of me." She pushed back her chair and stood. She crossed to the window and stared out with her arms wrapped around herself. "But I'm hoping you'll be interested enough to hear me out."

"Go on." He remained where he was, still leaning back in his chair, considering.

She turned back to face him. "I don't want you thinking I'm behaving impulsively. On the contrary. I've spent many months searching for answers. The idea took shape overnight, and I spent most of today thinking it through, lining out objections, and ultimately, I think it's a solid idea. That said, if you want to schedule a different time to talk, I understand. Mr. Thompson mentioned you have other appointments."

"You're here now." He watched the battle rage across her face. A slight frown became pursed lips. No doubt it had cost her something to show up at his office uninvited. Earlier she'd mentioned a sleepless night, not that there was any trace of it on her beautiful face.

"BHI's communications division is in serious trouble."

He knew that. Before he asked for a definition, she added, "Three consecutive quarters of losses."

Which was worse than he'd surmised. "Mostly from the retail stores," he guessed. "People buy their gadgets in different ways than they did years ago."

She didn't deny that, but she didn't say he was right, either.

"Since you don't own the land under most of the stores, you can't win."

"Regardless, we own some patents. We do some things really well and there's plenty of potential."

All of which was true. He waited, wondering how this had led her to the idea of marriage.

"Options should be considered. Consolidation, mergers, a sale, acquisitions, infusion of cash, shake-up in leadership." She paused. "That's where you come in. I need your brain."

"Why mine?"

"You approached my father. It's clear you've already seen the possibilities. You're smart and aggressive, brilliant even."

"That's flattering—"

"As my husband, you'd have a seat on the board." She'd dug out the corporation's bylaws and confirmed that. To be certain, she had a corporate attorney going through the document as well, looking for pitfalls. "You could exert influence. I have years of insight I can offer you. It could be a marriage in name only. I'd be willing to negotiate a prenuptial agreement with you that we'd both sign. We'd naturally include a predetermined divorce date. Of course, we would keep our finances separate. We don't even have to live together."

He took it all in. "Very generous of you." In his most considered way, he allowed the tension to stretch. "And what do I get out of it?"

She lowered her hands to her sides. "I'm not sure what you mean. I've already said you stand to make a tremendous amount of money. And I'm sure those patents are very attractive."

"It's not all about financial considerations."

"You're a businessman," she replied. "This is an unprecedented chance for you to influence BHI's decisions on potential mergers with Donovan Worldwide. We're not just talking communications. Really, on any decision, we need you, myself, my mother and only one other person. We're only talking about a year, maybe two at the outside. And like I said, I'll make it as easy for you as possible. You'd be free to live your life as you do now."

He noticed that the shakiness had left her voice. She was now a woman in control again, and more, someone with what she believed was a solid business proposition. Lara was clearly operating from her strength. It appealed—*she* appealed—to him on a number of levels. But her suggestion would never work for him. "I have a different view of marriage than you do."

"Oh?"

"I'd want a few things from you in return. Please sit back down." His words weren't a polite request.

Seeming to recognize the authority in his words, she complied without hesitation. He considered that a positive first step. "Before you persist with this idea, there are some things you need to know."

"I'm listening."

"If we were to get married, we would live together as man and wife."

"I've already said that wouldn't be necessary."

"And I'm saying it will be." He picked up a pen and threaded it through his fingers. "And that point wouldn't be negotiable. I'd expect you to move into my loft."

"That seems like a lot of effort. I'd only be moving back out again."

"Non-negotiable," he reasserted. "You can accept this term and keep the conversation moving forward, or I can thank you for coming to see me."

"This isn't how a negotiation works," she protested.

"You want something. I'm telling you what I expect in return."

"You stand to be the biggest winner here," she said. "I think you can afford to be a bit more magnanimous."

"I'm afraid that's not something I'm known for. You'd do well to remember that."

She opened her mouth as if to speak but closed it again almost right away.

"I will not have speculation about either of us or the nature of our relationship."

"Meaning?"

"You won't be dating other men," he said bluntly.

She nodded. "As long as you're discreet, I'm okay with you maintaining your friendships."

"There would be no cheating in this relationship. For either of us."

"The hypothetical relationship," she corrected, feeling a bit breathless.

He was getting to her, unnerving her, giving him the position of strength. Couldn't be better. "And we would sleep together."

"I..." She cleared her throat.

"Let me be more specific. We would fuck."

Her breath caught.

"Often." He dropped the pen and leaned toward her. "Is that a problem? Hypothetically?"

"No." She met his gaze. And he heard hesitation in her tone when she added, "None."

"Hypothetically, what do you know about BDSM?"

"Some," she admitted. Then her eyes widened. "Are you into it?"

"Into it? I wouldn't say that." He waited, choosing his words with great care, moving slowly. It was crucial she understood this and what it meant. He knew that might take time, and he was willing to be as patient as required. "I'm a Dominant. It isn't something I'm into. It's part of who I am. A part of my personality."

"And you'd expect..." She trailed off.

"That you'd be my submissive?" he finished. "Yes."

She started again. "You'd want..."

"I would."

Her earlier poise had worn off, and her breathing was ragged. This was what he liked. Women who were honest.

"Tell me what you know about it," he prompted.

She stalled before saying, "This doesn't seem to be the right time or place for this discussion."

"I'm happy to move it to my house. Or yours."

"How about a coffee shop or restaurant?" she suggested. "Where we're not totally alone."

He shook his head. "You'd be free to leave at any time if you're uncomfortable, or to ask me to go."

"On second thought, your office is fine."

"So tell me what your understanding is."

"I know what the initials mean."

When she'd first arrived, her voice had been confident, made so by her rehearsed speech. But now… Her words were more carefully spaced, and her voice was a bit higher pitched, as if her vocal cords were stressed. She was real, more open, perhaps feeling a bit vulnerable.

"And I've had a little experience, well, maybe not what you'd consider experience."

He waited.

"I dated a guy who used a flogger on me. Once he used a blindfold. He tied my wrists together with some rope."

He slowly sat back. "Anything else?"

"A spanking, over his knees." She fidgeted, a trait he found charming.

"What were your thoughts about the experience?"

She finished the coffee that had to be cold by now. He let her stall for as long as she needed.

"The whole thing?" she asked finally. "Or just the spanking?"

"The whole thing."

"It was fine."

"Those are damning words."

"To be honest, I was disappointed. I didn't understand what all the fuss was about. I liked the blindfold and having my hands secured, but the flogger damn well hurt. If there was supposed to be any pleasure, I never experienced it. And when I was over his knee, I'm afraid I had an attack of the giggles."

Another answer Connor hadn't been expecting.

After sliding the mug back onto the coaster, she met his gaze. "Maybe I was hoping for something more. When he spanked me hard enough to stop the giggles, it freaking stung."

"I imagine it was supposed to," he said wryly.

"Other than feeling the pain, I came away with nothing. Afterward we had sex, but—" Abruptly, she stopped talking.

"We have to talk openly."

"Even if it's embarrassing?"

"Especially then."

"How did I know you were going to say that?" She crossed her arms over her chest and held onto her shoulders. Then, obviously realizing she was betraying herself, she lowered her arms. "I expected more from the sex, I guess, but it was the same old thing." Her face was a lovely shade of pink. "Missionary. Over too soon. After that relationship, I dated another guy and things were... I'm trying to be polite."

"Go on."

"I guess the best word for it is predictable."

"Boring?"

"Boring," she repeated. "I asked him if we could experiment a little. When I told him what I wanted, he tried. He tied me up, but the knots were so loose that I could slip my hands out. It sort of lost something when I had to work to keep them in place. He placed a tie over my eyes, and that was as close as he got to a blindfold. When I asked him to spank me, he untied me and told me I was too extreme for him. He seemed really disturbed by it, and I never saw him again. The last guy I dated...well, let's say there was no chemistry."

He wasn't sure what to think of a man who had a willing woman in his arms and didn't attempt to give her what she wanted, whether he was into it or not. "I can guarantee that

I will be willing to at least talk about anything you want to try. We'll have plenty of discussions about that." Connor saw her shudder. From thrill, he hoped. "Have you ever been to a club? A play party?"

She shook her head and he caught the glitter of an earring. For a wild, wicked moment, he wanted to see his initials there, in diamonds. "Is there anything you wanted to experience?"

She hesitated, and he waited. Finally, she tipped back her head. "When I masturbate, I think about a man's belt."

"I think we could arrange that."

"I might hate it. It could ruin the fantasy."

"It could," he agreed. "And it could make it even better. Anything else?"

"You're asking a lot of questions, Mr. Donovan. Tell me about you, what it is you think I need to know."

"As I mentioned, BDSM isn't something I'm merely into. Kinky sex like you're suggesting is fine. Awesome, in fact. I definitely enjoy it. I'd love to see your body spread wide, held open for me. But I see that as an extension of a relationship rather than replacing it."

"I'm a bit confused. I thought it was all about the tying up and beating."

"To some people, it is. And that's fine. To me, it's much, much more. Tell me, do you consider yourself compassionate?"

She blinked. "Of course."

"Loyal to your family and friends?"

"Naturally."

"Someone who likes chocolate?"

"Adores it," she said, softly, as if it were a confession. "And pizza."

That little bit of information, he hung onto. "They're part of who you are."

"Yes."

"The D/s dynamic is the same thing to me. I can't separate it from my personality. Nurturer. Protector. Dominant."

"That sounds a bit scary."

"It doesn't have to be. In fact, I'd insist you have a safe word, a way to immediately stop anything we were doing. You'd also have a word to slow things down, whether to give you a break or to reconnect emotionally or just to talk about how you're doing."

"I'm not used to hearing men use the word emotional."

"It's part of a real relationship," he said. "I may not be as good at recognizing my emotions as you are yours, but I do have them, I promise you."

She gave him a soft smile, and he recognized that they'd had a small connection. He—they—could build from there.

She looked out of the window for a few seconds, in silence. When she glanced back, a thoughtful frown was burrowed between her dark eyebrows. "So if we were to marry... You'd expect..." She squirmed a little. "You'd want to spank me? Blindfold me? Tie me up?"

"All that, yes. We'd talk about which you were comfortable with, find your limits. But it goes beyond that for me."

"Beyond it, how?"

So she was curious. Considering it, at least. "I'd expect that, while we were married, you would be my wife, but also my submissive."

"Isn't that synonymous with servant? Slave? Yes-man? I'm not a puppet for anyone," she said, scooting her chair back a little, putting distance between them. "I can't be. I refuse to be."

"I wouldn't expect that." He kept his voice easy, moderated. "It's clear that you're intelligent as well as brave. I wouldn't want anything less."

"Do you ever have...I don't know how to put this. Regular sex?"

"Regular?"

"You know. Wham-bam. Wipe up with a tissue and you're done?"

"No," he said bluntly.

"Not ever? No quickies? Something where we can just get it over with?"

"Lara, I'm not sure what kind of sex you've been having,

but I promise you, you won't want to just get it over with."

"That sounds a little overconfident."

He smiled. "I don't think so. I will be so focused on you that you'll want it to go on and on."

She laced her fingers in her lap, as if unsure what to do with them. "It's clear that I don't have any idea what it would mean to be a submissive or whether I'd like it or not. Like you said, whether it's part of my personality."

"We'll also talk about that, all of it. I'll let you know my expectations, requirements."

"And what about mine?"

He took her, her challenge—her tilted chin and narrowed eyes—very seriously. He recognized she was a novice, and fuck, he had to admit that it appealed to him. He hadn't had a serious relationship since his father had passed. Until Lara, he hadn't even been attracted to anyone.

Recently, he'd gone to a local club with his friends Reece and Sarah. Julien Bonds had flown in to meet them. While Connor had enjoyed being there, he hadn't scened. Without a relationship, it was sexy, but not significant.

Watching Reece flog Sarah had made him restless. The two had seemed unaware of anyone else, and the way Reece had interacted with her, even carrying her to a comfort couch for her aftercare, had spoken of an intimacy that was missing in his own life. "No doubt you will have needs," he agreed finally. "I would do anything in my power to meet them."

"That doesn't sound very Dom-like."

He grinned. "Be that as it may, taking care of a sub gives me fulfillment." When she didn't say anything, he continued, "To me, D/s relationships are different from others on many levels, and they require tremendous trust. I will work to ensure that I deserve your trust by honoring my word, letting you know what to expect and never taking you further than you're comfortable with or have agreed to go."

After pausing for a moment, he added, "I will be the Dom you need, the Dom you require, the Dom you want.

In return, I expect you to accord me your respect and utter loyalty, at home as well as in public. I don't anticipate that you'd agree with me on all matters, but I would demand that we handle disagreements discreetly. Details of our relationship would remain between us. Always. As part of our prenuptial, you would agree that there would be no tell-all book. No interviews with the press."

"If you even think such a thing, Mr. Donovan—"

"I leave nothing to chance, Ms. Bertrand, not when it comes to my family. I expect you're the same way and that's why you approached me."

She gave a nod, slow, as if reluctant.

"That said, I promise you I would be a patient Dom and honorable husband. I even know how to do laundry and load the dishwasher."

"All that?"

"And I give excellent foot rubs."

A delicate flush stained her cheeks. That was another thing he hadn't expected. The contradiction between sophistication and innocence ensnared him.

For a moment, the tension eased.

Then, as he waited, it grew again.

"You were right when you said I had no idea what I was suggesting when I came to you with my proposal."

"It's a lot to take in," he agreed. "You're free to leave and think about it. Or perhaps you'd like a taste of what you'd be in for as my wife, my sub?"

"What are you suggesting?"

"That you give me the chance to tantalize you. To see if it might be in your personality. After that, if you still want to pursue the possibility of getting married, we'll set up another meeting outside of work, where we'll have adequate time to talk about details and get more intimately acquainted."

She hesitated.

He didn't push. But damn, part of him hoped, really hoped she was interested enough to accept his challenge. And he admitted he wanted to touch her, make her respond to him.

"I feel like I've entered a maze. This is a bit of a mind fuck."

He didn't disagree with her statement.

"What do you want me to do?"

He pointed to a spot in front of the couch. "Go stand over there. Take off your suit jacket."

Eventually she stood.

"Lock the door first."

She gave a small nod before pivoting and heading toward the door. As she walked, he stared.

Her hips were rounded, and he noticed the way her buttocks were emphasized by the tight fit of her skirt. Connor considered that maybe his earlier thought had been wrong. Maybe she hadn't chosen the red suit for power. Or Christ, maybe she had, her power over him. Those heels, those stockings… "Seams up the back?" *Damn.*

"Problem?" She turned the big lock. The bolt made a purposeful sound as it slammed home. Then she faced him again, resting her shoulders against one of the floor-to-ceiling double doors. She brushed back her hair and boldly met his gaze.

Any earlier doubt was erased. This woman had chosen her outfit intentionally. She'd known the effect that skirt would have on any male with a pulse. And hell, if he didn't have one, it would restart it. "You're lovely." And smart. He made a mental note never to underestimate her as an adversary, as a lover.

Without being asked a second time, she moved to the center of the room. The sight of her calves, accentuated by those heels, gave him palpitations.

But it wasn't just the heels. It was the entire package. She had flawless posture, and she walked with a little strut that spoke of confidence.

Was there anything hotter?

She stopped where he'd indicated then shrugged out of her suit coat. She took her time—her sweet, sweet time—draping the red material over the arm of the couch.

Then she rolled back her shoulders, making her breasts

thrust toward him a bit, causing the button across her chest to strain. God help him.

Connor stood and walked toward her.

As he drew closer, her scent slipped past his defenses. Pheromones, he reminded himself. They made rational people insane.

He couldn't take his gaze from her. Often, he preferred his submissives to look downward, but he loved seeing her eyes, all the emotions and reactions that she didn't hide quickly enough. Uncertainty, sure. But mixed with a bit of curiosity. It created a heady elixir that he suddenly hungered for.

Only a few inches from her, he stopped. "Put your hands behind you."

Nothing existed but the sound of her breathing and the heat of his sudden desire.

She did as instructed.

He placed his index finger on the hollow of her throat. Her lips parted slightly. "If you're scared about anything, just say the word yellow."

She nodded.

"As we get to know one another better, as you gain experience and build your trust, things that might have made you nervous will no longer bother you. Yellow will slow me down, give us chance to regroup, discuss. Tell me you understand."

"I understand."

"When we're in a scene, in private, you'll address me as Sir."

She gently pursed her lips but didn't object. "I understand, Sir."

Over the years, at clubs, at parties, with subs he'd played with, he'd been called Sir. But the term hadn't had any impact on him. It had held no power. Coming from her now, it was like a slam to the solar plexus. That she'd called no one else Sir did crazy things to his brain circuitry.

He opened her top two buttons. Though he could see the flutter of her pulse in her throat, she said nothing.

Then he parted the material.

Her demi-bra lifted her breasts, leaving most of her flesh bare, but her nipples were hidden. She was lace, innocence, seduction. He knew this image of her would be seared into his mind.

Unable to resist the temptation of the woman who might be his future bride, he brushed the pads of his thumbs across her honey-kissed skin.

Her eyes drifted shut.

Emboldened by her sensual reaction, he stroked inside her bra and gently rolled her nipples.

She swayed toward him.

"Lovely," he said, exerting more pressure.

"Yum," she said.

"Yum?" He wasn't sure he'd ever had that reaction from a woman before. He liked it. "More?"

"Maybe." She opened her eyes and looked up at him. "I might be too chicken."

Looking at her to gauge her reactions, he squeezed her nipples a tiny bit harder. Before she could process what he'd done, he backed off.

"That..."

"You liked it?"

"Yes."

He teased, waited.

"Yes, Sir," she amended.

"Good girl." He gave her what she'd asked for, this time holding on a little longer. "Too much?" he asked when he'd released her.

"No," she admitted. "Not at all."

She had at least a small taste for pain. *Intoxicating.*

This time, he rolled her nipples, pinched them, pulled on them, drew her onto her toes. In reaction, she bent her knees. "Oh, yes," he said. He pushed her bra down, out of the way, then bent to lave each nipple with his tongue, sucking on each tip to soothe it.

She reached for him, hands on his shoulders. "Nice," he told her. He waited until her breathing had steadied a bit before saying, "But I'd told you to keep your arms behind your back."

Her eyes widened but she didn't immediately pull away. "You know what that means?"

"No." She drew a breath. "No, Sir. But I'm afraid I can guess."

"Yeah, you can. Tonight, if you dare, you can be punished for not following orders."

She scowled, tiny lines digging in between her eyebrows. "I don't think I'd like that."

"You weren't sure whether you wanted your nipples squeezed like that, either."

"True." She slowly uncurled her hands from his shoulders.

Part of him was tempted to tell her to leave them there.

She put her arms behind her back again.

"Very nice," he said. "Now I'm going to kiss you."

"Am I supposed to just stand here?" she asked.

"As opposed to…?"

"Participating?"

He lifted an eyebrow.

"I liked having my hands on you," she admitted. "And I've been wanting to mess up that very perfect hair of yours."

"You need to do a little reading up on submission."

"Oh?"

"No talking without permission."

"I see."

He frowned.

She laughed, a genuine, seductive sound. "I told you I'm new. No experience. I'm bound to make mistakes, Sir."

Connor reminded himself he'd already learned not to underestimate her.

"May I?" she asked. "Touch you?"

As he leaned toward her, she lifted herself onto her toes and met him. "Wrap your arms around me, Lara."

She parted her lips in anticipation and he claimed them. The force of their kiss took him aback. He'd kissed dozens of women, but he'd never felt a searing connection.

Lara wasn't tentative. She met his tongue, tasting, testing as deeply as he was. It was as hungry as it was natural.

When she laced her fingers behind his neck, he fisted a hand in her long hair and pulled her head back a little so he could deepen the kiss.

She offered herself to him with no resistance, not struggling, but rather, inviting. He accepted, lowering one hand to her derrière and drawing her against him, softness to sinew.

As she'd promised, she dug her hands into his hair, holding tight, the way he wanted her to. Having her there seemed right.

Her body went slack, and he took advantage. Coffee tasted sweet in her mouth, but it was the headiness of her surrender he appreciated most.

Suddenly he hoped she was brave enough to play with him later this evening.

With more reluctance than he'd ever felt, he ended the kiss and helped her to stand.

She blinked as she released his hair. After she was steady, she took a step back and smoothed her skirt, avoiding eye contact. Finally, she cleared her throat and looked up.

"May I?" He moved toward her and reached inside her blouse.

"Connor..."

He smoothed a hand down her chest and straightened her bra. Her nipples were still hard, and because he knew himself well, he resisted the temptation to tease them one more time. Nothing about her, or this, was simple. He already desired her. If he continued, he'd want more, and he wouldn't be satisfied until he touched every inch of her skin as he bared it. He'd want to lick her cunt from back to front to memorize her scent. And he'd want to mark her.

Being a gentleman, he rebuttoned her blouse. Then, to distract himself, he said, "Give me your cell phone."

"Er, it's in my purse."

He crossed the room, then picked up the clutch and placed it on his desk before unhooking the metal clasp. "May I?"

"I have a feeling I won't have many secrets from you." She tucked her shirt tails into her waistband.

"Not if I have my way." He pulled out her phone.

"Make a Z-shape across the keyboard to unlock it."

A few moments later, he had saved his cell phone and office numbers in her contacts list. For good measure, he added his personal email address. He was a bit disappointed she hadn't done that herself yesterday, when he'd given her his business card. "No excuses not to call me."

"I figured that was what you were doing."

"You'll also notice that I didn't ask for your information."

"Is that supposed to make me feel better? I've no doubt you could have it in less than a minute if you wanted it. From Erin, if nothing else."

"I could," he agreed. "But I won't." He propped a hip on the edge of the desk. She hadn't moved from the center of the room, but her clothing and jewelry were once again in place, and she'd smoothed back her hair. Her shoulders, though, were curved slightly forward.

The beautiful Lara Bertrand—who'd just had a sample of what he'd require from her submission—wasn't quite as in control as she probably hoped to appear.

"The point is, the next step is yours. You've had a tiny taste of what it would be like with me. A small amount of pain on your nipples. Hopefully a sensual, arousing pain?" If the way she'd responded to his kiss was any indication, it had been. "Text me, call me, shoot me an email if you want to explore more. Eight o'clock. What area of town do you live in?"

"You move fast."

"We'll go at your speed," he assured her. "Tonight. Tomorrow. Next week. It's your call. It was my understanding you were anxious to get to the marriage part. I'm willing to wait as long as it takes."

"The Heights," she said after a long sigh.

"If you're agreeable, I'll have my driver pick you up around seven-thirty."

"I always prefer to drive myself so that I'm free to come

and go as I choose."

Her words were tacit agreement, but he was smart enough to realize he didn't have her. Yet. "Of course. Keep in mind, April is at your disposal. Even if it's late, you'd be safe. And if you'd like a glass of wine, you wouldn't have to worry about driving. I'd be more comfortable."

"What if I wanted you to pick me up?"

He recognized what she was doing. Showing her independence, an obligatory objection to ceding control to him. "As if it were a date, rather than an introduction to my form of seduction?"

She caught her breath.

"If that makes you happy, Lara, I'd be delighted to pick you up."

"I'll let you know what I decide." She reached for her jacket. "But I still may not come at all."

He didn't argue. "Let me help with that. Please." His words were light. His tone was commanding. His expectation allowed no argument.

Responding as he'd hoped, she waited while he crossed the room, picked the jacket up and held it for her.

"Are you always so mannerly?" she asked as she turned back to face him.

"With my woman? Yes."

"Your woman? *Your* woman?" Her voice held a touch of indignation and outrage, but the question had emerged shaky.

"That's what you want to be," he reminded her. "Isn't it?" He smoothed her lapels.

"No." She shook her head.

"My wife? What do you think it means?" For a few moments, he let her think about it. Now, he saw, with the way she was rubbing her upper arms, realization was settling in. When she'd walked into his office, she'd obviously had an abstract idea of what she was proposing. Business had been her focus, and apparently it hadn't occurred to her that he'd expect something more.

He walked back to his desk, and she followed. He picked

up her phone then dropped it back in her bag. He re-clasped it before returning it to her.

"Thank you. It's been memorable."

"It has, indeed." He went to the door and unlocked it. His hand on the knob, he paused. "And I won't forget I owe you a punishment."

Her grip whitened on the bag.

"I'll be waiting to hear from you." He opened the door and she walked past without another word.

Lara kept her composure until he'd closed the door behind her.

Then, realizing Thompson wasn't in the room, she exhaled raggedly and sank into a chair.

What the hell had she been thinking in coming here, proposing to Connor Donovan when she knew nothing, *nothing* about him?

Even after he'd revealed that he was a Dominant, she'd stayed. Not only that, but she'd made things worse by following his soft-spoken commands. She'd all but invited his touch then she'd surrendered to his kiss.

Worse, she'd done it willingly. And she wanted to do it again.

If she were smarter, she'd get away and stay away.

She drew a breath. Last night, as insomnia had stalked her, Erin's words had seemed to play on an endless loop. Somewhere around midnight, Lara had started to consider the idea of marriage to Connor. For the next hour or two, she'd come up with a dozen reasons why that was a ridiculous idea, including her outrageous attraction to him. From the night she'd first met him, she'd recognized he was dangerous. Despite that, she'd been ensnared by his steely gray eyes.

Eventually, she'd fallen into a restless sleep. After dawn had awakened and she'd guzzled half a pot of coffee, she'd hit the shower. Thoughts of Connor hadn't been far away.

Then she'd received a copy of an email one of their attorneys had sent to her father. The woman had raised concerns regarding several clauses on a contract her father intended to sign. The news had startled Lara, though it shouldn't have. It was simply another in a string of decisions she disagreed with.

While she'd been dressing, she'd reached the inevitable conclusion. She did, indeed, need an ally on the board. A strong, powerful one. And Erin was right. Connor was brilliant. He had the financial resources and strategic thinking skills to help her out.

But was marriage the logical solution?

After breakfast, she'd pulled out a file containing BHI's legal documents and realized there were only two ways to get him a seat on the board. One was through her father's invitation. She didn't see that happening. Family members, on the other hand, were automatically accorded a seat.

She'd spent hours thinking it through and had decided that a marriage of convenience would be a wise move for both of them. For her, especially.

There had been a definite spark between her and Connor the other night outside the elevator. She knew she hadn't imagined it. So she'd decided to exploit it.

Even though she hadn't worn those heels or that suit in months, she'd selected both. The skirt was a bit too tight, and a look in the mirror had shown her that it flaunted her buttocks. Generally she didn't wear the outfit because it was a bit risqué but, with Connor, that was exactly why she'd selected it.

She just hadn't expected his all-too-male reaction.

For the second time, she wondered what the hell she'd gotten herself into.

Lara exhaled.

The outer door opened and Thompson entered the room. "Is everything okay, Ms. Bertrand?" A ferocious line was buried between his eyebrows, making him appear scary.

She totally understood what Erin had been talking about. He was extremely large, and she had no problem imagining him in military garb. With his broad shoulders and jagged scar on his bald head, he looked to be equal measures protector and kick-ass intimidator. That he was so refined in his mannerisms made her feel somewhat discombobulated. "I'm fine. Thank you." She stood, wondering if the man had any idea what his boss was into. Had he been shocked when she'd locked the door?

Embarrassment tore through her.

How often did something like that happen? How many women came to Connor's office long enough for him to seduce them? Was she one of many?

Reminding herself no one had the ability to dictate her emotional state, Lara squared her shoulders as an outward show of pulling herself back together. "Thanks again for the coffee," she said as she was leaving the room.

"My pleasure. Next time I'll have biscotti for you."

"Sounds heavenly," she replied. She closed the door, knowing she wouldn't be back.

Lara kept her focus as she waited for the elevator. She avoided eye contact with other occupants and kept her head back as she strode through the lobby.

At the main entrance, a woman took a step forward. "Ms. Bertrand?"

"Yes?"

"I'm April Martinez. Mr. Donovan asked me to give you a ride back to your offices."

The gesture startled her, but she realized it shouldn't have surprised her. From her very first interaction with him, she'd felt something mesmerizing and seductive about the way he took charge of situations. Now she could add *unsettling* to the mix. The man liked to be in charge. Part of his dominant nature? Another sample of what it would be like if she were his woman?

"Ma'am?"

Humidity had made the afternoon feel like a swamp. The idea of air-conditioning appealed in a way that made the idea of resistance futile. "Thank you."

April indicated the sedan near the curb. Lara recognized

it from the night he'd offered to rescue her from the rain.

Heat suddenly slid down her spine. Over her shoulder, she glanced up at the building, unable to shake the feeling she was being watched. Maybe she was. More likely, she was being fanciful. Connor Donovan had more important things to do than watch her drive off.

Unless he was waiting to see if she complied with his wishes?

She entered the car and a few moments later, the driver merged into traffic. "Do you have the address?" Lara asked.

"Mr. Donovan provided it." April rattled it off. "Unless you'd like to make any stops?"

In the rearview mirror, she met the woman's eyes. Lara wondered, again, how often Connor did this kind of thing. "The office is fine." Even though something to fortify her nerves appealed—the bakery or a bar. At this point, she'd settle for either.

After April dropped her off, Lara hesitated. She realized she wasn't mentally prepared to go back to work.

Instead of entering the building, she sent text messages to her administrative assistant and to her father, letting them know she was taking the afternoon off.

The drive home seemed interminable. The traffic didn't distract her, and neither did cranking up an oldies station on the radio.

And of course, when she arrived, Mrs. Fuhrman was outside with her five dogs. It didn't matter that the eccentric woman wasn't supposed to have that many. After her husband had died, Mrs. Fuhrman had signed up to be a foster parent for rescued dogs. And she couldn't always allow herself to be parted from them, especially the ones with physical ailments. The dogs were all shapes, sizes, temperaments and ages. The oldest, Happy, only had three legs.

Lara closed her car door just as Suzy-Q, an apricot-colored mastiff mix, yanked on her leash and broke free, dashing over toward Lara.

Even though Mrs. Fuhrman was yelling at the dog to

come back and to be nice, Suzy-Q jumped up, paws landing in the middle of Lara's chest, knocking her back so that she rested on the car's fender. The dog seemed to smile before licking her face and slobbering on her blazer.

She grinned. There was nothing like puppy love to change her attitude.

"Get down right now, Suzy-Q!"

The dog ignored her owner. Instead, she put her big head on Lara's shoulder.

"I'm so sorry, Lara," Mrs. Fuhrman called out. "I don't know what's gotten into her. She hears your car and starts to lose her mind, I'm afraid."

"She's fine." She stroked the dog behind one of her ears then told her to get down. Immediately Suzy-Q complied.

Since four leashes were totally tangled and some of the dogs were excitedly barking, Lara returned Suzy-Q to Mrs. Fuhrman.

"Thank you, dear. She must love you." Mrs. Fuhrman shook her head, but not a single one of her blueish-purple hairs moved. "She's usually much better behaved than that, as you know," the woman said.

Lara didn't correct her neighbor even though Suzy-Q visited, in her exuberant, behaviorally challenged way, almost every day.

Once Suzy-Q's leash was back in the older lady's hand and the woman had slipped back into one of the shoes she'd somehow lost, Lara went inside to change and wipe off the dog's expression of affection.

An hour later, she wasn't convinced that coming home early had been the right choice. Being alone, with too much time and not enough to do, was never a good thing.

She'd already weeded the garden, pruned some flowers and tidied the house. And she hadn't been able to escape her thoughts.

She grabbed her laptop and did an Internet search on submission and Dominance.

Images populated the results, some of them appealing, most of them a bit frightening. She read a few well-written articles that explained both, from different perspectives. And it seemed that people did have varying expectations.

But she was quite certain that, despite what he'd said, she'd have to become a bit of a puppet to him.

She told herself that there was no way she was going to his home this evening. A marriage of convenience was a business deal that should be discussed in a boardroom or a neutral place. And that way, she could make sure he kept his hands off her. She'd already learned that a single touch from him could undo her.

Decision made, she closed the computer's lid.

Now she only had a few more hours she needed to fill before she could start getting ready for the next day.

After changing into running clothes and securing her hair into a ponytail, she headed out, down the street, focusing on her footfalls, looking ahead, trying to shut out the world as she normally did.

It didn't work. Unbidden, Connor's words returned to tumble through her memory. It wasn't just what he'd said. It was the certainty with which he'd said them, and the corresponding reaction that had slid through her.

Lara turned a corner and picked up the pace, even though her breathing was already labored.

As he'd suggested it might, his introductory taste had tantalized her. The way he'd tugged on her nipples had made her clench her thighs. Other men she'd been with had been afraid of giving her what she wanted, but clearly Connor wouldn't be. She wasn't sure if the idea appealed to her or terrified her.

Despite her best intentions, her mind wandered back to his talk about punishment. What the hell had he meant by that? Part of her railed against the idea. Who the hell did he think he was? What gave him any idea that she'd be agreeable?

And still... Curiosity made her panties damp.

In that moment, she wondered who she was fighting—Connor or herself?

She slowed her pace and headed for home.

Running in Houston's signature blend of heat and humidity was never a good idea. It zapped strength and energy. And it hadn't banished a single thought of Connor.

She let herself back into the house but nixed the thought of sitting on her leather couch in her damp clothes. Instead she filled a glass with filtered water before going outside to sit on the swing.

The overhead fan provided a welcome relief as she took several long drinks.

A hummingbird darted by, distracting her. With its unmistakable fluttering sound, it hovered for a second, then paused to sip some nectar from one of her lantanas before darting off.

She pulled out her scrunchie and told herself she wasn't going to Connor's loft tonight. Not only that, but she wasn't going to call him until tomorrow. Or the weekend. When she talked to him, it would be to let him know that a business arrangement was a solid idea but that she had no intention of being a submissive. That would complicate things far too much.

Decision made, she went back inside to take a long, cool shower.

It wasn't until afterward that she checked her cell phone.

She'd missed a call from her mother, presumably to confirm their lunch date tomorrow. Either that or her intuition had warned her that her only child was thinking of doing something potentially dangerous.

There were no emails or texts from Connor. While that didn't surprise her, she admitted it did disappoint her, even though she hadn't given him her number. But it reinforced his point. He was a man of his word, something he felt essential to building trust.

As she towel-dried her hair, she recognized she was playing games with herself. The fact she'd been disappointed that he hadn't reached out to her forced her to realize that she wanted to see him. She'd liked being in his arms, liked his teasing introduction to the sex they would have.

Still, she desperately needed some semblance of control.

Instead of letting him send his driver, she planned to take her own car. And she wasn't going to show up at eight.

She keyed in her message and sent it before she could change her mind and do things his way.

Less than thirty seconds later, he responded with his address and a code for entry to the parking garage.

That was it? She stared at the phone, waiting for something more. Anything. But her screen remained blank.

Seriously?

She'd expected him to object, insist on sending April, or at least remind her that he was a big bad Dom and that he'd suggested eight o'clock. And he'd given her no arguments. The confounding man made it difficult to get frustrated with him.

After dropping the phone onto the counter, she hurried into the bedroom.

She chose her favorite bra. It was a nude color and covered with black lace. She'd paid a small fortune for it at a lingerie shop, and she wore it only on special occasions. Then she grabbed a pair of black underwear, something modest. Not that it mattered, she told herself. She wasn't intending that Connor would ever see them.

Then she went into her closet to search for the right outfit. Something that said this was a discussion, not a prelude to his seduction. Something that kept her covered up.

After sorting through all of the hangers and digging through her drawers, she selected a sleeveless maxidress. She added platform sandals and a little jacket that covered her shoulders.

Her hair was the next big decision. Up? Loose? She sighed, remembering the way he'd held her when he'd kissed her.

She opened a drawer and took out a couple of clips to pull it back. Lingering dampness from her shower caused strands to curl around her cheekbones. She pushed them away, hoping they'd stay in place.

After a minimal brush of mascara and a touch of lipstick, she studied herself then wiped off the lipstick.

She left her house at seven-thirty and found his place with

no delays, meaning she arrived right on time. So she drove around the block several times.

By the time she entered the parking garage, the clock read eight-oh-five.

She pulled in and saw him standing near a car that she recognized as the sedan from earlier. He was lazing against a concrete wall, one booted foot propped on the wall behind him.

He wore a tight, long-sleeved charcoal T-shirt. The shirt had three small buttons, and he'd left the top two open. As if that weren't bad enough, well-worn blue jeans hugged his legs.

Lara had to force herself to concentrate. It was impossible to believe she'd asked this man to marry her.

Her heart did a slow thud in her chest as she imagined coming home to him every day. This just wasn't possible.

She took her time parking, aware of him there, arms folded, watching her. She even stalled for a few seconds, gathering her purse, unfastening her safety belt, checking that she had everything.

Evidently he grew tired of waiting. He pushed away from the wall and strode forward to open her door.

He offered his hand. She slid hers into his. His touch and strength simultaneously made her feel protected and overwhelmed. Never had she experienced anything like that. "You scare me just a little," she admitted.

"Good."

Her heart skidded to a stop. "That response made things worse."

"I want you clear on what you're getting into." He drew her hand to his lips. "I'm glad you came."

"I wasn't sure I was going to." And she still wasn't sure she should stay.

He smiled. "I like bravery."

If he hadn't added the end part, she might have turned and run like her feminine intuition was urging. Instead, she extricated her hand and he closed the car door.

"Shall we?"

Before she lost what remained of her brain cells, Lara tucked her keys into her purse. Once she was situated, he placed his fingers at the small of her back and guided her toward an elevator.

She'd never had a man do that before. She found it a little intimate and, damn it, a bit sexy.

He pushed the button for the thirtieth floor, and she took a step to the side to put some distance between them.

They exited into a hallway and he indicated she should precede him to the end.

His loft was considerably more modest than she'd expected for a man of his stature. Though there was no doubt that his furnishings and the few decorations were pricey, nothing was ostentatious.

A small but functional kitchen was off to the right. Everywhere she looked, bricks and beams were exposed, giving the main living area an industrial feel. He had several large paintings all hanging from a picture rail. Each was accentuated by individual lighting.

The loft's furnishings were sparse, making the space seem large and airy. A low-slung leather grouping was arranged in front of the fireplace, creating an inviting area for conversation or relaxation. Windows offered a view that was all city, with its vibrancy. Somehow it suited him.

"Feel free to make yourself at home," he encouraged. "After all, I'm hoping you'll be spending a considerable amount of time here."

She didn't respond to that.

"You're welcome to put your purse over there." He pointed to an interesting piece of furniture. It was crafted from mahogany and had a tall back with hooks placed at various intervals and a bench opened for storage.

She laid her purse on it, near an iPod and his fitness watch.

"Shall I show you around? Nothing's off limits to my potential bride."

"About that..." She turned back to face him.

He waited.

"We need to talk."

"That's why you're here," he agreed.

Damn. He was devastating.

This evening was the first time she'd seen him without a suit. And he was no less appealing for it. His shirt could have been custom-made, the fit was that good. She noticed his biceps were well formed. She'd previously guessed that he was a runner or biker, but she now knew his slender physique was a result of a tremendous amount of exercise.

The ends of his hair were damp, but he obviously hadn't shaved. The stubble on his jaw was masculine. As if that wasn't enough, he smelled of danger laced with an undercurrent of invitation.

"Something to drink? Wine?" he offered. "Red? White?"

"Water," she replied. "I need to keep my wits about me."

"Bottled? Or maybe some mineral water?"

"That would be wonderful." She gave a polite half smile.

The loft was open, so she could watch as he went into the kitchen and pulled out a bottle from the fridge. Then he grabbed a lime, a knife and a cutting board.

He cut the fruit into precise pieces and dropped one into the bottom of a thick glass before adding the sparkling water. He nicked another piece of lime to garnish the rim.

"That was more work than you needed to go through," she said as she accepted the drink.

She took a sip then toyed with the lime piece as she watched him pour a glass of wine.

"Something wrong?" he asked.

"I feel like you're being polite. Overly polite, maybe."

"Are you waiting for my evil twin to show up?" He grinned, and she felt completely disarmed.

"Sounds ridiculous that way."

"But?"

"Yes."

"You're wondering when I rip your clothes off and beat you? How the whole BDSM experience fits with your expectations of marriage and what I mean when I ask you to submit to me?"

Her finger slipped, and the lime piece splashed into the

mineral water.

"The answer to the first question is the moment you ask me."

Her mouth dried. "I think I made it clear earlier. I'm afraid you've got the wrong woman if you think I'm going to ask you to rip my clothes off and beat me."

"Perhaps." He walked into the living room and invited, "Join me?"

She took a chair near the fireplace, her back to the window. Her choice was meant to keep as much distance between them as possible.

As she'd planned, he sat on the couch. "Tell me what you were hoping for when you came here."

"I don't know. What happened this afternoon bothered me."

"In a good way? Bad way?"

"Both." She placed her drink on one of several coasters that were scattered across the glass coffee table. "And truthfully, I want to appeal to your business sense and reiterate—"

"You have."

She closed her mouth.

"Let's start where we agree. Having me on BHI's board will provide you with needed support and give the company some valuable feedback and direction."

She nodded.

"Further, both companies benefit."

"Yes."

"So your hesitation is due to the fact I'm a Dom."

"It is. I'm willing to make some arrangements with you. Maybe you could go to clubs, get your needs met that way?"

"I'm open to discussion, to explaining, to moving slowly, to introducing you to my world a step at a time."

"That's not how negotiation works, Mr. Donovan. I'm supposed to ask for something, you're supposed to counter with something else. Then we meet somewhere in the middle. You don't get everything you want," she said dryly.

"You're exactly right. That's how it's supposed to work."

Did he have to be so damn agreeable? The man undid her.

"You want marriage," he continued. "My condition is your submission." He extended his left arm across the back of the couch then propped an ankle on the opposite knee. With his wineglass in his right hand, he looked totally in charge and completely at ease.

"If I say no, is the discussion over?"

"You're considering running away before finding out what I mean, want I want, what I demand. And you're assuming you'd hate it. Did you hate what we shared this afternoon? Were you frightened by the way I kissed you? Maybe by the way I played with your nipples?"

Memories scalded her.

He leaned forward to put down his glass before leveling his gaze on her. There was no quarter in those gray eyes.

"What's it to be, Lara?"

Lara hesitated.

He didn't press, didn't say anything further, allowing the silence to become its own force.

A battle waged inside her, self-preservation versus desire. "No," she confessed. "I wasn't scared. Nervous, yes. But a kiss can hardly be considered submission."

"Oh?"

"It's not like I was on my knees." Yet she was picturing it. Lord help her. "Or naked. Or being beaten."

"But you did go to the door to lock it. Then you went to the center of the room. And you waited for me. You trusted me. You responded when I asked if the way I pulled on your nipples was too much."

His words made her burn for him.

"Did I take you further than you could go?"

"Of course not."

"Further than you wanted? Or were you left craving more, imagining more?"

She looked away, severing herself from the power of his eyes.

"We talked in my office about the fact D/s relationships need tremendous amounts of trust. I outlined what I'm willing to do for you to feel safe, but it goes two ways. You will need to be scrupulously honest with me. More importantly, Lara, the only way we can have a successful relationship is if you're honest with yourself." After pausing for a moment, he added, "That can be the most difficult obstacle."

His words, so accurate, gave her a chill. She'd been so busy fighting herself and her responses that she'd buried honesty several layers deep. What he'd done to her, with her, had made her panties damp. She'd been aroused even though she was apprehensive.

"Curiosity is part of the reason you're here," he said. The words were a statement, not a question.

"And nervousness about what you'd demand is something that almost kept me away."

"Fair enough. Ask me the dozens of questions that are going through your mind. Ask how I'd punish you."

"Does that have to be part of it?"

"For me, yes. But here's the important part. Any relationship we enter into will have rules. I will follow them as well."

"The idea that you would even consider punishing me is a deal-breaker."

"Is it? Let's consider the crime. Do you remember?"

She did. In detail. "You told me to keep my hands behind my back, and I didn't."

"And on a scale of one to ten, where would that fall as a real infraction?"

"One. You weren't angry, at least you didn't seem to be."

"So, what kind of punishment do you think fits with what you did?"

"A spanking? And if you remember, I've had two and hated them."

"I remember everything you've said to me."

With each word, he drew her more under his spell.

"And you haven't had a spanking from me. Or it could be that I'd tie your hands to my bedposts and keep them there as I licked and sucked your pussy."

For a moment, she wasn't sure she'd heard him correctly.

"Would you hate that?" Before she could answer, he continued, "You have a very narrow definition of punishment. I like to be a bit more creative than that. And I promise you, Lara, you'll have to ask for it."

She shivered.

"Let me show you the rest of the loft."

He'd intentionally changed the subject, she was sure, just

to keep her guessing. "I haven't said whether I agree to..." She couldn't find the right word. "This whole thing."

"Just giving you more information to help make your decision." He stood.

Slowly, she did, too, then she followed him down a hallway.

"Workout room," he said, opening the first door.

"Nice," she approved. He had a couple of pieces of cardio equipment, some free weights and a giant television along with a stereo and a fridge. The area was small, but organized well.

"You're free to use it whenever."

"I never said—"

"I know. This way." He opened a door to reveal his office. "There's room for a second desk."

Despite herself and without invitation, she entered. He had exposed brickwork, as she'd expected. But this place reflected the private Connor Donovan.

His college degree was framed and hung on a wall. At an angle was his college pennant. He had shelves that were filled with memorabilia—a baseball, an autographed football, a conch shell.

Another shelf was filled with pictures in all different sizes. Frames were crafted from every possible material... metal, glossy wood, plastic. Some were painted, others were ornate.

One photograph showed him in college graduation garb, flanked by his parents. Another showed him on horseback, wearing denim and a straw cowboy hat. There was a picture of a groundbreaking. He was holding a ceremonial silver-colored shovel. Standing near him was an older gentleman and two other men. His brothers, if she wasn't mistaken. "This is your grandfather, right?" she asked, pointing. "Erin calls him the Colonel."

"We all do."

"Rather formal."

"You've never met him?"

"No. I've met your mom, but no one else. I'm guessing

this one is Cade, right? Lives on the ranch in west Texas?"

He nodded.

"And Nathan?" The brothers were almost equal in height and they shared a similar, strong set to their jaws. Cade was the largest, and Nathan was the only one smiling. They all radiated strength and the aura that came with being born into power.

Behind several frames, she saw a snapshot of him with Erin. "May I?"

"Of course."

Lara picked it up.

They were on vacation, if their outfits were anything to go by. Erin was dressed in a floral sarong. He wore shorts, a sleeveless T-shirt and a jauntily tilted sombrero. Rather than looking at the camera, he and Erin were facing each other and both had big, goofy smiles. She had never seen this side of him, and it made him more real, less scary. Though trusting that could be dangerous for her, she realized. "Were you in Mexico?" Lara guessed.

"Yeah." He nodded. "Cozumel. It was a port of call while on a family cruise."

"You look happy."

"I was." He was silent for a moment. "I didn't know it would be the last family trip we'd ever take. My father died months afterward."

"I can't even imagine what that's like." Erin had said that Connor was taking life too seriously, that he'd become a hard-ass in recent years. The sight of a more carefree Connor melted her heart a little. It was easier to think of him as a formidable opponent, a man who was uncompromising and demanding.

"Some things are difficult to recover from. So now I try even harder to appreciate all of life."

She felt a bit humbled that he'd allowed her a glimpse into his private hell.

He returned the picture to its rightful spot. "I'll make room for you," he said. "In here, on the shelves. I don't want you feeling as if it's just my space."

"You're not playing fair," she protested.

"I play to win."

He continued the tour, showing her the master suite. A large bed with a padded bench at the end dominated the room. He had nightstands, but no television, books or even a clock.

"Your room is for sleeping."

"Among other things."

Like he'd intimated earlier, the headboard did have posts. She just wasn't sure if he'd been serious about wanting to attach her to them. The idea sent a chill through her.

"I don't say things unless I mean them."

"Is mind reading one of your many talents?"

"No. Your eyes tell me everything I want to know."

He continued the tour by opening the door to the closet. His clothing and shoes filled less than half of the available space. She wondered if he'd made room for her today or if he always kept his belongings confined to one area. It could be the latter, if the rest of his loft was anything to judge by.

The master bathroom had a soaker tub. She was afraid she might drool.

"Maybe I should have mentioned that at the beginning," he said.

"If it came with wine service…"

"It could."

"And the foot rub…?"

"It could."

"You really do fight to win."

At that, he grinned.

She looked up at Connor and knew she was doomed. Attraction zipped through her, much like it had earlier this afternoon when he'd told her to lock the door and go to the middle of his office. No matter how nervous he made her, she wanted what he offered.

"Now you have a big choice."

"Oh?"

"We can explore the last room."

"What's in the last room?"

"It was a bonus space, mostly used for storage. But I've converted it to a playroom of sorts."

Her blood became a bit sluggish. "I assume you're not talking about board games."

"You're correct."

"And the second choice?" Her voice sounded tremulous even though she was trying to pretend she was unaffected by him. Truth was, she was dizzy with desire.

"You can lift up your skirt and bend over the bench at the end of my bed and beg for your punishment."

Her knees went weak. "I don't suppose 'none of the above' is a choice?"

"As I told you, you always have a choice. I'm not a beast."

Shocking herself, she then said, "And what if I say *all* of the above?"

He arched one eyebrow. "I'd say which order do you prefer?"

"Um, the playroom," she suggested.

"And I'd respond that the correct answer is, whichever you prefer, Sir."

She swallowed deeply. "That means…"

"In future it will mean additional punishment. Tonight, we'll just consider that I'm instructing you about my expectations." He paused. "Would you like to answer the question again?"

"Whichever you prefer, Sir."

"You couldn't be more perfect. Come here."

She took a step, closing the distance between them.

Each time she interacted with him, she found him more compelling, more dangerous. Logic should dictate that familiarity would make her feel more certain, but it had the opposite effect.

"You look beautiful," he told her.

As he focused on her, his gray eyes seemed darker in color than they had appeared earlier.

With his large palms, he framed her face. She parted her lips slightly, silently praying he'd move in for a kiss.

He brushed back strands of hair that were curled around

her cheekbones, and she reached up to place her hands on his wrists.

"Behind your back," he said.

"Is that a rule?"

"Not always. Only if you're told."

"I like to touch."

"I like to be obeyed," he countered.

Reluctantly, she put her hands behind her.

His kiss started slowly, softly.

She closed her eyes and swayed toward him. He offered his body as support, and his strength flowed into her.

Though she ached to run her fingers through his hair, she took pleasure from doing as he said. Her body became more pliant as she stopped fighting herself.

He deepened the kiss, forcing her lips apart, tasting, touching, demanding. She was helpless. The combination of his determination and masculine power silenced her deepest objections. She wanted this man.

Though he only touched her face, her nipples hardened.

He ended the kiss before she was ready, but the way he drew his eyebrows together kept her silent. He stared at her intently, as if seeking an answer to a question so deep that he didn't know how to ask it.

Before she could possibly be prepared, he moved in again, this time with force, demanding her compliance.

She was lost. She wanted it. Him.

Keeping her hands in place took every bit of her mental energy. Physical sensation bombarded her, and she ached to participate.

When her breathing was erratic and her body responsive, he eased back.

"I could kiss you all night, and it wouldn't be enough."

"For me, either," she confessed.

He lowered his hands. "You pleased me."

The words were heady, and she exhaled an unsteady breath.

"You can put your hands at your sides. I'll show you the playroom."

She'd never admit that she was a bit disappointed that he hadn't suggested she bend over the bench.

He moved past her, and she followed.

In the bedroom, he stopped near the foot of the bed, and said, "But first, I want to see you on the bench."

Her heart skidded to a halt.

"What do you say?"

"Yes, Sir."

"Damn."

The approval in his tone made excitement trip through her.

"You remember that we talked about safe words?"

She couldn't believe they were having this conversation. "Yes."

"Unless there are words you want to use, we can use red and yellow. Red for stop immediately, yellow for slow down, we need to talk, I'm scared, or to let me know you need something."

"That works for me."

"Tell me what we're going to do," he said.

"Ah..." She could hardly make herself use the words. "You're going to punish me in some way for not keeping my hands behind my back earlier this afternoon."

He nodded. "I want you to face the bed and hold onto the bench. I expect you to stay in place. Tell me you understand."

She nodded.

Earlier today, she'd realized that having him order her around was a mind fuck. He'd agreed. Lara realized that he knew what he was doing, what to say, how to act. This was part of the whole seduction, she realized, the part that made BDSM relationships different. Her previous boyfriend had just dragged her across his lap and started wailing on her buttocks. There'd been no discussion, no exquisite anticipation or demands for compliance. In contrast, everything Connor did heightened her arousal.

Unhurriedly, she got into place and he drew up her dress.

She bit her lower lip.

"Your ass was made for a beating, Lara," he said as he outlined the top part of her panties. "I'm going to take these off."

She closed her eyes.

He drew her underwear down then tossed them on top of the bed. "Gorgeous. Now spread your legs as far as you can and turn your toes inward."

Lara found it impossible to breathe.

"So lovely."

He rubbed her buttocks, light, then quick. Abruptly, he stopped.

She was anticipating that he'd strike her then, but he didn't. Instead, he slid a finger back and forth against her clit. Shocked, she drew her legs together.

"Stay in position," he warned.

He'd moistened his finger before touching her, and since she was already a little damp, it only took a few seconds for her to become slick.

She began to sway in response to his touch. It'd been a long time since she'd had sex and his touch aroused her quickly.

Before she expected it, he entered.

In response, she moaned. If this was punishment...

He began to finger-fuck her. She rose up but was careful not to let her legs close. Then she felt him push his thumb against her clit. The pressure was unbearably wonderful. "Mmm," she said.

"Do you like this, my responsive little Lara?"

"So, so much," she said, feeling an orgasm beginning.

But instead of driving her to completion, he pulled back then slapped her right buttock, hard.

She yelped.

Almost right away, the pain receded. Then it vanished when he pushed his finger back into her. The orgasm began to unfurl again. "Yes..."

He kept one hand between her legs but slapped her left ass cheek with the other.

The shocking sting added to the throbbing in her pussy.

"Oh, yes," he said. "Tell me what you want."

She shoved her pussy backward, wordlessly asking for more. "An orgasm."

"An orgasm, *Sir,*" he coached.

"Yes! An orgasm, Sir."

"Ask."

She locked her knees for a moment as she fought for rational thought. "Please. Please, may I have an orgasm? Sir?"

"Have you earned it yet?" He spanked her right cheek again.

The orgasm started to burn in her. "More. Please."

"Beg," he told her.

"Please, will you spank me? Please will you give me an orgasm, Sir?"

"Absolutely perfect responses, little Lara," he approved.

He smacked her left cheek, and he kept the punishment going, slapping the right side of her ass five times in quick succession before moving back to the left. "I..."

"Come when you're ready," he said.

He continued to rain the blows on her bare skin, and the climax gathered force.

"I want your juices all over me," he told her.

His words, the small amount of pain, the way he ground his thumb against her, the speed with which he fingered her all combined to make her thighs tremble.

She cried out, choking on a sob as she thrust her hips back, demanding he go deeper, harder, and he gave her what she needed.

The orgasm plowed into her with a force she'd never experienced. She screamed out his name as she came, her pussy clenching.

He stayed there, saying things quietly, words that were so far away that she couldn't make them out.

It took her a long time to return to reality and start breathing normally again.

Eventually he moved, picking her up, then he turned to sit on the bench with her on his lap.

Lara rested her cheek on his chest while he stroked her hair, brushing back her confounding, curly tendrils.

"I enjoyed that," he said.

"I bet you did," she agreed. She moved so she could look at him. "It's not your ass that's sore."

"True." He raised a finger to his mouth and licked her juices from it.

She'd never seen anything as shockingly erotic. It made her needy all over again.

"You survived your first punishment."

"Are they all like that?"

"Depends on the infraction," he said. "I told you I want the punishment to fit the crime. Your infraction was wanting to touch me, so I forced you to keep your hands on the bench. But you won't always get an orgasm with a punishment. In fact, most times you won't. I'll want you to think about what you did." He put his hand in her hair and pulled her head back a little. "You have one promise from me. You will never, ever be punished when either of us are angry. You'll always know the reason as we will have talked about it ahead of time, and you will have agreed to it. At times, you may get to choose it."

"I actually don't intend to be punished ever again." Even as she said it, she wriggled around on his lap, aware of the scratchy denim of his jeans and the tenderness of her skin.

"Would you like to see the playroom?"

"If you wish, Sir."

He helped her to stand. A little embarrassed, she straightened her dress and reached for her underwear.

"Leave them. I like knowing you're still damp, and I'm hoping your dress keeps reminding you of the handprints on your buttocks."

"Diabolical."

"Never underestimate that trait," he warned, and she knew she'd do well to heed the words.

He led her to the playroom.

"Feel free to touch and hold anything."

"I'm not sure I'm that brave." She wandered around.

A slender chest of drawers was pushed against one wall. Despite the fact there were no windows, the space seemed light and airy. The wooden floor was polished and, as she expected, all of the items in the room were obsessively organized.

"What is that?" she pointed to an odd-looking contraption in the corner. It had two different pads, set at different heights. It was covered in red vinyl, and the metal stand was painted a glossy black.

"Spanking bench."

"It looks like a chair." She considered it. "Of sorts."

"It's a versatile piece. The knobs on the side allow the back platform to be adjusted by about a foot and the lower portion can be unlocked so it folds down. Eyehooks allow the Dom to bind a sub in any number of ways. You can kneel on the bottom part and be secured to the top. I can have you stand and grab the top. From the opposite side, you can be fastened to the lower end so that you're bent over more. I can even make it all the same height. The possibilities are almost endless."

She realized he'd started out by talking about the spanking bench in general terms. But then he'd become more specific. Instead of discussing how a Dom restrained a sub, now he was being explicit about what he expected from her. "This place seems pretty kinky for a man who says he's only looking for a submissive to show him respect."

"I did say I enjoyed kinky sex," he reminded her, his eyes dancing with a devilment that made her shiver.

"You did." A number of floggers hung on the walls, along with other scary-looking implements of pain.

"You indicated you'd had some experience with a flogger."

"It didn't look quite like those. It was shorter, not as..." She searched for the right word. "Sturdy. Less expensive, maybe?" She doubted it had even been made of leather. Even from a few feet away, there was no mistaking the scent of these. "I'm not really sure what everything else is. Some, I can guess." *The cane, for example.*

He took down a coiled piece of leather. It was black, braided and fearsome.

"This is a single tail," he said. "It's a type of whip."

"Looks like something out of an action-adventure movie." She stared, fascinated. "Do you carry it when you go looking for the Holy Grail?"

"This whip does know how to get to the bottom of things. It's particularly attracted to smart-asses."

She hadn't seen this side of him, a ferocious scowl softened by an easy tone. It made him more complex, more real, approachable. "You know, I kind of like that image," she teased. *Maybe a little too much.* "I can see you as a dashing moving hero. *Sir* Indiana Jones, perhaps?" Damn if all of this didn't add to his appeal, not that she needed any more reasons to be attracted to him.

"Let's see if I can be as accurate with it as Indy was, shall we?" He shook out the single tail.

She took a step back, her laughter dying. He still looked dashing, but more than a smidgeon of intimidation had been mixed in. The whip portion had to be several feet long. "I promise to behave."

"Like most things, it can be gentle or it can sting, depending. This one in particular is meant for beginners. For you."

"It never occurred to me that there would be different kinds."

"Some I would probably never use on you. I'd enjoy it if you asked for a session with it."

"Until you, Mr. Donovan, I had thought I was at least a little adventurous."

"Your choice."

She was curious. Very much. And scared.

He waited.

"One?" she suggested.

"How would you like it?"

"I feel like I'm at a bar ordering a drink."

"A brush of the tip? A crack?"

That suggestion made her clench her buttocks. "The first.

Just a brush."

"Let's go over there, where there's more room."

Nerves and a swarm of excitement collided in her belly.

"I'm going to have a couple of practice strokes. Go ahead and sit on the spanking bench and watch."

Lara recognized how smart he was. Letting her be a voyeur, getting her accustomed to his space in a nonthreatening way.

Since she wasn't sure exactly sure how to sit on the thing, she chose the lower platform. The padding was surprisingly thick and firm. As she got comfortable, she couldn't banish images of herself over it, face up, face down. In all her wild scenarios he'd immobilized her. Even though she'd had an orgasm a few minutes ago, she started to get aroused again.

He brought out a towel from one of the drawers and hung it from a hook secured to the wall, presumably as a target. Then he turned his body at a slight angle, put one foot forward, held the whip over his shoulder. A moment later, he brought it forward in a single gentle motion. The stroke landed right in the middle of the towel.

She stared, fascinated.

He turned and repeated the process, using his backhand.

"That sounded…quiet." Not what she expected.

"You wanted the Hollywood version?"

Imagining him as the rakish hero, she said, "Yes."

He turned to use his forehand again. This time, he cracked the whip.

She gasped, even though it had been nowhere near her. "Okay. That was scary."

"It's all in the touch, the force. Precision. Control."

"That's a word that suits you. Is that the way you run your life?"

"You could say that. Now bring that sweet rear of yours over here."

"I might have changed my mind."

He lowered his head a little and regarded her. With the look and using no words, he called her out as a coward, someone who wouldn't do more than put a little toe into the water.

"Okay," she said. "But just the brush part." She stood. "You promise?"

"Lara."

That uncompromising note galvanized her and she moved into the middle of the room.

"Your choice. You can get on all fours or lean up against the wall with your hands above you. Or you can bend over. I recommend one of the first two options because you're more likely to stay in place. And I want your dress out of the way."

"All fours," she said.

She got into position and pulled up her dress. She felt scandalously exposed with her bare rear and still-damp pussy.

"Which cheek?"

"Left." Backhand. Theoretically a weaker stroke.

"And the correct answer is…?"

Oh my God. "Whichever you prefer, Sir." She looked over her shoulder. "Does that earn me a punishment?"

"It does. One stroke on each ass cheek."

"Yes, Sir," she said miserably. She brought her head back to neutral and looked at the floor.

The first landed on her left buttock. A brush, something sensual that she barely felt. He followed it by a stroke on her right side. It bit and made her gasp. But it reignited her arousal.

"How was that?"

She hesitated. He'd left her hungry for more. But she was reluctant to reveal that she'd liked it. "Better than I imagined."

He rubbed a thumb over each place he'd landed the strokes then said, "You can get back up."

She accepted his hand.

Her dress fell back into place, and she rubbed her right butt cheek through the material.

He coiled up the whip and rehung it on the wall. It didn't surprise her that he retrieved the towel, folded it and returned it to its rightful place.

Control was definitely the correct word to define his personality.

"These are crops." He pointed to the far side, continuing his earlier conversation as if he hadn't just delivered two exquisite lashes that made her mind spin. "This is a spanker." He took it down and offered it to her.

At first glance it looked like a leather paddle. But he showed her it was actually two different pieces. "This one, you may actually like."

Which meant there could be others she wouldn't.

"This weekend, we can experiment with anything you choose. In fact, we can use all of them if you're up for it."

She couldn't breathe.

"Spend Saturday with me. We'll have some instructional time followed by a nice dinner, like a normal date, be seen in public together so that the announcement of our marriage will seems more realistic."

"If it happens."

"My lawyer is drawing up the prenuptial. I assume you've spoken to yours?"

"I was waiting until tomorrow." She shook her head. "I mean, until after we'd been alone." He, on the other hand, had known or at least suspected she'd respond well to him. Lara supposed she should be heartened by his confidence, but she was feeling slightly out of control and had been since the moment she'd walked into his office with her proposal. She'd had no idea what she was getting into.

"That's fine. You can expect mine tomorrow, and you can make any amendments, have your lawyer review it and send it back."

"Of course." She reminded herself they were talking about a business transaction. But that was difficult to remember with the way her buttocks still burned. She'd felt the impact of his single tail and she was staring at countless other instruments of torture.

"This…"

He waited.

Lara was beginning to realize what a strength his silence could be. It forced someone else to speak, gave him the opportunity to think, respond and strategize. She vowed to learn from him.

Time stretched, and she wondered what kind of commitment he was demanding from her. He'd said Dominance was part of his personality, and this underscored it. "How often would we use this room?"

"Daily."

Her heart stopped. "Are you serious?"

"No." He grinned.

She closed her eyes to regroup.

"I anticipate we would use it often. At least once a week."

Which meant, even if they were only married a year, fifty-two times. "You expect a lot."

"I want you to be clear about what I will demand from you."

"I think I've seen enough."

He nodded.

She left the room, and he closed the door behind them.

In the living room, she was able to breathe properly again. "It's been a long day," she said by way of excusing herself.

"Would you like me to drive you home?"

"I need my car for tomorrow."

He nodded. "Call me with any questions about the contract. I'll plan on picking you up Saturday around one?"

None of this was proceeding as she'd planned. She'd figured they'd hammer out an agreement in a roomful of lawyers, announce their marriage then each go on with their regular lives.

She hadn't counted on Connor being a Dominant and taking marriage vows seriously. On one hand, it felt like they were moving too fast. On the other, she was anxious to get the whole thing behind them so he could join the BHI board.

"I'll walk you down."

Already she knew better than to argue.

Since there were other people in the elevator, they

remained silent on the ride down.

As she slid behind the wheel of her car, he said, "Pack an overnight bag for Saturday."

True to his word, the first draft of Connor's prenuptial agreement appeared in Lara's inbox before ten o'clock in the morning. He'd encrypted it and sent the password under separate cover.

She opened the document. Not surprisingly, it was almost twenty pages long and each section was complete. Even though she didn't have time to read each line, she scanned the highlights.

As she'd had a preliminary meeting with her family attorney, she'd known this prenuptial would be a bit different from many others. Most people entered a marriage assuming it would last rather than setting a termination date. That should make it more straightforward. At least theoretically.

Since that appeared to be the case, she searched out the pertinent parts. As he'd mentioned yesterday in his office, he'd included the fact that everything that happened between them was confidential, not to be disclosed to the press, and he'd backdated that to yesterday.

Then she read the addendum.

Item A outlined her role as a submissive.

Shocked, she leaned forward to study the screen. He insisted she wear a collar if they attended lifestyle events. She was required to address him as Sir during their BDSM scenes. And she would submit to predetermined punishments when necessary. They would live together and sleep in the same bed.

The idea that he'd discussed the intimate details with his lawyer mortified her.

She was willing to bet that a sympathetic judge would rule

that the addition was unconscionable, thereby rendering it unenforceable. It could threaten the entirety of the rest of the agreement. On the other hand, if she didn't sign it, he might refuse to marry her.

He was damn shrewd.

Item B contained his requirements of his wife. She was free to keep her own last name, but she was welcome to take his if that suited her. Regardless, they would be known as Mr. and Mrs. Donovan to their colleagues. She would be expected to accompany him at times to various events and perform other duties such as hosting dinner parties.

Outside of immediate members of his family, no one would know about the marriage of convenience. That rocked her. His family could know, but hers couldn't? She understood that his concern was practical from a business standpoint. But keeping it from her mother might be difficult. The woman seemed to have psychic skills where Lara was concerned.

She froze when she reached the bottom line.

The length of the contract was for three years unless both parties agreed to negotiate a longer term.

Three years?

She'd been thinking one, two at the most.

She dug out her cell phone, scrolled through her recent contacts, found his number then dialed.

"You read the contract."

Did he ever engage in niceties? "And there are certain things I don't like."

"Have your attorney contact mine."

She expelled a deep breath. "There are only a few points we need to talk through. I'm sure you can guess what they are."

"I need to ensure you have adequate time to review the document," he said. "And you'll need to have your lawyer look at it. I'm happy to discuss it when we meet tomorrow," he said.

When she was at his house, worrying that he might secure her to the spanking bench?

"Surely there's nothing you didn't expect?" he continued.

After last night, the addendum shouldn't have surprised her. "Can we meet for coffee?"

"Of course."

"On second thought, no." She didn't want anyone overhearing. She thought about suggesting her office, but she didn't want her father knowing Connor was in the building. And the idea of going back to his office...

"Thompson has some biscotti for you."

He couldn't be serious.

"Two o'clock?" he suggested. "I can have my attorney with me, if you'd like."

"That won't be necessary."

"Shall I send April?"

He was giving her all sorts of choices, yet she still couldn't help but feel as if he were totally in control. It unnerved her.

"Lara?"

"Yes. Please do."

"I look forward to seeing you." He ended the call.

She sighed. Even when she got what she wanted, it seemed to be on his terms.

Lara printed off a copy of the contract then closed the document. She grabbed a yellow pen to highlight her biggest concerns before putting the packet of papers in her briefcase.

Afterward, she joined her father for a short meeting in his office to set the priorities for the coming week.

"Anything new?"

"No."

"Nothing back from Connor Donovan?" she asked eventually.

"He'll come back," Pernell said, linking two paper clips together.

Her last hope was to convince him to take a great big swallow of pride. "You're not willing to relent, call him, maybe? I could be part of the meeting. Maybe organize a time for him to talk to the board."

"That's not how business is done, Lara Marie."

"What if I set it up?"

He straightened his spine. "I won't hear of it."

"This could be an excellent opportunity."

"It was an insulting offer. He'll come around. Or another company will. We can start making overtures."

Which wouldn't put them in a position of strength. She was torn. Part of her wanted to confess what she'd done. A larger part was distressed over her father's continual state of denial. His wire inbox was filled with paper and he was wearing a golf shirt and casual pants, his usual Friday attire. "You're heading out?"

He checked his watch. "Meeting some colleagues. We have a tee time just after lunch."

"Will you be back this afternoon?"

"No sense. I'll be most of the way home by then."

"I have a meeting with the VP of Technology at three-thirty."

"Good. Bring me a report on Monday."

"I'd like you to be there. He says he has some interesting ideas to discuss."

"No doubt I'll be playing the back nine by then. Should have some good weather for it."

With a brief nod, she stood. At the doorway, she paused, and looked over her shoulder. "You know, Dad, if you started to work on your exit strategy—"

"I still have years to think about that."

"You could consider a part-time retirement. Have more time to play golf and spend time at the club."

"You'll be CEO soon enough, Lara Marie."

"That's not my point, and you know it. I'm far better as the CFO."

"You'll inherit eventually."

"That's not what this is about," she said. "I want you around for a long, long time. But we need to be able to make decisions and execute faster. Have the ability to spin off bad divisions." With an exasperated motion, she tucked strands of hair behind her ears. This wasn't a new argument. She softened her tone and continued, "We need some new energy. We could consider at least beginning a search for a president. You can remain as CEO. Even chairman of the board." Intuition warned her that anyone they hired for that position would end up resigning in frustration, unless Pernell was able to release some control.

"Have that report to me by Monday."

Frustration still simmered, but she knew it would be helped by lunch with her mother.

She went straight from the office to an Italian bistro in a nearby boutique hotel. Service was typically European style with plenty of time to relax. Menu prices were about fifty percent higher than comparable restaurants, but the food was wonderful, and the location was rarely crowded at lunch. It was an excellent place to visit and catch up.

Helene breezed in five minutes late, looking radiant in a yellow, slim-fitting dress and matching heels. She'd obviously been to the beauty salon. Her dark, shoulder-length hair fell in perfectly trimmed layers, and overhead lights seemed to bounce off the golden highlights. Her nails were manicured and her face glowed. Maybe she'd had both a salon and spa morning.

"Hello, darling," Helene said.

Lara stood, and her mother kissed both of her cheeks.

"You're looking well," Helene said.

She didn't, and she knew it. Since she'd run into Connor two nights ago, she hadn't slept enough, and she knew it had taken a toll. "You look positively radiant, Mother."

"Divorce made me what I am today. Happily single."

Being away from Pernell agreed with Helene. She'd spent years as his hostess and greatest supporter. In return, she'd been ignored and forgotten on many occasions. When Pernell's health began to suffer, she'd asked him to cut back on his schedule, eat better, spend time with the family. In response, he'd worked longer hours, scheduled more meetings then canceled their anniversary trip to Australia.

Helene hadn't cried or gotten angry. Instead, she'd taken control of her own life. She'd bought a two-bedroom townhome in River Oaks and furnished it with brand-new pieces.

She'd taken only her personal items, cosmetics, jewelry, favorite clothes and shoes. At first, Pernell hadn't realized she'd left him. Being served divorce papers on the golf course had been his dose of reality.

Lara took her chair while a waiter pulled back one for Helene.

After he'd filled both water glasses and described the specials, he took their drink order.

"Unsweetened iced tea with a slice of lemon," Lara said.

"House chianti for me," Helene requested.

The moment he walked away, she said, "Tell me everything. You didn't call me back last night. It's your father, isn't it?"

Lara settled for a half-truth. "Connor Donovan came to make an offer on the communications division." Helene knew all the intricacies of the businesses since she still held a seat, not that she attended meetings, but she occasionally read the notes, especially since it impacted her income.

"The old goat kicked him out?" she guessed. "Without the board ever hearing the information."

"Precisely."

The waiter returned with drinks and a basket of bread.

After he'd taken their order, Helene broke off a piece of the loaf and dipped it in some olive oil.

"Wait a minute. If your father didn't tell the board…?"

"I had dinner with Erin Wednesday night, and I went back to the office to tie up a few things. I bumped into Connor as I was getting off the elevator."

"When you see her again, give her my regards. Now, back to Connor. He stopped and just happened to tell you he made an offer on the communications division?"

Her mother's ability to juggle multiple conversations and ideas was one of things that had made her indispensable to Pernell. Lara wasn't sure he appreciated that, even now. "He didn't volunteer it. I asked why he was there."

"What did you think of him? He's a handsome young man, isn't he? More like his grandfather in temperament.

Very serious. Not given to romantic notions."

Lara wasn't so sure of that. Serious, yes. But some of the things he said were charmingly antiquated, bordering on romantic.

"Did he tell you what the offer was?"

"No." Lara toyed with a piece of bread, dipping it in the plate of olive oil, then setting it back down again.

"There's something you're not telling me."

It wasn't like her to hedge. Then again, she'd never been in a situation like this. She wasn't sure where she'd even start to describe her relationship with the complicated man.

"I imagine you confronted your father," Helene said. "Wish I could have seen that."

"He said the offer was missing some zeros and a comma."

"Which you don't know for sure."

"Correct."

"And taking it to the board won't gain you anything. So you might as well treat yourself to a spa day. Nothing is solved by dwelling on it."

Lara shook her head. A massage didn't solve every problem. On the other hand, it might help her to sleep better. "This is our company, your future, as well."

"You got nowhere with your father. Which means you need to go to Connor and ask." Helene was lifting her glass to her mouth when she froze. "You already have, haven't you? Clever girl." Helene put her glass back down. "In fact, that's why you didn't call me back last night. You were with Connor."

"How the hell do you do that?"

"DNA."

"DNA?"

"You get your brain from me. That's precisely what I would have done. Besides, you're generally more forthcoming with information. You went to his home? Had dinner, maybe?"

When she didn't answer, Helene went on, "What's he like in private?"

She discarded about a dozen adjectives before settling on,

"Smart."

"You don't take a company like Donovan Worldwide and make it bigger than it was without being intelligent. Surely you discussed the offer?"

"No. We didn't. Honestly. He said it was no longer on the table."

"For your father, perhaps. You'll know how to make it happen, if it's possible. I don't suppose the old goat is talking about retiring yet?"

"If you're referring to my father, the answer is no." She didn't mention the way he continually shut down the discussions about hiring his successor. Like him, the rest of the board likely assumed that she would step into his position, but that side of the business didn't play to her strong suit. Though she'd become somewhat adept at strategy, vision and leadership, it wasn't what she really wanted to do. She preferred to figure out how to make it happen.

Helene squeezed Lara's hand. "What you're trying to do is admirable, but sometimes walking away is for the best. You owe BHI nothing. You can start your own business or become CFO for another company. You've got mad talent, my girl. Don't let it be buried."

Though she appreciated what her mother was saying, Lara's sense of duty wouldn't let her walk away. All the days at BHI with her father, all the studying, years of schooling, all were to one end, helping her father succeed.

"You can only help people who want to be helped," Helene added as if reading Lara's mind.

Her mother had learned that lesson, Lara knew.

Lara moved the conversation away from work. "You have your ladies' soirée today?" She suspected her mother realized it was a defensive tactic, but she didn't argue.

"Today we're having a mixer. We'll be having men in attendance."

"Oh?" The information startled her. "Anyone in particular?"

"We're not particular. As long as they're single and

rich. Well, knowing how to dance is nice. Nice, but not necessary."

Lara hadn't ever considered that her mother might eventually want to date again. After leaving Pernell, she'd started traveling with friends, and she'd even taken the desired trip to Australia. "Mom? Is there something you're not saying?"

"You'll be the first to know, darling." But she looked into the depths of her wine.

At least Lara was temporarily distracted from her own problems.

Her mother picked at her salad and skipped dessert, which told Lara plenty. But it also kept Helene from mentioning how little Lara ate.

Over coffee, Helene said, "You know, Erin's mother, Angela, might like to join us in future. I should invite her." She pulled out her phone and recorded a voice message to do just that. "Could be good to have her as a friend."

Lara went still. From her mother's standpoint that made a lot of sense, but she wasn't sure she liked the idea of the two of them being friends.

"I'm sure one of the ladies has her number. If not, I'll have you get it from Erin."

Helene picked up the check, then they said their goodbyes.

By the time Lara arrived back at the office, she only had time to respond to a few emails before grabbing her briefcase and going back to the lobby to meet April.

The woman was already parked in front of the building, standing on the curb with the back door open.

There were parts of Connor's need to control things that she could get accustomed to, maybe even appreciate, Lara realized. "Good afternoon, April."

"A pleasure, Ms. Bertrand," she replied before closing the door.

After asking to be sure the car's interior was a comfortable temperature, April eased into traffic.

It took little more than five minutes to reach the building that housed Donovan Worldwide.

April said she was at Lara's disposal. After thanking her, Lara went inside the building.

No matter how calm she pretended to be, nerves swarmed Lara as she rode the elevator. As she waited for it to stop and the doors to open, an odd feeling settled over her. She'd made this trip twice in two days. As Connor's wife, his sub, it might not be that unusual. The idea of calling him husband seemed intimate, frightening, exhilarating, all in one.

Again with confidence she didn't feel, she exited the elevator then walked toward Connor's office. Unlike yesterday, Thompson stood to greet her when she arrived in the reception area.

"The biscotti was a nasty lie, something just to entice me, wasn't it?" she asked him.

"Not at all. I baked it last night."

"You..." She opened her mouth, stunned. This big, burly former military man brewed the best coffee on the planet, and he baked? But instead of finishing her sentence, she said, "Impressive."

"I have many talents, Ms. Bertrand."

"As I'm learning. But aren't they complicated to make?"

"Time consuming," he replied. "Helped that I had all the ingredients on hand."

She was moved in a way she rarely was. That he'd gone out of his way for her, that he assumed—or knew—she'd be back, that he was giving his tacit approval to her, touched her. "I'm not quite sure how to thank you."

"By eating them," he said with a big grin.

"I shall. Ah... Is Mr. Donovan available?"

"He is. Said to send you right in."

The anxiousness that had settled somewhat suddenly took flight. Yesterday, Thompson had walked with her. Today, it was as if she were a regular guest.

"Decaf or regular?" Thompson asked.

"Decaf, if it's not too much trouble."

"No trouble at all."

She pulled back her shoulders and knocked before

entering Connor's office.

The sight of him all but stopped time.

He was back in professional dress, wearing a charcoal suit that was so dark it was nearly black. His white shirt was starched, and his tie was a contrasting silver. His eyes were a shade lighter than his suit, and his smile was as broad as it was welcoming. How could she resist him?

It took her a moment to realize he wasn't alone.

Connor stood, and so did his guest. Even if she hadn't seen a picture of Nathan, she would have recognized him.

"Lara," Connor said, coming around his desk. "Welcome."

She hadn't been sure of her reception, but he took her in his arms and kissed the top of her head. Stress and anxiety faded as she leaned into him. How did he manage to simultaneously make things so difficult and yet so easy for her?

"People will believe this is real if you keep that up," Nathan said.

Connor stepped back. With a slight frown, he said, "Lara, I apologize for this ill-mannered lout. My younger brother, Nathan."

Nathan's grin was relaxed, making it impossible to take offense at his words.

"I kicked him out five minutes ago, but he's used every stall tactic available so that he could drag out the meeting long enough to run into you."

Unapologetically, he shrugged. "Erin speaks highly of you, and so does Connor. I had to meet you." He extended his hand.

She put down the bag and took it—his grip was strong, but not overly so…welcoming.

Conversation was interrupted by the arrival of Thompson.

He put down the tray on the small table. After pouring a cup for Lara, he carried it and a biscotti to her.

"No cream and sugar?" Nathan asked.

"The lady is tough," Thompson replied.

Nathan and Connor exchanged shrugs.

"Cup for you, Mr. Nathan? I did bring cream."

"My brother was just leaving," Connor said.

"Can I have one of those cookies?" Nathan asked.

"It's a biscotti," Thompson corrected. "Chocolate chip or almond?"

"Both."

Connor sighed and took his seat behind the desk. Nathan sat back. Enjoying the exchange, Lara hid her grin behind the cup. It appeared that Nathan was just as stubborn as his brother, and she liked that.

"Are you still jittery from earlier, sir?" Thompson asked as he gave Nathan a cup, saucer and a small pile of biscuits.

"I'm switching to Scotch," Connor said. "And that doesn't go with cookies."

His annoyance was charming, showing her the dynamic with his family and employee. He might be a bit sarcastic, but he wasn't short or unkind.

Lara dunked her biscotti in the coffee and savored the bite. "I was serious yesterday. If you're ever looking for a new job, please call me. Name your price."

"Thompson, contact Erin. In fact, bring the lawyers in. I need to amend your employment contract. I want the option to match any other offer you receive."

Thompson grinned before leaving, closing the door behind him.

"And as for you, future wife, we can change our agreement, as well. There shall be no stealing my employees."

"What's yours is ours, I thought?" she replied cheekily.

"You're fortunate we have company."

"Oh, go ahead," Nathan encouraged. "I'll enjoy the show."

"Why are you still here?" Connor asked. "Other than eating my cookies and drinking my coffee?"

Unapologetically, Nathan took a bite from his second biscotti.

"When you arrived, Nathan was reminding me that we have a family get-together on Sunday morning for my mother's birthday. We think it's a good idea for you to accompany me."

She put down her cup and saucer and glanced between the brothers. As much as she might have preferred to keep the discussion between them, she realized there were very real strategic considerations. No matter how much she'd thought she'd prepared for this, she couldn't have thought through everything. "We have some details we need to work through," she replied, making no promises.

"There's my cue to leave," Nathan said.

"There've been many that you've missed," Connor replied.

"Oh. You wanted to be alone? Why didn't you say so?" After shooting her a disarming grin, he finished his coffee. "Hope to see you Sunday, Lara." Any further conversation was cut off when Connor showed Nathan out.

This time, the door was closed and locked with a decisive click.

He returned and moved aside the chair Nathan had been sitting in. Connor propped his hips on the edge of the desk with his legs spread. "Now, come here." He pointed to a spot directly in front of him. "Let me greet you properly."

She wanted to object. They hadn't hammered out their agreement. Getting ensnared by him put her in a worse bargaining position. Then she told herself that it was too late. She was already captivated by him.

"Come here, sub."

"I'm not your submissive."

"Yet."

Letting the objections die unspoken, she did as he requested.

"Good," he approved. He put his hands on her hips and drew her a bit closer. "Kiss me."

Lara wondered if she was capable of denying him anything.

He claimed her lips.

His first touch was a soft, sensual joining that demolished her resistance. It was sweet with the promise of tenderness.

Then, that accomplished, he threaded a hand through her hair so he could cradle her head while holding her captive.

He plunged his tongue into her mouth, tasting, exploring, demanding her surrender.

Even if she wanted to withhold it, her body would betray her. She *wanted* him.

He tasted of determination as he all but fucked her with his tongue. Her knees weakened and she leaned into him for support. Since he hadn't told her otherwise, she held onto him, grabbing handfuls of his silk suit. As always his support was absolute.

She was unable to breathe, unable to think. The only thing she recognized was her total capitulation to him. The more he gave, the more she wanted.

When he finally ended the kiss and drew away, she released him. She pressed her fingers to her mouth, not because he'd been too rough but because she wanted to remember the exquisite sensations.

"How's your ass?"

"I'm sorry?"

"Any pain from yesterday's spanking?"

The only thing she'd received from that was a restless night as the memories had tormented her. It had hurt, but in a way that had left her woozy for more. He was brilliant, she conceded. He only gave her enough to keep her curious. "I'm fine."

"Show me."

She knew it would be useless to ask him to repeat what he'd said or to question the order. Connor Donovan always meant what he said. She could argue with him, insisting that she wouldn't do anything until they'd sorted out things between them. But what would that gain her?

A newly found devilish part of her personality drove her on. Each experience she'd had with him was hot.

"I'm waiting," he prompted her.

Slowly, she turned. She pulled her hem up around her waist.

"Fuck me." He sucked in a breath. "Panties over the garter straps. You dressed that way on purpose."

Yes, she had.

On that long-ago trip to the lingerie store, she'd bought a black bra, garter belt and matching panties set. She'd added several pairs of stockings. Until this morning, they'd remained at the bottom of her lingerie drawer.

Connor's reaction to her unusual boldness made her giddy.

He stroked her buttocks then skimmed the insides of her thighs, stopping just millimeters from her pussy.

Her breath caught.

"There's not even a single mark. No reminders."

"No physical marks." She looked at him over her shoulder. "But I have plenty of memories."

"Do you?"

His eyes were narrowed, and she felt the sensuality simmer between them.

"Shall I give you some more?"

When he'd said that he'd make her beg, she'd scoffed at the idea. But need was becoming its own, clawing thing. "Yes," she whispered.

"Ask."

"Mark me."

In response, he growled then pulled down the bikini panties. His gruffness caught her off guard, turned her on.

She stepped out of the silk and lace underwear, and he wadded them into a ball which he stuffed into his pocket. "I may need to go shopping if you keep confiscating my underwear."

"Feel free to bill any lingerie to me."

With his thumb, he outlined the straps of her garter belt, igniting her skin, arousing her. In unspoken plea, she spread her legs.

Accepting her invitation, he pressed a finger to her clit then gently began to move back and forth.

She clenched her hands on the top of the desk.

"You're so very responsive, little Lara."

Until him, it had never been like this.

Deep inside, an orgasm took form. But before she could climax, he pulled back and slapped her right ass cheek, striking from the bottom up. There was pain, but so much more pleasure, and it heated her pussy. "Please..."

Connor leaned forward and bit the side of her neck.

"My God," she cried out.

He put a hand across her mouth before slapping her left buttock. That one would leave a mark, she was sure.

By slow measures, the man was driving her mad. "Now, now, now..."

"Yes." He plunged two fingers inside her, and he pumped them hard and fast.

Thrusting backward and grinding against him, she sought more. The combination of her scalding ass and the way he tormented her pushed her over the edge. She came, the explosion ripping through her. She screamed, but the sound was muffled by his palm.

He held her while she struggled to regain a normal breathing pattern. For a minute longer than she needed to, Lara stayed where she was.

She was starting to realize how much she enjoyed being in his arms. His strength soothed her. The last few years she'd been mostly alone, fighting constant battles with her father at work while having no one to lean on. Because of the situation between her parents, she couldn't even turn to her mother for advice.

Connor was the first person who'd really offered help and support. She just wished the costs weren't so high.

He helped Lara to stand, and he straightened her clothes. "Do you always dress like that?"

"Rarely."

"I'm torn between telling you to do it every day and forbidding you from ever doing it again."

That she had the power to arouse him made her breathless. "I wrinkled your jacket earlier," she said, smoothing out the material.

"Small price," he said, "for that kind of response to my kiss. Now, about the contract?"

Of course he brought it up when her thoughts were filled with him. "Are you going to give me my panties back?"

"No chance." His grin was smug.

So she was supposed to negotiate while her pussy was damp? Would her next few years be spent this way?

After tucking her skirt beneath her, she resumed her seat. Instead of sitting behind his desk, he took the chair Nathan had vacated. He sat back, index fingers pressed together, an inch or so in front of his face. "I assume you have a copy of the agreement in your briefcase?"

It would be easier to look at the pages together, but his proximity was distracting. Calling on her years of professional experience, she pulled out the document and flipped to the pages in question. She decided to start with the small things. "I understand that you don't want my father to know the details of our arrangement—"

"Or the press or the general public," he clarified.

"And I understand that you need your family to know since, I assume, they're also on your board of directors."

He nodded.

"I didn't realize you'd start telling people so early."

"Just Nathan."

"It's important to me that my mother knows the truth."

"Ah." He tapped his fingers together. "Tell me why."

"DNA."

He looked at her over the tops of his hands.

"ESP is more like it," she said wryly. "She knows everything about me."

He laughed.

"It's really not funny," she insisted. "More than anything, it's scary. What she doesn't know, she guesses, and she's right. I'm not sure, honestly, that I'll be able to keep it secret. I've never really kept anything big from her."

"I'd like to meet her first."

"I had the impression you were anxious to get the contract signed."

"We could see her this evening. Or over the weekend."

His answer was more than she'd expected and less than she'd hoped. "She'll be an ally."

"If she agrees with the union. It could be that she wants

her only child to be happy and to marry for love and not to sacrifice herself for the family business. Her ex-husband's family business."

That argument was probably valid, she conceded. Even Lara liked the idea of marrying for love. "I'd be willing to bet she'd support me. She's also a member of the board. Hasn't been to a meeting in over a year, but she retained her seat as part of the divorce settlement. If she's on our side, she can be vocal as well as persuasive. The people my father appointed are also lifelong friends of hers."

"I look forward to meeting her, then," he reiterated.

She sighed.

"Next point?"

"Your addendum. Neither item A nor item B will hold up in court."

"Probably not."

"So why are they there?"

"Our signatures both matter. It shows we've discussed these things and that we both have the same understandings. I want you clear about my expectations. It will make our marriage happier."

"About that..."

It appeared as if he was struggling to hold back a grin.

"Three years?"

"Longer is probably better. Company turnarounds often work on a five or ten year plan. Is that what you wanted to suggest?"

Suddenly three seemed wonderful. "That's a long time to tie up our futures." And a long time for her to be his submissive.

"In personal time, it is. In terms of business, successive quarters, mergers, acquisitions, sales, due diligence reports, it's nothing."

Which brought her to item B again. "Loyalty to you as a husband... I love my father. Our marriage will end, but he's my father forever."

"Turn to me. My shoulders are broad. You may see it as a conflict, but the truth is, this is for him, as well. There's no more selfless act than to help save the business that matters so much to him."

The paper was between them, and she met his gaze. "You make it sound easy."

"It doesn't have to be difficult. He's cantankerous and perhaps overwhelmed."

"Stubborn. Which makes you two a bit alike."

"I think that was meant as an insult." But there was no acrimony in his tone.

"It wasn't meant that way."

"I believe you."

"As for my house, I'd like to keep it."

"You could rent it out."

"I'm not sure I want to put my belongings in storage for that long. And I'd hate to sell it. I shopped for it for years, and... It may seem ridiculous, but it's mine. I want somewhere to go back to when this is over. Would you consider moving in with me?" The idea made her blood heat. She pictured him naked, enjoying Saturday breakfast, coming home after a business trip.

"I prefer to be downtown near the office."

"I understand that, especially for a single man. And my yard is my respite from the world. I have enough room for you to be comfortable. Will you think about it, at least?"

"Lara—"

"For me?"

"Now who's not fighting fair?"

"Thank you." She leaned toward him and kissed his forehead.

His eyes widened for a moment before he schooled his reaction. But she'd had a glimpse. For all his gruffness, he did have a softer side. If she weren't careful, she might start to fall for this man. Nothing could be more dangerous to her emotional and mental health.

"That's it? No further objections?"

"The financials are fairly straightforward. I'll get you mine. But we have to sort all of these things out."

"Do you have plans this evening?"

"No."

"Do you shower or bathe before bed?"

"Generally I take a bath to help me relax." Which is why she had fallen in love with his soaker tub.

"Good. Call me before you climb into bed. Be naked."

She looked at him, knew she was falling under his spell, taking another step toward being his submissive and not objecting to the journey. "Is there a reason?"

"Yes."

"Care to enlighten me?" she asked when he allowed the silence to stretch.

"No."

She needed to be careful, she realized, or else she'd give him anything he asked for.

"Let me know when you've set up that meeting with your mother so we can get our agreement over to your lawyer. I'm looking forward to talking to you tonight."

Just before ten, Connor's phone rang.

He answered immediately, "Good evening, Lara." *Wife-to-be.* Ridiculous how much he liked that thought.

"I..." She paused.

He waited.

"I had a bath."

She had an amazing, appealing combination of innocence and boldness. Even before the marriage proposal, she'd intrigued him. With it, she'd snared him. "Tell me what you're wearing."

"A towel. Peach colored."

The addition of the detail made him hard. He imagined the shade made her honeyed skin seem even more sun-kissed.

All evening, he'd been thinking of Lara, remembering the sight of her bent over his desk, his bed.

He'd dove into the building's swimming pool soon after he'd gotten home. As he'd cut through the water with powerful strokes, he'd realized that he was thinking of the future. The thought had startled him. Since the loss of his father, he'd exercised to keep the grief at bay or to sort through the numerous difficulties he faced running a multinational company. "Where are you in your house?"

"My bedroom."

"Drop the towel and lie on your bed. Face down so that you can put the phone next to you on speaker." He wondered if she'd protest.

Moments later she murmured, "Yes, Sir."

"You're so wonderful, Lara." He sat back against the living room sofa and reached for his glass of brandy. He took a sip while he listened to her movements. The sounds grew louder as she found the speaker button and he heard a faint whisper that might have been her towel falling to the floor.

In the past, he hadn't thought a lot about getting married. Rather, it had been an abstract thought. The only thing he'd known for sure was that D/s would be a part of any union. But he'd had no idea how rewarding it would be. Having this woman, so smart, courageous, beautiful as his submissive? The reality was sublime.

"I'm in position, Sir," she said.

"You're right-handed?"

"I am."

"I want you to use your left hand to part your labia. Then use your right to stroke your clit, make sure it's exposed, meaning pull back the hood. I want you to feel this deeply."

She moaned.

"Touch only the outside of your pussy."

"This feels strange to be doing this with you, like..."

While she was searching for words, he instructed her, reassured her by saying, "Do as you're told, Lara. There's no room for you to be embarrassed when you're pleasing me. Imagine I'm there."

"I wish you were. This was easier when you were doing it."

"Some time when we're together, I'll watch you do it and give you some pointers."

"You would?"

"Yeah. I will. Stroke yourself, little Lara. Now."

Her soft moans told him she was doing as he said. Despite the fact he expected exactly that, he still found it gratifying. "A little faster."

"Ah..."

She'd obviously shoved aside her hesitation and was focusing on what he'd asked of her. "That's it." His words were as approving as he was. "Imagine me spanking your ass, hard. With my hand, blazing across your skin."

"Sir!"

"Don't you dare put a finger in your cunt."

She groaned. "I won't."

"I took off my belt earlier," he continued, "and I thought about using it on you, starting just above the backs of your knees. You'd have marks from that, wouldn't you?"

"Yes. Oh, yes. Oh..."

"No coming yet." His cock throbbed. Ignoring it, focusing on her and only her, he took a sip of his brandy. "Faster, little Lara. Italian leather was made for your derrière. Are you grinding your pelvis against the sheets and making a mess of them? If not, you'd better be. I don't like polite little orgasms. I want everything. No holding back. I don't want you to be a lady in my bed. I want you to be a wanton submissive. Focus on bringing your Dom joy. And that comes from raunchy sex."

"I... Sir... Oh, God, Connor..."

"Hold off," he snapped. How far could he push her? And did he want to make her wait, maybe see if she climaxed despite his command? "Think about me, Lara."

"I am. I am."

"Pinch your clit."

The sound of her breathing filled his ears and his senses. He pictured her thighs shaking, vividly imagined her thrusting her pubis against her hand. "Put two fingers inside your pussy. *Do it now.* And keep up the action on your clit. Use your thumb if you need to."

For a full thirty seconds, he listened to her suffering, knowing she was close, hearing her fight it off. She made tiny, unfeminine grunts and her moans begged him for satisfaction. "Now," he told her. "Come for me."

There was silence for few moments, then she gasped. The sound quickly became a soft scream. He remembered earlier, in his office, when he'd had to put his hand over her mouth. Now, as then, she ended on a soft sigh with ragged breathing. Everything about her was desirable. "Very, very good."

He heard odd noises, as if she was picking up the phone, taking it off speaker, maybe rolling over onto her back. He pictured her breasts heaving from the exertion. Tomorrow couldn't arrive soon enough.

"I've never done anything quite like that," she said.

"There's much more to come. Sleep well, Lara."

"Wait. That's it?"

"What more do you want?"

"I don't know. Something. That was incredible."

The connection, he knew. That's what she wanted. Him to be there, just for a bit. A form of aftercare he hadn't really thought through. Earlier, he'd encouraged her to turn to him, and she had. Definitely a step he appreciated. "You couldn't have been better. Are you ready for bed? Doors locked? Lights off?"

"I need to turn off the light in the kitchen."

"Take me with you. But don't put any clothes on. And don't try to be sneaky. I can hear everything you're doing. And I'll know if you put it on mute."

"Does anything get by you?"

"Not where you're concerned." He swirled his glass and heard the change in her breathing as she walked.

"Okay. The light's off."

"Now back to bed." There was quiet and he took the final drink of his brandy. He wasn't feeling tired at all. In fact, he was rather consumed by the idea of curling her against him tomorrow night.

"Okay, I'm there. In bed, I mean."

"Sleep naked."

"I usually wear a nightshirt."

"Did I ask that?"

She made a sound he identified as part sigh, part exhalation of frustration. He was fine with that, as long as she did as she was told.

"Lara?"

"I got it. Naked. Even if I freeze."

"Overnight low should be in the high sixties or maybe low seventies." He put down his glass, stifling a laugh. "I think you're safe."

"Heartless."

"You'll find out just how much tomorrow."

"Is that a promise or a threat, Sir?"

Her words were sultry and effective. "That's a little brave, considering whose ass will be upturned over my spanking bench tomorrow."

"Would an apology help?"

"Not at all." He shook his head, even though she couldn't see him.

"I was afraid of that."

He confirmed her address and confirmed the fact he'd be picking her up around one o'clock before asking, "How are you doing?"

Maybe because of the night or because of the distance, her answer sounded as if she had been emboldened. "Restless. Wondering about tomorrow, a bit nervous about it, maybe a bit excited, as well. And I'm still a little aroused."

"If another orgasm would help you sleep, go ahead. And about tomorrow? You're right to be a bit nervous *and* a bit excited."

It'd been a hell of a night. Talking to Lara before bed last night, listening to her get off, had interfered with his rest.

As a result, he'd slept later than normal and he'd spent a good portion of his morning scheduling a telephone conference call with his family members to discuss her proposal.

Erin had been shocked into silence, maybe for the first time in her life. His grandfather had warned him to get a solid prenuptial. Cade had been noncommittal and Aunt Kathryn had cautioned him not to overextend his workload. Nathan had said he thought they would make a significant amount of money if they could secure the patents.

Connor phoned his mother separately. She'd never wanted to be involved in the business, but since he planned to take Lara to her home, he owed her the courtesy of a heads-up.

His mother had been the only one to urge caution, to be sure he wasn't making decisions he couldn't live with later.

Coming from her, the advice was solid. She spoke from the pain of feeling like an outsider in her own marriage. Even though she'd known how much his father had cared for Stormy, Angela had still married him. She'd been a model wife and wonderful mother. But he wondered if she thought the cost was worth it.

He'd still been focused more on the past than the future when he'd left the house to pick up Lara, and it had taken some determination to channel his thoughts in a more productive direction.

As he'd gotten closer, though, it had become easier.

The anticipation of having the lovely Lara under his lash had a way of changing his focus.

Since he knew what he had in store for her and how much energy she'd need to get through it, he stopped at a local coffee shop and bought her a cup of the strongest brew they had.

He still managed to arrive a few minutes early.

Connor exited the car and heard barks, growls, yips and even a high-pitched mewl. It sounded as if one of the neighbors was running an animal rescue.

Lara was already outside on the porch, upper arm propped against one of the white columns that supported the porch's roof.

She wore an ankle-length navy dress. It had white horizontal stripes that wrapped around her. Rather than disguising her curves, the clingy material showed them off.

No matter what she wore, she appealed to him. She had a way of being both elegant and sexy at the same time. As much as anything, her classy demeanor turned him on. Well, her perfect ass didn't hurt, either.

Her hair was soft and curling, a result of the Texas humidity, and it brushed her bare shoulders. She wore heels. Bright red heels. Sweet God, help him.

She lifted one hand in a wave.

The sounds of dogs grew increasingly louder.

"Watch out!" she warned, eyes wide. "Suzy-Q, *no*."

He looked to his left in time to see a lion racing full speed in his direction. Not quite sure what to do in the event of a wild animal attacking in suburbia, he stopped, turned toward it and raised his arms, lifting the coffee to safety. He was a bit more afraid of spilling the drink than the charging four-legged ferocity.

Lara hurried down the stairs. "Suzy-Q, *no*," she repeated more forcefully.

"Suzyyyyyyyy!" a disembodied voice yelled.

The oversized animal skidded to halt.

"She's harmless," Lara promised, nearing him.

"What is it?" On second glance, it looked a bit like a yellow bear.

"Mastiff and Great Dane. Could be something else in her background, too."

Now that he was closer, he saw that the creature resembled a dog, of sorts. It was considerably larger than anything he'd ever seen before, and he'd bet the beast weighed somewhere close to his own weight. Its hackles were raised, teeth were bared, and drool hung from its mouth. "I think it's preparing to digest me."

"I promise. She's a love."

Just then, it jumped. Its paws landed on his shoulders, shoving him back a step. The canine's gigantic face loomed in front of him. "Nice doggie?"

"Suzy-Q!" Lara shouted.

A cacophony of barks and yips and animals broke loose, as if the hounds of hell had been unleashed.

Dogs in every yard added their noise, and three other animals dashed over to encourage the massive mutt on.

He fought to keep his balance and retain his grip on Lara's drink.

She kicked off her heels to run the last few steps, and she reached for the dog. Obviously sensing her approach, the beast swiped its oversized tongue across his face, leaving a trail of drool.

Then, apparently unsatisfied, it licked his ear.

He closed his eyes against the enthusiastic assault. He'd had a dog as a child. Something smaller. Well, hell, anything was smaller than this thing. But he'd never experienced anything this surreal.

Lara grabbed the dog's collar and admonished, "Down, girl."

The thing didn't budge.

He had to put his hand on the collar to help guide the dog back to the earth. It was a long trip, he mused.

"I think she likes you," Lara said, not even attempting to hide a smile.

The dog tried to jump again. "That's quite enough," he said evenly. "Sit, Suzy-Q."

Immediately, she did, tail thumping. "Good girl," he approved, scratching behind one of her floppy ears.

"Oh my goodness! Goodness' sakes! Goodness. Oh my goodness' sakes." The woman running toward them completed her dash.

Her arrival seemed to have happened in slow motion, but that couldn't have been possible. Although, with her baby blue slippers flopping around, maybe it was.

"Oh, Suzy-Q! Thank you! Thank you for protecting the neighborhood like that." She crossed her hands in front of her chest, as if in prayer. "I'm so glad to know we're safe from intruders. What a good doggie."

He looked at her. She was thanking the *dog?*

Lara tried to hide her snicker.

"I'll deal with you later," he warned.

"Yes, Sir." But her eyes danced, and she pressed her lips together, presumably to keep the laughter from spilling out.

The neighbor scolded the other dogs, telling them to settle down. A couple across the street came out to see what was going on, another man had halted his lawn mowing while he watched.

Finally, another dog joined the fracas, part limping, part running, all wagging. It wasn't just his missing leg that slowed him down, it was his detour through the flower garden.

"Here comes Happy," Lara said.

He, too, jumped up and smeared a muddy paw on Connor's slacks. "Not a word," he told Lara. But even he had to be impressed by the yellow pansy that Happy dropped on his shoe.

The short, wobbly thing set its tail in motion again. Its entire body followed. "How does it not fall over?"

"Mystery of nature," Lara agreed. "Welcome to my home. I'd like you to meet Mrs. Fuhrman."

The lady with the so-blue-it-was-almost-purple hair was still not apologetic. In fact, she narrowed her eyes at him. "Who are you?"

"He's my friend."

"Fiancé," he corrected.

Lara flushed and the other woman's mouth fell open.

She looked at them over her horn-rimmed, rhinestone-studded glasses. "Your what?"

"Connor Donovan," he said, extending his hand.

She ignored it.

"From Donovan Worldwide," Lara supplied.

"The moving company?"

Lara shook her head.

"I'm the guy who's hoping to marry Lara."

"It's a secret for now," Lara stressed.

"Well, the dog thinks you're all right. She's usually a good judge. But I'm reserving comment."

"Fair enough," he agreed. "We'll let Suzy-Q make the decision."

At the sound of her name, Suzy-Q tipped her head to one side, looked up at him and whimpered. "Stay," he told her.

She broke their grips on her collar to lie on the floor at his feet. After extending her dessert-plate sized paws, she dropped her head on top of them with a soft whimper.

"Don't get used to it," Lara whispered.

"Obedience is heady," he responded.

"What did you say?" Mrs. Fuhrman asked, putting her hand to her ear.

"Everyone likes a well-behaved dog," he lied.

Lara smothered a laugh.

"They do, indeed."

"Can I help you get them all back home?" Lara offered.

None of the five had leashes, he noted.

"They're fine," Mrs. Fuhrman said.

"Everything okay?" the man with the lawnmower shouted out.

"Lara's talking to the moving company," Mrs. Fuhrman replied.

"You putting the house for sale?" he asked.

"I'm not going anywhere," she replied.

Connor felt as if he'd stepped onto a movie set. And, he had to admit, Lara made a hell of a leading lady. He couldn't remember when he'd been more charmed.

"Come along," Mrs. Fuhrman said to her pack as she started to walk away. Three followed immediately. Happy wagged its whole body a few times before trailing behind.

Suzy-Q remained in place.

"Go home," he said, pointing toward the house next door.

Instead, she inched closer to him. How she managed that with her massive bulk, he had no idea.

"Suzyyyyyyyy!"

"Go," he repeated.

Lara crouched to stroke the dog behind the ears. With obvious reluctance, Suzy-Q stood and started to walk home. She stopped midway to look back.

"Go."

Finally, she started to gallop toward Mrs. Fuhrman, who was standing on the stoop with her hands on her hips.

"She's quite the animal," he said, brushing hair, dirt and flowers from his clothes.

"She is. They're all rescues. Mrs. Fuhrman has a big heart."

He heard the woman usher the dogs back inside. On the other side of the house, the lawn mowing resumed.

"About that coffee that you've been so carefully protecting…"

"No one said it's coffee."

"It is," she insisted. "You're a smart man. You wouldn't

bring a cup with that logo and not have the elixir of life in it. And it's mine. Right? Tell me it's mine."

How could he not want to wrap up the moon and give it to her? He offered her the cup. "I think it's only half full at this point."

"I don't care how full it is." She accepted it and took a long drink. "You could spoil me. Three days in a row with great coffee?"

"Sorry I don't have a biscotti in my pocket."

"Suzy-Q would have ferreted it out. And, I apologize for the wild welcome. That didn't go quite the way I'd thought it would."

"It was memorable, and I'll be thinking of ways you can top it."

Her mouth parted.

"Show me," he said.

Her eyes darkened, almost imperceptibly.

"Inside. Now."

Their gazes locked. Yeah, she understood, recognized what was happening here, if not on a conscious level, then on an instinctive feminine one.

She finally looked away and turned toward the house. He picked up her shoes for her. They had those little cutouts at the front that would show off her painted toenails. Until today, he couldn't have said that he'd ever noticed anything other than a spiked heel, but these took sexy to another dimension.

Inside, the house was cool, and he took the time to turn the front door lock to keep out neighbors and four-legged friends.

He dropped her shoes in the entryway alongside a pair of running shoes then followed her into the kitchen. "Mind if I wash up here?"

"That's fine. I have a lint roller to clean your slacks and jacket." She put her cup on the counter. "Be right back."

By the time he was finished washing and drying his hands and face, she'd returned, holding out the promised roller. He thought about accepting then changed his mind. "Why don't you do it? An act of your submission."

She hesitated for a second. He saw a hidden doubt in her eyes but then she seemed to come to terms with it. She'd have a dozen objections, he knew. But they were just that, objections, nothing real.

Finally, she nodded.

"Start with the jacket." Now he was glad he'd worn a lightweight blazer, despite the weather. No telling the damage Suzy-Q would have done to a shirt.

Lara, with her entirely unique scent that reminded him of the promise of summer nights, moved toward him.

She looked up at him for a second. He liked the differences in their sizes. It made him feel even more protective over her.

Without a word, she lifted a lapel and rolled the sticky tape over it. She took her time moving to the next.

He enjoyed how deliberate she was. She continued to move over the rest of the material, ensuring every dog hair was gone.

"Pants, too?" she asked, her tone a bit hesitant.

"Yes."

She peeled off the used sheet, wadded it then dropped it to the floor.

With the same kind of dedication as earlier, she began just below his belt. She took more time than necessary around his crotch area. And if she kept it up, he might be taking her here rather than waiting until they were back at his place. Or, hell, maybe both.

Lara bent to roll the tape over his thighs, front, inside, then reaching through to the back. In less than a minute, his slacks looked as if they'd just come from the dry cleaners.

"Put down the roller then go get that throw rug," he instructed, pointing to the place in front of the stove.

Without question, she did.

"Kneel on it."

She complied with that stunning grace that so captivated him. Fuck. She belonged there, and by his side, in his life.

"Earlier," he said, "I mentioned that you could greet me

properly. Stay where you are," he added when she moved as if to stand. "Hand me the roller." He took it and placed it on the counter. "Many times subs will be on their knees to greet their Dom."

"Is that what you expect?"

He heard the note of doubt in her question. "Not always. But it's certainly a preference. It's hard to deny that it reinforces our roles, though. True?"

"I'm not sure I like it."

"I do." And damn, he did. "You have no idea how stunning you look to me. How much I desire you. Do you like that? And be ruthlessly honest with yourself."

She was thoughtful for a moment. "That it turns you on appeals to me, yes."

"That's part of the beauty about submission. You may not enjoy certain things, at least not when you first think about them. But would knowing that you please me also fulfill you?"

"Yes. On some level. But..."

"Let me relate it to you in a different way."

"I wish you would. I'm fighting this a bit, thinking it's ridiculous, wondering what the hell I've gotten myself into."

Despite that, she'd stayed in position. "I appreciate the way you're working through your struggle." He thumbed a piece of hair back from her forehead. "I stopped at the coffee shop and waited in line with about six thousand other people, a number of them girls from a softball team and their overwhelmed parents."

"A Saturday hazard."

"I didn't mind at all. But it was more than that. Before leaving, I not only looked up your address but also the closest place that was actually on my way. I left early enough to ensure I was still on time so I didn't keep you waiting."

"I'm sorry." She shifted restlessly, but she didn't get up. "Maybe I'm missing your point, but I'm not following you."

"I stopped because I knew it would please you. Today,

everything is about giving you a memorable day. My point is this... In any successful relationship, D/s or vanilla, each partner makes tiny sacrifices, does small things, acts of service as it were, because it makes the other person happy. I didn't have to bring coffee. You don't have to look so ravishing. You don't have to greet me on your knees, but it makes me happy, encourages me to think of even greater ways to show you my pleasure."

She smiled. "This is definitely not worse than being with six thousand kids at the local coffee shop. And that location doesn't even have a drive-through, if I remember?"

"I'd stand in the line three times to see that look on your face when you realized I was carrying a coffee cup. In fact, one day I hope that you will smile at me the same way."

"The smile was for you," she reassured him.

"Nice try."

She grinned.

"Now, to greet me properly..."

"Yes?"

That was exactly the response he'd hoped for. "I'd like you kneeling up, not back."

She'd been resting on her calves, and she straightened her posture.

"Nice. Legs farther apart."

The dress constricted her a little, but she did as he asked.

"Within these guidelines, I'll leave the rest to your discretion. Your hands can be by your sides or on your thighs, but with your palms up and gaze cast down."

She nodded.

"Or, you can link your hands behind your back or neck. Either way, I want you to tip your head back."

"So no direct eye contact."

"Until I speak, no." He heard her breath catch, which told him this was becoming more real to her. "At any rate, I always want your shoulders back. Now show me."

Her motions were a bit unsteady, as if she were concentrating on his instructions, trying to remember and, if he was right, she also had a good deal of nerves mixed in.

She placed her hands on her thighs, palms up, shoulders back, gaze down.

"Couldn't be any better. Now with your hands by your sides."

Just as wonderfully, she did that, as well.

"And behind your back."

It took her a few seconds to remember to tip her head back.

"And now behind your neck."

When she did, he caught his breath. She'd moved aside her hair, and it cascaded down her back. It took every bit of control not to fist his hand in it and, instead, remain at a distance while he acquainted her to his form of Dominance. "What did I tell you about your gaze?"

"No eye contact. Sir."

He walked around her twice, slowly.

Once, she turned her head to follow him, but when he raised an eyebrow, she returned to the correct position. "Good. Now look at me."

She did. Her eye color appeared a bit lighter. Unless it was his imagination, they had a dreamy quality, perhaps meaning that she was surrendering to her internal battle. "You've done this correctly, and the last requirement is that you be nude."

Lara sucked in a breath.

"Show me that."

She blinked a couple of times, looked down at the floor, then back up.

"We can go in the living room if you're more comfortable."

"I'm not comfortable being naked anywhere," she said.

"You'll learn. And don't tarry, otherwise I will take away your clothes when we're at my house."

"You wouldn't!"

"Oh absolutely I would. Your confidence is my aphrodisiac." He offered his hand and helped her to stand.

He held her hand until they reached the living room. The blinds were closed, and it looked as if she'd prepared the house for her absence. The air-conditioning had been turned off, and a bag sat near the door. Fortunately, an overhead fan churned through the heat.

Connor sat on the couch and watched her twist her hands together. He waited, and he'd do so as long as it took.

"Am I allowed a rug or anything?"

"If you're greeting me when I've been out, absolutely. If you're kneeling for my pleasure, serving me perhaps, then no."

"Right now, I mean."

"You tell me."

"Right. No rug."

"Good girl."

"I've never done a striptease before."

"Don't start now. Skip that and go straight to a *strip now*."

Despite his urging, she took her time, exposing her skin a satiny inch at a time. Finally, when she'd pulled the dress over her head, she draped it over the back of a nearby chair.

Her champagne-colored bra was demure—understated and sexy because of it. Her thong was nothing more than a scrap of dark blue silk. Tonight, he knew, he'd make this woman his.

She reached back to unhook her bra then allowed the straps to fall down her shoulders. After shrugging, she tossed the bra on top of the dress.

"You've got great breasts, Lara. Have you ever worn nipple clamps?

"No."

The way she'd responded to his touch yesterday, he'd bet she'd enjoy them.

She removed her thong and tossed it on the pile.

"Before you kneel, please turn. Slowly."

A gorgeous pink colored her cheeks.

"Think of me," he reminded her. "Not yourself."

"That's not all that easy."

"Think of the feeling of accomplishment, then."

She shook her head but did as he said.

"Wait. Stop." Her back was to him. "I've got to look at your ass." He imagined her closing her eyes or sighing. But it didn't matter since he couldn't see her reaction. "Spread your legs a little farther. Then grab your ankles."

"Maybe your other women were super flexible."

"Do your best. Your knees or calves are fine."

She managed to hold onto herself just above her ankles. Her hair touched the floor, and her pussy and ass were on perfect display. And yet, he demanded more. "Reach back and spread your buttocks for me."

Once she had, his balls pulsed. "You asked once if I ever had regular sex. This is why I don't. The way you respond, the way you're so gorgeously displayed for me... I would absolutely have no interest in having you just get into bed at the end of the day and lie there while you're thinking of something else. I have no interest in just sticking my dick in you and getting off. I want this. I love seeing your body spread wide open for me. The sight of your asshole..."

Her knees wobbled.

"And I'm imagining fucking it."

She released her grip.

"That's what you want, too. What you've been looking for. You told me before that you were left unfulfilled, *wanting* might have been your word. This... This, Lara. For today, just today, don't fight it. We owe it to ourselves before we sign the contract. Put aside your inhibitions, doubts, fear, and just go with the experience. Get everything possible out of it. Can you do that?"

7

Lara considered her answer. His words—naughty and slightly dirty—aroused her, and that shocked her. He ordered her to do things she'd never done before, and they thrilled her. He was right. Until Connor, she'd been wanting more, wondering if her lackluster sexual experiences were typical. But now…

She had to know.

He was offering her the opportunity to experience things she might otherwise know nothing about.

So far, the things they'd done had turned her on, even the spanking, and the slight sting from the harder single tail strike. Even if they ultimately didn't marry, she knew she'd be sorry if she missed this opportunity.

He was right that she wanted everything he'd mentioned, no matter how scandalous the suggestion.

He'd told her previously that being honest with herself might be her biggest challenge. She'd had no idea how prophetic those words were. "Yes," she admitted aloud.

"Give me today?"

She nodded.

"Good. Now kneel as if you're greeting me."

Lara had to focus on his instructions and ignore her embarrassment. After what they'd shared and she'd just done, there couldn't be anything more to worry about.

She knelt, spread her knees wide, put her hands behind her neck then tipped her head back. A bit belatedly, she remembered to draw her shoulders together.

"Very nice."

Her hair flowed down her back and she stayed in position as he stood over her and looked down.

She avoided eye contact but not the awareness of his proximity and power…or that of her own arousal.

He slowly walked around her. Even though he'd done so in the kitchen, here, with her being naked, she experienced it in a whole new way.

When he was in front of her again, he stopped. "I like the way your body is open for me.

He crouched in front of her. Staying in position was more difficult than she could have imagined. Gently, he cupped her breasts.

She started to sway toward him, but caught herself.

"Damn." He took hold of her nipples and rolled them gently.

"Mmm," she said, the sound part moan, part plea.

Connor responded by tugging up on her nipples, pulling them away from her body.

It hurt, ached, but it also felt exquisite.

"You like that," he said.

She closed her eyes, just allowing herself to enjoy the moment.

"I'm going to slap your cunt."

In a moment of panic, she started to close her legs.

"What's your word if you need me to slow down?"

The question jolted her out of her momentary fear.

"Bring your head to neutral and look at me."

She took a steadying breath. He was right there, looking directly at her. At one time she'd thought his eyes were cold. Now the gray seemed molten. She drew strength from him as well as reassurance.

He stroked a finger across her cheekbone. "What do you say if you're lost, need to connect, need a break?" he repeated.

"Yellow."

"And if you need to stop immediately?"

"Red."

"And where are you now?"

"I'm fine." Her voice sounded surprisingly strong. "A little apprehensive, honestly. I know it will hurt. But I'm willing to try."

"Have I asked you to do anything that's caused you more pain than pleasure?"

Even the single tail had been enjoyable. The sting had faded quickly. "No, Sir."

"Are you ready to continue?"

In that moment, she realized that he'd read her slight nervousness and had responded to it. He'd let her know what he was doing and made sure she was okay. "Yes." She nodded. "Yes, Sir. I am."

"Let's go back to where we were. I want you to give yourself over. Keep your body as relaxed as you can. Great posture, please, so that you're thrusting your breasts out. And tip your head back."

Chastened, she returned to the correct, open stance, and he started to torment her pussy. She was beginning to really understand his version of Dominance and how he ensured her compliance.

His touches, squeezes, pulls and the strokes against her swollen clit all were starting to drive her mad. She could do nothing but endure. And, she admitted, enjoy.

Lara concentrated on her breathing and she closed her eyes. That seemed to help her stay focused.

He palmed her breasts again, teasing. He tugged on each nipple in turn, and he pulled them high. Little pulses of exquisite torture ran through her.

"Do you like that?"

"Yes, Sir." And she did. She'd never known how much.

"Most times, if we're having a scene, I'll keep you tied. Right now, I want you to work on keeping your arms where I told you. Consider that you're tied, by my will. More of a challenge, and you may have to fight your own reactions. But if you really can't endure this, you can move."

She felt him slide a dampened finger between her pussy folds and she rocked her hips forward a bit.

"That's it." In response, he moved his hand.

Lara groaned.

Her body began to shake as he brought her to the edge of

an orgasm and kept her there.

"I enjoy playing with you, little Lara, learning about your responses."

"This is incredible for me, Sir," she admitted. Part of her wanted to hold onto him, look at him, but another part felt free to just savor, not worrying about what he thought or what his facial expressions meant. This was what she had been hoping for when she'd played with a blindfold, the ability to simply experience rather than anticipate what was next.

"Are you on the edge?"

"Right there," she admitted.

"What would it take? A little more pressure on a nipple?"

She couldn't give voice to the truth. That just a little more pain would tip her over the edge.

"Maybe my thumbnail across your clit?"

In response to his vivid description, she jerked.

"A finger inside you? Two? Three? Forcing your cunt wider, letting me feel your G-spot?"

Lara pursed her lips to hold back a whimper. Even the suggestion was enough to make her mad.

"Maybe one up your ass?"

All that. All of it.

He slapped her pussy, hard. She gasped, screamed, but no matter what, she stayed where she was, open, her arms behind her, available for his torment.

"I want your orgasm," he ordered, words biting, as if sharpened by jagged glass. He slapped her again.

She screamed as she came.

"Gorgeous," he approved, catching her body as she pitched forward. "In every way."

"That..." Lara couldn't think.

"Put your arms around me."

She was only peripherally aware of doing what he said. As if it came from far away, she felt his soothing touch and absorbed his mumbled words of reassurance. He stroked her hair, then put a hand behind her head to hold her protectively against his chest.

There was nowhere she would rather be.

It took her a few minutes for her breathing to regain its normal pattern. The whole time, Connor held onto her. Part of her never wanted him to let go.

"I think I liked that," she admitted. Eventually she pulled away. "When you first mentioned that you were going to slap me there—"

"On your cunt?"

"On my cunt," she repeated somewhat hesitantly. "I wasn't sure if I could take it. But it was amazing. You know, in future it may help me if you don't tell me what you're planning to do." But she was greedy. Everything else he'd said, she wanted it, too. His words lingered and tantalized. Now that she'd discovered this side of sex, she was ravenous.

"It's a balance," he agreed. "To prepare you, let you know what to expect. But if you know something's coming, your brain can supply the rest and fills in the blanks with fears."

"I understand that."

"Fear is one of the most powerful of all emotions. To conquer it is to succeed in life."

"You're sounding a bit like a philosopher." Or a man who'd been through a big test. She put her hands on his chest and pushed back a little so she could look at his face. He believed what he was saying, clearly. "Do you tell yourself that every day?"

"It's a mantra."

"Fear can be useful," she argued. "Without it, you can behave recklessly."

"Indeed. That's where discernment comes in. But it's easy to let fear keep us stuck where we are."

"Sometimes the boogeyman really is out there," she replied.

"Most times he's in your head. Take the last scene, for example. In just a few seconds, you built it up to be something worse than the experience actually was. In fact, you could have said no and not had that shattering orgasm."

And the after-effects still lingered.

"Let's get you to my house."

She nodded.

He stood and helped her up.

"I should take a quick shower."

"Do you have a handheld showerhead?"

"Don't get any ideas. I'll be right back."

He picked up her clothes and didn't offer them to her. "Show me the way."

His jaw was set, meaning that any argument would be futile. She sighed. Another thing she could learn from. The man didn't waste time with disagreements. He just asserted his will until it became a force in and of itself.

Connor followed her as she walked toward the back of the house and into her bedroom. Being naked was beginning to feel more normal, but it was still a bit startling to know he was behind, watching her.

He deposited her clothing on the bed. "Through there?"

She nodded, and he led the way into the small master bathroom. Since the house was older, it had been an addition. Her space wasn't luxurious, like his.

Maybe moving into his home would be better. She'd miss her neighbors and the backyard, but the soaker tub was an enticing trade-off.

He moved the shower curtain aside and reached into the stall to turn on the water. A few seconds later he said, "In with you."

She moved past him. "You're going to get wet."

"I'll worry about that."

Connor directed the gentle spray just below her breasts. "Soap?"

She grabbed the tiny bar and made a lather.

"What's the scent?"

"Magnolia," she said, returning the sliver to the wire rack.

"Haunting," he said. "And now it will be on my sheets."

The idea that he intended to sleep with her took their relationship to a new level of intimacy.

He watched her run the lather across her torso, then

lower. As she washed, he rinsed. He took care not to wet her hair or ruin her makeup more than she already had.

"Grab the soap again."

She picked it up and held it while he ran his fingers across it and slid off a small amount. "Done?" At his nod, she replaced it.

"Now turn around." He washed and rinsed her back and buttocks. "There's no indication that I spanked you." He trailed his fingers lower. "Maybe this tiny mark from the single tail?" He pushed on her buttock.

"I don't feel anything," she admitted. This morning, she'd looked at her rear in a full-length mirror. She hadn't seen anything. She'd never tell him that she'd been slightly disappointed.

He took his time, slowly moving across her skin.

"This isn't what I thought of when you mentioned Dominance and submission." She rolled her head from side to side as she enjoyed the feel of his hands on her.

"Every relationship is unique. I enjoy caring for you. I do it as much for myself as I do for you." He rinsed her off. "Now let's make sure your pussy is clean."

She turned to face him and she spread her legs without argument.

"Part your labia."

The man was a torment. He directed the water near her clit then moved his hand away. He repeated his action a couple more times and arousal began to churn inside her. "Connor!"

"Hmm?"

"It's…" This seemed impossible. But because her skin was so tender from his sharp slap, even the small amount of water had her on edge. She'd never thought of herself as particularly orgasmic, but he was proving she was.

Abruptly, he moved the showerhead.

She felt like a rubber band that had been stretched too far then pinned there. He couldn't seriously be planning to stop there? "I want…"

He met her gaze. "I know. I know exactly what you want."

"And you won't let me climax? Are you serious?"

"Think of how much more intense it will be later when I let you come."

She bit her lower lip in frustration. "You're not showing any remorse."

"Or feeling the slightest bit of guilt."

His quick grin was wicked, toe-curling.

She tried one more tactic. "This seems really cruel."

"Cruel is a harsh description."

"Try feeling what's going on inside me."

"That much, little Lara, I do know," he assured her.

Probably true. But the man had been skillful. She wanted an orgasm. And she wanted him. Last night, before she'd fallen asleep, she'd thought about that. She'd wondered why they hadn't had sex. She was certain it wasn't because he wasn't attracted to her. No doubt, he was. She'd already noted how controlled he was, and maybe this was another extension of it.

After he'd made sure all the soap was gone, he turned off the faucet. She shucked the water from her skin while he grabbed a towel from the rack.

He offered it and she wrapped it around herself.

Stunning her, he leaned forward and kissed her shoulder. "You smell delectable."

"It's the soap."

"It's you. That scent wouldn't be the same on anyone else."

He followed her to the bedroom, and he made himself comfortable on a small wooden chair while she dried off and re-dressed.

She tried to ignore him while she concentrated on what she was doing, but it was difficult. Even when he was silent, he was an enigmatic force.

Finally ready, she said, "Let's go."

He picked up her towel from the floor.

"I'm afraid you've discovered that I can be somewhat messy in the bedroom." She hoped he didn't look in the closet. Instead of tidying it, she'd moved a pair of discarded jeans so that she could close the door. As for the bed, she'd assumed that he'd want to see the house, so she'd made it for a change, even grabbing the throw pillows from her office. "I'm organized at work and with most things. I think this is the one place I forget about my responsibilities."

"Among your many charms."

"As neat as you are, I'd be surprised if it doesn't drive you crazy."

"I wouldn't let it. If we need a rake to dig out your side of the closet, we'll get a rake."

She didn't respond. No matter what she said or didn't say, he kept making plans for their future.

He turned off the light and overhead fan and followed her from the room. As they passed the kitchen, she snatched up her abandoned coffee cup.

"I could get you a fresh one," he said.

"This will do."

Near the front door, Lara slipped back into her shoes and grabbed her purse while he collected her overnight bag.

"Tell me you put soap in there."

"I have a travel size, yes."

"We'll order you a box of them for my house."

He opened the door then waited while she locked the deadbolt.

Lara followed Connor down the path. He opened the car door for her and helped her inside. After stowing the bag in the trunk, he slid in beside her. It seemed natural to be together.

As they drove across town, he turned the conversation toward business then their potential marriage.

"Tell me how you see this unfolding," he invited. Then, before she could remind him it might not happen, he added, "Assuming we're able to work out an agreement."

"I'd need to tell my dad, obviously. But I'm not sure if I should do it before or after the wedding." The word made her tummy jump. Ignoring the reaction, she took a drink of the coffee and continued. "I'd suggest we hold an emergency board meeting. I'm sure my mother would back the request. If needed, we can contact the individual members. I don't necessarily expect him to like it, and it's certainly possible that he'd do something, anything to block your seat. But there's really no way around that."

The idea of being at odds with her father like that made her heart ache. But she recalled him trying to get her to take medication when she was ill as a child, insisting it was for her own good. In a way, she supposed, the roles were reversed now. The knowledge didn't make the idea any more palatable.

"It would definitely be good for me to meet your mother," he said, repeating his words from yesterday.

"She texted this morning, asking how I was doing. Then she sent another one. She's part of a ladies' group. They call themselves the Friday Afternoon Soirée. They get together and do things like getting facials, going shopping, meet for happy hour. She managed to get your mother's phone number from a mutual friend and plans to invite her to join the group."

"How did that transpire?"

"We had lunch yesterday and I mentioned the fact I'd seen Erin. Since my mother's in charge of outreach, she's always looking for fresh blood. Er, I mean, new members." He grinned.

"And if your mom mentions we're going to be getting married... Especially if she knows it's a sham and my mother doesn't—"

"Sham?"

His tone chilled her. "That's what it would be."

"It's an arrangement."

"Really, Connor, I'm not sure why you're objecting to the term," she said, turning to face him.

"While we're married, we'll be married. I take all my commitments seriously."

"You're splitting hairs," she told him.

"If you think anything about the time we're together will be inherently dishonest, you're wrong."

Traffic ground to a temporary stop, and he looked at her.

To distract herself, she took another drink of coffee. And she ignored the way her hand trembled. Instead of responding to his statement, she said, "I won't call it a sham again."

The car ahead of them began to move again. "See that you don't." He eased into first gear.

She sat back. At times, his rigid responses caught her off guard. She'd seen the softer side of him with his brother, interacting with Thompson, with Mrs. Fuhrman, even Suzy-Q. But she knew better than to think that was the real him. Connor's spine was made of steel, and it seemed he never bent.

All too soon, they arrived at the parking garage.

He grabbed her bag from the trunk. Instead of waiting for him to come around to her side of the car, she climbed out, headed for the trash can to discard her empty cup then met him at the elevator.

The car had already arrived, and he was holding it open, waiting for her.

Everything he did spoke of control. She realized that, even if he was angry, he wouldn't show it. He was a difficult man to read.

She moved past him and stood at the back of the elevator. When the doors closed, she said, "I'll choose my words with more care in the future."

"It's over. Forgotten."

"Is that it?" She searched his features. "Are you that able to compartmentalize?"

"Yes. I rarely take anything personally. When it comes to you, doubly so. We'll get along much better through the years if we don't harbor resentment. Do you agree?"

"That's a great theory," she replied. "I'm afraid I'm a little more likely to hold onto things, though. It can take me a while to think things through and move on. I should probably try to be more like you."

He swept his gaze over her. "Don't change a single thing."

In response to his perusal, his words, her thought process slowed.

The elevator dinged, signaling that they'd reached his

floor. The ride had been less than a minute, and in just that small amount of time, he'd managed to take an awkward-feeling situation and turn it around in a way that made her feel really good about herself.

She reminded herself that she'd never had much luck in the love area, and when she did commit, it would be to a man who was more spontaneous, less emotionally distant, a man capable of giving as much as she was.

Once they were inside his loft, he said, "Feel free to make yourself comfortable. The built-in drawers on your side of the closet are empty. You'll find empty drawers and cupboards in the bathroom for your toiletries. We'll take the weekend to figure out whose house we'll live in. Can I pour you a glass of wine?"

"Please." She hesitated. "Back to my mother for a minute."

He gave her his attention.

"I'd prefer just to tell her myself."

"I said I was willing to meet her."

In frustration, she sighed. "Do you ever relent?"

"I already have."

He probably believed that.

"Originally," he reminded her, "I said you couldn't talk about it to anyone. I'm willing to consider that perhaps that's unreasonable. So I need more information."

"I still don't like it."

"I don't like letting anyone else know."

"Fine. I'll message her and set up a time to see her. Is there anything on your schedule I need to know about?"

"I'll rearrange things if I need to in order to make time. I'll also have Thompson add you as an administrator on my calendar so you'll always know where I am."

Every step made the whole thing seem more real. "I... uhm...I'll put my things away if that's okay?"

He nodded. While he went to the kitchen, she sent her mother a message then walked toward his bedroom. If he had his way, it would be their room.

The place was so masculine, from the forest-green bedspread to the dark furnishings. Being in his closet was even more disquieting.

Everything was organized. On the far left were his suits, ranging in color from black to charcoal to light gray. His dress shirts were hung next to them. All were starched, all were white. Even from a distance she saw they were monogramed.

In the center of the closet, a few blazers divided the casual clothes from the business ones. His chinos were either khaki or navy. He'd hung the polo shirts together, grouped by color. Golf shirts were next. Off to the side were a handful of long-sleeved, soft-looking T-shirts. She noticed that every garment and hanger faced the same direction.

Connor joined her. She'd been so fixated on his level of order and precision that she hadn't started to unpack her bag. "Did you have a professional help you organize the closet?"

He shook his head. "Judging me to be too regimental?"

"I wouldn't say that out loud."

"Which means I read your mind."

She flushed, but she shrugged. "I've honestly never seen anything like it."

"I found ways to cope in the last few years."

"Since your father passed?"

His gaze shuttered, but surprisingly, he didn't close her out. "That's part of it, certainly."

"And the rest?"

"Ask again over dinner."

He offered the wine and she accepted, taking a small sip. She put the glass on top of the dresser and unpacked her things. She hung a dress on a rail. "It looks a little odd."

"For now."

"Are you sure you're okay with me cluttering your space like this?"

"It won't bother me in the least."

Next she went into the bathroom to put away her personal items. "I've never done anything like this," she said when she saw his reflection in one of the mirrors.

He lazed against the doorjamb, at ease. "What part?"

"Putting my stuff away at a man's house. I hadn't thought about it until now, but I rarely sleep over with a man. And I've never lived with anyone."

"It'll take some adjustment, but we'll figure it out."

Doubts and reality collided, crashing into her. She dropped her makeup bag onto the counter.

"Easy," he said.

She turned to face him. "I'd really imagined we'd..."

He waited.

"Go to a justice of the peace or a judge. Some sort of civil ceremony. Then I'd see you at board meetings." She pursed her lips.

"Lara, the day you walked in my office and I saw you in that delirium-inducing skirt, that became an impossibility. I was determined to have you. You will be waking up next to me for the next four years."

"Three!"

He grinned. "Ends that argument."

"Your contract said three years, Mr. Donovan."

"And now you think it's an excellent idea," he said.

"Coercion is grounds to nullify the entire agreement."

"That *wasn't* coercion."

"But it is trickery."

"Lara, I've already told you I play to win. You'd do well to remember it." In contradiction to his words, she saw a small smile playing at the corner of his mouth.

The crack in his hardened, careful veneer had a way of melting every bit of resolve. Unfortunately for her emotional well-being, it also drew her in closer.

"Have a drink of your wine. Relax a little, cut us both some slack. I didn't pour you much because I want you of sound mind when we enter the playroom."

Even though cool air whispered from the vents, she got very, very warm. "I thought what happened at my house sort of took the place of your plans for the afternoon."

"It was only an appetizer."

He left her alone, and it took all of her concentration to finish putting away her things. Her little bottles of shampoo and conditioner fit on one shelf inside the shower. But the soap she put in the dish near the bathtub.

After taking another sip of her drink, she went in search of him.

He was in the living room, sitting on the couch. "In our contract, we didn't address birth control."

She sank onto a chair. "I'm on the pill."

"I always wear condoms, but since we're going to be married, I expect we'll want to forgo them sometime in the future."

Lara nodded.

"And if you plan to get off the birth control pills, you'll discuss it with me first?"

He'd said it so matter-of-factly that it was impossible to feel embarrassed. "Of course."

"Good. Anything else you need to talk about before we go in the playroom?"

Her insides suddenly became molten. He was a master at using his voice and tone. He gave a slight emphasis to the word playroom, and he managed to change the subject from serious to sensual in only a few seconds.

"In that case, go in our bedroom and strip then join me in the playroom. Get in one of the positions I taught you earlier and wait patiently for my attention."

Something in her responded to him completely. She nodded.

She walked down the hallway, her shoes echoing off the hardwood boards. And she was aware of his gaze the entire way.

In his closet—their closet—she hung up her dress and put her panties in a laundry bag that she'd brought along. Then she put her bra in a drawer with the rest of her lingerie. It was interesting, being with him. In just a few days, she'd become more adept at keeping her focus even while things seemed a little out of control. Perhaps she understood him better. Being methodical was a skill, one that could serve her well. At the least, the thought kept her calm while she smoothed her hair and went to rejoin him.

He was already in the playroom, but he looked totally different, astoundingly Dominant.

Even though he'd given her instructions, her step faltered, and it took all her control not to speak to him.

He'd removed his jacket and turned back his sleeves, leaving his forearms bare. She drank in the sight of him—lean, commanding.

His legs were spread wide and his thighs looked powerful. He had the whip coiled in one hand.

If she'd ever had a sexual fantasy about a man, he was it.

He gave an almost imperceptible nod toward the floor.

Galvanized, she crossed to the center of the room and knelt. She settled in, this time with her gaze cast down. Having her head back would make it all but impossible not to look at him.

She pulled her shoulders back and rested her hands, palms upturned, on her thighs. The entire time, he'd been silent, but she was conscious of him standing over her.

"Even better than I could have hoped," he said.

Lara took a breath to school her thoughts.

He allowed the time and distance to stretch. And she took her cue from him. Her heart beat faster than normal, and her breaths were shallow, but she forced herself to wait.

She heard him moving things around and the sound of something being dragged across the floor. The spanking bench, maybe? She was almost glad she couldn't tell exactly what he was doing. Then she remembered what he'd said about fear. The images her imagination was supplying were probably much worse than anything he would actually do to her.

"Tell me what you're thinking." Though he'd spoken softly, the words seemed to reverberate.

"I'm trying not to."

"And?"

"It's working, but only a little. I'm wondering what you're doing. Feeling a little apprehension, then I'm reminding myself that I have words I can use and that I've liked everything we've done. And some of those things I would have said I didn't want to do." She paused. "There's a tiny amount of curiosity mixed in, too."

"Stand and come to me."

She didn't rise as elegantly as she would have liked. No doubt he intended for her to get plenty more practice. If he had his way, he'd have years to school her.

His eyebrows were furrowed. She'd noticed that he did that when he was intent or thoughtful. It unnerved her to realize he watched every single one of her moves.

She took a few steps and stopped in front of him, aware of their height difference, how much bigger he was.

He took the whip handle and put it beneath her chin. In response, she shuddered.

"I want to get you better acquainted with my single tail."

Despite her intention to be calm, she looked at it. She wasn't a fool. He'd only used it on her twice. One had been a tease. The second had been harsher. And she'd heard the way he cracked it. The thing was an extension of him, and he could wield it any way he chose. "I'd ask what you had in mind, but the answer may scare me."

"I will promise you'll like the experience. And I promise you'll feel it. A sting, maybe a burn. If you're lucky, you'll have a few marks when we go to dinner."

"Lucky?" she repeated, her voice coming out as a squeal.

"It's my hope that you'll learn to like my marks, savor them, even."

"Again, as I keep telling you, Mr. Donovan, you have the wrong woman."

"Do I? Is that why your breathing is so shallow?"

She glanced down, severing their gazes. He seemed to look too deeply into her, all the way to her heart, her mind.

He moved the hilt of the whip, tracing it down the column of her neck and pausing at the hollow of her throat.

This man, her future husband, made it impossible to hide. She reached up and held onto his wrists.

"I think, Ms. Bertrand, that you please me immensely."

After she released her grip, he drew the handle lower, between her breasts, she pictured him tracing the same path with his cock. She shuddered, and her nipples hardened. As he ignited something that had been latent within her, intimacy was created. Connor made her feel as if she were the only one who mattered to him.

He made circles around her breasts then continued past her belly button, arrowing toward her pelvis.

For a moment, she forgot to breathe entirely.

He angled the hilt against her pussy, parting her labia, teasing her clit.

No matter what she said, her body wasn't capable of lying to him. She was already moist.

Easily, he slid the handle back and forth, making her tingle.

"Tell me again how I have the wrong woman."

She moaned as he increased the friction.

"That's it." He eased a tiny bit of the handle inside her.

"Oh, God." She closed her eyes.

"Do you want it?"

She reached for his shoulders.

"Tell me," he said, voice harsher.

"Yes… Please, Sir. Please."

He drove her wild, fucking her with the handle, plunging it in and out, making her squirm, drawing it back out so he could play with her clit, talking to her, encouraging her.

She leaned into him, rising onto her toes in silent plea.

"Such heat. I can smell your arousal, little Lara."

"Con-nor!" His name emerged as two distinct syllables. The things he was doing to her became her entire world.

"Come for me, Lara. Do it *now.*"

She was lost.

The orgasm crashed over her, and her legs lost the ability to hold her up. As always, he was there, offering support, wrapping her up.

When her brain function returned to normal, Lara realized she was clinging to him, holding on to fistfuls of his shirt.

He had her head cradled and a palm pressed against the small of her back.

"I'm not sure what happens to me," she admitted.

"Connection," he said. Then he smiled as he stroked her arm. "And I think that ends the conversation as to whether I have the right woman or not."

She tried to pull away, but he only tightened his grip.

"Be easy."

She exhaled.

"Relax." His words were gentle with reassurance and patience. "Stop thinking."

Slowly, she nodded.

He continued to offer his strength until she totally relaxed in his arms. She curled into his chest and uncurled her fists.

"Yeah. That's it."

She'd never had a man so in tune with her. The feeling amazed her.

"When you're ready, go over to the bench," he instructed.

Lara stayed where she was for a little longer then followed his directions. He'd placed it near a wall, probably to give himself ample room to swing the whip. The taller section faced her.

Cuffs dangled from either side of the metal frame, one set close to the floor, the other at the far side of the bench.

He came up behind her and laid the whip on the lower platform, where she could see it. Her pussy juices were still on the handle.

"When we were at your house and I was preparing to spank your pussy, I told you that you were being tied by my will."

She turned her head to look at him.

"I wanted to make you feel more secure, to build trust. Mentally that can be more difficult than being restrained because you need to make a conscious effort to remain in place. When you're tied, you're free to struggle, to pull. There's a certain freedom in it."

"Sounds contradictory." Everything about this journey was more complex than she might have imagined.

"Your right hand, please."

In less than thirty seconds, he had both of her hands restrained to the far side of the bench, forcing her body into a small stretch. Even though she knew she couldn't pull away, some sort of doubting instinct made her test them.

"Ankles next."

That made her much more nervous.

He crouched to fasten her into the second set of cuffs.

"What are your safe words?"

"Crap and oh fuck?"

"Lara," he warned.

Judging from the near-growl in his voice, he obviously had little appreciation for her sense of fear-based humor.

"Yellow and red, Sir."

She waited for him to pick up the whip but he didn't. Instead he rubbed her thighs and buttocks, starting slowly then becoming more vigorous.

He spanked her then, and with each touch, tension left her body.

"How are you doing?"

"Good." Unbelievably, she started to settle in. Just days ago, she wouldn't have believed this to be possible.

"I wish you could see yourself as I see you. I adore the sight of you, tied in your submission."

His words made her damp.

After a few more targeted hits, he crouched next to her.

She turned her head toward him.

"This won't be like last night. More intense. More prolonged."

She nodded.

"I'll be watching you the whole time. And I want you to stay with me. Count it out."

"Is there a number we're going to?"

"Twenty, if you can tolerate it." He picked up the whip and stood.

Instinctively she pulled on the restraints and tried to get more comfortable.

"I'd tell you to stay still, but you look so hot like that. Feel free to move. I want to see you dance for my single tail."

The first few were a sensual feast. His pressure was light, like a leather caress.

"How many is that?"

"Four," she replied. Two on each of her ass cheeks.

He brought the whip forward and let it snap against her right thigh. She swallowed a scream. *This is for beginners?*

"How many?" he demanded.

"Five." Then she remembered... "Sir."

"Much better."

She heard him take a step, then he stroked a hand between her legs.

"I might have lied when I said I only want you in here once a week," he said. "I love beating you."

He moved away and struck each of her upper thighs.

They were somewhat harder, and she swayed a little. "Six and seven, Sir."

"Beautiful. Come back to neutral when you can."

She realized he was giving her time to absorb each stroke, to be lost in her thoughts. Once the pain receded, a warm glow replaced it. And she felt ready to continue. A few seconds later, she got back into position.

The next three were dizzying, this time somewhat lower on her legs, alternating sides, and the third landed somewhere in the middle. "W-w-ow." She forced out a jagged breath. "Eight, nine, ten," she said, eventually remembering.

He dragged a thumb across each tiny bite, reigniting the pain.

"Cruel and unusual, Sir."

"You'll remember them more."

As if she'd ever forget anything they shared. She was responding to Connor more than she had any man, ever. The idea of finding another lover after him was daunting.

"Ask me to continue."

In that moment, she realized what was happening. She wasn't simply enduring this. She wanted it. Him. His whip. "Please. I want more. Sir."

"The pleasure is mine."

He marked her, just above the area he'd scorched. "Eleven." She gasped. Then he moved to the other side. "Twelve, Sir."

Methodically, he continued, placing each about an inch above the last. They were biting, burning. "Thirteen. Fourteen." She'd lost count. "Fifteen? Sir?"

"Stop counting," he told her. "Simply surrender."

The next stole her breath.

Then he caught the inside of her thigh and she screamed.

"I'm waiting to hear you say yellow if you don't want me to continue," he said.

She didn't give it to him. She wanted this. Instead, she struggled back into the correct position.

She felt him at her pussy, his fingers, his mouth.

The pain drove the arousal to stunning new heights. Combined with the way he'd denied her earlier, she wanted to crawl out of her own skin.

She pulled against the restraints, trying to push her hips back so she could force him to lick more of her pussy.

With a small laugh, he moved away.

The ankle cuffs made it impossible for her to close her legs to assuage the throbbing demand.

He continued the beating. Sensations merged, desire and anguish becoming one. His stripes went higher, until he'd covered her ass. He was no longer gentle, and she loved it.

When she knew she could take no more, he tossed the whip onto the bench.

Then he fingered her pussy, and she felt his fingers get slicker. Before she realized what was happening, he withdrew, moved back and slowly pushed one of them into her ass.

She froze.

"Go with it," he suggested.

He fondled her with his other hand, sliding a thumb against her clit. He overwhelmed her, slipping in and out of her pussy while he simultaneously finger-fucked her ass.

She trembled, fighting against the restraints and needing them for reassurance and balance. "This..."

"The reward."

"I'd do anything for this," she confessed.

He continued the relentless drive. Then she felt him turn

a finger slightly to find her G-spot.

"Fuck."

"Yes."

He pushed against that sensitive spot inside her and her whole body convulsed in response. She screamed his name.

Connor continued his assault until she collapsed forward and dropped her head.

He placed a light kiss on her bare shoulder then eased his fingers out of her, "Give me one second. I'm not going away."

She heard him wiping his hands. She'd barely noticed that he'd gone before he returned to her and unfastened her wrists.

Her legs were slightly cramped, and he rubbed them gently after he released them. "Tell me you brought a miniskirt or short dress for dinner tonight?"

"I'm afraid not."

"We can go buy you something. I want to see those bite marks from my whip."

He helped her to sit on the top platform of the bench. Against the vinyl, she felt the marks. A chill went through her, and she rubbed her arms.

Connor unbuttoned his shirt and stripped it off so he could put it around her shoulders. She snuggled into its comfort. The feeling didn't just come from the warmth, she realized. It was also because the shirt bore his scent.

The sight of him half-naked made her mouth water. She knew he worked out, but she hadn't expected his abs to be so well defined. There wasn't a trace of excess weight on him, reminding her of how disciplined he was in every area of his life.

It terrified her how much she was attracted to him, how much she wanted his possession. She wasn't sure why he was waiting to take her to bed. Maybe to build her anticipation, making sure she didn't feel rushed? At any rate, she was getting restless. She couldn't take her gaze off him. "Tell me you're not saving yourself for marriage," she said.

He grinned. "No chance. I fully intend to fuck you tonight, Lara. Be thinking about it."

Now she wasn't sure she could think about anything else.

"Can you walk in the shoes you brought?"

"Not far. But I have a pair of sandals, too."

"Let's get cleaned up and head out. There's a boutique just down the street."

She scowled. "You were serious about something short?"

"I always mean what I say." He looked at her purposefully.

She'd never gone shopping with a man before. Then again, she hadn't done a lot of the things that he demanded from her.

He wiped down the bench then the hilt of the whip before putting it away. "Shall we?"

Connor stepped aside and allowed her to pass. As she was walking, he pinched her butt.

She squealed, stopped, turned and glared. "You may not joke, but you're an awful torment. I bet your siblings have stories about you."

"I couldn't have been a better big brother. They nominated me for awards."

"I bet."

He grinned beatifically.

In the master suite, she cleaned up then dressed again before slipping into sandals.

He dressed in khakis and a golf shirt with the Donovan Worldwide logo on it.

"I'm not sure whether you look like we're going on a yacht or whether you're going to quote a moving job for someone."

"I'm warning you, Lara," he said. But he shook his head. "You know, maybe it's not a bad idea. We should have Nathan look at acquiring a moving company. You can be our first client and make Mrs. Fuhrman look like a psychic."

"I'm not moving."

"Soaker tub," he said, adjusting his collar in the mirror.

She met his gaze in the glass. His eyes were frosty, serious. Mesmerizing.

"I've already told you I intend to have your total submissive surrender. I will do anything to ensure I get it."

"Try it on."

"It will barely cover my ass," Lara protested.

"My point entirely." He smiled. "Don't make me repeat myself."

She walked over to a nearby mirror and held the tiny dress in front of her.

It was black, clingy, plunging, skimpy. The triumvirate of cock-swelling perfection.

"You've got to be kidding me."

He merely lifted an eyebrow.

"Connor, there's no way that this will work for me."

He said nothing. Over the years, he'd found that to be a solid technique. But with her, it was even more effective. She sorted through options quicker than average people. In his experience, she arrived at the right decisions.

"Fine." She turned back to face him. "I'll try it on, but I'm already telling you it will look terrible. My butt…"

"A lot of women would pay for a world-class behind like that."

"I think you're just horny."

"You've got me there. Doesn't mean I'm wrong, though."

"I want a couple of other things, too."

"That's fine." He moved to another section of the rack.

"You could sit on that chair over there. It's for aggrieved husbands and…friends." She pointed to a plush chair cleverly situated near some jewelry.

"Which I'm neither. I'm a highly sexed almost-fiancé. They help with the shopping."

"Is it possible for you to be more annoying?"

"Lara, darling, I haven't started yet." He selected a slinky thing in red. "Reminds me of your suit that first day."

"It's nothing like it," she protested.

"I want to see it on you."

She glowered but accepted the garment. Then she went to a rack and picked out something that looked like it would hit her below the knee. It was a putrid light brown. "My future wife is not wearing puce."

"It's taupe."

He said nothing.

With a sigh, she returned it and pulled out a purple dress that was more than adequate for the office. It was sleeveless and had a square neckline. In short it was classy and elegant, her signature style. No doubt it was also figure flattering. "You can have that in addition to something else. That will be good for tomorrow's gathering with my family."

"I can't afford two new dresses," she protested.

"You don't need to."

"You're not buying my clothes."

"Then maybe you can arrange for some overtime at the office. Or just buy one."

The clerk who'd just finished ringing up a sale came over. "Can I start a dressing room for you?"

"Thank you." Lara gave the three outfits to the woman.

The clerk unlocked a wooden door, hung up the dresses, then said, "Let me know if I can do anything to help."

After Lara promised to do so, the clerk wandered off to greet a new customer.

"Go ahead and try them on," he encouraged. Unless you want to buy new shoes as well, the black is probably the best choice." Those red heels with that dress? He wondered if he'd survive it. "And we do have reservations."

She entered the dressing room and closed the door. Since it didn't go all the way to the floor, he saw her place her purse on the carpet. Next he heard the sound of her pulling off her dress. He gave her about sixty seconds before saying, "Show me."

A few seconds later, she did. She'd put on the purple dress. As always, she knew exactly what was right for her.

"Elegant." He'd be so damn proud to have her at his side as his bride and partner.

She surveyed herself critically in the mirror, smoothing out an imaginary wrinkle. "I love it," she said.

A few minutes later, she returned wearing the red dress. "I don't like it," she said.

He shook his head.

"What? You're not going to tell me everything I put on is wonderful?"

"Why would I do that? I want you to feel confident. And it bunches around the hip. Your body is perfect. The dress isn't."

She sighed.

"Honesty," he reminded her. "It's the only way to build trust. So admit it. You like the black dress."

"It's nice. But it's not my style."

"It could be if you're brave enough." He enjoyed the thrust and parry with Lara. This woman wasn't just steamily sexy, she was savvy. Brains and beauty were a combination he was finding delicious.

After the way she'd responded yesterday in the playroom, he'd suspected she would enjoy this afternoon's scene. Then, he'd trained her how to greet him. When he'd smacked her cunt, her reaction had astounded him. She'd come hard, fast, wet. It had cost him plenty in terms of restraint to be polite and hold a conversation in the car. His blood had blazed in his brain, demanding he take her. He'd left her on the verge of a climax at her house. But he hadn't told her that all her suffering made his dick ache.

Then she'd presented herself in the playroom. Her innocence and nudity would undo the hardest heart.

The way she'd taken his single tail had given him immense satisfaction, a feeling of pride, even. He'd intended to go slowly, but he'd listened to her moans. He'd allowed her to drive the scene, and he'd given her what she asked for.

That she was willing to please him caused a mad demand and protective need to collide in him. He'd wanted to fuck her then, when she was striped, burning, on the edge. It'd been days since he'd jacked off, and thoughts of taking her were beginning to consume him. It would no doubt blow his mind. But a quick joining wouldn't do it for him. He wanted time to explore her and learn more about her. Which meant he had to wait. "Quit stalling. Or I'm coming in."

"You wouldn't."

His hand was on the door handle when she pulled it open.

"You would have," she amended.

He started to answer, but she interrupted, "You do what you say you're going to do."

"Count on it. Count on me. Now let me see you."

"I need a bigger size."

He moved back so that she had room. "Step out."

Slowly she did so.

"Hands behind your neck and turn all the way around."

She glanced around to see if anyone was staring.

"Gaze on me."

When she looked at him, he continued, "No one else matters. Even if you're momentarily embarrassed, you'll still be pleasing me. People aren't watching you as much as you think they are. And you'll never see them again. Worry about me."

She put her hands behind her neck and slowly turned.

"Stop." Because of where the floor-length mirror was positioned, he saw her reflection. She was worrying her lower lip. "I can see a couple of marks. Before you wear it again, I'll use a cane first."

"It's too..." Lara tugged on the neckline then the hem. "I was going to say it's too much, but the truth is, it's too damn little. There's not enough of it to cover anything."

"It was made for you."

She completed her circle and looked at him. "Do you know how much this thing costs per square inch?"

"Spoken like a CFO. They're the only ones who would calculate a dress that way."

"Anyone with a brain would," she countered as she let her hands fall to her sides. "At least cost per wear. How many times would I wear something like this?"

He shrugged. "Dozens?"

"Real life isn't like that." She rolled her eyes. "No one dresses like this on a regular basis."

"My wife damn well will."

The clerk came over. "Your husband is right. It's beautiful on you."

"He's not my—"

"Yet," he finished. "She'll take it and the other one."

"I'll pay for the purple one. But since the black one is yours, you can pay for it."

"Excellent solution." He told the clerk to ring them up, giving Lara no further opportunity for argument. "The only thing missing is jewelry."

"Absolutely not," Lara said.

"We have some nice costume pieces," the woman supplied helpfully.

He wandered to the necklaces while Lara changed back into her own clothes and paid for the purple dress. A little while later, she joined him.

"No arguments," he said before she could open her mouth. "Try this." He removed the triangle-shaped pendant and fastened the choker around her neck. It was ridiculous how much he liked the way it looked. "It'll do until we can get you a real collar."

Her eyes widened. "You're scaring the crap out of me. Your contract said that would only be for when we attended lifestyle events."

He nodded. "We'll talk about it. Will you wear the necklace? Not as a symbol, but because it will look nice with the dress?"

"Connor."

"Your choice, Lara. I won't force you."

"I'll consider it," she hedged.

"Fair enough." He unfastened the clasp then went to pay for his purchases.

Within five minutes, they were on the way home. The tissue-wrapped necklace was stowed inside the garment bag, but he'd left the pendant behind.

"So you bought me a dress instead of paying off the debt of a medium-sized corporation?"

"A small one," he agreed.

He let them both into the house, and he said, "Can I pour you a fresh glass of wine before I take my shower?"

"I can get it, if you'd like?"

"Yeah." He wanted her to feel totally at ease, find her way around the kitchen, make her mark on it like he intended to leave his on her.

He left the bag in the bedroom closet before heading into the shower.

She joined him in the bathroom. "Is it okay if I fix my makeup in here? Or do you want me to do it somewhere else?"

"This is fine." The intimacy of the scene didn't escape him. She was the first woman he'd had in his loft. If things worked the way he envisioned, this would become a habit.

After rinsing off the soap, he sluiced the water off then exited the stall. Belatedly, he reached for a white towel and wrapped it around his hips.

She had turned and was looking at him. She was wearing the black dress. She'd layered on a smoky gray eye shadow, touched up her mascara, and a tube of lipstick was suspended in front of her. She'd swiped a touch of red across her lower lip, but the top was alluringly bare. "Ah..."

"Yeah. Don't think that beating your hot ass and licking your pussy hasn't affected me."

She put down the lipstick. "You say stuff like that on purpose."

He crooked a finger at her and she went to him.

He kissed her, sucking her lip into his mouth then devouring her. She lifted up to thread her hands into his hair.

The towel fell and his cock pressed against her dress.

With her eyes closed, she responded completely to him. No matter the words that sometimes came out of her mouth, her body told the truth. She wanted him, and she was willing to submit.

Since they still needed to make it to dinner, he reluctantly ended the kiss. "I'm afraid I've made a mess of your lipstick."

"I'm more than okay with that."

As he dried himself, he watched her. She was reapplying the red while she looked at him out of the corner of her eye. The little tease was taking her time, going back and forth, intentionally driving him mad. "You'll pay for that," he vowed.

"What?" She opened her eyes, wide and innocent, watching him watch her. "I'm just making sure I don't miss a spot."

She blotted off the excess and dropped the tissue onto the countertop. The shape of her lips was there, in tormenting glory.

"You're going to get what you're asking for if you keep that up," he told her.

In response, she reached for the dress's hem and pulled it up above her hips. She had no panties on underneath. He saw bites from his whip. It had to hurt still. And she was asking for more. Heat, molten and demanding, pulsed in him. "Careful," he warned.

"I'm being nothing but, Sir," she responded.

He dropped his towel and moved to her left side.

Again without being told, she grabbed hold of the countertop.

"How many, Lara?"

She turned her head to look at him. "Whatever you say, Sir."

"Six." *Fuck.* His cock throbbed, its tip pressing against her skin.

She moved to spread her legs wider. He had to have a taste.

He touched her pussy. She was already damp, and as he stroked, she became wetter. He brought his finger to his mouth and sucked it.

This time, he didn't warm her up. Instead, he put a hand

on her butt cheek. Then, satisfied with the placement, drew back and landed it.

She gasped at the force and moved away.

Just as fast, she wiggled back and presented her ass.

Connor put the next two on top of the first, offering no quarter, delivering what she craved, making sure she'd feel it as she sat in his car then later on a chair at dinner.

"That hurts...so good."

He moved farther away and repositioned himself slightly so he could use his forehand to spank her other buttock. She pulled away after the first to regroup, but then looked at him, straight in the eye. Hunger was etched on her face.

"Ready, Sir."

He couldn't fathom there being anyone more suited to him. Whatever he offered, she accepted.

He finished her off, and she took it with nothing more than a quick inhalation. "That ought to hold you, sub."

"For a while," she agreed.

"Shall I cancel the reservations?"

"I'm afraid I'll wear you out if you do, Sir."

"Do you have any idea the danger you're inviting?" he asked.

"Probably not." She reached out to put a fingertip on his jaw. "But I'm learning to trust you."

Potent words. "I may have to choose some sort of other punishment for you," he said. "Like standing in the corner."

She wrinkled her nose. "Then you couldn't touch me."

"You're too clever by far, Lara. Finish getting ready."

"Yes, Sir." She gave a quick, sassy grin before leaving him in the bathroom.

When he joined her, she was wearing the dress and her shoes. "It's even better with the heels," he said. Her calves were accentuated, and her legs seemed to go on forever. "I may never let you wear anything else. When you're done with that dress, the cost per wear will be about twelve cents. Did you put on panties?"

"No."

"I shouldn't have asked."

She picked up her glass of wine and told him she'd meet him in the living room.

He dressed, and he grabbed the necklace as he left the closet. He found her near the window, looking out. "It's one of my favorite views," he said.

"It's a lot different from my slice of heaven," she said, turning to face him.

He nodded. "Will you wear this?" He held up the necklace.

"Only because I think you're right. It will look good with the dress."

Lara turned her back to him then lifted her hair for him to fasten the clasp.

"Let's see." He put his hands on her shoulders and turned her to face him. "Couldn't be any better. There's a mirror near the coat stand."

He went with her and stood behind her. While she fingered it, he experienced an unusual feeling of possessiveness. He wasn't sure he liked the sensation. Over the years, he'd told himself that he didn't get involved because relationships were owed an investment of his time and energy that he didn't have to give.

Now he wondered if he'd been honest with himself.

He'd never been in love. Maybe because he'd never given himself that opportunity. Experience had taught him that emotion could be a messy thing. It could cause damage. And initially, perhaps that had been part of the appeal of Lara's proposal. After all, a business arrangement, he understood.

But with the sight of her, his hands on her shoulders, the dress and jewelry he'd purchased adorning her body, he recognized that this—Lara—had become much more than that.

"I think I'd like it better if it had the pendant on it."

"I'm sure you would." Before she could begin an argument, he said, "Are you ready to go?"

She collected her purse and headed for the parking garage. "Are you driving us?"

"I gave April the weekend off."

Traffic through downtown wasn't as big of a challenge as he'd assumed it would be, and they arrived at the luxury hotel a few minutes ahead of schedule. After turning over the car to a valet, Connor rounded the hood to meet Lara.

He placed his fingertips against the small of her back and guided her inside. He saw two marks on the backs of her legs. Neither was really obvious, but to him, they were significant. "Thank you for wearing this dress." With the patent red peek-a-boo heels, straight spine, hair flirting with her shoulders, she was breathtaking. To her credit, she didn't tug on the hem. She'd apparently grown accustomed to it, and she wore the outfit like no one else could.

Once they stepped off the elevator on the nineteenth floor, he gave the hostess his name, and they were immediately led to a table next to the window.

He pulled back her chair, and she sat then adjusted her weight.

"Everything okay?" he asked.

She gave him a wry smile. "Ouch," she mouthed.

He took his seat across from her.

The city lay beneath them. From their vantage point, they looked east—an endless panorama dotted by occasional buildings. Pure potential was there, untapped and waiting.

"I've heard of this restaurant," she said, "but I've never been here."

"They're famous for their seafood and steaks."

"And the views, obviously," she added. "I love my hometown. I'm glad I went away at times. It made me appreciate it more."

"Part of the reason you care deeply about BHI."

"Roots," she agreed. "Connection. It matters."

"I couldn't have said it better."

She ordered the Gulf shrimp platter, and he had a medium-rare steak. Once she'd consumed half a glass of wine, her posture became a little more relaxed and she became more animated than usual.

"I understand why you like living downtown. Everything's close, and it's got a certain energy, doesn't it?"

"Yeah. It's become part of me."

She swirled her finger around the rim of her glass. "What do you do to relax?"

"I exercise," he said. "Swim. Use the rowing machine you saw in my workout room. On rare occasions, I walk to work."

"That's it? The pictures in your home office… There was one with you and Erin in Cozumel. But that was a few years ago."

She was treading in territory he'd rather keep private, but if she was going to spend the next few years with him, she had that right. "I haven't taken a vacation recently."

"Not even a getaway, like to New Orleans? Galveston? South Padre Island?"

"No. You?"

Lara sat back and crossed her legs. "We were talking about you."

"Which I'm not accustomed to doing." Business, yes. But with the exceptions of Nathan and a few close friends, Connor kept conversation general, sports, business, weather.

"Even when we're intimate, you seem to be somewhat distant. Like you're holding yourself back."

Perceptive.

She tipped her head to one side. "It makes me wonder if you've always been like that. Or if it's because we don't have a…" She paused.

Since he had never supplied information that he didn't need to, he waited while she searched for the right words.

Finally, she settled for, "This relationship hasn't progressed like normal ones."

He noticed, appreciated, that she hadn't called it a sham again.

"Most times you get to know someone, and all along the way you're trying to decide whether things will work, whether or not there's chemistry, whether values align, whether you want the same things out of the future. If that all works out, you may decide to live together or get married."

"You forgot the part about whether the sub is gorgeous and well-behaved."

She took a long drink of her water then scowled at him. "My point is that most relationships don't start with a marriage proposal."

"Especially from the bride." When she pursed her lips, he relented. "In modern times in this part of the world, you're right. Through history, plenty of marriages have been arranged, either for political or financial gain. There's not much different about us."

"I'm not wrong, am I?" she asked. "About you holding yourself back?"

"It's nothing personal," he assured her. In fact, he'd already let her in closer than any other person.

"Where does love fit into for you?"

"It doesn't."

"You've never been in love?"

"No."

"Because you haven't let yourself?" she asked.

"Love is a messy thing."

"What makes you say that?"

He thought about changing the subject. It wasn't a particularly easy one for him. Yet it was best if she understood him. "What do you know about my dad and Cade's mother?"

"Not much. I mean, obviously I know you have a stepbrother and his mom's name is Stormy. I know Erin adores him, but she doesn't get to see him a lot."

"My father was supposed to marry my mother. Not exactly an arranged marriage, but certainly one that made sense. Their parents were friends. As such, they'd spent a lot of time together as they grew up. They dated, seemed very suited. Everyone expected him to propose right after college. But he actually never finished school."

Their food arrived, delaying conversation for a few minutes.

Lara took a bite out of a crab-stuffed shrimp and closed

her eyes in rapture. He wasn't sure he'd ever been with a woman who enjoyed experiences so fully.

"How's your steak?"

"I don't know," he responded. "I'm too busy watching you eat."

She paused, a forkful halfway to her mouth.

"Please. For the love of God, don't stop."

She blushed, but she finished the bite. "If I move in with you, can we eat every meal here?"

"I might starve," he said. "But that's a small price to pay."

After one more shrimp, she put down her fork.

"I notice you didn't touch the asparagus."

"No way am I filling up on green stuff."

A while later, the waiter returned to collect the plates. She skipped dessert, but asked for coffee. "Back to you," she said. Showing that she'd been listening to every word, she prompted him by saying, "Your dad never finished college..."

"I'm going to back up a little. My grandfather believes all of us should have real, working knowledge of the business."

"Makes sense."

"We have some ranching interests."

"I think that's another one of your under-statements," she said.

He shrugged. "My great-great-grandfather acquired a number of acres. We're fortunate to enjoy some success." But they all knew it took hard work to keep it successful and profitable. No one took the responsibility lightly. "As part of my grandfather's desire for us to know about that part of the business, he sent Dad to the ranch one summer. That's where he fell in love with Stormy."

"She worked on the ranch?"

The waiter put the coffee on the table, but Lara never took her gaze from Connor. Talking to her was a pleasure. She didn't interrupt, didn't make any soothing sounds. She just gave him her complete attention.

He thanked the waiter, told him to wait a few minutes before bringing the bill then tried to pick up where he'd left of. "She was a wrangler. By the end of the summer, she was pregnant. My dad proposed to her, but she refused. She said she didn't want to be part of the Donovan family. Too many obligations and responsibilities went with it. I'd be willing to bet my grandfather had something to do with that, though no one discusses it."

When he paused, she took a drink of coffee then moved the cup aside.

"Cade was born. Dad eventually married my mother, though no one is sure why. Probably out of a sense of obligation or some sort of coercion."

She winced sympathetically but said nothing.

"The truth is, Dad never stopped loving Stormy. I'm sure he attempted to be a good husband, and I know he was the best damn father he could be, to all four of us."

"I'm not sure how anyone can juggle something like that. Split loyalties. Being in love with a woman who isn't your wife?"

It hadn't been until after his dad's funeral and dealing with his own grief that he'd thought to ask those questions. His grandfather hadn't filled in much information. Since his stroke, Connor had stopped asking.

His mother was always friendly toward Cade, but there were times she spent more time in her room with a headache than with the family. "Though she never said, it had to be difficult for Mom to have Cade around, especially when Stormy brought him. Couldn't have been any easier when Dad drove to Corpus Christi to get Cade. Sometimes they met halfway." He took a breath. "Occasionally, I went with him and so did Nathan, even Erin. And he attended all of Cade's important events. You probably know that Cade was driving the car when Dad was killed."

"Yes. Erin mentioned that." She drew her cup and saucer toward her. "I'm sure it never gets easier."

He appreciated her quiet understanding. "The days pass. Grief doesn't consume every waking hour, but the reality is always there. You cope. You go on."

She was quiet for a while before saying, "After hearing

all that, I'm surprised that you'd want to get married to anyone."

"As you said, this is a smart business arrangement. If I hadn't already seen the possibilities for BHI's communications division, it might have been a tougher sell. And had it been anyone other than you..." With that necklace, the plunging dress, her natural beauty, the way he knew her buttocks and thighs bore his marks...

"It explains your reticence as well as your rules...your morals."

"And their inflexibility."

She took a drink of her coffee. "I understand."

"Finish up," he said. "I'm ready to go home." He signaled for the check then settled the bill.

Since the valet service was quick, he had her back at his loft within twenty minutes. "I've been waiting all day for this," he said when they were in his living room. "I want you to present yourself, in the bedroom." He dug his fingers into her hair on either side of her face. "Will you do that for me?"

"Yes. I will."

He moved his right hand lower so he could trace the outline of her necklace. "Go."

Once he released her, she started walking away from him. When she was a few feet away, he said, "Lara?"

She stopped and turned back to face him, her head tilted in question.

"Leave the dress on."

With a brief smile, she said, "I might have guessed you'd say that."

Before joining her, he gave her time to get settled.

A few minutes later, after he'd turned off the lights and secured the locks, he walked into the master suite. Seeing her there, near his bed, hands behind her neck, with her hair in glorious disarray, made his blood pound.

Without being told, she remained in place, her breaths gentle. She was the image of submissive perfection and he vowed to do everything he could to care for her, to cherish her.

He sat on the bench and told her, "Crawl over here."

With a whispered, "Yes, Sir," she did.

"Over my knees."

With the same grace that had first appealed to him, she draped herself over him.

He pulled up her dress and caressed her soft skin. "You told me once that you had a spanking and you weren't impressed by it. I'm going to try to change your opinion."

"I'm liking it already."

His handprints from this afternoon had faded, but a couple of single tail bites still marred her skin. "Do you feel this?" He pressed his thumb to one of them, and she jerked. Her movement was followed immediately by a sigh. "Fair warning, Lara. I'm going to want to see marks all the time."

He began to rub her more vigorously, bringing color into her ass cheeks. "Do you have any idea how much this sight of you over my knees turns me on?"

She shook her head.

"You will." He teased her cunt with his fingers then began to cover her buttocks and upper thighs with spanks, some light, others more robust. "Count them for me."

He rained them down fast, the blows coming one after another.

"One, Sir. Two…"

Relentlessly, he continued, increasing the frequency until she couldn't keep up and her words jumbled into an incoherent sentence and the word Sir sounded like a mantra.

He was aware of her grabbing hold of his ankle for support.

"You're made for this. For me," he said. He landed some spanks on her pussy. When she skittered away, he lifted his knees to roll her back toward him.

"Oh, Sir!"

"One of my favorite words," he informed her.

He tormented her pussy, brought her to orgasm then drove her toward another.

Only when she was thrashing around, gasping for air to breathe, did he help her to sit up.

He pulled her against him and wrapped her up completely in his arms, not letting her go.

With a shuddering exhalation, she curled into his chest. He liked the way she turned to him. It was the stuff of his Dominant fantasies.

"I had no idea. When I fantasized about a spanking, that's what I'd hoped it would be like."

"I'll give you anything you want, Lara. I'll try to make it as good for you as I can. But that kind of spanking is a reward."

She put one hand on his chest and pushed herself back a little so she could look up at him. "Yeah. I'd find ways to misbehave everyday if I had a guarantee that you'd punish me in that way."

"Ask for it any time."

"I might."

He brushed her hair back. "Doing okay?"

"I think my legs can hold me upright, if that's the question."

He helped her to stand, and he added, "I want you to go into the playroom and get a pair of wrist cuffs. They're in a drawer." He wasn't more specific than that.

While she was gone, he stripped the comforter from the bed and placed it over a rail in the closet. Then he removed his clothes. When he returned, she was waiting, kneeling, cuffs on the floor in front of her. "Well done. Now take off your dress."

She stood and looked at him for a moment. "Impressive, Sir."

Her feminine approval made his cock even harder.

"I've waited as long as I can. Naked, Lara. Now."

She smiled in a saucy, teasing way and slowly reached for the hem. Still taking her sweet time, she pulled the dress up while wiggling.

"You're doing that on purpose."

"Just following orders, Sir."

As if he'd never been with a woman before, he watched without blinking. Moments later, she was wearing only a bra and she was dangling the dress from one hand.

"The bra, too."

"Tell me we're going to have sex," she said.

"Oh, yeah." He took the dress from her and tossed it over the bench. "We're going to have sex."

In response, she unfastened the bra.

Her beautiful, dusky nipples were already erect, begging for attention.

He sucked one into his mouth, laving it, stretching it. He saw her bra fall to the floor.

Lara put her hand on his shoulders, and he felt her legs jerk.

"So good," she murmured.

As he continued to bathe the nipple with attention, he rolled her other nipple between his thumb and forefinger, elongating the hardened nub.

Then he changed it up, sucking on the other and toying with the dampened one.

"I've never known anything like this," she confessed. "Never had any idea."

Honestly, he hadn't either. The longer they interacted, the more he wanted. Even though that violated his rules, he refused to change anything about it.

Pulsing desire driving him, Connor left her long enough to pick up the cuffs. Without protest, she offered her wrists to him.

"Behind you."

"Oh?" Her eyes widened, and he saw neediness in the deep brown depths.

She turned, and he fastened her into the cuffs. In addition to the intoxicating scent of her arousal, he caught a gentle whiff of magnolia. He succumbed to the urge to gently sink his teeth into her neck, increasing the pressure until she moaned.

"Onto the mattress." With his hands on her shoulders, he guided her toward the bed.

When the backs of her knees hit the mattress, he helped her to sit. Then he gently pushed her over. "I love having you helpless."

He grabbed a condom from the nightstand and rolled it down his cock before joining her on the bed.

Her eyes captivated him as she intently studied him.

It took all his resolve not to skip the foreplay. "Spread your legs. How does your pussy feel?"

"Other than a bit tender from those spanks you just gave me, it's fine."

"Lift up your legs and keep them up." He moved between her thighs. "Higher," he instructed.

"I'm going to have to step up my abdominal work," she said wryly. "Being with you requires being in shape."

"Are you complaining, little Lara?"

"Ah." She obviously thought better of it. "Not if this is the reward. This is more like incentive, Sir."

"Well said, sub." With his mouth, he claimed her cunt, licking, nipping, using his tongue to fuck her pussy.

She cried out, turning her head to one side. "I want to touch you."

When she allowed her legs to rest on his shoulders, he pinched one of her thighs.

"Damn," she protested.

"Stay in position," he warned, putting his hands beneath her buttocks. He lifted and squeezed, trying to reignite the pain from the spanking and tipping her pelvis to give him a better angle.

"This… I want to touch you."

"I want your orgasm," he countered.

He pulled one hand from beneath her and inserted three fingers into her heat. He spread them apart, forcing her wider, making her accept more.

She whimpered, but he felt her pussy clench.

He was relentless, torturing her, driving into her.

"I need to come."

"Do it."

"I…can't."

naked around me all the time, Mr. Donovan."

He grinned.

"And you're really, really good in bed." She brought her arms around in front of her, moving slowly as she stretched her shoulders.

"My question was really about the handcuffs," he clarified.

"I may be starting to understand what you were talking about the other day…the freedom that comes from being bound."

"Go on."

"You're the one who told me it would happen," she protested.

"But I want to hear about it from your perspective."

"Since I couldn't touch you, it was as if…I don't know. I had no choice other than to let go. It allows me to get out of my mind more. I wasn't thinking much, just enjoying all the sensations." She paused for a second as if to sort through her thoughts. "I'm not sure that makes sense. Touching you, holding you would be a whole different experience. I guess being bound gives me permission to enjoy it more. I liked it. But it doesn't mean I don't want my hands all over you."

"I promise you'll have plenty of opportunity for that." And he had a few ideas along those lines. "Let me draw you a bath. May help with those kinks."

As he entered the bathroom, she said, "Damn. Nice ass."

He turned back to face her and said, "I feel the same about yours. Especially when it's red."

After he'd disposed of the condom, he turned the faucet on full blast.

A few minutes later, she joined him in the bathroom. Her hair was mussed, and she yawned. He couldn't wait to pull her against him as they slept.

She grabbed a clip and secured her hair. Then, instead of waiting for the tub to finish filling, she climbed in. She sank down and sighed. "If you can't find me, try looking here," she said. "I may never get out."

Lara closed her eyes, and he gazed at her. She still wore

the necklace, and he liked the way it nestled against her skin.

Who was he fooling? He liked everything about her, from the way she tipped back her head, to her sun-bronzed shoulders, to the way her breasts looked with their dusky, peaked nipples.

He let her soak in peace while he showered.

When he'd finished, she was soaping her body.

He kept an eye on her while he dried off. A few stubborn tendrils of hair had escaped to curl against her cheekbones. A few others lay against her nape. He realized he liked having her in his space and watching her savor the bath.

He walked over, picked up a sponge and soaked it in the water. He squeezed it out just inches over her body, rinsing the soap from her skin.

"Be very careful," she warned him. "I'm this close"—she held her thumb and index finger about an inch apart—"this close to getting spoiled."

She sat up, and he ran the sponge over her shoulders, down her back. "Getting closer," she told him. "You know, if the whole deal with you owning a moving company doesn't work out, you can apply for a position as my personal assistant."

"I'll keep that in mind." He put the sponge back on the shelf.

"Thank you." Her voice had a soft husk.

"Always," he replied. Since the water had started to chill, he offered her a towel.

Lara stepped out and he wrapped it around her.

He went into the closet to put on a pair of shorts then went back into the bedroom and waited for her.

A few minutes later, wearing a pastel pink shirt that barely covered her butt, she joined him.

"I've told you I would prefer you come to bed naked."

"I..." Color drained from her face and she reached for the hem. "I thought it was just for that one night."

"Leave it on." He pulled back the covers on her side of the bed. "I'm not sure I can endure the temptation." The truth was, he'd desire her no matter what.

He turned off the light then pulled her close, spooning her. Her bare legs pressed against him. "That thing you're wearing. Is it called a no-sleep shirt?"

"In case you were wondering, I don't have any panties on."

"Keep up that kind of talk and I'll have to put you in a chastity belt for your own protection."

She wriggled provocatively.

Fuck. It was going to be a hell of a long night and an interesting future.

In gentle waves, awareness crept in, and Lara spent a few moments in that blissful, unnamed space between awake and asleep.

She stretched, then curled back into herself when she noticed some small aches.

That realization brought her back to consciousness and she opened her eyes. She was in Connor's bed, but she exhaled when she saw that he was gone. His pillow had a small indentation, and the covers were stamped with his spicy, masculine scent. She listened carefully, but there was no indication he was anywhere in the suite.

She forced herself up onto her elbows. The effort caused her a twinge of pain in her abdominal muscles, and she suddenly recalled the way he'd forced her to hold her legs up while he'd licked her pussy.

Her heart pounded and memories rushed in. The session with the single tail, shopping together, conversation, his sensual spanking and, God, the sex…

Even though she tried to put a stop to them, the visions persisted, as if they were on a slideshow. She recalled the hot way he'd fucked her, holding nothing back. Just as quickly, though, he was capable of tenderness. He'd drawn her a bath, even rinsed her off before pulling her against him in bed. She'd never met a more complex, confounding man.

It was impossible to fathom she was actually thinking about getting married to him. Though the union wouldn't last, she was recognizing that it might be impossible for her to keep her emotions under control. Getting entangled with a man who had his feelings walled off was nothing short of insane.

Unable to shake the feeling that she'd set something in motion that she had no idea how to stop, she tossed back the covers and climbed out of bed, determined to find coffee before being friendly to the day.

She heard music from down the hall, indicating he was probably working out.

Despite her own best intentions, she was drawn toward the exercise space.

For a moment, he was unaware of her, and she stood in the doorway, watching him. Seventies rock music pulsed through the space and he pulled the handle on the rowing machine in keeping with the tempo. He stared at the television, even though the sound was muted.

He didn't have a shirt on, and she saw a sheen of perspiration on his upper body. It was his shorts, though, that arrested her attention. They were compression skins, and she'd never known a man to wear them unless they were layered under something else. The black material hugged his legs and his genitals. Her heart raced so fast that she wondered if watching him work out would count toward her daily cardio goal.

Suddenly he looked over, and she was a bit embarrassed to be caught staring.

"Morning," he said, his smooth pulls never faltering. "I'm almost done here."

"No hurry," she said. "The music drew me."

"Sorry if I woke you."

"You didn't." Or maybe he had, because she'd been aware of his absence.

"I made a pot of coffee for you."

"Okay, that's final. I will marry you," she said.

He grinned.

Right now, she wasn't sure which was more important, watching him or grabbing a cup of coffee.

He focused his steel-gray eyes on her. Silent promise radiated from them, simmering and pulsing even across the distance.

Her stomach plunging in anticipation, she escaped to the kitchen.

He'd thoughtfully set out a couple of mugs, and she filled one from the thermal carafe. Instead of carrying it to the table or the living room, she simply leaned against the counter while she took the first restorative sips. There'd be time to move after the caffeine hit her bloodstream.

A couple of minutes later, he joined her. He had a towel draped over his shoulders, and he was still wearing those lust-inducing shorts.

"How'd you sleep?"

"Never better," she admitted. It had been a long time since she'd slept the night through. Much as she was loath to admit it, his presence had helped her. Well, that and the exhaustion that had clobbered her after they'd had sex. It wasn't just the physical exertion, she knew. It was the way he pushed her, emotionally, mentally, demanding trust, taking her places that she'd never been.

"Is it okay if I go near the coffeepot?" he asked. "I promise you a refill."

"Am I that scary?"

"Your refill comes before I take any," he said by way of answer.

She looked into her cup. "It's almost empty."

"There's enough for both of us," he promised.

He grabbed the carafe, and Lara moved away. As ridiculous as it seemed, there was something about starting the day together that made her feel more vulnerable.

True to his word, he topped off her mug before pouring his own.

He leaned against the stove, across from her. They were close, but not touching, and she was grateful for the distance.

"How are you doing this morning?"

"A little tender. Aware that I may need to hire a personal trainer to get me in shape to have sex with you."

"Yeah. You'll want to be prepared for the acrobatics."

"Acrobatics?" She narrowed her eyes.

"Drink up. You'd have figured out that was a joke if you were awake."

"It's not me," she protested. "It's you. You don't joke."

"Rarely," he conceded.

But it had happened, she remembered. A few times, in fact.

"We're all meeting at my mother's house around eleven. I thought you might want to go and grab a bagel and a cappuccino to hold you until then. There's a small place a few blocks away. It's overcast, so it's a nice day to walk."

"Sounds perfect." She liked the idea of getting out of the house, having something ordinary to do after everything they'd been through. And it would keep her mind occupied, allowing her less time to stress out about meeting his family. "Will Erin be there?"

"She'll be dying to see you, I imagine."

"So she knows? About us, I mean."

"We had a family conference call yesterday morning. I'm surprised she hasn't called you."

"So am I." Soon, everyone would know. "My mom sent me a text last night. She can see us this afternoon if that works for you."

"Name the time."

"How about two? Will that give us enough time?"

He nodded.

"I'll let her know."

"Good. Now breakfast. Can you be ready to go in fifteen minutes?"

"If I can shower and put on my makeup after we get back."

"Deal."

She excused herself and returned to the bedroom to get dressed in a pair of yoga pants and a T-shirt emblazoned with the Houston city skyline. She was tying her athletic shoes when she heard him enter the bathroom then, almost immediately afterward, the sound of the shower. He was already done by the time she went to pull her hair into a ponytail. "I think you take the fastest showers known to mankind."

"It'd be different if you were in there with me."

Her pussy tingled at the thought.

Five minutes later, they were walking side-by-side down the street. This was the kind of relationship she'd been looking for, something easy, where two people were working toward the same goals, passion...

She looked over at him. Sunglasses shaded his eyes. A dark golf shirt showed off his biceps and his lean torso. His pants conformed to his muscular thighs. He hadn't taken the time to shave, and the shadow on his jaw appealed to her. Connor Donovan was a mouth-wateringly handsome man.

This weekend, she'd had a glimpse of what a life together might be like, waking up in his bed, having coffee together, watching him work out, sharing breakfast, spending time together. If this were real, it would be so good.

As he held open the door to the coffee shop, she shook off her melancholy. This whole thing had been her idea, and she had to deal with the consequences.

He selected a healthy power bagel, loaded with nuts, fruits and seeds. She went straight for the maple scone iced with maple frosting.

"The biscotti should have clued me in to your sweet tooth," he said.

"Not only that, but I don't share." She broke off a piece and popped it into her mouth, savoring the bite.

The barista called out their order and he went to claim it before returning to the table with the drinks.

"I think your definition of submission is different from what I expected," she told him after she'd taken a sip.

"How so?"

"I guess I thought you would have expected me to go get the drinks. Maybe to have brewed the coffee this morning." She shrugged. "I'm not sure. It seems like you're always doing little things for me."

"First of all, it makes sense that the first person out of bed would make the coffee."

She shook her head. "It makes more sense to set it up the night before, put it on a timer and have it waiting when you get out of bed."

"I forgot I was dealing with an expert. We should do that." He took a drink from his smoothie. "Back to your question. Some relationships include that, certainly, just like many vanilla relationships do. But we're both busy executives. Working together will make our lives together easier. To me, the most important part of the D/s dynamic is the respect. When something matters to me, I want you to very carefully consider what I say. And sexually..." He looked at her.

She felt the full force of his personality.

"I think you know what I expect."

"To be in charge."

"That has enormous responsibilities with it. I take them seriously. Your safety and well-being are paramount."

She'd already seen the proof of that.

"But if you ever feel the overwhelming urge to get up before me, after I work out, I have coffee and an omelet, three eggs, fresh veggies, including onions and green peppers. Red ones are nice for color. Heat them in olive oil before adding the eggs."

"I keep telling you that you have the wrong woman."

He took the final bite of his bagel. "Couldn't hurt to ask."

Her phone rang and she checked the caller identification. "Erin," she said.

"Surprised she waited this long."

"Uhm..."

"Go ahead and take it. I'm sure I have email, and I've got newspapers to read." He pulled out his own phone.

She left the coffee shop and moved to a shady area beneath a tree, away from potential eavesdroppers.

"What the hell?"

"Good morning to you too, Erin."

"Are you kidding me? You're marrying my brother and I have to find out from him? And I've been waiting twenty-four hours to hear from you. Isn't that cruel and unusual punishment? What about chicks before dicks? Hmm? I'm not waiting another minute. Spill it. Now. Every detail."

She stood and began to pace. "Nothing much to tell. There's been no decision yet, and I'm not sure we'll be able to come to terms."

"What, did you two sign a blood oath to stick to the same story?"

Lara laughed. "It's the truth."

"Okay, fine. I'll pry. Who proposed?"

"I did."

"What? Did you at least buy him dinner first before frying his male mind?"

She shook her head. No matter what was happening, Erin kept her outrageous attitude. Lara was reminded of their times in college where Erin would dramatically enter their dorm room, throw herself on the bed, hug a pillow and regale her with stories. "Nothing like that. After I met with you—"

"So you weren't playing it cool on Wednesday night? It was my idea all along?"

"I went back to the office after I had dinner with you. I ran into Connor. He was getting on the elevator as I was exiting."

"So you knew he visited your dad?"

Her breath froze. "You knew?"

"No! Are you kidding me? Me? Keep a secret? Come on, Lara."

That much was true.

"I didn't find out he had any interest in BHI until Thursday when we had our monthly meeting. I've missed some updates, so I wasn't in the loop. Your dad kicked Connor out, right? My big brother wouldn't have liked that much."

"I started thinking about what you'd said."

"And...? Give me the details. Where are the negotiations stalled?"

Lara remembered what he'd said about loyalty and protecting their relationship. Keeping it from Erin was a huge test. She settled for telling parts of the truth. "He wants me to live with him."

"He's a neat freak, but other than that, he doesn't do anything weird like leave toenail clippings in the bathtub."

Erin had had a boyfriend in college who'd done that. After she'd seen it, she'd been unable to shower. After putting her clothes back on at two a.m., she'd called Lara to pick her up. Since then, they'd judged all men by that standard.

"So why can't you live with him?"

"The marriage will have an end date."

There was so much silence that Lara thought the call had dropped.

"So you don't mean for this to be a long-term thing?"

"No. I never did. He's okay with that. But I thought we'd live separately."

"He wants the appearances. Shit, Lara."

Erin understood. Over the years, they'd shared their frustrations. Erin knew her better than anyone else did.

"I was hoping you'd cracked his shell, that he wanted to have a real marriage."

"No. He was clear that there's no love involved. But he wants me to move in."

"This is kind of like putting your life in limbo, isn't it? You can't date anyone else, and you have to be with a man who doesn't love you but acts like he does."

"That's a good way to explain it."

"Well, crap. So you're thinking about BHI and nothing else."

"And it will be good for Donovan Worldwide. Connor will buy the communications division, at a more than fair price. And the patents."

"You know, Lara, you've made a lot of choices in your life because they were the best for your dad. Maybe you should start making ones that are the best for you. There's a whole world out there. You don't have to do this. Don't set yourself up to be miserable."

"On the other hand, it's only for a few years," Lara replied, serving as her own devil's advocate. "Fewer years than college."

"But no spring breaks," Erin quipped.

"It's not like I've been dating much anyway."

"So? That doesn't mean you should put your life on hold. This didn't work out the way I envisioned it," she said. "I'm not happy."

Lara agreed with that. Then she saw Connor coming in her direction. "I need to go."

"I'll see you at my mom's later. Oh, by the way, did you know your mother called my mother? This is getting really weird."

"Yeah. Sorry about that."

"It's your fault?"

"Not intentionally." She paced beneath some shade trees as she explained about the Friday Afternoon Soirée and the fact her mother was spearheading membership growth.

"If she gets Mom out of the house and ripped-ass drunk, that would be great."

"I'm not even sure how to say this, but they're planning to invite men to future events."

"Even better."

"Seriously?"

"Yeah. Mom needs to stop hanging around the house. The more incentive, the better. Before she gets a yippy dog and a Prada to put it in."

"Ouch," Lara said.

"Yes," Erin said unapologetically. "I was talking about your mother's pampered princess."

Lara was pretty sure princesses weren't treated as well as Diva. To be fair, Erin didn't dislike all small dogs, just Diva. She'd babysat the animal one time when the regular nanny had been unavailable. Erin had shown up to pick her up, and Diva had bitten her toe. After sending her sincere apologies to Erin through Lara, Helene had taken Diva to the veterinarian to make sure her teeth hadn't been injured.

They said goodbye, and she ended the call.

"I thought my sister was going to keep you into the next century. I read three newspapers and responded to six hundred emails."

"Six hundred?"

"At least."

"Was that another joke, Mr. Donovan?"

"I don't joke, Ms. Bertrand."

"Um-hmm," she replied.

They walked home and got ready for the drive across town. Last night, she'd taken off the necklace and put it on top of her dresser. It was a pretty piece, more expensive than it should have been. She considered wearing it again since it would look nice with the dress she'd brought. But to him, it had meaning that she didn't want to encourage.

She met him near the door.

Even casual, he managed to look professional and... delicious. She couldn't think of another word for it.

He wore a white shirt and lightweight blazer. He'd added a blue tie shot with pinstripes several shades lighter. He smelled of spice-laced mint, and he hadn't shaved. The combination said urban sophistication, and it was all she could do not to run her fingers in his hair and ask him to take her back to bed.

Before they left the loft, he grabbed three bottles of champagne from the pantry. "For the mimosas," he explained.

"My kind of party."

"I figured it was."

Once they were on the road, she asked, "What should I expect from your family?"

"That everyone will be polite. You'll meet my grandparents, my Aunt Kathryn and my Mom. You already know Nathan, and we already talked about Erin. There will be lots of food. And plenty of mimosas."

"Your grandmother's name is Libby. Libby Sykes, if I remember?" In Texas, the Sykes name was legend and connected to the Texas Revolution.

"That's correct."

"And it was a great romance, like he wasn't good enough for her, but Grandma Libby wouldn't be dissuaded. Erin told me the story, but it was years ago."

"I wouldn't call it a big romance, but that doesn't mean Erin wouldn't," he said dryly. "They met at a church dance when he was home on leave from the army. He was a lieutenant at the time. Rumor has it, she asked him to dance. They continued to see each other whenever he came home. He left the military when he was a captain."

"I thought you called him the Colonel?"

"It's a nickname, not a title." He changed lanes to go around a slow-moving truck.

"But he worked hard and proved himself in the business or something?"

"He took over one of the shipping divisions. Once he'd doubled its worth, he was allowed to propose to my grandmother"—he shrugged—"I'm guessing it was during that time he earned the title of Colonel. I can imagine how disciplined he was, what a hard-ass."

That part, at least, the man had passed down.

"My great-grandfather's wedding gift was one of the divisions of the company the Colonel had built. Because of his own sense of pride, he renamed it Donovan, US. Over time, it's grown. About ten years ago, he renamed it Donovan Worldwide. Humble beginnings, but my grandfather's devotion and sense of obligation have made it what it is."

"I think you're underestimating your own contribution."

He shrugged. "I have had a good example to follow."

She was beginning to see a pattern with the Donovans and their easy humility.

They had to park down the street, and just before they entered the house, Erin opened the door and yanked her inside the house and into a big hug.

"I think you needed that," Erin said.

No matter what, she'd always been able to count on her friend.

The party was better than she expected. Angela, Connor's mother, was a wonderful hostess, even though the gathering was in her honor. She'd assigned each person to bring something, and it was a feast. Nathan had brought quiches from the local delicatessen, Erin had brought fresh-cut watermelon and honeydew, Kathryn had brought dozens of croissants from a local bakery.

Lara felt no more uncomfortable than she was at any business meeting. And it helped her to think about it in those terms.

No one asked about the contract details or wedding arrangements.

Erin mentioned that she'd decided to invest her own money into a friend's corset shop in Kemah.

"I'm not surprised," Nathan replied.

"We're planning to open for the Fourth of July weekend."

"Then spend September through May wondering how to pay the rent?" he replied.

Erin shook her head. "You're forgetting Christmas. And all kinds of different events. Street festivals, that kind of thing."

"If you have a good online presence, that will help, too," Lara added. "Custom orders."

"Who knew those things would come back in style?" Libby shook her head. "I remember celebrating their demise."

"I'll come to your grand opening," Aunt Kathryn promised.

"It's your trust fund," Nathan replied.

The conversation ended, and the family worked together to clean the table, put away the leftovers and load the dishwasher.

She wandered over to Erin, who mixed them each a strong mimosa. "I was hoping to celebrate your engagement, but we can just as easily use it to forget your sorrows."

"It's not all that bad."

"Call me anytime. Unlike you, I remember to keep chicks before dicks."

"The dick in question is your brother. You realize that, right?"

Erin rolled her eyes. "And the chick is my best friend. If you need to complain about Conn, I'll listen."

They clinked their glasses together.

"I'd like a moment of your time, young lady," the Colonel said as he joined them.

"Granddaddy," Erin warned.

"I won't bite her," he said, thumping his cane on the floor.

"It's okay," Lara said with a smile that encompassed both of them. "If you do, I'll bite back."

"Spunk," he said. "I like that."

"I'll be with Grandmother, but I'm telling Connor you've stolen Lara away."

"There's a quiet place on the patio," the Colonel said.

She took her mimosa with her and followed the older gentleman outside.

"Family means a lot to you," he said without preamble as he lowered himself into a chair. "Otherwise you wouldn't be doing this. I understand why you went to Connor."

She glanced back inside the house. Connor was still sitting with his mother, but he was looking back at her.

"Connor told me you will be working out an ending date to the marriage. I don't necessarily support that. But as long as that's confidential, it can work. But I want you to hear my thoughts with no polite bullshit. Marriage should be forever."

"I agree with you, in theory. As you know, this is more of a business arrangement."

"Things have a way of becoming more complicated. Unexpected consequences." He, too, looked through the window, back inside the house. His gaze fixed on Connor's mother, his own daughter-in-law.

She wondered if he was talking about his own regrets, the way he'd influenced past events. Suddenly she saw the Colonel as a more complex man. He'd lost a son, and because of his own health issues, Connor had been forced into a prominent role at Donovan Worldwide.

"Time can't go backward."

"I think I understand what you're saying." And more, she had greater respect for what Connor had said yesterday. Love could be a messy thing. The after-effects of Jeffrey's love for Stormy continued to ripple through the generations.

Before she could say anything else, the patio door opened, and she saw Connor walking toward them.

"Ready to go?" he asked, standing behind her and squeezing her shoulders. "We still have to see your mother."

Lara said her goodbyes to the Colonel then she and Connor went inside to give their farewells to the rest of the family.

"He's gruff, but well-meaning," Connor's grandmother said. "There's a softie under that bluster. A man who cares, someone as flawed as the rest of us."

Lara hugged the older lady then allowed Connor to guide her outside.

Once they were alone, he pinned her against the side of the car and allowed his gaze to flow over her body. "No nicks or bruises?" he asked.

"Everyone was very polite."

"Good. Any nicks or bruises will come from me," he replied.

Just that fast, he'd created simmering tension between them. She swallowed deeply.

"Open your mouth for me."

When she didn't immediately comply, he added, "Now, Lara."

Instead of looking away, she did as he instructed.

He grabbed her hands and raised them high, pinning her wrists to the top of the car in a powerful grip.

She was lost.

His kiss consumed her. He demanded everything she had to offer, then he asked for more.

With only the slightest hesitation, she gave it, pressing herself against him, opening her mouth wider. He tasted of determination. He consumed her.

Connor inserted a thigh between her legs and she rode him, seeking, rubbing, grinding.

With his free hand, he brought her more fully against him. Right here, she was close to coming.

As quickly as he'd fanned the burn, he pulled back, ending the kiss and releasing her wrists.

"That's a hint of what's to come later," he said.

She still couldn't think when he helped her inside the car. "That was in public," she said when they were on the road again.

"Yeah. And I made sure there were no kids outside and no one was watching. I'll always protect you."

To busy herself, she dug a lipstick out of her purse and flipped down the visor for its mirror.

"Keep it up. Just makes me want to kiss you again."

Her bigger concern was that she wanted it, too.

"Where are we meeting your mother?" he asked when they were exiting the neighborhood.

"I figured we'd go by her house." She programmed the address into the GPS.

"She knows I'm with you?"

"Yes. And she's dying to know why."

"Anything I need to know about your mother? Does she still go by Bertrand?"

"She does. Dad told her to change it back to her maiden name. Until then she was going to. But because Dad didn't want an ex-Mrs. Bertrand out there, she decided to keep it. That about sums up her personality. Other than that, she has a dog that thinks it's royalty. Fair warning, it bit Erin."

"This is my lucky weekend." He looked at her. "What kind of dog?"

"Pomeranian."

"I have no idea what that is."

"Purse dog. But she's really adorable."

"Other than the biting thing," he added.

"She has little teeth."

"Anything else?"

"That about covers it."

"Except for the part about the DNA connection to you."

She smiled. "There is that."

Helene met them at the door, holding Diva in her arms. The dog was wearing a pretty ribbon that was the same hot pink color as her mother's dress.

"You both look beautiful," Lara said.

"Diva went to the spa yesterday."

Of course the dog had been to a spa, rather than the groomer.

"Come in, come in."

Connor closed the door behind them, and Lara kissed her mother's cheek. Diva moved in to add her own kiss. "See? She's sweet," Lara said to Connor.

"I assume you're Connor Donovan," Helene said, rather than waiting for an introduction.

"Pleasure to meet you, Ms. Bertrand." He extended his hand.

Not to be ignored, Diva put out her paw.

Lara was surprised to notice that he didn't hesitate. Instead, he stroked behind the dog's ears.

"What a good girl!" Helene approved.

Diva turned her head toward his hand. Lara sympathized with the pooch. She was afraid her response was much the same when he dug his hands into her hair.

"Since it's cool enough and not too windy, let's sit outside." Helene led the way through the house and out onto her porch.

A pitcher of lemonade sat in the middle of a table, along with three glasses.

"Fresh squeezed?"

"Your favorite," Helene replied.

Once Helene set Diva on the slate, the animal wound herself in and out of their legs, yipping and all but dancing in circles.

"Oh, Diva, darling. You'll wear yourself out." Obviously not having any of that, Helene picked up the pooch and held her close.

Lara poured everyone a glass of lemonade, and her mother wasted no time with pleasantries.

"So what's this about a wedding?"

Suddenly Lara wished she'd smuggled in one of the mimosas.

"I spoke with Angela Donovan yesterday," Helene continued. "She said the two of you are getting married. One might have thought my daughter would have mentioned it herself. At least in passing."

Before she could answer, Connor touched her leg.

"My fault entirely," he said. "I wanted to tell you in person. It's been everything Lara could do to keep it secret."

"How about we skip the bullshit, shall we?"

Lara's mouth fell open.

"This is a scheme you two concocted to get Connor a seat on BHI's board, isn't it?"

"Actually—"

"You're not a good fibber, Lara, so don't even try."

"Mother!"

"Well, that solves one of our three sticking points," Connor said. "Lara said she'd never be able to keep it from you. Something about DNA. We're hoping you'll be agreeable and work as an ally on the board."

She smiled and readjusted Diva's bow. "And have the chance to help drag BHI into the twenty-first century? Tell me what you want from me."

Lara hadn't been sure what her mother's reaction was going to be to the wedding, but other than being slightly miffed that she had not been the first to know, she was rather accepting. Excited, even.

They discussed strategy, and it had been years since Lara had seen her mother so animated. She promised to personally contact the board members and ensure they were in BHI's meeting room at five o'clock on Tuesday afternoon.

"What about Pernell?" Connor asked.

"Oh, he won't have any choice." She grinned. "I won't let him know about it until after everything is all arranged. Manipulation is my favorite pastime."

Connor evidently noticed Lara's lack of feedback.

"Lara?" he prompted.

Even though this was exactly what she wanted, and still believed necessary, part of her couldn't help but think it seemed as if they were plotting a coup. "I wish we didn't have to do this."

He touched her leg in reassurance. "Doubts?"

"Not really. More like..." She trailed off.

"You can either fight for BHI, Lara," her mother said, "or you know it will become a shadow of its potential. I support you, either way. You know that. I'd be just as happy if I was supporting your position to leave. But under the current structure, BHI cannot thrive. Something has to change. You've been working there long enough to have realized that."

Lara picked up a spoon and stirred her drink. "It's the right thing."

"That doesn't mean it's easy," Connor said.

She drank in reassurance from his strength. "I'm not sure I realized just how difficult it would be."

"You can rely on me," he reminded her.

When the conversation was wrapping up, Helene lifted her lemonade glass in a toast. "I really do hope you two find happiness."

"It's more complicated than that, Mom," Lara said.

"Again, Lara. You're a terrible fibber. I've seen the way Connor looks at you. And when you spoke about him the other day..."

"Go on," Connor encouraged.

"Enough," Lara warned her mother.

Helene relented with a small smile. "I imagine you'll just handle the wedding privately?"

"If we work out the rest of the sticking points," Lara clarified. "And I'll still want to see a copy of your original proposal to my father," she said to Connor.

"I'd like a copy, too."

He nodded.

A few minutes later, she and Connor left.

"Until now, I hadn't really believed that whole DNA thing," he admitted when they were driving.

"Even when I was at college. She knew if I'd stayed out too late. Guarantee my phone would ring before seven a.m."

He grinned. "And you have confidence that we can have

this all pulled together by Tuesday afternoon?"

"She's good," Lara said. "She'll use whatever means she needs to get people to the meeting." There was a reason she'd been the Mom of the Year at all of Lara's schools. The woman knew how to get people involved, and she knew how to fundraise. She was an absolute social maven. "If nothing else, she'll intrigue them. Or bribe them with chocolate chip cookies."

Conversation moved from strategy on to the proposal he'd prepared for her father. It was low, like her father had said, but it was far from offensive. And it was a good starting point. The BHI board had deserved to hear it. At the very least, she, as Pernell's daughter and CFO, should have been informed of the offer.

"You told your mother about meeting me," he prompted after that.

"If you want details, you can forget it. None. Zero. Your ego's big enough," she said.

"So you told her something that would feed my ego?"

She rolled her eyes. "My lips are sealed. Nothing is escaping."

"When you bumped into me after I'd seen your dad, I was thinking of having you on your knees."

Her breath tangled in her chest.

"I'm glad it was mutual. Let's get back to my place."

She shifted. "I was planning to spend the night at home tonight. I don't have work clothes, and I need my car."

"I'm not done with you yet. There's plenty of the afternoon left, and we still have some details to discuss before tomorrow. It's your call, Lara. Tell me to take you home, or ask me to beat you."

There was seduction in his gaze, and she was helpless to resist him.

Connor poured her a glass of wine. He enjoyed having her here, and already it was natural. She'd come in and put her purse on the coatrack then slipped off her heels while he'd hung his blazer from one of the hooks. He'd loosened his tie and unfastened the top button on his shirt.

She'd followed him into the kitchen and pulled the merlot from the refrigerator. It was a small step, but teamwork nonetheless. Whether she knew it or not, he was wearing down her defenses. The woman was going to be his wife on Friday, if not before. He'd have her moved in by Wednesday or Thursday. In a little over a week, he'd have a legitimate place on BHI's board. Within six months, Donovan Worldwide would have acquired BHI Communications and its patents. "We've had a number of successes today," he said. "And hopefully more to come." He offered her a glass.

"Thank you," she said as she accepted it.

"What do you say we order a pizza for dinner?"

"I'd say that sounds rather mundane."

"We need to eat."

"Pepperoni."

"Anchovies," he countered.

"What? No. Eww." She shook her head. "No."

He couldn't keep his grin confined.

"You were joking? You?"

"Sausage," he said, relenting.

"Half and half?"

"See? We do know how to negotiate."

"Yeah, you hijack the deal with anchovies. You get anything you want after that."

He ordered while she carried her wineglass into the living room. As usual, she sat in the chair, something he intended to change.

After he'd hung up, he walked into the living room and grabbed the remote control to select an easy-listening station.

He closed the blinds then said, "Show me how you masturbate."

"Right now?"

"The pizza will be here in forty-five minutes. Do you need

longer?" He removed the stack of magazines that had been on top of the coffee table. "After you take off your clothes, get on here."

She put down her glass, untouched. "Your requests continue to get more outrageous."

"Unless you want to be naked when the pizza delivery person arrives, I suggest you get on with it."

"I'm not quite sure what to do."

"The next time we have phone sex, I want to be able to picture what you're doing," he said. "Do what you normally do."

"When you mentioned before that you wanted to watch me, you threatened to provide pointers."

"Don't think I won't."

Lara stood then pulled off her dress and draped it over the arm of the chair. Her bra and panties matched, but today she'd chosen briefs. Though he generally preferred skimpy lingerie, he appreciated how classy they looked as well as how nicely she filled them out.

Swaying a little to the classic love song, she reached back and unfastened her bra. As the chilled air whispered over her skin, he watched her nipples tighten.

He expected her to shimmy out of her panties, but she didn't. Instead she cupped her breasts, pushing them together, lifting them. Closing her eyes, she tipped her head and let her hair fall down her back. He could imagine coming home to this every night.

His cock stirred.

Determined not to be focused on his own needs, he propped one knee on the opposing leg then picked up his glass of wine.

While still holding her breasts cupped together, she rolled her nipples, then pulled on them like he might, hard, then harder.

He looked away to take a drink.

She sighed so softly, he wasn't sure he'd actually heard it. But she made the same sound again when she twisted her nipples.

"You like that?" he asked.
"I do."
"Don't stop." He went to the playroom for a pair of lightweight nipple clamps. "You'll like these," he said when he returned.
"I used clothespins a couple of times, but I hated them when they twisted."
"These won't do that." They were alligators, joined by a lightweight chain. They wouldn't stand up to a lot of tugging, but for extra pressure while she was masturbating, they'd probably be ideal. "May I?"
She held her breasts for him, and he couldn't resist the opportunity to squeeze her nipples, loving the feel of her flesh between his fingers. Emboldened from the way he'd seen her torment them, he gave a much more brutal twist.
"Oh, Sir." She moaned, actually pulling away to increase the pressure.
He smelled her arousal.
"My clit is throbbing," she admitted.
"So's my dick."
She looked at him, at his crotch. Unexpectedly, she reached for him. "It is," she said, stroking him.
"Hands off," he warned.
"And if I don't?"
"I'll withhold your orgasm."
"I'd prefer a spanking," she said.
"I'd prefer to give you a spanking, too, but it's not happening unless you're very well behaved."
Reluctantly, she pulled back her hand.
He took hold of her right nipple, pulled on it then held it while he put a clamp in place. "If you want more of a bite, you can put it closer to the tip."
"This is good," she told him.
He placed the second one, then stepped back. "Not only are they effective, they're quite beautiful on you."
She shrugged and stretched to test them. "I like them. I may have to get a pair."
"They're yours."

"Thank you."

The song transitioned into something a bit more up-tempo.

Without him saying anything, she licked her finger then slid it in beneath her panties. She moved her hand back and forth and rocked onto the balls of her feet as she moved her hand quicker and quicker.

When he was sure she was going to orgasm, she swayed to a stop then slowly drew down her underwear before using her toes to pick them up and drop the fabric in his lap.

Maybe forty-five minutes wasn't enough time for this.

She sat on the edge of the coffee table then brought up her legs. Casting a sly glance at him out of the corner of her eye, she leaned back and parted her thighs, giving him a view of her glistening cunt.

Even though the clips were on her breasts, she still squeezed her nipples and alternated that with plumping her pussy lips, sliding fingers between her labia. As he watched, she drew back the hood of her clit, showing off that that swollen bundle of nerves. He was tempted to smack it, lick it, anything just to get her off and put him out of his misery.

Not just from the sight of her pleasuring herself, this woman was getting to him. Days ago, he'd told her that he wanted to be able to imagine her masturbating when they had phone sex. Now he knew that he'd never get anything done if he thought about it at all.

She continued the motions, pinching her tits, touching her pussy, sliding inside herself.

He loosened his tie even more.

"I'm waiting, Sir. Did you want to give me any hints?" she teased.

That was it.

He moved quick, grabbing her up, pulling her over his lap.

"Connor!" She squealed.

He blazed his hands on her buttocks while she sought

purchase with her feet and hands. The chain swayed toward the floor, and her cry of shock became one of demand.

"I've got to have…"

He gave her what she didn't have words for, completion, raining smacks on her buttocks, a few on her upper thighs, a couple above her knees.

In silent demand, she parted her legs, and he arrowed two fingers into her cunt then forcefully pulled them back, repeatedly fucking her.

She pushed her toes against the floor, changing the angle of her hips and letting him in farther.

"Oh… God. Please. I'm going to come."

Before she'd finished speaking, he felt her vaginal walls clench. He moved his hand slightly so he could find her G-spot, and once he had, he pressed it.

She came, her orgasm dampening his fingers.

He'd never known anything so sublimely erotic.

Her chest heaved, and he left her there for a short while before turning her over. "You did a damn fine job, little Lara."

"Does that make me a master masturbator?"

"Let's see what other skills you have."

She pushed away a little and asked, "What did you have in mind?"

He pulled off his tie and dropped it next to them on the couch.

"Mmm," she said.

Without being asked, she unfastened his buttons, not stopping until they were all open and she had her hands on his chest.

"Condom, in the nightstand," he said.

"I'll get one." She nodded and slid off his lap.

She took a step and swayed slightly, then put her forearm under her breasts—likely to stop the clips from swaying. They'd been on there long enough for her to really feel them, but she didn't protest.

He stood and undressed. "Put it on me," he instructed when she returned.

Lara, in her naked, clamped glory, knelt in front of him.

Instead of tearing the packet, she reached for him, closing her hand around his shaft and moving in full strokes that made him even harder.

Then she took him in her mouth, swirling her tongue around the head before pressing it to the tender, most sensitive part underneath.

He pulled on her hair and she continued to lick and suck him, drawing him deep. "You're damn sexy, little Lara."

She moaned against his glans, and the resulting sensation almost made him come.

Connor rocked his hips, pushing himself into her mouth, and she knelt up and took more.

As he went deeper, tears streamed down her face, smearing her mascara. He'd never been more aroused. "I want to be in your cunt," he said.

For a few seconds, she continued, while looking up at him through her lashes.

"I'm warning you," he said, voice gruff.

"Yes, Sir," she whispered after she'd eased back.

She managed to tear the packet then pull out the lubricated latex. Watching her roll the condom down his cock kept him turned on.

He sat on the couch and helped her up before settling her over his lap, facing him.

Lara moved a hand between him to help guide his cock into her wet and willing pussy.

"I like having you in me, Sir," she said. She sank all the way down and exhaled a breathy sigh before holding onto his shoulders.

"Wait." He reached over and picked up his tie. "Hands behind you."

She adjusted her position, pushing off, working her hips backward so she could support her weight. Each motion made him even hotter for her.

He reached around her to secure her wrists with the silk tie. "Tight enough?"

She pulled against the fabric, and that caused her to arch,

forcing her breasts out more. The chain attached to her nipple clamps swung gently.

"Yes," she replied.

"Now ride me, girl." He put his hands on her hips to guide her, and she rocked to and fro, lifting up, allowing herself to drift down.

"You feel bigger this way. Deeper."

They moved together, building a forceful rhythm.

"Yes, yes," she said. "So hard. So good."

He lifted her higher, brought her down harder.

"Sir!"

"Yeah," he said. "Come. Squeeze my dick."

Her legs began to tremble. He reached up to yank off the alligators and she screamed, pitching forward, clamping down on his shaft.

Her orgasm drove his, and he ejaculated, the pulse of each stream making him jerk. She stayed where she was, as if immobilized, and he continued to push up inside her for several more seconds.

Finally, tension left her body.

She rested her head on his shoulder. "I had no idea."

He hadn't, either.

Because he'd never spent this much time with a woman, he hadn't known what it was like to be constantly intrigued by someone so eager. Not just any woman, but a submissive one.

He held her for a bit. While he'd always enjoyed giving aftercare, until her, it hadn't felt so essential.

He removed her silken bond, and she put her hands on either side of his face. "How are your nipples?" he asked.

"Sore." She looked at him, and there was a wry twist to her lips. "That was mean."

"If they had been a different type of clamp, maybe," he replied. "Those are lightweight, and they came off easily."

"In your opinion," she countered.

"Made you climax."

She sought a response, wrinkling her nose. "There is that."

He juggled her off his lap and put his hands on her waist

to support her until she found her footing.

The doorbell rang from the lobby.

"Pizza," a voice said when he answered.

"That was fast."

Lara scooped up her clothes and scampered toward the bedroom while he quickly disposed of the condom and yanked his pants on then buzzed the guy up.

When she returned, he inhaled the faint scent of magnolias, and her hair was piled on top of her head. Her skin was slightly damp and she had on one of his long-sleeved shirts. She'd rolled up the sleeves and secured the cuffs above her elbows. The top button was open, and she'd skipped the bottom two, as well.

Since the material didn't appear to be starched, he guessed she'd grabbed the shirt from the dry-cleaning bag. "You could have chosen an unworn one," he said.

"This one smelled like you."

Everything in his body became slow-moving. He looked at her a second time. "You're not wearing any undergarments."

"No, Sir. I'm not."

God help him.

He deliberately focused on dinner. Anything other than the sensual daze she'd plunged him into.

When he'd insisted she move in with him, he hadn't thought through everything that would be involved. He'd figured out how to share the closet and the bathroom and mentally sorted through the logistics of sharing an office. But he hadn't considered the small, intimate moments such as sharing a pot of coffee, a fine merlot, or deciding what to eat for dinner. He'd never imagined she'd put on his clothes, or that she'd look so fucking hot when she did.

He had the sensation that he was in emotional quicksand, and he'd walked in willingly.

"Where are the plates?" she asked.

When he didn't respond right away, she drew her eyebrows together. "What? Seeing me half-naked is bothering you?" she asked, voice light with teasing.

"I may put you in a snowsuit," he said.

"But then you won't see my nipples, all hard from the scratchiness of your shirt."

"Some Doms like to put electrical tape on their sub's nipples."

She gasped.

"Don't push me, little Lara. I will find a way to avoid temptation." Or maybe he'd skip that and just keep her tied up and fucked all day, every day. The second thought appealed to him most of all.

"Looks yummy," she said, flipping open the lid of the pizza box. "You were in charge of the plates," she reminded him.

"Plates," he repeated, and she laughed.

He shook his head to clear his brain circuits and took down plates from a cabinet. Then he pulled a shaker of Parmesan cheese from the refrigerator and put it on the counter.

She scooped out a slice of the pizza for him then selected one for herself.

"Cheese?" he offered.

"No, thanks." The box had several packets of crushed red pepper tucked inside. She picked up one, ripped it open, then she covered her entire slice with the spicy stuff.

"I wouldn't be able to eat for a week if I did that."

"They're delicious. Lots of nutrients."

"Sure."

"No. Really. They have vitamin A"—she tipped her head to the side—"and anti-inflammatory properties." Not waiting until they moved from the kitchen counter, she took a big bite, and her eyes instantly watered. "That one was hot." She started to cough.

"CPR is not on the menu," he cautioned.

"How about mouth-to-mouth?"

"That could be."

She looked at the pizza then back at him. That made her laugh, and the combination of that with her coughing made him hurry to fetch her a small glass of milk.

"Drink."

She downed it in two gulps, and the coughing stopped.

"Your milk mustache is attractive."

She ripped off a square from the paper towel roll and immediately pressed it to her lips. After she pulled it back, she looked at it then glared at him. "There was no milk mustache."

"No. There wasn't. But that look on your face was priceless."

She wadded the paper towel and threw it at him.

He caught it and tossed it in the trash can.

"Peppers?" she offered, holding up her half-empty packet.

"I think I'll skip them." He added a couple of liberal shakes of cheese to his slice, then closed up the box. "Let's eat in the living room."

She wrinkled her nose. "That seems like it should be off limits for you."

"Pizza is the exception to almost every rule."

"What other rules?"

He pretended not to notice the way she shook some of the peppers from her slice. "The ones about healthy eating and watching television."

"Television?"

"And I'll let you pick the movie."

"I like chick flicks," she warned. Then she floored him by adding, "Like *Indiana Jones*."

"I object. *Indiana Jones* is action-adventure, not a chick flick," he protested. "That franchise is the coolest thing on the planet for men."

"So why is Indy so appealing to women?" she demanded. "Besides the whip?"

"You tell me."

"He's gorgeous, for one. And the hat. Did I mention the whip?"

"I have a great whip."

"And you're pretty good with it, too. Well, as far as I can tell, that is. Maybe if I had a little more experience, I'd be a better judge." She ripped a couple of more pieces of paper towel to use as napkins then followed him into the living room.

He sat. In invitation, he patted the couch cushion next to him. Her hesitation was slight, but discernible.

With a small shrug that he wouldn't have noticed if he hadn't been watching, she joined him. "What else?" he asked.

"He's a pretty good dresser. Well, for an archeologist. You've got better taste. But you don't have a hat. A hat would complete your whip outfit."

"I'll keep it in mind." He picked up the remote and scrolled through the available movie titles, though he had to admit, the earlier music had been an excellent idea.

"Stop," she ordered when she saw her choice of movie.

He pushed the button to make the selection, and the familiar theme began to play. "You haven't convinced me it's a chick flick."

"Chick flicks make women all melty," she said. "And thinking about your single tail and a hat makes me all melty. I win."

He shook his head. "Maybe I should take a whip to the office."

"Only if you want me visiting you at work every day."

"You know..." He studied her.

She was ripping a piece off her pizza crust, and she paused.

"You, over my desk, begging for my lash? Show up anytime."

Something heated throbbed between them. Not that it surprised him. It was always there, just waiting. "Let me get your wine," he said to divert both of them.

"Thanks."

He retrieved her glass from the far side of the room then set it down in front of them. "I'll never look at the coffee table the same way again," he said.

She snuggled into him, but pulled away and sat up to cheer when she saw Indy and his whip for the first time. "Can you really do things like him? Like wrap it around people's wrists and yank swords out of their hands?"

"I imagine you can with a bullwhip."

She shivered then settled back against his body.

For the next couple of hours, while they kept reality at bay—the upcoming board meeting, Lara going behind her father's back and working out the final details of their agreement—he had a glimpse of what the future might look like.

As the credits eventually scrolled, reality encroached.

She moved out of his arms, and he reached for the remote to kill the television.

Lara picked up the dishes and carried them into the kitchen.

"It's late," she told him.

"You could stay."

"We'd have to get up ridiculously early so that you could get me home in time for me to get ready and pick up my car."

He nodded. The drive time would allow them to talk, as well. "You're welcome to leave anything you want here."

Explaining that she needed everything at home, she repacked her bag. More than anything, it was a reminder that she still hadn't agreed to move in.

Once they were on the road, he brought that up. "Have you given any further thought to our living arrangements?"

She tightened her grip on her purse.

Since the evening was breezy, she was using his shirt as a jacket over her dress. He liked the combination.

"I see your point about living downtown," she said hesitatingly. "But I already come in every day. We could commute together."

"Or walk in ten minutes."

"Honestly, it's more than that. I'd have a difficult time giving up my place. Even if it was only for a couple of years."

"Three years," he corrected.

She turned toward him. In the shadows of the setting sun, she added, "And the whole thing about being a submissive..."

"You hated this weekend?"

"That's not it. It's a lot of responsibility."

"And something that will evolve as we work on it."

"I left your necklace on the dresser."

"I see."

"It's a beautiful piece," she hastened to say. "But a hell of a representation about our relationship that I'm not ready to make."

"Understood." That didn't mean he liked the sting of her rejection, especially after what they'd shared. "You know, Lara, I'm not going to force any of this. You came to me with a proposal. If you've changed your mind, I understand. I can drop you off and we can part friends. Think about it. If you still want to pursue it, I want this agreement signed before Tuesday's board meeting."

An hour before the alarm clock rang, Lara gave up the battle and climbed out of bed. As she moved, her abdominal muscles protested the quick movement. In fact, her entire body carried reminders of the weekend. Her buttocks hurt, from his spankings as well as his single tail. Her pussy was tender. Even her ass felt a little sensitive from being reamed by his finger.

She paused for a moment, unable to decide whether a shower or a cup of coffee was the first order of business.

Shower, she eventually decided, since it would help with the soreness in her shoulder muscles. It seemed no part of her body had escaped his particular brand of torment.

And damn it, she'd enjoyed it all.

She turned the shower spray on full blast and set the heat to as high as she could tolerate.

Last night, she'd hardly slept, and she'd awakened a dozen times. She'd tossed, turned, punched the pillow, tried to shove away thoughts of Connor. Even when she'd drifted off, thoughts of him had haunted her. She'd recalled his touch, the feel of his hand blazing across her bare buttocks, the bite from the alligator clamps, the salty taste of his pre-cum spilling into her mouth, the constriction of her vaginal muscles as she'd sat in his lap and ridden him.

In the middle of the night, his words about their potential marriage had returned to haunt her.

And now, she had to face them.

Like Connor had said, if she were serious about moving BHI forward, she needed to commit to a plan of action with him.

She'd recognized that he was right. Once a course of action

was set, it made sense not to deviate unless a compelling reason presented itself.

That meant signing their agreement.

So what was she willing to concede?

The whole submission thing? Living arrangements? The next few years of her life?

The weekend had shown her how difficult things might be, and not because she disliked him, but because she was starting to care about him. Watching television together, snuggling, oohing and ahhing over Indy's antics—particularly the ones that involved his kangaroo-hide bullwhip had been fun—more fun than she'd ever had with a man. For someone so rigid, he'd laughed with her, teased her. The way he'd interacted with her mother and his family had shown her how much respect he had for other people. His reaction to Suzy-Q's enthusiasm had been the magical ingredient that had really melted her heart.

Even now, she craved his touch.

She took a minute to consider the thoughts that had loomed so large last night. Other than her feminine fear of Connor and the power he would wield in her life, there was no reason for her to abandon her course of action. That didn't mean the threat he posed wasn't real. It just meant that she had to figure out how to deal with him, give him just enough for him to feel as if he had what he needed. At the same time, that meant she had to figure out how to protect her emotions.

That, she realized, would be the most difficult thing of all.

No matter what, Connor was determined not to fall in love. She understood, particularly after being around his family, understanding the dynamics, his very real obligations and the loss they'd all endured. But none of that made it easier for her.

The water ran cold before she turned it off.

Still, she had obligations, as well, to herself, to BHI, to her father, to their thousands of employees. And being with Connor for a few years would provide real, solid solutions. She could sacrifice for a while. Learn to compartmentalize the way he did.

With a new sense of determination, she dried off.

Connor's shirt was draped across one of the rods in her closet. Instead of putting on a robe, she reached for the shirt and fastened only the middle few buttons.

Since it was still early, she waited for the coffee to brew then took her first cup out onto the patio, along with her phone.

There was a message from her mother saying she'd already contacted the board members and that they would be at the meeting. As Lara had expected, her mother had wasted no time.

But Connor hadn't sent either an email or a text. Though it didn't surprise her, it left her somewhat disappointed. She told herself that maybe he was waiting for her to reach out to him with a firm decision. She understood that he wasn't a man who liked to waste time. Then again, maybe he hadn't spent the entire night thinking about her the way she'd been consumed by him.

A small part of her wished she'd spent the night. None of these thoughts would be burrowing around in her brain. No matter what she battled, she knew he'd be there with her. And it was so damn easy to give in to the temptation of turning to him.

The sun had lightened the sky enough for her to walk around the yard, deadheading flowers and watering the potted plants. She fed the few fish that remained in the pond then grabbed her empty cup and phone and went inside to finish getting ready for the day. All the while, she expected Connor to contact her, but he didn't.

She drove to a coffee shop for an extra-large, quadruple-shot caramel latte and a breakfast sandwich. After one sip, she knew she would have preferred one of Thompson's excellent coffees. Funny, until now, a latte had been her daily favorite.

At nine o'clock, she grabbed the report she'd put together after Friday's meeting with the VP of Technology and walked to the conference room for her regular Monday meeting with her father.

When he hadn't arrived by ten after the hour, she wandered down to his office.

Venessa, his assistant, said he'd just called to say he was running late. He'd breakfasted with one of his civic groups and gotten caught in conversation.

"Can we reschedule for ten o'clock?" Lara asked.

"He's leaving for lunch at ten-thirty. Does half an hour give you enough time?"

To grab an ibuprofen for the headache that was gathering, perhaps. "Just tell him to call when he arrives."

Venessa jotted a note to do so.

Back in her office, Lara's cell phone was blinking. There was a message from Connor informing her that Texas had a mandatory seventy-two hour waiting period for marriage licenses.

He suggested they pick it up today if they wanted to execute it by the end of the week.

Execute was never a word she would have put in the same sentence with the certificate of her marriage, and it summed up her confusion. A business arrangement where they lived separately made sense in her mind. But living with him, watching a movie, having sex, sleeping in the same bed, sharing the same space, made it so much more.

Telling herself she was being ridiculous, she replied that his suggestion made sense.

He immediately responded with an address on Caroline Street downtown, and he added, third floor. He suggested they meet at two o'clock, after the lunch rush, and added that April was driving him and they could pick her up, if that would be easier for her.

Lara was still considering his offer, thinking through her options of accepting the ride, searching for parking or hailing a cab, when she received an emailed invitation to be an administrator on his calendar.

She had a vague recollection of him making that suggestion over the weekend but that he'd remembered to have Thompson handle it surprised her. How Connor kept his millions of promises straight, she had no idea.

Realizing she was taking one more step toward him, she accepted.

As the template in front of her populated, she was shocked. He had a dizzying array of appointments, some of them with BHI competitors. He also had chunks of time blocked out for planning, budgeting and strategy. Some afternoons, he had meetings scheduled every forty-five minutes. The BHI board meeting was already on there, as was their upcoming appointment, and a few hours on Friday afternoon marked as personal and unavailable.

A phone call from Venessa interrupted her study. Venessa said that Pernell had decided to work from his country club rather than driving all over town. He suggested they meet tomorrow morning instead.

Any doubts that she was doing the right thing vanished.

For whatever reasons he had, Pernell was no longer fully engaged in the business. Maybe fear? Maybe lack of interest? Maybe a mistaken belief that things ran well without his input. It didn't matter where the truth was. He was impeding the ability to get business done.

She realized that she should have been pushing even harder for him to retire, or at least semi-retire. "Actually, if you can, put a board meeting on his calendar for tomorrow at five."

"I don't see any conflicts," Venessa said. "But he doesn't always tell me if he has things in the evenings."

"Understood. Thanks, Venessa."

Lara reached her father's voicemail and requested he return her call. She said she would be in his office at four o'clock tomorrow for a private meeting, and she added that it was urgent.

Finally she messaged Connor to let him know she'd appreciate a ride this afternoon. That done, she waited for a feeling of relief.

It didn't come. Instead, she had the sensation she'd just stepped onto a rollercoaster.

"A genius is trying to reach you."

Music shattered the silence. All of a sudden, Connor's office sounded like the inside of a movie theater, with a decibel level to match. "What the hell?" Connor demanded, looking over at Thompson.

"I think that's your phone, sir," the man replied with a grin.

Connor grabbed his phone from the desktop. He went to turn off the ringer, but it was already in silent mode.

"Has to be Mr. Bonds," Thompson said. "Right on!"

Around them, the action-adventure theme increased in volume. Connor realized it was now also coming from the computer's speaker.

"That's some shit," Thompson approved.

Having no other choice, Connor answered the call. Rather than all the noise instantly ceasing, the music coming from the computer gently faded. "I'm done using your prototypes," Connor said, instead of greeting his old friend.

"I'll take them," Thompson said.

Connor scowled and Thompson's expression sobered. "I'll be handling some filing in my office," he said.

Thompson closed the door behind him.

"What?" Julien demanded. "You don't like my theme song? It's gone through a lot of revisions. We're up to eighty-three percent of respondents saying it's very identifiable. Astounding number. Thinking about using it on a game, as well. Imagine, me as a video game hero. I wasn't happy with the jawline. They didn't quite do a good enough job."

"How the hell did you know I wasn't in the middle of something pressing?" Connor demanded.

"That's not possible. I hadn't called you yet."

"There are things in the world other than you that are important."

A moment of silence followed. "There are?"

Having no other option, Connor sat back. "What gives?" Besides the fact Julien wanted to own a piece of technology developed by Donovan Worldwide. He insisted it would give his next generation phone an edge in the Holy Grail of electronics. Battery life.

"You tell me. There's only one reason you're going to Caroline Street with one Ms. Lara Marie Bertrand this afternoon."

Christ. Even Connor didn't know Lara's middle name. And wait… "How the hell do you know…?" He trailed off as tension settled at the base of his skull. "The calendar program," he guessed.

"It's something, isn't it? We developed the initial app for a restaurant in New Mexico. Thompson agreed to beta test an upgrade for corporate use."

"And gave you direct access to my personal life."

"It's for your own good. I was planning a trip to Houston, so I thought I'd see when it was best for you."

"Instead of calling and asking?"

"And inconvenience both of us? What would be the point in that?" Julien countered. "But then I figured out you were getting married, so I wanted to talk about that. Hence the call."

"I never said I was getting married."

"You and Ms. Bertrand are going to the courthouse building today. There are a limited number of offices there."

"All civil," Connor countered.

"True. And I considered that, actually. But there's a seventy-two hour cooling off period in your state. Which means a logical time for you to get married would be Thursday or Friday. And you blocked Friday afternoon out for personal reasons. And…tomorrow, after hours, you have a meeting with the BHI board of directors."

"You should have been a spy."

"I would make a good one, wouldn't I?"

"Still, assuming Lara and I are getting married is a big stretch."

"And Ms. Bertrand has been added as an administrator on your calendar. The only people who get that right are personal assistants and spouses."

He thought to ask if there was anything Julien didn't know. But the answer was obvious.

"I assume my invitation is in the mail," Julien said.

Connor sighed. Sitting back in his chair, he explained, "It's a business matter."

"Ah."

"I looked her up. I wouldn't poke my eye out if she crawled into bed next to me."

"One more crack and this conversation is over."

"You're marrying a beautiful woman, Connor. And it's a *business matter*? Then you are either blind or stupid. She's Pernell's only heir. And according to sources, she's fucking brilliant with money."

"Sources?"

"She was an intern at one of my companies."

No surprise there. Connor nodded.

"She doesn't consider herself an entrepreneur," Julien continued.

"That wouldn't have come from a confidential HR file, would it?"

"Perish the thought. I'd never be so crass."

Connor remained skeptical.

"She can do amazing analytics and risk assessments, but developing new ideas isn't something she has a desire to do. And, my friend, that's your forte. So why is it simply a business arrangement? It looks like a match made in corporate heaven."

"You ever met a relationship you didn't want to meddle in?"

"What's the sticking point? I mean, besides you being an asshole."

Nothing like old friends to give you medicine without sugar. "You know better than anyone that love is messy."

"It is. And that's what makes it so...oozingly delicious."

Connor shook his head. "It's not that easy."

"Be bold," Julien said. "You're not responsible for anyone else's mess. It's time you saw that. You're a different person than your father. You wouldn't make the same choices he did."

He recoiled. No one else but Julien Bonds would have the guts to say words like that. But he supposed it was easy to be a sage when you were examining someone else's life and didn't have to live with the consequences.

"So I take it I'm not on the guest list after saying that. No, wait. I'm confused. I was never on it, anyway. I might as well say anything I want."

"There is no guest list."

"Pity. Every woman wants a wedding."

"This one would prefer there was nothing other than a legal certificate. Wants to live in her own house and pretend we're not married."

"Can you blame her?"

The tension sledgehammered the back of his neck. "I might add it was her idea to begin with."

"Judging by what we know of Pernell, I'm guessing your bride-to-be needed some support. So my guess is she offered you something in return, a seat on the board, the opportunity for you to acquire the communications division. A sacrificial lamb, as it were. Unless you'd bend a little and offer some love, I wouldn't want to live with you, either."

"Thanks for that."

"Anyway, I'll be in Houston sometime next week. I have a real estate investor who wants me to look at sites for a new retail store."

"Galleria area?"

"Among them, yes."

He was intrigued.

"I'd love to meet the new Mrs. Donovan while I'm there."

"I'll keep you advised."

"No need. I'll calendar it for you. Let me know what changes. I do love shopping for wedding gifts."

"Save your money." He ended the call.

Julien's words haunted the rest of his morning and they were still on his mind when he and April arrived in front of Lara's office building.

She was standing inside the revolving door, and she pushed through it the moment he opened the car door.

At the sight of her, something sparked inside him, a recognition, an attraction, a feeling of possession. Today she wore classic pumps, an above-the-knee skirt, white blouse and a blazer. Her purse hung from her shoulder.

No matter what she put on, from that slinky thing on Saturday evening to one of his shirts last night, he responded to her.

She'd covered her eyes with sunglasses.

Her smile looked polite. He knew enough to realize it was strained.

He kissed her cheek, but she didn't respond.

Instead, she accepted his hand into the car and told April how much she appreciated the ride.

He slid in beside her, and she removed the sunglasses. It was then that he noticed the tension edged beside her mouth and eyes.

Julien's words plowed into him again. "Anything I can do for you?" he asked.

"No." She shook her head. "I just need to get through tomorrow."

"Trouble?"

She updated him on the fact her father hadn't shown up for work this morning so she hadn't had the opportunity to discuss the report she'd compiled after her Friday meeting with BHI's VP of Technology. "I can work on the financials," she said, "begin some due diligence, but if my father won't consider the proposal to sell the package of patents to Bonds—"

"Patents for?"

She closed her mouth. "I shouldn't have said that much. I forgot that you know him. You and I haven't signed anything yet. At the very least, we need a non-disclosure in place before I tell you anything else."

"Are they part of the communications deal?"

"No."

Then it was technology. And if they had value to Julien,

they could have value to Donovan. He admired her determination to protect BHI. As CFO, that was paramount. And yet, as the man she'd ridden yesterday afternoon, the man who'd guided her through her first submissive steps, he wanted her to turn to him. He wanted to help her battle the dragons.

"You received a copy of the invitation I sent to the board. I listed you as a special presenter. I left Dad a message about the whole thing, and I scheduled a four o'clock with him tomorrow."

"Any response?"

"No." She rubbed her arms.

He could only imagine what was going on inside her head. He knew there was a part of her that felt as if she was doing something dishonorable. "No matter how he reacts, you're doing the right thing."

"I know. Or at least I think I do."

"There's no guarantee the board will agree with my communications proposal," he reminded her.

"True."

"But they have a right to hear it."

"Damn right. And we certainly do need your input." She tipped her head back. "What if it's all for nothing? What if we can't convince them and the company keeps going the way it has?"

"That could happen," he agreed.

She pulled away and turned so she could face him. "That's reassuring."

"I've told you, Lara. I don't lie to you. It is a possibility. A real one. But it's the worst possible outcome. More likely we'll end up with less than we want and more than we expected. But know this, we'll do the best we can. We'll send the strategy to your mother in the morning for her feedback. And we'll consider what you'll say to your father. If it's not good enough, we'll regroup. I'll still have a place at the table for several years. Change is inevitable."

"You never give up."

"What's that saying? With enough time and determination,

you can piss a hole in a rock."

"Thank you for that." She grinned and allowed her shoulders to rest against the seat.

"Have you heard from your mother this morning?"

"A couple of times. She mentioned that you sent over a copy of the communications division proposal. She's got almost everyone lined up for tomorrow's meeting. She has a couple of calls in to my dad, but he hasn't spoken to her, either. And before you ask, no. I'm not surprised."

They arrived at the county building, and they rode to the third floor in silence. She held on to her purse and stared straight ahead.

The tension that he'd thought had left her was back, judging by the set of her chin.

There was another couple already with the clerk, so he and Lara took a seat. The pair had their hands linked, and they kept looking at each other. They were informing the clerk of their honeymoon plans. Then the soon-to-be groom leaned over and kissed his fiancée.

Lara turned away and busied herself flipping through the pages of a popular personal finance magazine.

The couple stood, and the man hugged his future bride.

Lara didn't look up.

Finally, the clerk called out, "Next!" and waved them over.

Connor held Lara's chair, and they each dug out their driver's licenses and answered the required battery of questions. He paid the fee.

A few minutes later, the clerk gave them some final instructions for returning the signed document then wished them much happiness for the future.

He scooped up the manila envelope containing the oversized document and followed Lara to the elevator.

"It took longer to drive over here than it did to get the license," she said.

Far less time than he'd budgeted.

In the car, he asked, "Do you have time for a coffee?"

"Yes. I was actually hoping we'd have a chance to talk."

April whisked them to a local coffee shop.

Surprising him, Lara ordered a large raspberry lemonade. "I need to be able to sleep tonight," she said. "Last night was rough."

"You never have to do it alone," he said.

Because of the time of day, they were able to find a quiet table in a back corner.

"I've decided you're right," she said. "Let's get the agreement over to our lawyers. I'll move in with you. I can rent out my place, put my things in storage. But the limit is two years."

"I was willing to consider moving into your house."

"I've changed my mind about that."

He noticed that she kept stirring the lemonade rather than drinking it. "Any particular reason?" he asked.

"The soaker tub."

He looked at her. "And if you were more serious?"

She sighed. "My place is better for families, for entertaining. Your loft suits our lifestyle better."

Connor nodded.

"And if the rumors about your prowess are true..."

He raised his eyebrows.

"Which I'm inclined to believe they are..." She gave a small smile that erased the uneasiness that had been bubbling.

"Go on."

"Then two years is plenty of time for you to set plans in motion for BHI's future, help my father see we need some restructuring. I'm not suggesting it won't be a lot of work. But I've already seen what you can do when you focus your energy."

"Well played," he approved.

"As for addendum A—"

"The one outlining your role as my submissive."

A pretty shade of pink stained her cheeks, and she swirled her straw before looking up at him. "I'm willing to agree to all of that in exchange for the two-year concession."

"You drive a hard bargain."

"Which means we have an agreement," she said.

"I'll send you a revised copy today. We can be married Friday afternoon."

Slowly, she nodded. "I wondered about that time you had blocked off on your calendar."

"For you." Then he amended, "Us."

"You'll handle the arrangements?"

"If that's what you want. If it's important to you that you make the plans—"

"It's not."

He wondered how true that was. But her eyes gave nothing away. "I have a friend who's a judge. We can go to his office. Or I'm sure he'll be willing to meet at mine."

"Let's go to his. Fewer people that we may have to explain to."

"As for witnesses?"

For long minutes, she toyed with her straw. He wondered belatedly if she'd even taken a sip. "I don't want to invite anyone."

Julien's words about every woman wanting a wedding haunted him again. But then, he reminded himself, it didn't mean she wouldn't have a real one. Just not to him.

That thought brought him up short. The idea of her with someone else, looking forward to the future with another man, pissed him off, though rationally he knew it shouldn't. "I'd like you to move in sooner, rather than later."

"How soon?"

"Tonight."

This time, she met his gaze fully.

"We'll need to touch base with your mother and ensure we have an agenda put together for the meeting. We have a script that we need to write, and we'll want to practice it so it flows well. It would be nice to have your mother's feedback on it."

"She'd love that."

"It will be easier to do if we're together."

He saw the battle rage across her face. First came her frown of denial. It was followed by her rolling her head in a slow motion. Finally, she gave him a sharp nod. "Agreed."

What he didn't tell her was that he'd be there to hold her, protect her, shore her up when doubt about her dad, about them, crept in. "You can pick me up after work, and we'll go to your house to pack up a few things."

"With the way you're dressed?"

"I have a change of clothes in my office."

"Of course you do."

"We'll get a crew for anything big, but the two of us should be able to manage the personal items that you'll be needing."

She moved the drink to the side. It was still full, and condensation dripped down the outside of the plastic cup. "Is fast the only speed you know?"

"I've learned that we don't always have as much time on the earth as we think we do. Tomorrow we have the board meeting. Wednesday we need to select rings. Pick me up at five?"

"I should get back," she told him, and her voice sounded strained.

He nodded.

After dropping her back in front of BHI, he returned to work. The first thing he did was call up their prenuptial agreement. He changed the term of the contract to two years and made the confidentiality agreement more expansive, noting the information could be shared as long as they were in accord. Before he sent it to her for perusal, he couldn't help but scan addendum A.

Already, she'd been incredible during their sex play, adventurous and eager. He couldn't remember having been with anyone who was more perfect for him.

The opportunity to have her in his bed every night vanquished the doubts that Julien's words had raised.

Satisfied, he sent it over to her then got back to work.

A few minutes later, she sent him a fairly standard non-disclosure agreement. Smart woman. Within half an hour, she sent him back the prenuptial contract.

Confused, he opened it and didn't immediately see any

changes. Instead of assuming there were none, he opened a program to compare the two documents. There was a change, to addendum B.

Wife does not cook.

He grinned.
Instead of revising the contract, he sent her an email.

Husband agrees.

Within minutes, she informed him that their duly revised prenuptial had been forwarded to her personal attorney for further review and reminded him that the lawyer would no doubt advise that his addenda would never stand up in court.

In that case, I'd like dinner on the table at 5:30 every night.

Her reply was almost instant.

What do attorneys know, anyway?

He appreciated her attempts to make things easier between them. She didn't have to, he knew. So her efforts were doubly appreciated.
By the time she pulled up to the curb a few hours later, he was dressed in casual clothes and waiting for her. To her credit, she was two minutes early.
"You don't mind if I drive?" she asked when he shut his door.
"Why? Are you terrible at it?"
"Of course not." She checked her mirrors before pulling onto the street. "I thought it might be something that you wanted to control."
"I appreciate that. But, no. My father's accident was a random-odds thing. A tire cut by debris, combined with speed and the angle of impact." He could discuss that part

of it dispassionately. He'd read the report, saw the logic, could recite the facts. It was the emotional loss that he'd never sorted through.

She stopped for a traffic signal, and he looked at her. Since it was after hours, she'd taken off her jacket, leaving her arms bare.

"What?" she asked, glancing over at him.

"I'm thinking about later."

"What part?"

He swept his gaze over her, his intention clear, and her breath caught.

"Oh. That," she said.

That was real—and good—between them.

He suggested they stop at the local hardware store for boxes then he asked a customer service representative for help finding the black electrical tape.

"Electrical tape?" Lara asked as they headed toward the appropriate aisle.

"For your nipples," he reminded her.

She gasped. "You can't be serious."

"You never know."

The whole time they checked out, she looked from him, to the tape, then back.

While they drove to her house, he asked if she had a favorite local Chinese restaurant.

She handed over her phone and told him the name. "It's under my favorites tab."

"What do you want?"

"Mongolian beef. Spicy. And crab wontons. And eggrolls."

"You hungry?"

She shrugged. "I missed lunch."

He called in the order and asked for it to be delivered around six-thirty. After he hung up, he said to her, "Why am I not surprised you ordered the spiciest thing on the menu?"

"How do you know that?"

"The man on the phone said so."

Suzy-Q greeted them when they got out of the car.

First, she put her giant paws on his shoulders and gave him a sloppy upstroke kiss. Then she did the same to Lara.

Mrs. Fuhrman came running out of her house, wearing pink rollers in her blueish-purple hair and waving a leash.

"I've no idea what's gotten into her," the woman said. "She never misbehaves."

Connor met Lara's gaze and they both suppressed their smiles.

Connor clipped the mastiff mix back onto her leash and turned her over to Mrs. Fuhrman.

"You're the moving man, aren't you?"

"You could say that," he replied, grabbing a handful of boxes from the trunk.

"We'll miss you, Lara," Mrs. Fuhrman said. Then, making soothing sounds to Suzy-Q, she took the dog home.

"I'm convinced she sends the dog over here," Connor said.

"It's the only way she gets to talk to a handsome man."

"In that case—"

"Wait. I take it back."

"You think I'm handsome," he said.

"I forgot about the colossal ego."

He grinned. "Can you grab the bag with the electrical tape?"

She shot him a scowl, but did as he asked.

Inside, he began to tape boxes together, and she answered the door when the food arrived.

She set it all out on the counter, then took out paper plates and napkins and two bottles of Shiner Bock, his favorite beer. And it was Texas made.

The whole time she worked, her gaze kept straying to the electrical tape. "Seriously, what's it for?"

"Your nipples."

She sighed.

They went into the backyard to eat, and he had to concede the place was gorgeous.

He uncapped the beers, and they touched the tops together.

She demolished a couple of wontons and an eggroll before diving into the Mongolian beef. The amount that she consumed before taking a drink surprised him. "So the choking thing on the crushed red peppers last night was an isolated incident."

"I told you."

For a few minutes, they sat together on the swing, and he understood what she meant about her house. It was an ideal place for backyard barbecues, for family time. Definitely a contrast to his urban fervor.

"Only thing that could make it perfect is a hot tub," she said.

If he lived here, he'd definitely install one.

They returned inside and she cleaned up the kitchen.

"What are the most important things for you to take for now? We need to get through the next few days and we should get back to my place as soon as we can to give us adequate time to work. We can come back over the weekend and take care of the rest of the stuff."

She nodded. "Shoes. Clothing. My notebook computer. Well, all my electronics. Running shoes. Workout clothes. My curling iron. Brushes. Makeup. Shampoo."

"Magnolia soap."

"I think I left some at your house."

"It will be all gone tonight."

"It will? Okay, then. Magnolia soap."

"What do you want me to pack?"

"Actually…none of it. I want to be sure I have what I need."

"Okay. You pack. I'll load the car."

"That will work."

"But first…"

She was headed toward the bedroom, but she stopped. "Yes?"

He cut off four pieces of the electrical tape and lined them up along the kitchen counter. "Unfasten your bra."

"What…?" she asked, but her voice had a dreamy, rather than outraged, quality.

"I want you aware of addendum A. And nipple clamps would be cruel. You'll be aware of the tape, though."

"Connor... Sir..."

"Unfasten your bra, Lara."

She reached beneath her shirt and did so.

"Now lift your shirt." He picked off two of the pieces and went to her.

He squeezed her nipple gently, then harder. Then, when she closed her eyes, with even more force. He tugged it, yanked it, made it hard, pulled her onto her toes and caught her when she moaned and wrapped her arms around his neck.

He kissed the side of her neck, inhaled her scent, unable to get enough of her. She'd said she'd had a rough night, but the truth was, so had he. He'd wanted her with him, thought about her, considered all the ways he wanted to claim her and make sure she knew she was his.

He set her back from him. While her nipple was still like a tiny rock, he put the tape on, in the shape of an X.

"That's..."

"How is it?"

"Tight. Uncomfortable."

"On a scale of one to ten. The lower end merely being an irritant."

"Two," she replied after some consideration.

"Good. Now the other one." He repeated the process, tormenting her until she moaned and begged him to either stop or let her have an orgasm. "That's the reward for finishing the move," he replied. He went over to the kitchen counter for the other pieces of tape. After the second X was in place he nodded, pleased. "Incentive," he told her. For both of them. "You're welcome to refasten your bra or leave it off, your call. But if I had my way, you'd wear a white T-shirt and that demi-bra you wore to my office last Friday."

"I think a sports bra," she countered, "so I feel nothing and my breasts don't move at all."

He followed her into the bedroom and watched her

change into a pair of shorts. She hesitated before pulling out a white T-shirt. Then deliberately, very deliberately, she opened her second drawer and selected a demi-bra.

He was reminded, again, that she was the perfect sub.

She pulled off her blouse and tossed it onto the covers of her unmade bed. Then she removed the bra she'd worn to work.

Finally she put on the demi-bra, and he moved into adjust it for her, folding down the little line of lace and positioning her breasts in the cups so that he could see most of the electrical tape.

She didn't protest, and she kept her gaze on him. Trust was there, and he treasured it. Through her shirt, he traced the X on each of her breasts. "I can't wait to take it off later."

"I think it will hurt."

"I'm sure it will."

Lara closed her eyes and pressed her lips together.

"Your responses are intoxicating," he told her.

"I think the tape feels tighter."

"Even better. Now let's get on with it."

She turned away, and he swatted her ass. Giving a yelp, she headed for the bathroom.

A few minutes later, he took a box to her. She'd piled a bunch of personal effects on the vanity, and he said, "Go ahead and pack other stuff while I handle this."

For an hour, they worked together. She'd pull out her items, he'd put them in a box, seal it and stow it in the car. "Anything else?" he asked, heading back inside after filling up the trunk. "We've still got room on the back seat."

He found her on the floor, kneeling in front of her nightstand. She quickly closed the drawer.

"What do you have?"

"Nothing I need. It can stay here."

"Show me."

"This." She opened the drawer and pulled out a small bullet vibrator.

"Perfect." He held open his palm.

"I know that look," she said.

"Bring it to me."

On her knees, as he would have expected, she did so.

"You're an apt pupil. Now get on your back."

"I think whatever you have in mind is heartless," she protested.

"You can't begin to imagine how much."

She sucked in a breath.

"Are you doing to make me repeat my request?"

They both knew it wasn't a suggestion.

Lara sat on the bed then lay back. He went into the bathroom to clean the toy, and when he got back, she was still in the same position.

"Lift your hips."

She did, and he pulled her panties and shorts down to her knees.

"Now spread your legs."

Since she was already moist, the bullet slipped right into her pussy.

"What setting do you usually use?"

"I start on three. Sometimes I go as high as seven."

"And you stroke yourself while you use it? Or do you just fantasize while it's inside you?"

Her breaths were rapid. "I just imagine that I'm a captive." She turned her head to the side. "I can't believe I'm telling you this."

"And that your orgasm pleases your captor?"

"Yes," she whispered.

"Does he stand there and insist you come for him, or you'll be punished?"

She whimpered.

"Does he?" He turned the vibe on, to four.

She cried out, lifting her hips.

"What's the punishment if you displease him?"

"A spa…nking."

He flipped her over.

She screamed.

"Does he let you hump the mattress? Or does he make you stay still, miserably so? I bet he does both, doesn't he?"

She clawed at her rumpled sheets.

He took off his belt and wound it around her wrists, securing them together. Then he gave her hot little ass a sharp spank. *"Answer the question."*

"Both!"

"I bet he leaves it inside you, doesn't he, turning it up, wanting you to suffer for him first?"

"Yes. Yes."

"Does he like your misery?"

"He smiles."

"Oh, I imagine he does." He stood where he was sure she could see him. Then he turned the setting to five.

She writhed.

"And what then? Does he give you more?"

Lara scooted up, as if trying to escape the pressure.

"What happens if you come too soon, Lara, and ruin his fun? Captives are made for their master's pleasure, aren't they?"

"Yes, Sir." She turned her head.

"So you wouldn't ruin his fun, would you?"

"No. No!"

He turned up the intensity.

"Sir. Oh, Sir!"

"Rub yourself on the bed, Lara, like a needy captive."

As she moved, he turned it up again.

"What are you going to do now?"

She cried out, and the sound was garbled.

"Tell me what you want." He smacked her, right beneath the swell of her ass. The cracking sound rent the air.

"Sir! I need to come."

"Like a good little captive?"

"Yes, Sir."

"You want to please your master?"

He saw her body go rigid.

"Ask."

"Please. Please, Sir. If it pleases you, I'd like to come."

"What pleases me is to watch you suffer."

"*Oh, God.* Oh, God!"

"Count backward for me. From ten to one. Do not dare come before you get to one." His cock tented his pants. He was throbbing, almost in time to her wiggles and cries. Damn, she was everything he'd ever wanted.

"Eight."

"Hold it off or I'll make you give me five more. I don't care how much you cry and beg, captive."

His harsh words made her shout out.

"Five."

"Hold back that orgasm, my dirty princess."

She started to gulp huge sobs.

"Four."

Relentlessly, he turned the vibration up full force.

"Th…ree." She choked.

"Wait."

"Two." She locked her knees.

He reached over and pinched her clit.

Lara screeched and clamped her thighs, coming against his hand, helplessly fisting the sheets.

"Beautiful, beautiful," he soothed as he shut off the vigorous bullet.

She gave another few involuntary jerks as aftershocks claimed her.

He stroked her back even as he released her wrists. "So, so pleasing." He talked to her, touched her and sat next to her until she let go of her powerful grip on the bedclothes. "In future, I may just keep you tied to my bed."

"That's what happens to captives," she said softly as she turned her head to him. "At least in my fantasies."

He left her only long enough to dampen a washcloth then he rejoined her to bathe her heated skin.

"Thank you for that," she said. "But now, when I masturbate, the sound of your voice will fill my head. And the way you spanked me…" She closed her eyes for a moment. "That was more than I could have ever hoped for."

"Maybe you thought I was joking about tying you to the bed and keeping you as my captive?"

She opened her eyes again, letting him see into her darkest secrets. "Maybe you thought I was joking that I'd let you."

"This is called a coup, Lara Marie." Pernell picked up a pencil, snapped it in half and threw both of the pieces against the wall. "A goddamn betrayal."

Lara took a deep breath but forced herself not to wince. Despite her father's brutal words, she didn't relent. Instead of arguing with his statements, she said, "I'm sorry you see it that way."

All day, she'd dreaded this meeting. Obviously having known that, Connor had called a couple of times to offer support and to help her refocus on other business matters. For the first time in the last few years, she'd felt as if she weren't so alone.

"I have a right to run my company in the manner I see fit," Pernell said.

"As long as you're executing your fiduciary duty," she countered.

"Which I am."

"I disagree." Though he hadn't responded to her repeated messages, she knew through her mother that he'd been busy talking to board members last night.

When she'd knocked on his door at four o'clock, she had been surprised when he'd answered.

He'd dispensed with any greeting and, instead, had demanded she take a seat.

She had, feeling prepared for anything.

Last night, she and Connor had role-played a dozen different scenarios, including the fact her father might resort to intimidation or bluster, even guilt. At one point, Helene had joined them via video conference call, just in case they'd missed something. Helene had warned that he might try to play on her emotions as a loyal daughter, saying it was her duty to support him.

Her mother and Connor had both coached her to remain resolute and not to succumb to emotional manipulation. Both had even offered to accompany her to the meeting. For a moment, before she'd knocked on Pernell's door, she'd almost changed her mind and called them.

But now that she was face-to-face with him and his stubbornness, she drew on her own fortitude, the same determination that had driven her to approach Connor. She knew, without doubt, an intervention was the only way to stop Pernell's thoughtless and potentially reckless actions. The only way she could live with herself was if she didn't take the coward's way out. "Connor will make a presentation. Mother will be there."

"No one has to listen to him."

"Not today," she agreed. "But after Friday, they will. Connor and I are getting married."

"You're what? That goddamn bastard!" He leaped to his feet, face red. He slammed his hands on the desktop and leaned toward her. "He did this. He got to you after I told him to get the fuck out. I'm going to rip his—"

"Enough." Then, more gently she added, "I love you, Daddy." Lara's emotions overflowed. She was still the little girl who'd happily jumped in the car for the ride downtown to follow him around. She was still the young executive who'd made her first presentation to the board. More than anything, she was still the person who loved her father too much to allow him to fail.

"He did this on purpose. When he couldn't get his insulting offer past me, he went behind my fucking back. The crazy bastard wants my company. And he'll do anything to get it."

She said nothing. She'd learned a thing or two from watching Connor.

Finally, he sank into his chair. His spine was erect, and she saw fire in the eyes that were so like her own.

Until now she hadn't noticed that the only time she'd

seen him so animated recently was the night he'd tossed Connor out. Otherwise, his eye color seemed dull. Having an identified target seemed to give her father his fire back. "Hear him out," she suggested. "You'll have your turn."

"I need to see the bylaws. Where the hell are my bylaws?" He yanked open the bottom desk drawer.

"Section eight," she replied. "The CFO can call an emergency meeting. So can a quorum. And section eleven, board members serve at the discretion of the chairman, which is you. But all immediate family members automatically have seats if they're over the age of twenty-one. And spouses are also included."

"Damn Helene had her fingers in that, too. That clause wasn't in there until we got married. Always was a conniving opportunist."

"That's my mother you're talking about," she reminded him. "I think she's quite clever."

"I never said she wasn't."

Finally, Lara sat. "You will always be heard. You will always be valued and respected. But it's time we considered some different directions and strategies. And if you want time to be on the golf course, you've earned it."

"If you think I'm staying away while that Donovan bastard sits in this chair—"

"I think he'd find it too uncomfortable. And so would I." After checking her watch, she said, "We're due in the conference room at five. We will start without you if necessary."

Lara Bertrand, his future bride, was a force to be reckoned with, and Connor had never been prouder.

At four-thirty, he'd stepped off the elevator on the eighteenth floor of the building that housed BHI. Helene had been waiting for him, and she'd shown him to Lara's office.

The place had taken him aback. He was accustomed to

seeing her in her personal surroundings, and the wide space with clean lines and its lack of clutter surprised him, showed him another dimension to her. The more he saw, the more he appreciated her.

She'd said the meeting with Pernell had gone as well as could be expected, and she had no predictions about the way he would behave at the board meeting.

Together, the three of them had walked to the conference room.

She'd already had water, agendas, copies of the corporation's bylaws, notepads and pens placed at each setting. True to Helene's nature, a plate of chocolate chip cookies had been set on a credenza, next to a pile of napkins.

If he'd had any doubt of the pair's ability to get things done, they'd have vanished in that moment.

The projector had been set up for his slide show. The whiteboard was empty and pens were lined up in the tray.

Lara and Helene greeted each board member as they arrived, and they introduced Connor. Between his brother's research, his own reading and information gleaned from Helene and Lara, he was able to smoothly interact with each member.

At five o'clock, each person had taken a seat.

By five after, Pernell still hadn't arrived, and Lara grabbed her phone and excused herself from the room.

When she returned, Connor was unable to read her expression. People started talking among themselves, and he heard whispers as they wondered about Pernell's absence and what Lara intended to do about it.

She waited five more minutes before she stood and thanked everyone for their attendance. Her voice rang with authority, and the board members looked to her for leadership. Despite the fact that this was a position she'd maintained she didn't want, it obviously came naturally.

He sat back now and watched her.

"Last week, Connor Donovan approached us with an offer to purchase the communications division."

He noticed she hadn't placed the blame on her father, an

astute and adept move.

"On further reflection, I'd like us to reconsider the offer. Yes, it's low." She looked at him. "But it's an excellent place to begin. Ultimately we may decide it's not in BHI's best interest, but we owe it to ourselves to look at it. I will have a copy for you at the end of the meeting, but with your permission, I'd like Connor to give us a short presentation, outlining potential benefits."

For the next hour, Connor went through his slides. His team had done an excellent job of animating the presentation. Thompson had admitted that they'd gotten some help from a couple of Julien's associates in his new movie division. In fact, Connor recognized the music that played at the end as a more refined version of Julien's theme song.

Regardless, it was both showy and informative.

He answered dozens of questions, and provided some quick math on the whiteboard.

When there was a natural break, Lara stood, as they'd planned. "BHI has had three quarters of losses, as you know. The time has come for us to fully explore the changing landscape of our business to create a workable and profitable future. We need to be ruthless and unflinching in our expectations and vision. We need to offload unprofitable divisions, sell them if possible. And we need to focus on the things we do well. Transportation, shipping, logistics, energy."

Mary, the woman at the far end of the table stood. "Pretty snazzy graphics, Lara and Connor." From her tone, it wasn't a compliment. "But we need more than cute cartoons."

One person laughed a bit nervously.

"Of course we do," Lara agreed. "Which is why you've got the last year's financials in your packet." She opened the manila folder that was in front of her and she had Helene distribute a new set of papers. "But since it can be difficult to make sense of it, I brought this." The page showed the last five years' profit and loss statements converted to a chart, by division. Out of six divisions, one was wildly profitable. Another had respectable earnings. One was hemorrhaging cash. "Of course, I'm more than happy to consider suggestions from the board. But I will tell you this much, while the communications division has some real value, we need to divest it. The longer we wait, the more employees we lose, the longer the patents sit unused, the less it will be worth. And that affects everyone's value. Even yours, Mary."

"So where does Pernell stand on all of this?" another man asked.

"You're welcome to ask him," she said. "The bylaws grant us the authority to act without the chairman if he's not in attendance."

Lara continued, "To be clear and reiterate a point, I'm not asking anyone to make any decisions today. That would be unfair. I wanted you to see and hear the Donovan Worldwide proposal, and I wanted you to have a chance to meet Connor. As of Friday afternoon, he will be my husband, and therefore entitled to a seat on the board."

Around the table, a few glances were exchanged, and one person nodded.

"We'll convene again in two weeks."

After Lara and Helene fielded a few more questions, Lara adjourned the meeting. As he'd suspected, there were numerous questions about the upcoming wedding.

A couple of times, he glanced across at Lara. He saw her talk to each person. She focused intently on them, actively listening.

She was a hell of a skilled communicator.

At first, the advantages of marrying her had been obvious. And now he saw the way she'd be an asset to Donovan Worldwide. She'd be an excellent hostess, as well as an adept partner. If he'd been looking to make a strategic move for Donovan, he couldn't have planned it better.

His musings were interrupted when Mary approached him. "I don't like surprises, Connor. And I don't know what the hell you've done to move Pernell out of the way, but I'm going to get to the bottom of it."

"Understood."

"I'm telling you, I don't like underhanded moves."

He offered his business card, but she ignored it.

Other than that, and Pernell's absence, the meeting had gone as well as any of them had dared hope.

The other members filtered out, leaving him alone with Helene and Lara.

"You've got my vote," Helene told them.

"Mary's going to be tricky," Lara warned.

"There's always one," Helene said. "I'll have lunch with her. Maybe invite her to be part of the Friday Afternoon Soirée." She promised to follow up with the other members of the board as well, then left them alone.

"You did well, Lara."

"As did you, Mr. Donovan."

"Quite the team." He opened his arms and she went into them. Nothing felt more right or seemed more natural.

Unable to keep his hands off her for one more minute, he put one hand on her ass cheeks and drew her closer.

She looped her hands around his neck.

Chemistry throbbed, demanding consummation. "I want to get you home," he said.

"What did you have in mind?"

"Something to make you forget, entirely, about today."

"That's a hell of a tall order."

"I'm sure you'll let me know how I do."

Unable to help herself, she initiated the contact, brushing her lips against his.

That seemed to be all the incentive he needed.

Connor claimed her mouth and her response. He tasted of success and promise, and every part of her intuitively responded to that.

More and more, the idea of having someone in her life to count on was becoming seductive. Though she'd tried to keep Connor and his determination to have more than a business arrangement at bay, when she succumbed, things were just easier.

At the board meeting, she'd been aware of his quiet

presence. Not only had he given support, he had been content to let her lead the meeting, never speaking up, except as they'd agreed. When her father hadn't shown up, he hadn't given any advice. Instead, he'd waited.

More than that, he'd been right when he'd said they'd been a good team.

She was beginning to wonder how she'd managed without him.

It was so, so tempting to lean in, count on his strength, but part of her knew better. In some ways, their two-year commitment seemed like an eternity. In other ways, it was only a wink of time. She had to remember to count on herself, not him.

But right now, forgetting today was a hell of an idea.

Facing her father had been necessary, and she had no regrets. But that didn't mean it hadn't cost her in terms of emotional energy.

Connor ended the kiss, but not until she was consumed with thoughts of him being inside her.

He had helped her clean up the conference room and power off all the electronics. Then they'd returned to her office so she could shred the financial statements and agendas that had been left behind.

While she slipped into more comfortable shoes and took off her blazer, he notified April they were ready to be picked up.

"Got everything?" he asked.

She tucked her purse and shoes into her work bag and slung it over her shoulder.

"Let me."

Even though she objected, he took the bag from her. "Is this part of your weightlifting program?" he asked.

"I move it from arm to arm all day," she teased back.

In the lobby, she waved goodnight to the security guard.

"It was nice to see your mom," the woman called out. "And she brought me a chocolate chip cookie. Can't believe she remembered that after all this time."

"I didn't get one," Lara told Connor when he opened the

door for her.
"Or dinner," he said. "Do you want to stop for something, or go straight for the sex?"
"After the way you kissed me? Is that really a question?" she asked.
April was already waiting, and she delivered them to the front of Connor's high-rise in under ten minutes.
"I could get used to this," Lara confessed.
"It saves significant amounts of time."
"And it's pretty damn luxurious." It would have taken longer to walk to the parking garage and get in her car than it did to get to Connor's home.
Once they were inside the loft, he locked the door.
At the purposeful sound, her pulse hitched.
"Join me in the playroom, little Lara, and present for me, there."
As always, his choice of those very specific words tripped something deep inside her. She knew he meant for her to have that reaction. Within seconds, they changed her focus and her state of mind. But it wasn't just the words, it was his tone. It allowed for no arguments or hesitations, and warmth rippled through her. "Yes, Sir," she said.
She followed him down the hallway. At some point, he'd moved the spanking bench so that it was almost in the middle of the floor. He'd also adjusted the platforms so that one was significantly higher than the other.
Instead of prompting her, he simply waited.
After kicking off her shoes, she removed her dress.
"You can put your clothes on top of the dresser."
Aware of his heated gaze on her, she moved past him and did as he said. He folded his arms and watched her shimmy out of her underwear and bra.
He didn't say a word as she went to middle of the room, near the bench, and knelt. She exhaled, spread her legs, then lowered her gaze and put her hands on her thighs.
For a long time, he allowed silence to stretch. She concentrated on her breathing, channeling her inner patience as she waited for him.

"Have you noticed how natural that's becoming?"

"Yes, Sir." She couldn't deny that. Her movements were more natural, and she felt significantly less embarrassed.

"So beautiful. Come to me, Lara."

Focusing on him and his command, she crawled to him.

"Kneel up," he instructed.

Once she had, he softly said, "Take off my belt."

Lara went totally still. He'd remembered her telling him about it, and he was making her fantasies come true. Even though she'd spent time visualizing it, nothing could have prepared her for the reality, the pulse of his command.

She looked up at him. He was staring at her intently. In an unguarded moment, she saw softness in his eyes. He might keep an emotional wall between them, but there was little doubt he felt something for her.

"Do it now, Lara."

Nerves and excitement combined and plummeted through her, as if she were on a carnival ride. She fumbled with the buckle, and he stood there, not helping her. She was aware of his cock pressing against his slacks and of his restrained power.

Finally, she got the belt loose. She pulled the leather through the loops, and she shivered.

Since she wasn't sure what to do next, she folded the length over and offered it to him.

"Exactly right," he told her, accepting the belt. "Now, to the bench."

She went to it and positioned herself on it, kneeling on the lower platform and putting her chest on the upper portion.

"Would you like to be secured in place?"

"It's up to you, Sir."

"Thank you for that. The choice is yours."

"This is going to hurt, isn't it?"

"Maybe more than the single tail. I didn't use a lot of force, and this will cover a wider area and leave more of a stripe than a bite."

"In that case, please tie me," she replied.

He put his belt on her back. The leather still bore his body heat.

After securing her, he said, "Now for the warm-up."

This part, she was starting to look forward to. She knew it was to help prevent bruising, but it created intimacy and helped her prepare her mind as much as her body.

"How many stripes would you like, Lara?"

In her fantasies, she'd never been asked that question. "Ah… I don't know how to answer." What was the number between too many and not enough? "Whatever you say, Sir."

He was still rubbing her skin, relaxing her with every touch. "Let's start with eight, with the option of another eight before I fuck your ass."

"What?" She turned her head to the side. Instinctively, she clenched her buttocks. "Sir. Connor."

He moved onto gentle smacks, and pressure built inside her. Since he'd teased her earlier, she'd already been somewhat aroused. He was a master at erotic seduction. "You're insane."

"Insane, Sir." He pinched her.

"You *are* insane, Sir."

"You'll ask for it," he vowed.

"I've never asked for it before, Sir."

"Have you ever done it?"

"No."

"You've had my finger up your ass."

"I think that's different."

"Relax your buttocks, sub."

Despite the instructions, his words kept her on edge.

He continued to rub her. "Close your eyes. Give up the fight."

She did.

Then she felt him take the belt off her.

"Stay in that same place."

She nodded.

"Eight," he reminded her.

He gave her the first two lightly, across the fleshiest part of her rear. It was no more than a tease. Seductive. "More," she said.

"That's two," he responded. "Now three and four." He placed another one, lower, then lower still.

This was a totally different experience from the spanking or the single tail. As he'd said, it covered a larger area, not just in terms of length, but in terms of width. There was so much more surface to connect with her skin, a broader area to burn into her.

"Halfway."

The next was harsher, and she yelped.

He paused for a moment and waited for her to nod.

The sixth, he seared across her buttocks. She screamed. It was more than she'd expected, everything she'd hoped.

"Seven," he said, counting in advance.

He landed it on an upstroke, forcing her forward, making her grab hold of her restraints for extra support.

"Damn!"

"One more," he promised.

It landed on top of the last, sizzling with ferocity.

He then gently stroked between her legs, made her wet. That he'd done it differently than she'd expected made the touch even more stunning and welcome.

"How are you doing?" he asked. "Do you want to stop? Continue? Need a break?"

"More," she whispered.

He moved his hand away before she could orgasm. Despite the pain—because of the pain—her body felt lighter.

This time, he started on her mid-thighs. She gasped, and she pulled on the restraints.

"Would you like to count them out?"

"No, Sir." She wanted to get lost, instead.

He put another stripe a little higher, and the next two he crisscrossed.

Then suddenly the only thing she was aware of was the color red, light and bright, seducing. She released her grip on the restraints and surrendered to him.

Her body moved in automatic response, and she no longer felt anything other than peace.

At some point, she became aware that he'd stopped the beating and that he was tracing her spine with his fingertips, back and forth.

She took a deep breath. The color red began to recede, becoming black, then gray. Finally, she opened her eyes to see him standing next to her. "I liked that," she admitted.

"Everything you desired?"

"More so."

He played with her pussy and instant desire arced through her. It was as if it had been there coiled, waiting.

It only took two strokes for her to be on the edge, waiting and wanting. "I need you," she told him.

He left her for a moment, and she moved her head to try to see what he was doing. The restraints limited her range of motion, and she had to settle for listening.

Something hit the floor. Maybe his shoes? Then a slight rustle, maybe his clothing. Her inability to see him was driving her crazy, heightening her anticipation.

There was another sound, then the scrape of wood. Perhaps a dresser drawer?

Eventually she heard the unmistakable sound of his footfall.

"I'm going to fuck your pussy then your ass."

Her stomach plummeted.

"Use your safe words if you can't handle it. Will you try?"

She nodded, the platform warm beneath her face.

He took his time, playing with her clit, using long, mesmerizing strokes.

Heat rose again, licking at her.

"You have no idea what it does for me," he said, "seeing you like this. Tied down. Helpless. Trusting."

He'd created that bond, by doing what he said he would.

She felt him move closer, and the tip of his cock teased her pussy. He began to slip in and out, inserting just the head then, as she started to moan, giving her longer strokes.

He rocked his hips.

As much as she was able, she pushed back, inviting him in.

He put one hand on her waist, and she savored his powerful grip.

"Yes. Yes!" she said.

He put a lubed finger into her ass, sliding in easily.

The combination made her feel full.

Then he inserted a second, spreading her wider as he continued to push his cock in and out.

She was lost. "I want… Want…"

"Tell me."

"Everything."

He pulled out his fingers out. Then she felt him at her rear, the solidness of him pushing into her, forcing her sphincter apart.

"I…I…"

Her abdominal muscles failed her and she collapsed her whole weight against the platform.

"Bear down."

"Arr…"

"Bear down," he repeated.

"Can't…"

"You can."

She pulled against the restraints, yanking up on them.

He eased back, and she exhaled in gratitude. Then he moved forward again.

"You can do this," he said softly. He let go of her waist and moved that hand under her so he could play with her pussy, distracting her.

Conflicting sensations short-circuited her brain. Anguish as he continued to force his cock inside her tight ass, unfurling desire in her belly from the way he played between her labia, the lingering pain from the beating and the consuming drive to transcend it all.

"You're doing great."

He pinched her clit. She yelped, squirmed, tried to twist away, and that was all it took. He rammed his cock all the way inside her ass, then he stopped for a minute.

"I've never…"

"You're there. Go with it."

He pinned her totally against the spanking bench. She was lost. Helpless. His.

Despite his urging, she thrust back, and he moaned.

"Damn, Lara."

His words drove her. She liked that she was making him as crazy as he'd made her. "Fuck me, Sir," she said.

He began to move inside her. He kept his hand between her thighs, continuing to pleasure her, even though his breathing became guttural.

"Fuck me, *please,* Sir." He'd said she would beg, and he was right. She had to have him filling her, claiming her.

"Lara, I'll give you anything you want."

It was overwhelming. *He* was overwhelming. She'd never endured anything like this. Her body felt as if she were being pulled apart and put back together again in a different order. She loved it. She hated it.

His cock thickened inside her, and she knew his orgasm was close. "I need to come."

"Do it," he said, moving his fingers faster.

In her ass, he made shorter movements and he swelled even more. His breaths were sharp.

Then she was lost as her orgasm seemed to tear her apart from the outside in.

She squeezed him tighter, and he moved his hand to her shoulder. He imprisoned her. Took her.

He came, and she felt every pulse as he ejaculated inside her.

Connor's body shuddered, and she felt his grip on her shoulder tighten then release several times in quick succession.

Then, seconds later, he flattened his palm on her back.

They stayed liked that for long minutes, breathing together, recovering. His penis became flaccid, and he eventually pulled out. "I'll be with you in a second," he promised.

True to his word, he was back almost instantly, and she felt moistened wipes against her skin. Part of her insisted that it should feel humiliating. A bigger part appreciated his tender act.

She'd just started to notice that her muscles were tight when he loosened her bonds.

"Move slow," he cautioned.

"As if I can do anything else," she replied when she tried to move her right leg and a twinge shot through her knee.

As he released each cuff, she gently tested her muscles. She wasn't able to support herself and he swept her from her feet. Instinctively, she turned toward him and soaked in his strength and comfort as he carried her to the bed.

"You were everything I imagined," he told her, sitting next to her and wrapping an arm around her.

"Now I have more things to fantasize about," she said. And more reasons she would have to work to keep her emotions separate from her physical responses. Everything they did in the D/s realm made her crave more, as if she couldn't get enough.

"No diamonds," Lara insisted as Connor drew her toward a large jeweler at the mall. It had a reputation as one of the higher-end retailers. There were a few other stores that catered to her budget, but he'd already dismissed that suggestion.

"If you want people to believe our marriage is real, you need a diamond," Connor insisted.

They entered the store, and were immediately greeted by a male clerk. "Is there anything I can show you?"

"Wedding rings," Connor said.

"Sets or just bands?"

"Sets," he replied.

The man smiled. "Right this way."

They followed him across the carpeted floor to a series of long glass cabinets.

"What kind of diamond are you looking for?"

Connor shrugged. "A big one."

"Any special shape?"

"Lara?"

She shook her head.

"Oval," he said, as if it were the first shape that came to mind.

The man nodded and went behind a counter.

Connor started to walk after him, but she put her hand on his forearm and squeezed. "Stop. Would you listen to me, please? I don't even wear jewelry."

"I imagine a lot of women say the same thing before they get a wedding ring."

"A ring, yes. I agree that I need a ring. It doesn't need to have diamonds and I certainly don't need a big-ass diamond."

"A big-ass oval diamond," he corrected.

She exhaled a ragged breath. "Connor, please."

"It's an investment."

"In a two-year marriage?" she countered. "Let's be serious. You're talking about a serious waste of money."

"Are you going to give me a cost-per-wear analysis?"

She saw a smile tugging at the corner of his lips. And it made it impossible to be mad at him. "I think you're making fun of me."

The clerk waited, a wad of keys in hand.

"We'll disappoint him if we don't at least look," Connor said.

"And be keeping him from making a commission from someone who may actually want to make a purchase."

"Humor me."

Which meant the argument was over. Just like the numerous others that had come up in the last forty-eight hours. What time to go to bed, the fact he insisted she take a bath to relax at the end of the day, the way he got her up in the morning to hit the treadmill while he rowed. He was right about the need to take care of herself, and about the benefits of them talking while she soaked in the tub.

Their nightly discussions helped keep her more focused at work the next day. He provided helpful suggestions when she wanted them, kept his mouth shut when she didn't want them. Impressively, he seemed to know the difference.

But that didn't mean she wouldn't rather have a glass of wine, eat a big hunk of chocolate for dinner, sleep in then drag through the day with no energy.

Connor pointed out a couple of rings and the man pulled out the first. He polished it with a cloth, then offered it to her. Connor intercepted it. "Is the other one bigger?"

"Slightly," the man said.

"We'd rather see that." He gave the ring back.

It was a good thing the marriage was temporary. There were parts of his high-handed antics that wore her down.

With a gracious smile that said he was happy to wait on them all night if necessary, the man took out the other ring, polished it and offered it to Lara.

This time, she accepted it.

She slipped the ring on, and the diamond caught her breath. Light seemed to explode from it, and as she moved her hand, it winked. It was so simple and elegant that she couldn't help but stare.

"It suits you," Connor said. "I can see you wearing this to work or with a certain black dress when we go to dinner."

No matter what she did, she couldn't look away.

He was right. It was her style—understated, timeless.

But she was also right. It was a terrible use of his financial resources. Even though she couldn't look away, she said, "A simple band is sufficient."

"And my wife will not wear something that's merely sufficient."

His implacable tones broke through her reverie and she took off the ring and handed it back to the clerk. Obviously sensing a conflict, the man locked the case and moved away to give them some privacy.

"Connor, will you listen to me?"

"I promise I've taken your objections into consideration."

"Is this the part where you act like the big bad Dom?"

"I assure you, Lara, this is no act." He signaled for the clerk to return. "We need it by noon tomorrow. Can you have it ready by then?"

"Of course, sir." He excused himself and went to fetch the sizer.

Still steaming, she tried on two different rings before they found the right fit.

As the man slipped it into a box, she couldn't help a last glance at it.

"This comes with a wedding band, right?" Connor asked.

"Matching," the man assured him.

"And is there a man's ring?"

"One is available, certainly, sir."

The man was a mad shopper. She'd wanted a simple band,

and he was buying everything available. "Is that included in that outrageous price?"

"Lara," Connor warned her.

She watched while Connor tried on the matching platinum band, and the sight of it took her aback. Somehow, when she'd been dazzled by the diamond then disagreeing with him over the budget, the reality of them getting married tomorrow had been pushed to the back of her mind.

It was moments like this that brought it to the front and stole her breath, reminding her of reality and its ball of lies.

Despite her resolve to treat their relationship as nothing more than a business arrangement, Lara's feelings were becoming more and more complex.

Sleeping with him, talking, brainstorming, strategizing, walking to the bakery for treats on Sunday morning and their fun sparring...all of that was what she wanted in a marriage. Until she'd met him, the idea of D/s had been foreign. She'd wanted some kinkier sex, but the world he'd introduced her to was one she found seductive. Now that she'd had the experience, she couldn't imagine wanting anything else.

"Lara?"

The sight of the ring on his hand made her feel as if a fist were squeezing her heart. She realized she'd lost the battle. She wasn't just starting to fall in love with him, she was all the way in the deep end without a life preserver. As if she were drowning, she couldn't breathe.

She wasn't sure what his question was, so she replied noncommittally. "It looks fine." Lara forced herself to smile, using the opportunity to look away and to regroup. She wondered where she was going to find the strength to go through with this.

Desperately, she wished there was another way...a chance for her to get out now, before the future devastated her.

Connor told the man to ring up the purchase, and she took the opportunity to escape. She left the store and waited for him on a nearby bench.

It took him a full ten minutes to complete the purchase.

"Everything okay?" he asked, sitting next to her.

This was neither the time nor the place to discuss her thoughts. He'd likely tell her she was just having the jitters, and maybe she was. She'd turn to him. He'd comfort her. And she'd be even more in love. "Fine." She lied to save her sanity.

"Is it the money?"

"It's…" She grabbed the excuse he was offering. "Eighteen dollars and fifty-seven cents," she said.

He frowned.

"That's the cost per wear. Without tax. I figure the tax adds another dollar, give or take."

"Give or take," he agreed. "And worth every penny. It really is beautiful on you."

It was. A beautiful sham that threatened to leave her heart in pieces.

"Is that what you're getting married in?" he asked, sweeping his gaze over her.

Heat simmered in his steely gray eyes, and she felt a corresponding pulse deep inside her. Her future husband, her Dom, always showed his appreciation. And tension constantly seemed to hover on a slow boil between them. "No. I figured I'd change after lunch."

"I'll pick you up around two?"

"I'll be ready." Physically, anyway.

Since he wasn't quite ready to leave, she asked if April could give her a ride.

"Absolutely. But if you think you're getting out of the house without saying goodbye, you're mistaken."

As always, when his tone was tinged with a slight edge of danger, she began to moisten.

"Yeah," he said.

Without him issuing a command, she went to him. He sat on a chair and parted his legs, and she stood between them.

"Lift your skirt."

She exhaled deeply and did as he instructed.

Through the scrap of her panties, he mouthed her. Suddenly off balance, she reached for him, grabbing handfuls of his workout shirt. "Oh, Sir." No matter what was on her mind, his brand of sensuality distracted her.

He thumbed aside the silk and swirled his tongue over her clit. "That's it, little Lara. Give me your orgasm."

She moved her hips, offering him more of her pussy. Sexually, she held nothing back from him.

He slipped a finger inside her and crooked it so that he touched her G-spot.

A hundred pinpricks of light exploded behind her eyelids and her knees weakened as the unexpected force of the orgasm rocked her.

"Now that's a good morning kiss," he said.

After she'd steadied herself, she leaned down and kissed his mouth, tasting her own passion. Everything about him was erotic.

He set her away from him, then stood and walked her to the door. "See you soon," he said.

She paused for a moment, and they looked at each other. "Connor, I..." The words, the confession were right there, between them. And she couldn't speak them even though he waited for her to go on. Instead, she picked up the garment bag she'd hung from the coatrack.

Thankfully, April refrained from chit-chat, and Lara checked email on the ride. One of the board members, Mary, had asked for more information about Connor's communications proposal, and she'd copied Pernell also.

The request had been sent late yesterday afternoon. Unsurprisingly, her father hadn't responded.

That continued to weigh on her.

To her knowledge, he hadn't been in the office since Tuesday. Even though Venessa had said he was absent, yesterday Lara had gone to see for herself. His inbox had grown by at least an inch and pink pieces of paper bearing phone messages littered his desktop. He still hadn't answered his phone or returned any of her messages.

Following her intuition, Lara asked April to drive to his house. "Do you have enough time to do that before you need to return for Connor?"

"That shouldn't be a problem, Ms. Bertrand."

Even though his car wasn't in the driveway, she still took the chance and went and knocked on the door. When there was no answer, she tried the knob to find it locked.

"Ready, ma'am?" April asked.

"Thanks, yes," she said, getting back in the car. She felt relieved to know that he wasn't at home brooding. More likely, he was at his golf club.

Traffic was still light when she reached her office building, and she made a stop at the coffee kiosk in the lobby before heading upstairs.

A little after eleven, there was a knock on her door.

"Come in." She pushed aside the revised marketing budget and looked up.

Pernell entered.

Shock kept her in her seat for a few seconds before she jolted herself and stood. "Dad," she said.

"Mind if I have a seat?"

She considered going over to the less formal area but changed her mind, opting to keep the desk between them. "Please come in," she said.

Uncertainty kept her on guard, but she forced herself to sit back in her chair rather than on its edge. Again taking a cue from Connor, she waited rather than fill the silence with nervous chatter.

"I've had some time for thinking," he said. "I despise your attempt to take over my board."

She wanted to correct him, to tell him it was the BHI board. Then she realized that his words helped identify the problem. He thought of himself and the corporation as the same entity.

In his place, perhaps she would have, too.

As a young man, he'd started working as a stockbroker. He'd done well enough that he'd left the large firm and started his own company, taking a number of clients with him. She'd heard that the beginning had been bumpy, but he'd had the love and support of Helene. She'd worked a full-time job in addition to being his secretary, and they'd lived in a small, suburban one-bedroom apartment while he'd built his empire. He'd owned ten rental houses and two commercial properties, all of which had produced a nice income, before he and Helene had even considered buying themselves a modest place to live.

They'd continued to work hard and invest, and it hadn't been until he'd made his first two million dollars that they'd even discussed the possibility of starting a family.

"I've never considered that you wouldn't want to take over as CEO." He held up his hand when she might have spoken. "I know. You've said it a hundred times. I haven't listened."

She nodded.

"You know, Lara, since your mother left, my heart hasn't been in it."

Suddenly she saw him in a different light. Stubborn, yes. Curmudgeonly, even. But until now, she hadn't seen him as a lonely man. "I'm not sure I understand."

"Helene has a certain amount of energy. I had no idea how much I fed on it. Over the years, she wasn't as involved in the day-to-day, but every night, we talked about the business. I bounced every idea off her. But about seven years ago, she started talking about spending more time together, traveling, maybe buying a second home in Europe. She said I could run the business just as easily from Tuscany as Houston. I was still wanting to build and she wanted to start paring back."

It occurred to her that her mother hadn't told her this much. But it explained a lot.

"The truth is, as your mother stepped back, I was looking for you to replace that enthusiasm for growth."

For a paralyzing moment, Lara wondered if he was going to fire her. Technically that would be within his rights and his power, but it was an outcome she'd never considered.

"You're not focused on expansion or acquisitions.

You don't have the risk tolerance I have. But you bring a steadiness that we need. It could be that both you and your mother are right. That it's time to look at the changing business landscape. There are times for growth, particularly into emerging markets, but there are also times to consolidate so that sustainable growth can occur."

"And that provides the capital to invest elsewhere." There was silence for a moment, then she continued, "You know, Mother is right about other things, too. You can focus your energies where you want, maybe go play a round of golf in Scotland like you've always wanted. And technology can be taught. You can work from Tuscany—"

He shuddered.

"Or the UK. Or your club."

He looked around. "I'm not ready to step down as chairman of the board."

"No one else wants that, either."

"I'm clear on one thing, Lara. I can't allow you to sacrifice yourself for this company."

She shook her head.

"Donovan," he explained. "The man's shrewd. Smart. And you're wrong about his communications offer. It was insulting."

"It was a starting point. And if you look at it as part of the whole, as a chance to have cash to put into our global capitalization efforts, into energy, it's well-worth considering."

"He stands to make millions."

"And so do we," she countered. "Frankly, I wish them well. It's a competitive marketplace, and it's not in our sweet spot. We don't have the cash to execute on some of our patents. And we've lost some of our key talent to competitors. This is the time to divest ourselves."

"It's not how I do business."

"No. It's not," she agreed.

"I'll agree to let you negotiate the sale."

She nodded, not betraying the way her inner executive was jumping up and down. She realized what the decision had cost her father.

"But I won't have you marrying Donovan."

Her shoulders sagged. "I beg your pardon?"

"I had a lot of good years with your mother. It's my fault the marriage ended. But marriage is hard enough when you love someone. I appreciate the sacrifice you were willing to make. But it won't be necessary. We'll begin the search for a president, maybe a CEO. I lost your mother, Lara. I won't lose you. Marry him and I'll show up to fight you every step." His jaw was set in determination.

"It's not like you think," she said, her thoughts fracturing.

"Did he get down on one knee and propose to you? Tell you he would love you forever? Then it's exactly as I think. I didn't work my entire life for you to give up yours. Not having the support of someone you love makes life a fucking quagmire." With that he stood and showed himself out.

As if frozen, she remained in place.

The idea that she didn't have to marry Connor shot relief through her, but the feeling was shrouded in grief. Already, being with him every day and knowing he would never love her was debilitating. A future of it might have destroyed her.

She knew she should be rejoicing. But she couldn't.

Lara pressed her trembling hands to her face as she sorted through her options, not that there were many. Sanity and saving her relationship with her father versus two years with a man who would never love her? Even she wasn't that strong.

This morning, she'd woken up knowing she'd end the day as Mrs. Donovan. The course for the next couple of years had been plotted, and her strategy had been in place. Now that the ground had shifted, she felt uncertain. And she still had an agreement with Connor.

She paced to the window and stared out, unseeing.

If she didn't love him, she wouldn't feel this conflicted. She could simply tell him she'd worked out her issues and thank him for his willingness to help.

But she did love him.

And that made this one of the most difficult things she'd ever had to do. She told herself better now than later, but that meant she'd miss out on two years of memories and experiences.

Her heart raced.

Wishing her hands would stop shaking, Lara went back to her desk. For a cowardly few minutes, she considered the idea of calling him or sending a text message. But he deserved better than that, even if seeing him made it more difficult for her. Thinking it would be bad taste to contact April, she instead telephoned a cab to take her to Connor's office.

On her way out of the door, she purposefully ignored the garment bag containing the dress she had planned to wear for their wedding.

The cab ride seemed to last forever, even though it had probably taken less than ten minutes.

All too soon, she was in Connor's reception area, and Thompson looked up.

He grinned. "Hello, Ms. Bertrand. I don't think he's expecting you. He was planning to leave in a couple of hours to pick you up."

She tried to smile at him, but failed. "My visit will be a surprise."

"Go right in."

"He doesn't have company?" she asked, remembering that Nathan had been with him last time she'd dropped by unexpectedly.

"No, ma'am."

After thanking him, she walked toward the door.

"Can I get you a coffee? And I hid some biscotti for you."

"I'd love to take you up on that, but I've had more than I should have today." And she wanted to get this over with.

She knocked on Connor's door then entered without waiting for an invitation.

On her way over, she'd focused on him and all the reasons he had to be relieved by her father's change of heart. He'd get the communications division, and he wouldn't have to go through with the marriage. He could have his loft to himself, not have to share his workout space, return the ring and get his money back.

All in all, it was the ideal solution.

He glanced up, and their eyes met.

His smile was slow and sure, and it beckoned her forward. "If it isn't my beautiful bride." He stood and rounded his desk to rest his hips against the corner.

She drank him in, and he stole the rest of her breath.

His shirtsleeves were rolled back, showing the sinew of his forearms, reminding her of the way he wielded a single tail. And a belt.

The knot in his silver tie had been yanked low. He was the picture of studiousness and determination. He was the picture of the man she wanted to love her.

She closed the door and walked toward him, her feet feeling as if they were as heavy as bricks.

His smile faded as she drew closer, then it became a frown. "Everything okay, Lara?"

It was one thing to be certain about her course of action when she was alone, but now that she was near him, resolve wavered. She pulled back a chair and sat, afraid to go close to him. She'd never want to leave his arms otherwise. "I had a meeting with my father," she began.

"You could have called. I would have been there."

She should have guessed he would say that. He'd warned her from the start that he was a protector. It wasn't hard to picture him in armor, slaying a maiden's dragons. "He stopped by my office. And it seems you're off the hook."

"I'm not sure I follow."

She gave him a small smile, it was as much false cheer as she could summon. "We'll get the communications deal done. And he's willing to allow me to start looking for someone to replace him as president, perhaps even CEO. All this means..." She paused to swallow the knot that had lodged in her throat. "What I'm trying to say is... There's no longer a need for us to get married."

He waited, his body still.

"Say something," she implored. "Anything."

Seconds later, when he hadn't, she went on, "I… Thank you." She stood. "I am more grateful than you'll ever know that you were willing to help me out. When I look back, I realize what I'd asked from you. You really are remarkable." *And unbearably handsome.* "I'll never forget it."

"Let me get this straight," he said, his voice so chilled that an icicle seemed to slide down her spine. "You left our place this morning as my bride-to-be, and now you're saying thanks, but no thanks?"

"That's not…" It was. Exactly. "Yes."

"And you're planning on… What? Collecting your stuff after work? Walking away? Pretending it didn't happen? Not asking for my thoughts? Seeking my council?"

She rose to her feet, pushing her chair back. "What's the point? Neither of us wanted the marriage."

"You certainly did when you benefitted." His words had the precision of one of his whips.

"I deserve that." She folded her arms to protect herself. "But that's not the point. Two years from today, we were going to amicably end it. This saves us some attorney fees, court costs, any legal maneuvering that might have come up. Our lives would have gotten more complicated, too, I'm sure. I'd like to keep this amicable since we'll be working together on the communications deal."

He looked at her for long seconds before finally speaking, "What the hell is this really about?"

"I'm not sure I know what you mean."

"I would have expected you to come in here and tell me that you and Pernell had spoken then ask my advice. We could have talked it through as a team, had a strategic meeting. But you didn't. You never gave me a chance. You came in here with one purpose, to cancel our wedding."

She went to the window, as far away from him as she could get. "Okay, Connor. You want the truth?" She twisted her hands together. "Here it is. Just remember, you asked for it. You're right. I came here to cancel our wedding.

When we made the arrangement" —*what seems like a lifetime ago*—"you were really clear about one thing. Love wasn't going to be a part of this."

He nodded.

"Well, I violated that. I fell totally, madly in love with you. Don't you see? I can't marry you. You keep telling me to be strong. The truth is, I'm not made of that kind of steel. I'm not. I can't stand to be close to you, all the time knowing that you are fucking me, dominating me, wanting me to wear your collar and no matter what I do, no matter how I behave, how much I try, you will never love me in return." Her voice cracked. "I'm destroyed right now. The times we've been together, going to the coffee shop, working out, talking, dating like a real couple...they've been magic, and they've been unbelievably difficult to endure because I know they're not real to you, that you don't have the same responses that I do."

She took a deep, steadying breath, but she knew it wouldn't help. Her voice was cracking with the force of her emotion. "I blame myself—"

"Lara."

"No. Don't. You warned me. I should have paid attention, but I didn't listen. After two more years of feeling your physical response and being denied your heart, I'd be decimated. I'm sorry. My dad's offering me a way out, and I have to take it."

With all of her resolve, she walked from his office.

As she closed the door, she heard him call, "Lara! Wait!"

Knowing that if she looked back, she'd be undone, she kept moving.

"You look like shit."

"Thanks, sis."

Uninvited, Erin walked into Connor's kitchen, opened the refrigerator, pulled out an unopened bottle of wine and uncorked it. She poured herself a great big glass. Then, still, uninvited, went and plopped herself onto his couch.

That she had shown up annoyed him, but it wasn't a shock. He hadn't responded to her texts or calls. In fact, he hadn't spoken to anyone in the family for almost a week.

When she'd arrived in the lobby, she'd buzzed for entrance, and he'd ignored her. Undeterred, she'd let herself in. And she hadn't been at all concerned to find him working out. Instead, she'd said she'd wait.

He'd stayed on the rower for another twenty minutes. But then he realized he might pass out from exhaustion before she gave up.

When he'd sought her out, he'd found her on the couch, in his spot, with his channel changer in hand watching some godawful tear-jerker channel. The movie had to be as old as she was, but she'd been staring at it as if it were a gripping drama filled with award-winning actors.

He'd plucked the remote from her hand then turned off the television.

But now that she was back in his spot with a full glass of wine, appearing that she'd settled in for the evening, he wished he'd gone about his business.

She slipped out of her shoes and folded herself into a semi-lotus position.

Resigning himself, he poured himself a glass of wine and took a chair across from her. "To what do I owe this honor?"

"I came to get Lara's stuff."

The statement made him blink. On some level, he'd expected she'd come herself. Hoped, maybe. Which was probably why he hadn't boxed it up and returned it himself. Instead, he'd left dresses hanging in the closet, lingerie in the laundry hamper, her hairbrush on the vanity, even a bar of soap in the bathtub tray. Everything as if she were coming back.

"So, tell me. What the hell happened between you two? We've all been waiting to hear news of the wedding, then poof, nothing. What are we supposed to think?"

"You'll need to ask Lara."

"I did."

"And?"

"Other than saying things had worked out for both companies and that it was no longer necessary, she was pretty quiet. Well, except for the tears part."

That got to him.

"So I asked her for details. She gave me none."

"And?"

"Hello, dumbnuts. She's been a friend for years. We share everything. That she's not telling me means she's protecting you. And that annoys the crap out of me. What did you do that you called off the wedding and she feels the need to protect you from my wrath?"

"Clearly that didn't work."

"Clearly." She took a long drink before putting her glass down. "I want the details, Conn. And you can skip the platitudes."

"You're assuming it was my fault."

She rolled her eyes.

"Really, Erin, it's none of your business."

"You hurt my friend," she countered. "And that makes it my business."

All week, Julien's words about Connor being an ass had returned to haunt him. Julien had said love was a messy thing and Connor's personal experience had proved him right.

After she'd left his office on Friday afternoon, Connor had been angry. He'd felt betrayed that she hadn't turned to him and that she'd made a decision about their future without consulting him.

Anger had built, and after he'd canceled the appointment with the judge and let his lawyer know that the prenuptial agreement was now void, he'd turned up the notch until he was pissed.

Saturday he'd woken up morose. It should have been his honeymoon. Instead, he'd been taunted by the sight of their rings on his dresser. He'd spent too much time that evening with a well-aged bottle of whisky.

He'd woken on Sunday with a determination to forget about her. He'd worked out, grabbed his bike and gone for a grueling ride in the punishing heat then had returned home to pump some iron and finally swim his way into exhaustion.

Sometime yesterday, he'd tried to convince himself that her decision had been a good one.

But no matter how hard he worked out, he couldn't outrun her last words. She loved him.

That statement had him tied in emotional knots.

And his little sister's visit wasn't helping.

"You know why I'm confused? I thought you liked her. She's the only woman you've ever brought to a family function."

"We were supposed to be getting married," he reminded her.

"But I saw the way you looked at her, the way you touched her."

"I was being polite and courteous."

"When you all but banged her up against the side of your car?"

Carefully, very carefully, he put down his wine. "You saw?"

"Nathan, too. He was walking me to my car. He had to work fast so that Grandfather didn't see you. He wanted to leave so he could go train for his five-k walk. You were so fixed on Lara that you never saw us leave the house. And she certainly looked as if she were a willing participant. So you can tell yourself whatever story you want, big brother, but something happened, and my friend is still upset. Now excuse me while I get her stuff. Do you still have the boxes? Or should I use bags?"

"Pantry," he replied.

She stood, hands on her hips. "Do you want to get them?" Without waiting for a response, she went into his bedroom.

By the time he got there with two boxes, she had Lara's clothing and personal effects spread out across his bed.

"You know, Conn, you could do this yourself." Her voice was softer than it had been since she arrived. "Take it to her, talk to her."

He shook his head, but he helped her pack it up. He sealed the boxes, then carried them down to her car.

After the last one was loaded, she looked at him. "I'm not sure what you're afraid of. Aunt Kathryn and I have been worried about you for a long time. Since Dad. It's okay to live. To move on."

"I have. I just remember the lessons."

"What lessons?" she asked. As they'd been working, her hair had come loose from a clip, and she took it out then re-secured it.

"The same ones we all learned."

"Which ones?" She frowned. "Everyone reacts differently. Grandfather decided to start focusing on his health so he'll be around a lot longer. Aunt Kathryn's learned to seize every moment, and that's why she's going to say fuck us all—and whatever we think—to run off with a guy thirty-something years younger than she is. As for me? I've learned that life is too short to stay on the sidelines. I'm going to give my friend a shot at opening her corset shop. Maybe I'm reckless, like Nathan says, but you know what? I don't care. If I burn through my money, I'll figure something else out. So tell me again, Connor. What's the lesson?"

He scowled.

She kissed his cheek. "You don't have to go through your

life being a dumbnuts. Relax a little. You don't have to be responsible for the whole world. The earth was in orbit when we got here, and it will be here when we leave. I love you." She got in her car. Before pulling away, she paused to wave.

Despite what she'd said, Connor wasn't persuaded.

Lara might have believed that she loved him. But he lived every day with the damages of trusting that seductive emotion.

In retrospect, the way she'd handled it was probably best. If she was in love with him, then it was better that they'd ended it now.

He went back inside to take a shower. Instead, he changed his mind and put on his swim trunks before heading for the pool. Anything to keep the demons at bay.

"That's it," Erin said, carrying in the last box.

"Wine?" Lara offered.

"Don't mind if I do. I opened a bottle of Connor's to irritate him, but I didn't have a chance to drink it all."

Lara gave her friend a quick hug and ignored the few boxes that were stacked in the kitchen. "Outside?"

"Sounds good."

She poured them each a glass, and they sat next to each other on the swing.

"Sorry," Erin said. "I feel like a heel."

"Why?"

"It's my fault. I was the one to suggest you two get married, but I had no idea how fucked up he really is."

"I don't know how true that is."

"Okay, so tell me. I want to hear your side. I've been unbelievably patient. And now that I've brought you a small fortune's worth of your stuff, you owe me."

"Was this your form of bribery?"

"I'm not above it. Now dish before I drink all your wine."

"He's your brother."

"Chicks before dicks," Erin reminded her.

Erin set the swing in motion, and Lara debated how much to say.

Her mother had stopped by twice, and she'd listened until Lara couldn't talk anymore. While her mother had been wonderful, she hadn't fully understood. Lara had kept the D/s part silent, and that information complicated things in a way that wasn't possible to explain. "I fell in love with your brother."

"I thought you were going to tell me something I didn't know." Erin rolled her eyes. "That was obvious at the family gathering."

She blinked. *So much for the big reveal.*

"And Connor has a big ol' chunk of lead where his heart is supposed to be," Erin added. "So, did you tell him?"

"Yeah." She took a small drink. "He said nothing."

"It's not you, Lara," Erin said. "It's him. He's always been reserved, but he's been worse since Dad died."

"The thing is, he's capable of showing great affection." In the short time they'd been together, she'd gotten accustomed to sleeping in his arms, to having him draw her a bath, and once, a foot rub while they'd talked.

"I can tell you this, he can pretend all he wants. But we all saw the way he looked at you, and it took him a long damn time to put your dresses in a box. Your underwear took even longer. There was a garter belt I wasn't sure I was going to be able to pry out of his hand." She snickered.

"You made him do that?"

"And carry down all the boxes."

They chatted for a few minutes about the progress on the BHI Communications sale before Erin stood to leave.

"You know, Lara, if anyone was going to melt his heart, I was sure it was going to be you."

"Thanks for that." She walked Erin outside. The two hugged, and Erin gave her a reassuring squeeze.

She'd barely pulled away when Suzy-Q made a break for it, bounding across the yard to plant her paws on Lara's shoulders and her lay her head on top of one. "BFF," she whispered to the dog.

Mrs. Fuhrman came over with a leash in hand. "I swear she loves you, Lara."

"It's mutual." She stroked behind the dog's massive ears. "What happened with the moving man?"

For weeks, Lara had wondered if Mrs. Fuhrman watched the neighborhood happenings from her window and sent the dog outside as an excuse to come and get her. The question confirmed her suspicions. "Things didn't work out," she said noncommittally.

"Well, the neighborhood wouldn't have been the same without you. But he was a strapping young thing, wasn't he? Odd that a moving company has their gentlemen wear such nice clothes."

She smiled, maybe for the first time in days.

After getting Suzy-Q on the leash, Lara went back inside.

The house seemed larger than usual, and emptier.

She was tempted to ignore the boxes, but it was better to have something to do than spend the rest of the evening moping.

Tucked inside her pile of lingerie, she found a jeweler's box. She opened it to see the wedding rings that he'd purchased.

Warning herself not to be stupid, she couldn't resist the impulse to try them on.

The fit was exact, and the setting suited her personality.

Light hit the diamond and refracted a hundred different directions. She traced a finger across the stone.

Touching the cold surface somehow made the ending of their relationship more final. When he'd packed her belongings, he'd included the things he'd bought for her, the ring, the black dress, the necklace.

The emotion she thought she'd been able to manage broke free. She sank onto the floor, curled her legs to her chest and began to cry.

Lara wished she could take back the last few weeks, pretend she'd never met Connor, never knelt before him or called him Sir, never felt his belt or experienced the uninhibited eroticism that came from letting him share a fantasy.

But as each memory returned, she wondered if that was true. If she hadn't gone to him, she would have missed the pain, but she would never have had the experiences that had changed who she was.

"You, my friend, don't look like a man who has been on his honeymoon."

Over the finest bottle of whisky distilled by one of Kennedy Aldrich's companies, Julien lifted his glass. *Fuck.*

"I was waiting for you to tell me about it. I've been pretending I didn't know that you'd removed Lara as an administrator from your calendar app. I've said nothing, nothing at all, not a single word about the fact no one has filed a completed certificate of matrimonial bliss with your name on it. Ergo..."

He waited.

"The wedding didn't happen. You're not married. In fact, you're behaving like a rather miserable lout who no one wants to be around." Julien lifted his glass. "How'd I do?"

"You're called a genius for a reason," Connor agreed, downing the drink in a single swallow.

Julien shuddered. "It's for sipping, you heathen. *Sipping.*" He put down his glass.

"What do you think of the club?" Julien asked.

Julien had flown in to look at potential retail outlets for the next Bonds store, but at Kennedy's behest, he was checking out the local lifestyle club. The place was on the market, and Kennedy was interested in either buying it or investing in it.

"It's not what I'm accustomed to," Connor replied. Most clubs he'd been to weren't this upscale. They were in warehouses where late-evening comings and goings didn't bother residents. This was a house on several acres of secluded wooded land in exurban Houston, not likely to bother neighbors and offering plenty of discretion.

The two-story home had been significantly modified, with beams installed for suspension play, and walls had been knocked out between former bedrooms, creating large, open spaces. There was a small lounge area with comfortable seating and small tables. Though alcohol wasn't generally served, they'd been allowed to bring in their own because they weren't participating in any scenes. "I'd say it has potential. I'd want to see the former owner's profit and loss, though, before I got giddy about the possibilities." From where they sat, they had a view of an open space that contained a spanking bench much like the one he had at home, one that he kept imagining Lara secured to.

"You don't get giddy about much. Never have."

"Why do I have a feeling I'm not going to like where this is going?" Connor asked.

"Because I'm going to meddle in your life. And you never like that. Let's just pretend this is a visit to the dentist and get it over with, shall we?"

A few couples wandered past. Two walked upstairs while another helped themselves to complimentary soft drinks and sat at a nearby table.

Since it was early, the music volume was still low, something he knew would change soon.

"Bad shit happens in life," Julien said.

And because Julien knew what the hell he was talking about, Connor agreed. "Random odds."

"You have choices along the way. Your father being in love with Stormy didn't get him killed."

He leveled a glance at his friend. "Proceed with caution."

"Oh, fuck bubbles. I didn't travel more than a thousand miles not to plow ahead with careless disregard for life or limb. How many mad, dashing affairs have you had? Oh, wait. Don't answer that. Dozens. So bloody many you need a statistician to help keep it straight."

"You have a point?"

"No matter who you married, you wouldn't have an affair. You wouldn't put yourself in that position."

In the main room, a woman entered, wearing ridiculously high heels. She had shapely calves, a nicely curved ass…

"You wouldn't promise yourself to one woman then get another pregnant."

He tore his gaze away to look at Julien. "Love doesn't cheat."

"There you are."

"There…? What?"

"Love doesn't have to be a messy thing. It can be uncomplicated. Pure. Sustaining. Something that keeps you going. Look at your grandfather and Miss Libby. They've birthed a dynasty and have looked out for each other for over half a century. Look to that. Look to them. You, Connor, are not capable of tearing apart families. It's not in your moral fiber."

He looked back at the woman in the slinky, tight dress and the long hair. He couldn't quite make out the color, but… "God *damn* you." Anger propelled him to his feet.

Julien grabbed him. "It's not her."

Connor looked again.

"It's not," Julien insisted.

He looked more closely. Julien was right. It couldn't possibly be Lara. The woman was much shorter, had a few more curves and her hair was significantly shorter. "How did you know?"

"For whatever reason, the woman says she loves you." With his finger, he made a little circle. "I know. Crazy talk, right? I'm sure she's still healing. She's not the type to go and replace you right away. I do question her judgment, though. Who the hell would give her heart to someone who wouldn't protect it?"

Those words ravaged him, as Julien had probably intended.

It was his obligation, as a Dom, to have handled it better. As a Dom? Fuck, as a human being. As a man.

The momentary blur of jealousy had taught him one thing. He could no longer deny the fact he loved Lara Bertrand. He just hoped his stupidity hadn't cost him the first woman who'd been brave enough to love him. He couldn't blame her if it had. He didn't deserve her.

The commotion of multiple dogs barking shattered the silence.

"Suzy-Q, *no!*"

Lara turned down the television volume. In one of her less-than spectacular moments, she'd chosen an *Indiana Jones* film to pass the evening. The theme music alone had been enough to send her back in time to Connor's loft and the memory of snuggling on his couch. The sight of Indy with his bullwhip had made her squirm.

Unbelievably, she still missed Connor with the same kind of intensity, even though she repeatedly soothed herself with the reminder that time healed everything. Anyone who believed that had not experienced the power of a single tail on her bare skin, delivered by a Dom who was skilled with his whip and generous with his orgasms.

She was about to turn the volume back up when her doorbell rang. Wondering if Mrs. Fuhrman needed some help with her dogs, she slipped on a pair of flip-flops and answered the door.

Suzy-Q stood there, a giant bouquet of flowers hanging from the side of her mouth.

Confused, she reached to take them from the dog, and just as she did, Connor stepped onto the porch.

Her breath froze as she straightened.

He looked every bit as disarming as he always did, in a light-gray sweater and charcoal-colored slacks.

His jaw was shadowed and his eyes were smudged with fatigue.

Suzy-Q jumped, banging her head into Lara's. Connor reached to steady her as she dropped the flowers.

"She never behaves like this," Mrs. Fuhrman said, taking her time walking over. She had curlers in her hair, slippers on her feet and a robe cinched around her middle. "She saw the moving guy and forced open the front door. I shouted at her, but I couldn't come over until I put a robe on. I'm so sorry, Lara. Are you all right? Suzy-Q, get down right now!"

The dog happily did so, and she crushed the flowers beneath her bear-sized paw.

"It was a much better idea in theory," Connor said.

"It was perfect."

He attached Suzy-Q's leash and gave the dog back to Mrs. Fuhrman.

"I think she wants to adopt you," Mrs. Fuhrman said before walking away. "Sometimes dogs do that, you know."

Suddenly, it was just her and Connor. She leaned against the doorjamb, uncertain what to think, what to say, how to proceed.

He picked up the bouquet. Some of the petals fell off and several of the heads had been severed. A few blooms drooped over the side of the protective cellophane.

He offered it to her.

"I'm not sure I've ever had a more perfect gift." She accepted it and pressed it against her chest. "Thank you."

"Can I come in?"

She hesitated. "If this is about the communications deal, it's probably best if we meet at work."

"It's about us."

Her heart seemed to stop beating. She held the bouquet so close she crushed the few remaining perfect blooms.

"I'll stand out here all night, if you want."

"Okay," she said. It might be the only way to preserve her sanity. When he stood close, her resolve melted.

As if they were a shield, she kept the flowers between them.

"I went to see your father."

"You did…? Why?"

"To ask for your hand in marriage."

She stared at him. She'd heard words come out of his mouth, but she was sure they'd been in the wrong order. Or maybe she'd heard what she wanted to hear instead of what he'd actually said. "What? Why?" Her emotions slammed into one another—doubt, fear, distrust, each made her reel a little harder.

"Erin came to see me. She handed me my ass."

"Chicks before dicks," she said.

"And I...?"

"You are not a chick. I'll let you work out the rest."

"I deserve that."

"Take it however you want."

"Then Julien Bonds came to town."

"Did you tell him he'll have to deal with you on the patents?"

"We didn't discuss them," he replied. "We talked about you."

"Me?"

"Well, me."

"You?" she asked.

"You as well."

"I'm lost."

"So am I," he confessed. He dragged his hand through his hair.

She didn't relent and invite him in.

"I've let events of my past drive my decisions, without realizing that I've never been capable of moral ambiguity. Even before my father's death, I would have never allowed myself to cheat on a woman."

"I believe that about you. You're honorable."

He winced. "After the way I've behaved, I'd need to prove I've earned that label."

"Okay, you're honorable in that you don't cheat."

"Julien suggested I look to my grandparents' relationship when it comes to love, and not that of my parents. After I pulled my head out of my ass—"

"Must have been the popping sound I heard."

"I talked to my grandfather about you. About us. He told

the story again of how hard he'd had to work in order to win approval to marry Libby. And he said, some fifty years later, he'd do it all over again." He dragged a hand through his hair. "My focus has been fucked up, Lara."

"Back to the part about my dad," she prompted, her heart thundering just a little louder with each word he said. She heard the cellophane crinkle as her hand shook.

"I realized, this time on my own, that something significant must have transpired for his change of heart and for you to call off our wedding. I wanted to know what it was. He told me he couldn't let you settle for a marriage that didn't start with love. Then there was this story about all the stuffed animals you owned as a child."

Heat chased up her cheeks.

"And the way you would choose the ones that had something wrong with them. You'd pick the one missing an eye, or if the stuffing was coming out."

"Childish stuff," she said.

"No. It's about your heart, the love you have." He glanced at the flowers. "For the neighbor's dopey dog."

"Hey! It's not her fault she grew so big and got abandoned."

"And it's about the way you offered to sacrifice your future for BHI. It took that for your father to realize what he'd allowed to happen. It took being alone, missing you, for me to know that I wanted what you offered, what I'd so foolishly sent away. I owed it to you to protect the gift, and I didn't. If you'll give me the chance, I'll spend my life making it up to you. I love you, Lara Bertrand." He lowered himself to one knee. "Will you honor me by being my bride?"

"Oh, Connor…"

"Is that a yes?"

"Yes."

He stood and gathered her into a hug that smothered the past hurts and promised a future. This was what she'd dreamed of. Connor. His love. Nothing to do with the business, just them.

She heard the sound of clapping and an excited woof. She

shook her head.

"Now can I come in?" he asked.

"I'm thinking you'd better," she said.

He picked her up then carried her across the threshold and kicked the door closed behind him. "Is that *Indiana Jones* on the television?" he asked.

"It could be," she said.

"Tell me you love me, little Lara."

"Or else, Sir?" she teased.

He jostled her and she grabbed hold of him with a frightened squeal. He tossed her over his shoulder and as he strode down the hallway, he swatted her ass, hard.

"Say it," he warned, the words all but a growl.

He tossed her on the bed, then climbed on top of her, forcing her legs apart while simultaneously pinning her hands above her head.

For her, all joking vanished. She was with the man she loved, and he'd broken through years of wounds to offer his heart. "I love you, Connor. I will spend a lifetime showing you just how much."

"How important is a big wedding to you?"

"Are you thinking the same thing I am?" she asked.

"The marriage license is still valid. I want to marry you tomorrow afternoon, before you come to your senses and tell me you won't marry me."

"We could have a reception where we invite all our friends and family at a later date?"

He nodded.

Her heart was pounding, unable to believe all this was happening. "Does this mean we're eloping?"

"The only thing that matters is what you want. If you want a big ceremony with half of Houston in attendance, that's fine." He stroked her hair back from her face so he could read her expression.

"You know, the only thing that's important to me, really? Living here rather than downtown."

"Only if we have a big, stupid dog in our backyard," he countered.

"Done." She couldn't help but smile. "Are you serious?"

"Suzy-Q chose us, I'd say."

Connor released her to pull down her shorts, and she reached for his belt. In seconds, their clothes were scattered across the bed and all over the floor. She wasn't sure he'd ever been so unrestrained. "Please, Connor. Fuck me," she said.

He touched her pussy, and she moaned a little. She was already wet, ready for him.

"I need you, Lara."

"Do it. Do me. *Now.*"

Responding to her urgent, emotional demand, be entered her with a single thrust, joining them, giving her what she craved.

He leaned down to capture her mouth.

Feeling as if a fevered pitch clawed at her, she lifted her hips and wrapped her legs around his waist. He fucked her hard, satisfyingly, making up for lost days, and the fact her heart had been broken. "Connor…Connor!"

"Come, Lara," he whispered.

His words, his claim, made her orgasm. She held onto him, the way he'd always encouraged.

Then, the urgency harnessed, he changed the pace, setting a more sensuous mood. He changed the kiss to match, and he slowly devoured her.

She followed his lead. The lovemaking wasn't as intense, but it was somehow more passionate for it.

He lifted off her a bit to capture her gaze. He silently mouthed, "I love you."

Inside her, his cock stiffened. His strokes grew shorter, harder.

Unbelievably, she felt the first tendrils of another orgasm unfurl in her.

His gaze riveted her, and he said was rough as he said, "Wait for me this time."

She felt desperate, but she held back, fighting her own responses to give him what he demanded. "Yes, yes, yes," she said as he changed position, placing his shoulders against the backs of her thighs so that he could keep her spread wide while he claimed her.

"You're mine, Lara."

"Sir, there was never any doubt."

Connor could not be more awed by the sight of Lara.

She opened her office door when he knocked, and she stood there, wearing the purple dress she'd bought that Saturday afternoon at the downtown boutique.

"Perfect choice," he said as his pulse turned thready.

Just like the first time she'd walked into his office, she was a vision of classic beauty. The dress flowed over her body as if designed for her. He hadn't remembered it being that exquisite.

In addition to the dress, she wore silk stockings and three-inch stilettoes.

He leaned forward and inhaled the barely perceptible trace of magnolia. "I've suddenly got another suggestion." He lifted her hair to kiss the side of her neck.

"I'm betting it has something to do with skipping the wedding and going straight to the honeymoon."

"Potentially."

She moaned softly. "You..."

With his tongue, he circled her earlobe.

"Oh, Connor..."

"We can let Joshua know we'll be late. The idea of doing you on your desk in your wedding dress has a certain appeal."

"Then we'd have to reschedule the ceremony again, you'd show up to pick me up, and you'd get all turned on again," she said. "See the problem?"

But her eyes were still closed, and he knew that if he caught the hem of her dress and pulled it up, she wouldn't protest.

"Or we can get it over with and you can have me naked in less than two hours."

"I've never been more tempted to speed up a clock," he confessed.

Reluctantly, he released her.

He'd never spent this much time thinking about a woman. Then again, he'd never been with a woman who'd pierced his defenses and worked her way inside them. Her love, and the courage to confess it, had changed him.

She gathered her purse, and he picked up her bag.

"No cracks about it."

"Wouldn't dare. Besides, I've stepped up my weight training."

She glared.

He appreciated the easy camaraderie. How had he thought his future would be better without it?

"Do you have the rings?" she asked.

He'd offered to buy her a different one, but she'd said hers was perfect. And after fifty years, the cost per wear would be less than a dollar a day.

The elevator stopped at the twelfth floor to let off another passenger. When the doors closed and he was alone with her, he took the opportunity to place a hand on her rear. He felt the faint outline of straps from a garter belt. "You could have worn pantyhose."

"But then I wouldn't have the pleasure of knowing you were going crazy picturing me with a bare ass."

"Which means you aren't wearing underwear?"

She tossed him a heart-attack-causing smile. "Brilliant, Mr. Donovan."

The elevator dinged as it reached the ground floor and she walked ahead of him. Yeah, he couldn't wait for later, a little marriage-night treat. *If he survived that long.*

April drove them to the courthouse, and they made their way to his friend's office.

They were shown in, and Connor performed the introductions.

"Good afternoon, Your Honor," she said. "Thanks for doing this."

"Call me Joshua," he replied. "Unless we meet in the

courtroom."

"Or Sir," Connor added.

She looked between them. "You're a Dom, too? How many of you are there?"

"It's not like we're werewolves or something," Connor protested.

"Werewolves only get randy around the full moon."

Joshua coughed and picked up the manila envelope containing their marriage certificate. "Do y'all have your own vows, or would you like to go with something informal that I normally suggest?"

"I have vows," Lara said.

Connor raised his eyebrows. "Other than what we've discussed, I'm not prepared," he admitted.

"No problem," Joshua said. "We'll work with it." He stepped into the hallway and invited in the two employees who had agreed to serve as witnesses.

Connor and Lara said hello and thanked them for taking time out of their schedules.

"It's my pleasure," one of the ladies assured them. "Makes me remember when Murph and I got married thirty-seven years ago."

Joshua registered their names and ensured everything on the license was in order before asking Connor to face Lara.

They turned toward one another. Even though she'd been relaxed on the way over, he now saw tension in the way she held her shoulders. If they had been in private, he would massage her until her head lolled and he'd eased away all the knots.

"Take Lara's right hand in yours," Joshua said.

Connor did, and it felt warm, reassuring. Not only was he offering his hand, she was holding his.

"Repeat after me."

Connor nodded.

"I, Connor, take you, Lara, to be my wife. To have and to hold, for better, for worse, for richer or poorer, to cherish and protect, to honor and to love."

As he repeated the words, he squeezed her hand tight,

conveying the emotion of his promise.

She pressed her lips together and momentarily looked away.

"Now, Lara," Joshua said. "You may proceed any time you're ready."

After nodding, she blinked a few times. When she spoke, her words wobbled with unshed emotion. "Connor, I take you as my husband. I promise to work with you, to honor you, to show you the respect you deserve."

A knot of emotion settled in his heart.

"I will make you proud. And just like we are in this moment, I will turn to you. And every day that we are married, I will show you my love and my utter devotion."

"Now the rings?"

Connor took the two bands out of his pocket and gave them to Joshua. "I have the other for later," he told her.

"Repeat after me," Joshua instructed. "Lara, I give you this ring as a symbol of my vow. With all that I am and all that I have, I will honor you."

Connor said the words and slid the ring on her finger.

Then Lara recited them with no further coaching. His ring slipped into place and felt shockingly right.

"You may kiss."

"Behave," Lara mouthed.

He kissed her, gently and tenderly and not at all like he intended to later.

The woman who was married to Murph patted her heart as she walked from the room. The other woman shook their hands.

Joshua took care of the legalities and refused payment. He wished them well and promised to be there for both of them in the future. "See you at the club?"

"Maybe in the next few weeks," he said. "I'm keeping Lara to myself for some time."

Connor guided her into the hallway. After making sure they were alone, he had her against a wall.

"Connor! Not here."

"Oh yes," he countered. "Open your mouth for me, wife."

He had to have her.

He kissed her hard and deep. Having his ring on her finger had shifted something inside him. He'd had a similar reaction when he'd put that necklace on her before they'd gone to dinner Saturday night. He identified the feeling as possessiveness, and he'd never had it with any other woman.

Within seconds, she became softer for him. She met his tongue, and he tasted her surrender. It wasn't enough to sate him. It was only enough to make him hungrier.

He ended the kiss and gave her a second to straighten her dress before taking her hand and guiding her to the elevator.

"Congratulations, Mr. and Mrs. Donovan," April told them with a smile as she opened the car's door for them. "Where can I take you, sir?"

"Home?" he asked Lara as she entered the car then slid across the seat to make room for him.

She nodded.

"Sir?"

"The Heights," he confirmed. "You can take some time off. We won't need you until next Monday."

"Thank you, sir, ma'am."

Afternoon traffic slowed them down, and the drive took an agonizingly long time.

"I was thinking about a soaker tub as a wedding gift to you," he said.

"That would add value to the house." She nodded. "So it's a good investment. And I was thinking about a hot tub for the backyard. That's an investment in us."

"You, the moonlight, no clothes?"

"Read my mind."

Once they were finally home, he locked the door. "As much as I'd like to let you settle and catch your breath, I've been having fantasies about your lingerie."

"Have you?" She set down her purse and faced him.

"Wait for me in the bedroom. Leave the dress on."

She left her shoes on, too, and her calf muscles flexed

enticingly as she led the way down the hallway.

Lara perched on the edge of the bed, her legs crossed. That first day in his office, he'd thought she could have been on a pinup calendar. Seeing her now only reinforced that vision.

Then he followed her gaze. The necklace he'd bought her was on the nightstand.

"I thought you might want to put this on me."

He paused. "You understand what it represents to me."

"I do. I'm still learning, but with you as my Dom, I'll be an eager submissive. I'd be honored to wear it."

She lifted her hair, and he put the necklace in place.

He took a step back and looked at her. His cock hardened as all blood left the rest of his body and went straight there. "You are spectacular."

She touched it. "I love it."

"Now take off your dress."

"I could use some help with the zipper." She turned her back to him and lifted her hair.

Within seconds, she wore only her lingerie, the necklace and the mile-high shoes. "I'd freeze this moment if I could," he said. "I'm going to fuck you."

Instantly the atmosphere changed, he felt her respond to him. Her breathing slowed and her eyes became wider.

"Kneel on the bed," he instructed. "Thrust your ass back toward me."

He moved to her side and rubbed her cheeks until they were a flushed shade of pink. Then he parted her and tongued her, diving in and out making her hot and wet for him.

As she started to sway, he rained spanks on her ass, heightening her frenzy. "Ask."

"Let me come, Sir! Please. Spank me. Fuck me. I want your cock."

He did, blazing her ass with another dozen brutal slaps and several on her heated cunt. He dropped his pants and thrust into her.

She gasped, cried out. "I love you, Connor, Sir."

There were no sweeter words.

He held her hips steady while he fucked her. "I love you, little Lara." The more he said it, the easier it became and the more natural it felt. He vowed to spend the rest of his life not just saying it, but proving it, by wrapping her up and binding in his love.

The Donovan Dynasty: Brand

Excerpt

Chapter One

"He's a fucking badass. A *hot* fucking badass. But still, a fucking badass."

"Who?" With a scowl, Sofia McBride looked up from her clipboard and glanced at her assistant.

"Cade Donovan."

She followed the direction of her assistant's gaze.

Sofia wasn't the type to swoon, but...

He was standing next to the registry station near the front door of the country club and was dressed in an athletic-cut black tuxedo that emphasized his broad his shoulders and trim waist.

Rather than a typical bow tie, a sexy Western bulldogger tie was fastened around his throat. Intricately crafted leather cowboy boots were polished to a shiny gleam, and he wore a black felt cowboy hat.

Even from down the hallway, she noted his rakishly appealing goatee.

Though she'd never met him, she'd grown up in Corpus Christi, less than fifty miles from the Running Wind Ranch. Because his last name was Donovan, he was local royalty, and she'd heard of his exploits—fast cars, bull-riding championships, women—all the privileges money could buy.

He was mouthwatering. Given how tempting he was, no doubt he'd earned every bit of his reputation.

The woman at the front pointed toward the Bayou Room where Sofia and Avery were putting the finishing touches on the preparations for Lara and Connor Donovan's wedding celebration. Cade touched the brim of his hat with old-world charm.

"He's heading this way," Avery said unnecessarily.

"You need to get going."

"How about we switch jobs for the evening?" Avery suggested. "You can go to the Oilman's Ball, and I'll stay here."

"No chance." Sofia's answer had nothing to do with Cade and everything to do with her friend Lara, who'd just married into the family.

Even though there would only be a couple of hundred people at this evening's reception and the country club was one of the best venues to work with, Sofia planned to be there for her friend.

"But, but… That's Cade Donovan." Avery exaggeratedly stuck out her lower lip.

And Sofia wanted to meet him. At dinner last week, Lara had mentioned that Connor was a Dominant. And Sofia was curious to know if the other brothers were as well. "I'll take care of him."

"You never were good at sharing, boss."

"Go."

"If you need anything, anything—"

"Good luck with Mrs. Davis." Honestly, Sofia needed Avery's skills at the Oilman's Ball. Five hundred people were on the guest list, and press would be in attendance.

Zoe, Sofia's sister, had been at a downtown Houston

hotel all afternoon, overseeing the setup of the challenging event. Mrs. Davis, the ball's chairwoman, was notoriously demanding, and she'd been making changes to the plans for the last month. Avery's ability to say no while keeping the client happy was a skill Sofia had yet to master. "You're a cruel, cruel boss."

"You might meet a rich oil baron."

"There is that," she conceded with a cheeky grin. Avery was twenty-nine, and she'd set a goal of being married by the time she was thirty. She didn't lack interest from men, but she wouldn't settle for just any man, insisting she wanted a man who could keep her in very expensive shoes and give her a monthly purse budget to match.

After gathering her belongings, Avery headed for the back exit through the kitchen.

Sofia straightened her shoulders and walked toward the front of the room to greet Cade, who had paused inside the doorway. His gaze locked on her. He didn't blink, didn't look away. Instead, he perused her as if she were the only person on the planet.

It was discombobulating and heady.

Her sensible black skirt suddenly felt a bit tight, her patent leather heels a little too tall. Still, she strove for professionalism she suddenly didn't feel. "Mr. Donovan." She gave him her best smile. "I'm Sofia McBride. Lara's friend and the event coordinator."

"I'm early." He offered his hand.

Because it was the polite thing to do, she accepted.

His hand was so much larger than hers. All of a sudden, his presence seemed to consume her. His scent was leather laced with strength. He was exceptionally tall with a chiseled jaw, and it appeared that his nose had been broken, maybe more than once.

She had to look up a long way to meet his gaze, and when she did, she saw that his eyes were a chilly gunmetal. His posture spoke of a confidence bordering on arrogance, and he wore power as comfortably as he did his tuxedo jacket.

The air around Cade all but crackled with intensity, and

part of her felt as if she'd been swept into some sort of vortex.

Last week, when she'd met up with Lara, her friend had confessed that she and Connor shared a BDSM relationship. The news had momentarily left Sofia speechless. She had read books and seen a couple of movies about the subject, but other than the fact sex was kinky, she hadn't known much about it, and she'd never known anyone who was into it.

Once she'd gotten past the initial shock, Sofia had started asking questions. Lara had responded quite matter-of-factly, sharing enough information that Sofia was more intrigued than ever. When she'd gone home that night, she'd powered up her computer and done an Internet search. Some of the things she'd seen had made her flinch, but the idea of being tied up had starred in a few of her recent fantasies.

Now, she wildly wondered if Cade was also into BDSM, and she had a disturbing, naughty image of being over his knee while he spanked her.

With a little shiver—part apprehension, part curiosity—she pulled back her hand. "We're just putting the finishing touches on before Connor and Lara arrive," she said, probably unnecessarily.

Because the couple had married a few weeks before, the order of the evening was a bit unusual. The family was planning to meet at five for pictures, and the cocktail hour was scheduled for six, with dinner following at seven.

"Anything I can do to help?"

The offer caught her off guard. "Thanks, but I think we've got it covered."

"If there's anything you need, let me know."

She questioned if she'd imagined a slight emphasis on the word anything.

The photographer shouted out a cheery hello as she arrived, and Sofia was grateful for the interruption. "There's a bar near the restaurant, if you'd be more comfortable waiting there?"

A hint of a smile teased his mouth. Rather than softening his expression, it only made him look all the more dangerous. "Are you trying to get rid of me, Ms. McBride?"

Yes. The man definitely unnerved her. "I just want you to be comfortable."

"Can I get you anything while I'm there?"

"Thank you." She shook her head. "But I don't drink while I work."

"Do you always follow the rules?"

Though his tone was light, the question sounded serious.

"I like rules," she replied.

"Do you?"

"It helps keep my life in order."

"That's a good thing?"

"Isn't it?" she countered. Even as she answered, she wasn't sure why she was having this conversation, why she was revealing parts of herself to a stranger.

"Have you ever been tempted to say the hell with everything and explore all that life had to offer?"

"When it comes to business, yes."

"And everything else?"

"No." But honestly, she was now.

The photographer placed her backpack on a chair then moved toward them, sparing Sofia from further discussion.

Sofia introduced the pair, then excused herself to greet the DJ and show him where to set up.

Over the next ten minutes, three generations of Donovans began to arrive, and Connor and Lara took her aside.

"We need your help with something," Lara said.

"Anything."

"Julien Bonds RSVP'd about ten minutes ago. He's an old friend of Connor's."

Only professionalism kept her from dropping her jaw. There were a number of high-profile Texans on tonight's guest list, including one senator, but Julien Bonds? The man's genius was legend. She'd waited in line several hours to buy his latest wearable device at the opening of his newest flagship store, and he'd been at the event for a short time. He'd left only minutes before she would have gotten to meet him.

About two years ago, she'd written to the company, wanting an app that allowed her to do more impressive business presentations. Surprising her, one of Bonds' engineers had responded. Within two weeks, two of her favorite programs had been fully integrated. The difference it had made in her success had been phenomenal, and she'd always wanted to tell him.

"He's requested no pictures," Lara continued.

"I see." And since almost every person in attendance would have a cell phone, that presented a challenge. "We can ensure Heather won't take any professional shots," she said. "How would you like me to handle the other guests?"

"I was hoping you'd have ideas."

"That's what I was afraid of." Especially when she, herself, wanted a photo with him. She nodded, hoping to convey confidence she wasn't feeling.

"He won't be arriving until nine."

She checked her schedule. By then, the alcohol would have been flowing for a couple of hours. "Will he have anyone with him?"

Lara and Connor exchanged glances.

"Like security?" Sofia clarified. "An entourage?" He'd had about half a dozen people surrounding him at the store opening.

"Not to my knowledge," Connor said.

"Can you find out?" People blocking views would probably be the best hope.

Connor stepped to the side to make a call.

"How are you doing?" Sofia asked Lara.

"Fine. Happy. Nervous." She said it all in the same breath.

"I'll be your designated worrier." Sofia squeezed Lara's hand reassuringly. "Your job is to enjoy the evening. I'll be nearby if you need anything."

Lara smiled.

"You look beautiful," Sofia said. "The perfect Mrs. Donovan." Lara radiated elegance and sophistication in her short, form-fitting, cream-colored lace dress. "Marriage is obviously still agreeing with you."

"More than I would have imagined." Her friend flushed and fingered the stunning gold choker around her neck.

A series of diamonds descended from the metal to snuggle against the hollow of her neck. Because of their discussion, Sofia knew it was more than a piece of jewelry. The necklace was an outward symbol of Lara's submission to her husband.

Sofia didn't quite understand it, but she couldn't argue that Lara seemed happy, satisfied in a way she had never been before. Even when Sofia had asked, Lara had said she wasn't sure whether the feeling came from being married, from the strength of her new husband's business acumen, or from submission. After a glass of wine, she'd mused that it was probably the combination of everything.

"It's been a whirlwind, and I couldn't have managed this without you," Lara said.

"I wouldn't have let you," Sofia replied. "Please let me know if there's anything you need."

Connor returned and lightly touched his wife's shoulder. "Julien will have two men with him. And it's my understanding he'll only be here a short time. Mostly he's coming by to gloat. He thinks he had a hand in making the relationship work, and he does enjoy feeling as if he's a genius."

"And did he? Have a hand in the relationship?"

"He's a good friend with good advice," Connor replied.

"I'll talk to the DJ. I'm thinking he can play a song that will engage a lot of people. The twist, perhaps. Other than that, I'll contact the country club personnel and security to see what we can do. Maybe we can bring him in the back way. Keep him on the patio or something."

"You'll work it out," Connor said, his voice holding no trace of doubt.

She asked for a contact number for one of Julien's people. "I'll do the best I can," she promised.

The photographer signaled she was ready for the bride

and groom, and Lara and Connor excused themselves.

While the couple was busy, Sofia went in search of the country club security team. They agreed that bringing in the Bonds entourage through the patio was the most feasible option and suggested she have a look for herself.

She greeted other arriving family members then confirmed the schedule change with the DJ and asked for his help in keeping the focus away from Julien.

"Not a problem," the man assured her. "We can do some things with lighting and announcements about the photo booth and video greeting cards for the couple."

"There's a reason I like working with you, Marvin."

"It's the voice." He dropped his tone until it sounded like honey drizzled over a jagged knife.

"You should have a radio gig," she told him. "Nights, on an all-romance, all-the-time station."

"I have the face for it."

"You're fishing," she said.

"Yeah." He shrugged.

"I'll bite, though. You're a handsome man."

He straightened his tie, preening. Then, professional that he was, he made notes on his schedule as she walked away.

Before leaving the room, she couldn't help but sneak a peek at Cade. Even though he stood next to his handsome brothers, he didn't completely fit. His smile wasn't as genuine as theirs, and his Western-style tux and hat set him apart. He was taller, broader, more... She considered herself pragmatic, but the only word she could think of was brooding.

After shaking her head, she went to check that everything was perfect for the cocktail hour in the other room.

The quartet was in place on a platform, and they were tuning up. Two servers stood behind an open bar. The banquet manager confirmed that hors d'oeuvres would be served at ten minutes after the hour. All the centerpieces and decorations were perfect.

Finally, she went outside to check the patio.

Right now, it was too hot and humid to be pleasant. The

overhead beams had pendant fans hanging from them, their blades seeming to slog through the thick air.

Later, though, the lights off the bayou and the view of downtown Houston, combined with cooler temperatures, would make this an ideal spot.

She ordered a sparkling water from the bartender, enjoying the last few minutes of peace that she was likely to get for the next couple of hours.

"Lemon? Lime?"

"Lime, thanks." After she had the drink in hand, Sofia walked around the patio. She found a gate that led to the side of the building. There was gravel there, with pavers. That could be the best way to get Julien into the party with as little disruption to the festivities as possible.

She paused at the back of the patio near a massive potted palm. If she could get some workers to move the plants around, they could block part of the area from view.

Cade emerged from inside. Without hesitating, he headed directly toward the bar.

Sofia told herself that he hadn't followed her, but she couldn't be sure.

The woman wrapped a napkin around a beer bottle and handed it to him.

Sofia watched as he dropped a bill into the tip jar. Judging by the bartender's wide-eyed expression, it had been a good one. If she hadn't already liked him, she would have changed her mind in that instant.

Then he turned toward her.

If she'd had any doubt that he'd followed her, it was erased.

He remained where he was.

Heat and feminine response chased through her. She shouldn't be attracted to him, but damn it, she was.

Maybe she should have handled the Oilman's Ball and left Cade to Avery. Even as the thought flashed through her mind, she banished it. No matter how badly he unnerved her, he ensnared her. Intuition told her to run before she couldn't. Yet her body refused obey her mind's orders.

She curved both hands around her glass as he approached.

"I would have gotten that for you," he said, indicating her drink.

"I think as the event planner, it's my job to make sure you're taken care of."

"Always the duty of a man to make sure a woman's needs are met."

He hadn't said anything provocative, so why was she responding as if he had? "Thank you. But I'm pretty accustomed to taking care of myself."

She noticed him glance toward her left hand.

"By choice?" he asked.

"That's nosy, Mr. Donovan."

"It is," he agreed.

But Cade didn't relent. Instead, he seemed genuinely interested in learning more about her. How long had it been since that had happened? Months? Maybe years? Then the truth hit her. She'd never had a man be so inquisitive and not back down when she called him out on it. He was unique among the men she'd known. That, more than anything, was what encouraged her to respond. "My mother was abandoned by my alcoholic father when I was very young."

He winced.

"I had to take care of my little sister. As soon I was able, I was helping my mother bake cakes and pies for local restaurants. Sometimes she'd stay up all night. I really don't know how she did it. She remarried a wonderful man a number of years later, but I learned some important lessons early, and I've never forgotten them. I went to school on a scholarship. And I worked my ass off to buy my mom's business and expand it." Traces of irritation buzzed through her. "So it's hard to say that anything was by choice. I've done what I needed to from necessity."

"It appears you've done a fine job." He never looked away. Instead, he tipped his beer bottle toward her in silent salute.

"I grew up in Corpus Christi," she admitted. "I know of your reputation."

"Yet you're still talking to me."
"Some of it was good," she replied.
"That surprises me."
"We come from very different backgrounds."
"Do we indeed?"
There was something in his voice, an ache maybe. Pain, perhaps.
Because of his approval, the expression of his own angst, something went out of her. The fight? The need to explain, justify, defend the way she'd grown up? It hadn't taken long for Cade Donovan to have an impact on her.
Her text message alert sounded, and she put her drink on the waist-high adobe wall while she took her phone from her jacket pocket. It was the country club manager, as she'd guessed.
"Duty calls?" Cade asked.
"Afraid so."
"I hope to see you again later."
She didn't reply. The words sounded more like a promise than a statement, and a secret part of her hoped he was serious. She wanted more time with the darkly mysterious Donovan brother.
He went inside. After collecting her wits, she asked the manager to meet her on the patio.
She offered her suggestions, and the manager nodded and summoned a few members of the banquet crew. They brought out a hand truck to move around the big pots, creating a secluded area not far from the gate.
Once she was satisfied with the result, she informed Julien's team of the plan then found Connor to update him.
The only part she disliked was the fact that once again she wouldn't get to meet the elusive Julien Bonds and get his autograph on her cell phone case. What could be better than his signature right below the Bonds logo?

* * * *

Shortly before nine o'clock, she received news that Julien's car had arrived.

After signaling the DJ and receiving Marvin's nod in reply, she went outside to the gate to greet the party.

A beefy-looking man—security if the earpiece was anything to judge by—had a quick look around before nodding at her and speaking into a microphone on his lapel.

A moment later, Lara and Connor joined them in the makeshift meeting area.

The security guard positioned himself between the bar and the plants. She couldn't have been more pleased with how the plan worked.

Sofia ordered another soda water. The sound of Lara's laugh drew her attention, and Sofia couldn't resist taking a peek.

Julien wore a loose-fitting jacket, a white shirt and a skinny little tie that was knotted loosely. His trademark athletic shoes were an obnoxious magenta color, and the yellow laces quite literally glowed. He'd taken his tacky footwear to a whole new level yet he still pulled off the casual style that he'd become known for.

A woman, tall and willowy, with blonde hair cascading halfway down her back, stood next to him. She wore an electric-blue dress that flared around her in a style Sofia associated with Marilyn Monroe.

Sofia hadn't heard that he was dating anyone, but the way his arm was draped around the woman's shoulders and the way she leaned into him hinted that this was something more than casual.

The bartender handed Sofia the drink, and she turned to see Erin heading toward the private area.

Since she was the groom's sister, Sofia didn't try to stop her, and she nodded to the security guard to let him know that Erin should be allowed to pass.

"Let me know if you need anything," she said to the security guy.

He nodded curtly but didn't respond.

Sofia went inside and stood near the back wall, surveying the festivities. More people than normal were on the floor, showing off their moves, and some were even snapping selfies. How they managed that, she wasn't sure.

It was less than two minutes later when Erin returned, a pained smile on her face, her shoulders slumped a little.

Sofia thought about seeing if there was anything she could do for Erin, but the woman headed straight out of the front door.

Other than that, Julien and his date's visit went smoother than she'd anticipated, but she still breathed a sigh of relief when the country club manager let her know that a limousine had whisked away the Bonds party.

Several times during the next couple of hours, she caught Cade watching her, and she had to force herself to concentrate on her job and not the wild, crazy things he did to her insides.

* * * *

"When is it your turn?"

In the waning hour of the reception, with strains of music spilling from inside the country club, Cade thumbed back his cowboy hat and turned to face his younger sister. Half-sister, really. But the fierce and loyal Erin Donovan would protest that distinction. In her mind, as well as those of his half-brothers Connor and Nathan, they were family, no arguments.

Cade loved all of his siblings, but Erin most of all. Ever since she'd been a toddler, she'd been a pest, smothering him with adoration and love even when he didn't want it or deserve it. "My turn?" he repeated, stalling.

"Don't play dumb. When is it your turn to get married?"

"Not happening," he replied, even though he knew she would push the point. Erin worried about him living all alone on the ranch. As far as she was concerned, there was nothing but cattle, deer, horses and wilderness in South Texas. It didn't matter to her that he employed dozens of people, many of whom he interacted with on a daily basis. He also traveled more often than he would like. He drove to Corpus Christi at least once a week, flew to Houston almost every month for family business meetings, and he spent more time in the nearby town of Waltham than he cared to.

"Are you at least finally seeing someone?" she pressed.

"You know the answer to that," he responded.

"I keep hoping."

His father's death had devastated him, shattering his sense of self in ways he was still trying to comprehend. It was almost as if that event had divided the old Cade from the new Cade. In his late teens and early twenties, he'd been a bit reckless. The whispers about him, the way he didn't deserve the life of privilege he'd ended up with, had gnawed at him. He'd set out to banish the voices as well as to prove himself. He'd lived hard, tried to make his mark on the world, taken unnecessary chances bull riding, racing motorcycles then eventually, cars.

When Jeffrey Donovan had been buried, Cade had resolved to be a better man, to live up to the expectations placed on him. He'd thrown himself into his responsibilities and obligations, letting them consume him as he attempted to redeem himself.

He'd shut himself off from distractions, including dating. At one time he'd been active in the local BDSM community. Until this evening, when he'd walked through the door and met the curvy, sexy Sofia McBride, he hadn't had much interest in women lately. His attraction to her had jolted him and he wasn't sure he liked it. Hell, it had been at least three months since he'd attended a leather party, even longer since he'd hosted a submissive at the ranch.

Penance was a bitch.

Realizing that Erin had rested her fingers consolingly on his wrist, he shook off the melancholy. Tonight was supposed to be a celebration of love, of marriage, of the future. He wouldn't be the one to bring it down. "How about you?" he asked, redirecting the conversation.

"Me? Seeing someone? Are you kidding me?" She dropped her hand. "I'm too busy helping Julie get the corset shop going in Kemah. And trying to find someone to run the foundation. I'm pinch-hitting for now, but..."

"You're exhausted," he guessed.

She shrugged. "It's a lot of hours."

As head of HR for Donovan Worldwide, Erin didn't have an easy job. Filling high-level vacancies was difficult at best, and their aunt's decision to spend more and more time with her younger beau complicated matters. The Donovan Foundation had always been run by a member of the family, but now they would have to look to an outsider to fill her position.

And, in spite of their youngest brother's objections, Erin had gone ahead with plans to assist a friend in opening a fancy lingerie shop. When the woman had admitted she didn't have the funds to open the store, Erin had supplied that, as well. No matter the challenge, she accepted it.

"How are plans coming for the centennial celebration?" she asked, changing topics to one Cade hated only slightly less than the subject of his non-existent love life.

The Running Wind Ranch, which had been in the family for five generations, was going to be celebrating its centennial in early fall. He would have pretended it wasn't happening, but his grandfather, the Colonel, had recently announced that he wanted the family to host a gala, inviting neighbors, friends, vendors and business associates. Many of them had never been to the ranch. Others remembered a time the Colonel and Miss Libby had hosted grand events, the last one about twenty-five years ago. It was a headache Cade didn't want, but a duty he knew he'd fulfill. "My mother said I personally have to check out the caterers."

Erin grinned. "Excellent idea."

"Not sure why she couldn't do it."

"You really expect Stormy to take the blame if the food is awful?"

"Well said." Around Erin, he freely spoke about his mother. Neither Connor nor Nathan had ever said a negative word about her. On the other hand, none of them had ever discussed her involvement in the business, either.

The Colonel had spoken fewer than a hundred words to her in over thirty years, and Stormy said she preferred it that way. When Cade's father had gotten her pregnant, she'd been offered a significant amount of money to go away quietly. If she'd been the type to do that, no doubt his father wouldn't have fallen in love in the first place.

"Do you have anyone lined up yet?"

"A new bakery opened in town, a couple of doors down from the pharmacy. So I stopped in."

"And?"

He'd never felt more helpless. Give him a complex piece of machinery to repair or a steer to brand and he had complete confidence. But when two women had started smiling and shoving food at him, flipping through pictures of weddings and birthdays, offering him tiny plates filled with bizarre concoctions, he'd been overwhelmed and speechless. "Buffalo chicken wing cupcakes?"

"Were they good?"

"I don't know. I couldn't bring myself to pull it out of the frosting. How the hell do you eat something like that?"

"I see your point. I guess she was going for something sweet and savory in the same bite."

"Cupcakes should be sweet," he said.

"The whole world isn't black and white, big brother."

"I have rules, Erin."

She grinned. "Got it. Cupcakes are sweet. Women are spicy?"

"Don't you have someone else you can bother?" he asked pointedly.

"Seriously, Cade, you don't have time to put an event together. You need a company to manage it, invitations, decorations—"

"Decorations?"

"Absolutely. Flags. Bunting. Maybe a take-home memento, like a Christmas ornament or something."

He blinked.

"Flowers," she continued. "And entertainment. Perhaps a band. Live music is always good. People will come just for that. Oh, and a bounce house for kids. Margarita machines, for sure. You've only got a few months."

Until now, he'd figured he'd need about ten minutes to put it together. Throw some burgers on the barbecue, smoke some brisket, maybe get some of the ranch hands to roast a pig… But with the scowl on Erin's face, he saw he'd made a huge miscalculation.

"Have you sent out a save-the-date announce-ment?"

"To whom?"

"Seriously?" She rolled her eyes. "Ask Grand-daddy and Grandmother for their guest lists, and Connor. Better yet, ask Connor and Thompson. Thompson has Connor pretty well organized. He'll know who's who. Don't forget Nathan. My mother may want to invite a few of her friends."

He hadn't considered that. But it made sense. Though he'd never spent much time with Angela, she had been married to his father.

"Do you want me to ask her?"

"That's thoughtful of you. But no. I'll do it." Or find someone else to do it.

"I have a few people I'll want to invite. And we'll need to contact the cousins. Granddaddy's the best person for that, too."

"Are you sure all of these people have to come?"

"You'll be haunted to the grave if you forget anyone. No matter what you say, who you apologize to, it will be taken as a personal affront. You're welcome to run the whole thing by me. We probably do need to limit it at some point."

"To a hundred?" he asked hopefully.

She scowled. "I was thinking a thousand."

"People?"

"And horses."

A cold frisson of panic clutched him. "What?"

"People, Cade. A thousand people. I was joking about the horses. Tell me you've at least decided on a date?" she persisted.

"I was thinking about October, maybe November. I don't suppose you—"

"Oh, hell and no. No chance. I can help you find someone, but I can't handle everything from a distance."

"What about Miss Libby?" He'd heard rumors that their grandmother used to host some of the best parties in South Texas. And she'd hosted many of them at the ranch.

"It's been too many years. She can give you pointers, but she doesn't know the companies down in that area any longer."

"Your mother?" he asked desperately.

"Again, too far away. You're welcome to meet with both of them, but your event person may want to do that."

"I see."

"I'll try to have some people for you to interview by the first part of the week."

He nodded. A runaway train was easier to stop than Erin. This time, he was grateful.

"You're going to be fine."

He'd rather climb on the back of a roaring, snorting sixteen-hundred-pound bull than deal with a guest list.

Inside, the DJ announced that it was time for a line dance, and Erin gave a quick excuse then hurried off.

He went to the bar and ordered his second beer of the evening. Other guests were reaching for glasses of champagne, but he preferred to drink Santo, a rich, thick brew that suited his personality.

Because of the heat and late spring humidity, there weren't a lot of people outside, but he still wandered to the far side of the courtyard and leaned against the outer adobe wall. In a crowd of any size, he tended to seek out quiet corners.

Now that the toasts and obligatory pictures were out of the way and the party was in full swing, he loosened his bulldogger tie and unfastened the top button of his Western shirt. He took a deep drink and glanced toward the clubhouse.

Inside, his new sister-in-law was also participating in the line dance. He wasn't sure what radiance looked like, but Lara had to come close. She and Connor had gotten married in a private ceremony weeks before. He'd only met her the previous evening, but he'd instantly seen why his brother had been attracted to her. She was witty, beautiful and elegant, a fitting partner for the ruler of the Donovan empire. Connor was clearly besotted, if the fact he couldn't keep his hands off Lara was any indication. When she'd briefly left the room, he'd followed her movements and momentarily lost track of the conversation.

Until he'd seen the two together, Cade had been a bit skeptical of love. To him, it seemed like an emotion that fucked with people's common sense, something with the power to be dark and destruct-tive.

No doubt his father had loved his mother, but he hadn't been strong enough to tell his own father to fuck off so he could be with the woman he loved. Instead, he'd married Angela Meyer. She was obviously a fine woman, if his half-siblings were anything to judge by, but Cade had seen the way Jeffrey looked at Stormy up until the day he died.

Love for a man she could never have had kept Stormy stuck, and it wasn't until a year ago that she'd even gone on a date.

But watching Connor opened Cade's jaded eyes, just a little.

A few minutes later, champagne in hand and a stupid smile on his face, Connor wandered over.

"Congratulations," Cade said.

"Glad you could make it."

"Wouldn't have missed it," he replied. He'd talked to Connor when Lara had approached him with her bold proposal to save her family's business. Cade had offered his support, but he'd urged his older brother to exercise caution. He'd sacrificed a lot to take the helm of Donovan Worldwide. He should have had years to travel, learn the business, date. But he'd never complained. He'd simply done what he'd needed to. All without blaming Cade for anything. "You look...happy."

Connor grinned like a fool. "I am."

"Here's to many joyful years together." He lifted his beer bottle and Connor tapped the rim of his glass against it.

"You're going back in the morning?"

"Figured I'd head out after breakfast. Get in a half-day's work, at least." Cade didn't have to explain. More than any of his half-siblings, Connor understood him, his need for solitude, to roam the land in endless search of healing. His grandfather, behaving more like a general than the colonel he was nicknamed after, often insisted that Cade needed to spend more time with the family, so it fell to Connor to cover and make excuses. Cade appreciated it. "I'm told I need to ask you for a guest list for the centennial."

"That'll take some thought. I'll try to remember to ask Thompson."

"Since you're technically on your honeymoon starting tonight, I'll get with him. He's here tonight, isn't he?"

"Somewhere. But wait until Monday. This is supposed to be his day off."

"I forget."

"It's a Donovan curse."

Cade nodded. Their father had always told them it was their responsibility not to fail. And none of them wanted to be one to let down the previous five generations. "Speaking of work..."

"I should have guessed."

"When you're back from your honeymoon, I could use some time to discuss some ideas for the ranch."

"What are you thinking?"

"Ah. You mentioned something about this being your reception?"

They exchanged shrugs.

Connor glanced back inside, evidently to ensure his wife was occupied. "Make it quick."

"I'm thinking of offering limited tourism. Maybe seasonal."

Connor took a drink and regarded Cade. "On the whole section?"

He shook his head. "Just section one."

"That one's yours. You don't need to run anything past me unless you're looking for a second opinion."

"It's your heritage, too. But there are fiscal aspects to consider. Could make money. Could lose it."

"What are the net benefits?"

"More people get to enjoy it. It provides employment opportunities for people living in town. Considering allowing tubing on the river. Horseback riding. That sort of thing. If it makes money, we could consider expanding the conservation area into section one."

"Negatives?"

"Because I live there, it could mean some loss of privacy. Increased insurance premiums. Environmental impacts, for sure. We'd need parking, restroom facilities, vans or some way to move people around." They already offered hunting, fishing and birding trips. But those were on the southernmost portion of the land. "There have to be another dozen things I haven't considered."

Connor nodded. "Have you consulted with Ricardo?"

Ricardo was the foreman of that section. More than anyone, he would know some of the pitfalls. "I was going to do that next."

"Good plan. Then have him contact Nathan. Nathan can work on a feasibility study, work up a cost analysis."

"You don't mind me asking?"

"Why the hell would I mind?"

"He's got real work to do for Donovan Worldwide. This would be a distraction."

Connor's eyes, so similar to Cade's, narrowed. "Don't make me knock some sense into you in front of the family." Connor's voice held shards of ice.

"I'm still bigger than you," Cade reminded him.

"But I'm more pissed. And you've fucking had it coming for a long time. Five years, at least."

Cade took a swig of his beer, considering. Connor was right. Something raw and nasty gnawed in Cade's gut. Guilt. Anger at the unfairness of it all. Part of him wanted Connor to take a swing. Maybe it'd give him some fucking release.

Nathan strolled over.

The tension between Cade and Connor continued to roil, just beneath a polished veneer.

"Private party?" Nathan asked.

"Brotherly love," Connor returned. "Welcome to the brawl."

"Damn. We haven't had one of those in what, seven, eight years?"

Cade remembered the fucking miserable summer night in Corpus Christi. Middle of August. Eighty-something degrees, ninety percent humidity, making the air as suffocating as a wet blanket. Only two things had been moving, rattlesnakes and tempers.

"What are we fighting about?" Nathan sounded interested.

"Same thing as last time," Connor replied.

"More or less," Cade agreed. Back then, Cade had been in college, and Connor had recently graduated from high school. Though their father had insisted Cade receive a good education, it had been clear that Connor would inherit the majority of the family's money and interests. Cade hadn't objected. After all, he'd had no desire to move to Houston. He'd liked his life the way it was. All he'd needed was the rodeo, his ridiculously fast cars and motorcycles and a place to stow his gear.

None of them had known that it would be the last time they'd all be together with their father still alive. The four had spent the day on the land. Their father, Jeffrey, had told them the history of ranch, shared his memories, the dreams he'd had for it. And they'd all heard the regret in his tone. He'd loved the ranch, and that he wasn't able to devote time to it had bothered him.

Connor had said that Cade would make it all happen. Cade, feeling like the outsider he was, hadn't wanted something that rightfully belonged to his brother. He'd said he'd be moving along after he'd earned his degree.

Later that night, Connor had sought him out, called him a quitter and told him he had the same obligations as any other Donovan.

All his life, Cade had heard the whispers. He was a

bastard, an imposter.

His frustration at being told to step up and behave like a member of the family had made him furious, and he'd thrown the first punch.

Connor had gone down, but he'd grabbed Cade's ankle and yanked him off balance, slamming him to the ground. He might have been bigger than Connor, more accustomed to barroom and street brawls, but he had been dazed, and Connor had taken advantage of that. He'd still been pummeling Cade when Nathan had joined them and pulled Connor away and stayed between them until the tensions had eased.

"I'd prefer not to spill any of this mighty fine cabernet. But if necessary..." Nathan put down the glass on a nearby table. "Whose side am I on? Or am I just supposed to separate the two of you?"

"Your choice, big brother," Connor said to Cade. "You can continue to be a jackass or you can lose the chip on your shoulder and realize no one objects to you owning section one." He narrowed his gaze. "Or the house. If you want to burn the thing down or sell it, turn it into a bordello, that's your right. You owe us nothing."

"A bordello?" Nathan asked. "Now there's an idea."

"Whether you like it or not, we're brothers," Connor persisted. He didn't even bother to direct his gaze toward Nathan. "If you have a personal business idea, we sure as hell should be the people you turn to first, for advice, feasibility studies, financing. It's what family does."

He got that Erin, Nathan and Connor did that for one another. But Cade spent the majority of his time alone. Always had.

"What's it going to be, Cade?" He put down his champagne glass. "You going to take the help? Or are you going to continue to be an asshole with some fucked-up version of reality in your head?"

The laughter and revelry from the reception spilled around them, yet the tension continued to draw and stretch. Cade had no doubt Connor was serious. He'd fight for family, even if Cade didn't think he deserved it. And Connor threw a wicked punch. He'd go for a quick one-two to the gut then the jaw. Cade was fast and big. Both had reserves of anger to draw from. But on principle, Cade wouldn't hit as hard. He wasn't sure he wanted to drive back to the ranch with a dislocated jaw.

In the end, it was Nathan, as always, who defused the situation. "My jacket is brand new. I'd hate for my biceps to tear it."

"Your biceps?" Cade repeated, feeling some of the tension begin to ease from his gut, even though Connor still looked pissed.

"Been keeping myself fit so I have the energy to shoot down the ideas that everyone else thinks will make millions of dollars," Nathan said.

He was damn good at it. Not only did he have the patience to drill down on the most mundane details, he had a sixth sense when it came to evaluating a company's place in the market.

"Takes talent to thrash the wheat from the chaff."

"True," Connor conceded.

"Let me at it," Nathan continued. "You can email me or I could come down."

A few seconds stretched, the silence tenuous.

"That'd be good. It's been a while," Cade agreed.

The angry tension drained from Connor's face, and the knot inside Cade began to dissipate. He was smart enough to realize that he didn't deserve the family who so lovingly accepted him.

"I'll email you on Monday and set up a time," Nathan said. "Maybe stay a couple of days."

"You've got a room waiting." More like a wing, and if he wanted even more privacy, there were an additional three guest cottages on the property. Eighty years ago, the size of the house had made sense. Now it stood mostly as a museum.

No matter what the will or Connor said, Cade believed it belonged to his siblings every bit as much as him.

"Lara and I might come down, too," Connor said, as if Cade hadn't just been on the edge of fracturing their relationship. "When he was here, Julien mentioned he may want some time to ride horses."

"Bonds gets his prissy ass on a horse?"

"Inconceivable," Nathan added.

Connor shrugged.

"He's welcome. I'll keep a guest house ready." The ranch had a short landing strip and a helicopter pad, making it easy in and out for a notorious recluse.

Any lingering emotional strain was shattered when Cade saw Lara and Erin heading toward them. Erin's hand was firmly clamped around Sofia's wrist.

Well, well.

The evening was looking better every moment.

About the Author

INTERNATIONAL BEST SELLING AUTHOR

Sierra Cartwright was born in Manchester, England and raised in Colorado. Moving to the United States was nothing like her young imagination had concocted. She expected to see cowboys everywhere, and a covered wagon or two would have been really nice!

Now she writes novels as untamed as the Rockies, while spending a fair amount of time in Texas...where, it turns out, the Texas Rangers law officers don't ride horses to roundup the bad guys, or have six-shooters strapped to their sexy thighs as she expected. And she's yet to see a poster that says Wanted: Dead or Alive. (Can you tell she has a vivid imagination?)

Sierra wrote her first book at age nine, a fanfic episode of Star Trek when she was fifteen, and she completed her first romance novel at nineteen. She actually kissed William Shatner (Captain Kirk) on the cheek once, and she says that's her biggest claim to fame. Her adventure through the turmoil of trust has taught her that love is the greatest gift. Like her image of the Old West, her writing is untamed, and nothing is off-limits.

She invites you to take a walk on the wild side...but only if you dare.

Sierra Cartwright loves to hear from readers. You can find her contact information, website details and author profile page at http://www.totallybound.com.

More books from Sierra Cartwright

The third and final in the engaging *Donovan Dynasty* series.

His erotic demands test everything she believes.

The first in the best-selling

Bonds series.

She still craved him…

The second in the captivating

Bonds series.

It had to be her. He won't be satisfied

until he claims her.

The final book in the

Bonds series.

With all she has to offer, she's his to command…